'Why did you infect Cain with a strain of the Marburg virus, Doctor?'

'Because the Central Intelligence Agency and the Pentagon gave me a mandate to create the ultimate soldier, Colonel. And the funds to do it.'

'And . . . did you do it?'

'Yes,' she said quietly. 'And then some.'

'How long do we have to find Cain, Doctor?'

'Ten days' was the answer, and genuine fear, for the first time, entered her voice.

'And if we don't?'

'Then,' she replied, 'Cain will be able to walk through the largest city in the world, Colonel, and kill everyone in it.'

James Byron Huggins is the author of *Leviathan*, *The Reckoning*, and *A Wolf Story*. He is now Hollywood's most sought-after new action film writer. A former soldier, policeman and award-winning journalist, he lives in Decatur Alabama with his wife and two children.

CAIN

James Byron Huggins

ORION

An Orion Paperback
First published in Great Britain by Orion in 1998
This paperback edition published in 1998 by
Orion Books Ltd,
Orion House, 5 Upper St Martin's Lane,
London WC2H 9EA

A CIP catalogue record for this book is available
from the British Library.

ISBN: 0 75281 615 2

Typeset by Deltatype Ltd, Birkenhead, Merseyside
Printed in Great Britain by
Clays Ltd, St Ives plc

ACKNOWLEDGEMENTS

This book could not have been written without the help of a great many friends, including Bob Liparilo, Frank Cohee, Jr., Bill Lamphere, my mother, and most of all, my wife and two children.

Jan Dennis deserves responsibility for the story's highest level of conception, and I remain in his debt. Robert Gottlieb of William Morris, who recognized the work, is also someone I am indebted to. And then there is my editor at Simon & Schuster, Bob Mecoy, who made so many suggestions that improved what I hoped would be a dark and contemporary gothic horror story.

I utilized well over a hundred reference materials, some contemporary, some going back as early as the Bronze Age. Then there was reliance upon the voluminous writings of philosophers from early Roman times through the Middle Ages until today, in addition to Catholic treatises governing the rites of formal exorcism. I have done my best to capture what we cannot see – the heart of an eternal war, if it be true, between the two most powerful beings in the cosmos.

to Jan Dennis

PROLOGUE

Wind roared with the wrath of a wounded god as the granite gateway of the grave shattered. Ancient air, hot with subterranean strength, flowed from the broken portal, and age-old volcanic dust rose around them like a vengeful, resurrected ghost.

Raising a hand against the heated blast of the tomb, the priest glared into a darkness that seemed to absorb their torches with stygian solidity. He glared as the world around them accepted the roaring blackness, a roaring blackness that continued for a long haunting moment rushing, releasing, breathing. Until . . . silence.

Stillness.

Holding a torch tight in a sweating fist, Father Marcelle faintly heard hushed, frightened words behind him and felt his own arms and legs trembling.

'*Ayya!*' an Israeli digger shouted as he pointed to a massive column inside the portal.

Marcelle saw Hebrew letters chiseled hatefully into stone and raised the torch high to read the cryptic inscription. He saw that it was from the hard and warlike Davidic period, a period consistent with this sealed, five-thousand-year-old demonic Temple of Dagon recently unearthed by a sandstorm in the white dunes of Megiddo.

'What says it, Father?'

Marcelle concentrated to decipher the words as the stench of ancient death and decay invaded his breath.

And after a moment he was certain that, yes, it was an archaic form of Hebrew not written in five millennia, its true meaning lost to a chaotic and forgotten age.

'*Father!* What says it!'

With a severe act of will Father Marcelle braced himself and walked forward to enter the tomb, a place grown inexplicably cold despite the volcanic breath that had swept over them but moments before. Struggling to contain a strange anxiety, Marcelle whispered, 'It is from the Davidic period. It is a warning.'

'*Ayya!* A warning! What says this warning?'

'It is . . . obscure,' Marcelle replied, trembling despite his control. 'But it is very clearly a warning. It says in Hebrew, "Let no man disturb the . . . the Neshamah, finally slain within these walls by the sword of David, Warrior-King of the Hebrews, a servant of Yahweh." '

'*Ayya! Ayya! Ayya!*' was all Marcelle heard behind him, and he fought to control his fierce excitement, staring into the blackness of the long corridor. In the distance, just beyond a crumbled arch of huge dimensions that was probably the original entrance of the tomb, he saw a burial chamber that held an even deeper gloom.

Slowly following the torch's too-small circle of light, Marcelle walked toward the soundless dark. He barely noticed those who moved, almost staggering, behind him.

'Neshamah? What is it, Father? What is Neshamah?'

Marcelle heard himself as if from a distance. 'It was used to describe a man that is not man,' he said as he neared the secretive entrance of the burial tomb. 'It describes a man without a soul. A man who lives but does not truly live . . . because he had no soul.'

Marcelle dimly heard the stampede of retreating footsteps but their panic didn't prevent him from moving closer to the burial chamber. Then he realized there was a single presence stepping beside him in almost utter silence. He glanced down to see that it was the chief digger, trembling violently, holding a shovel in tight fists.

Without expression, Marcelle turned to the entrance to behold what lay within. And he stared for a wild and uncanny moment before his mind could accept the reality of it. He didn't move as he heard the Israeli blessing himself.

Before them, it was there.

A gigantic skeleton lay bone-white upon a massive stone slab. Lordly it was, and nobly proportioned. But the skull had been severed to be spiked upon a lance, hatefully impaled in the floor. Marcelle stared at the severed skull and in the firelight the depthless eyes glimmered, burning with a bestial essence that could have held its own in the nethermost hell.

Still wearing proud armor of iron and brass, armor blackened by flame and savagely scarred by the sword of some unconquerable opponent, the skeleton was haunting and horrific in the torch. Struck to silence, Marcelle walked slowly forward, cautiously circling the enormous form.

Immense in stature, perhaps eight feet tall and of tremendous bone-strength, the man had obviously been a powerful warrior. A long iron sword, heavily notched by battle, lay coldly at his side. And a broad, double-edged dagger was clutched tight in a skeletal fist, as if the hate that commanded those bones in life could not release the blade even in death.

Shaking his head, Marcelle turned slowly to the skull and instantly saw something engraved in the broad forehead. Amazed and breathless, he raised the torch high and close over the flickering black eyes.

It was a single word:

GOLEM.

Carved deeply, the word was scarred by a savage dagger slash struck with kingly force across the thick white bone, as if to forever erase the power of the word from the world.

The digger whispered, 'What is it, Father? What is it?'

'It is the same as Neshamah,' Marcelle said, turning with a strange fear to the headless warrior, so heavily armed. 'It was once used to name a dead man that lives.'

CHAPTER I

White heat smoldered on the dunes of Death Valley as he ran with white sand burning his bare feet beneath the sun. And a vast white wasteland stretched before him to the horizon as distant sand dusted white air, dancing in the heat.

Here he had come so long ago, to rebuild himself. And as he ran, with his feet churning white on the dune, he knew that he had. He had rebuilt himself piece by piece with discipline, and heat, and desert, and sun.

Now, he knew, he was strong.

On and on he climbed, fiercely resisting the desert, holding his form as he fought the smothering air almost too hot to breathe.

Black glasses concealed his eyes and he was almost naked. His body, lean and muscular, was burned dark. His hair, brown and flecked with white to mark his age, was shorn almost to the scalp.

Without mercy he climbed, for mercy was something he would never show himself again. No, neither mercy nor rest because peace, if he should find it, would not come from either of these. No, peace could come only from embracing what he knew in his heart day by day with the haunting and silence and dreams, the faces, and the memories.

Death in heat raged over him and Soloman savagely rose against it, fighting and embracing, challenging until the sand and desert and sun finally surrendered to his strength once more as he reached the crest.

Standing alone he swayed, cold, *cold* now in the heat of the day. But he had won again. And for a long moment more he stood before he fell, hot sand scalding his hands.

Butcher … they had called him.

But he was no butcher. He had done only what he had to do, for vengeance. So that only this remained. This death.

But death, he knew, had to die hard.

◆　◆　◆

He had never seen light through human eyes.

Light.

At last!

The fools succeeded!

His eyes opening from the heart of hell he arose, and his dark, dark gaze fell over the living. Cries of terror heralded his arrival as they stared over him, and he beheld their horror.

And laughed.

He began to climb from the shadowed table, found that he could not. And with a frown he bent his head to see thick steel brackets holding both wrists to the metal slab, imprisoning him. It was something he had known already, and should have remembered.

Mortal fools.

His burning gaze swept over them, beholding the world as he had forever seen it, yet never with such … such *limitation*. And he realized that he had been correct: He would be limited in this form, yes, limited in sight and limited in knowledge. But it did not matter, he knew. Nothing mattered because even in this limited form he could destroy all of them.

Yes, all of them.

The portion of his cosmic mind that had survived the terrible merging with this flesh came to him slowly. And with the return of that first faint ghost of consciousness he saw again this hateful world as he had first beheld it. He remembered the roar and clash of battle as, wounded, he rose up only to be struck down again by that unwounded might; how, exhausted, he grappled with that eternal strength that could know no exhaustion, to be hurled headlong –

Like lightning …

Teeth clenched like the fangs of an angry lion, he growled as the black essence that was *him* flooded through the commandeered form, instantly command-ing the magnificent strength. And in seconds he held complete bioelectrical and mechanical control of the body as if he'd forever held it, for it was only flesh.

He tensed to feel the titanic power in his arms, chest, legs, and back. He sensed the limitless strength in his hands, strength that could crush steel like clay. Then he drew a deep breath as he felt his heart pumping the superoxygenated blood; blood rich with chemicals that strengthened his fantastic body even more. Frowning, he knew that *this* was the power he had coveted for so long; the pure physical power to conquer this world, to rule this world.

Or destroy what he could not rule.

Memories of distant days when he stalked the corridors of this world like a colossus risen from its monstrous throne of granite, feasting upon the weak, flooded through him. And he smiled at them before he remembered the painful defeat delivered to him in that bitter end. He frowned, glaring into shadow.

No …

Never again.

He would never be defeated again.

Nor did he fear the battle, because he had nothing to lose.

And he had learned from his mistake, knowing at last that he could never defeat that hated, omnipotent might with might alone. So he had long ago established a new plan, a plan where he could use the children ... to destroy the father. Movement to his side.

He smiled.

It is time.

Turning his lordly head he watched as the shocked, sweating scientist staggered closer, frightfully holding the large syringe in a trembling hand like a weapon.

Yes. Come to me.

Calm, he narrowed blood-red eyes and waited until the scientist was close, and he moved. Moved so quickly that the move was no move at all and the steel manacle holding his left wrist was sundered like paper as he gripped the man by the throat.

Immediately the scientist sought to escape. But there was no escape. At the first touch, as the remorseless iron fingers dug into his neck with the cold force of a vise, he knew he was dead.

Yet ... the man hesitated.

His eyes focused, studying the face.

Humans ... so frail ...

Curious despite his vast knowledge of all things past and present, the man held the scientist in his implacable grip, examining all that was in the face. His vision was limited in this form, he realized, but also ... fascinating. He drew the scientist closer, slowly turning the head in his hand to study the horrible fear that had always burned in the faces of these beings. And as he studied the fear he realized that although he had always seen this fear he had never seen it so ... so *pure*.

Yes, he could use this fear.

With a flick of his wrist he coldly snapped the scientist's neck and effortlessly shattered the steel brackets holding his ankles. Then without resistance he sundered the manacle holding his right wrist and rose gigantically among them as they ran screaming, screaming for someone to save them as they always screamed for someone to save them.

But no one could save them. For he was among them, now. And what was done could not be undone.

Towering dark and princely and immense in the gloom, he gazed at the fleeing forms of the humans as they ran from the room, seeking to escape his ageless wrath.

A steel vault shut, imprisoning him.

He laughed.

'Mortals ... such a feast.'

◆　◆　◆

Soloman sensed it before he heard it.

Sweating in the windless heat he paused atop the dune. Eyes narrowing, he turned to the horizon, attempting to still the sound of the blood rushing in his head. With his eyes protected from the sun by small black glasses, he looked for a long moment and saw nothing. Then, faintly, the sound came to him – the subdued whirring of helicopter blades.

Sweat and heat were smothering but Soloman ignored it, listening and watching. And after a moment spent to discern the helicopter's direction of travel, he was certain.

Yes. They're coming.

He did not know why they were coming. It had been almost seven years and they had never come to him before, nor had he wanted them to. But now they were coming and he knew he would be ready when they arrived. He didn't fear them because fear had been burned from him during the disciplined dark of the long desert nights.

Distant blades whispered in waving air.

Without expression Soloman ran down the dune,

feeling the hard strength of thirty-nine years in his legs; strength forged by the hard force of his will; strength that gave him comfort. For he had wisely used the years to build strength on strength – strength of body on mind on soul. And he knew he was stronger than he had ever been before.

He didn't look up as he ran down the dune.

Strength on strength.

◆ ◆ ◆

The giant stood, wearing the military BDUs taken from a soldier on the Army Pathfinder team. And the dead men sprawled across the rolling gypsum dunes of sand-blasted desert were too few, he felt, for he was accustomed to far, far more.

All he could remember was death; a universe, a galaxy of death. And for a moment he thought that in this limited form he could never kill enough of them, though he knew he could.

It was fortunate that the black BDUs of the slain soldier, a member of the Army's most elite tracking battalion, were large enough to accommodate his titanic form. Blackened by blood, the clothes strained against his flesh, still swelled from the exertion of slaying all of them with his hands.

Together they lay at his feet: thirty-three men.

The sight made him remember all the lives he'd taken during his short tenure in this world. The blood was delicious to him, yes, but there were also the weeping wives and fatherless children to dream about, such delicious dreams of death upon death, of pain upon pain delivered to the world by the strength that was his, and his alone.

The bodies were scattered over an area of low gray dune broken only by knee-high sedge that erupted at the base and crest of sand. And a few narrow crevices marked paths where rain rolled to pool in a tiny lake, now a shallow plain of dry bones. Every living thing had burrowed far beneath the crust, seeking shelter from the sun, which destroyed so completely.

He gazed up, listening to a flying search formation of helicopters as it passed close. Yes, they would be searching to find him but he knew their methods, how to defeat them. He had been certain to remember that much, to know the means of consummating his plan.

He would move behind the helicopters as they flew west or north, using his almost endless physical strength to carefully stay ahead of the ground teams that would be following close. He would stay between them, not moving at all through open terrain but using the dunes for cover until he reached the high cliffs bordering the northern edge of White Sands Military Reservation, where the fools created this magnificent body.

Within a day, he knew, he could reach the base of the San Andres Mountains, moving west and unhindered through the mesas and towering red cliffs with the speed and strength of a lion.

When he reached Albuquerque he would easily steal transportation and move further into Cortez, Colorado, avoiding the cold mountain roads where he could be too easily trapped. He was certain he would not be caught, for his plan had just begun.

He smiled as he felt blood raining from his hands; such sweet blood.

No, he could never have enough.

◆ ◆ ◆

Soloman wordlessly handed a glass of Glenlivet to General Benjamin Hawken and the general instantly threw back a sobering swallow, as if he fully intended to have another.

In front of Soloman's desert home a fast-flight Loach

with two slicks – unarmed choppers used for troop transport – rested on the ground, blades churning a cloud of man-made wind. And a platoon of Delta Force commandos had positioned themselves over the grounds, securing a close perimeter.

Against what, exactly, Soloman didn't know.

Sensing the seriousness of a situation he didn't understand, Soloman dropped two ice cubes in his glass, pouring himself a measure of Scotch. 'So tell me, Ben, what do you want? You didn't hop all the way from White Sands without a good reason.'

There was no immediate reply as Hawken grunted and threw down another mouthful, turning wearily to gaze at Soloman's enclosed courtyard.

Heavy slabs of weights were scattered over the chalky white cement, as if they were used regularly. And a heavybag reinforced with silver duct tape hung from a chain, combat boots and bag gloves beside it. The bag had been hit by so many murderous blows from hand and foot that the coarse canvas seemed smooth as silk.

'Keeping in shape, Sol?'

'A little.'

'Still running? What? Ten miles a day?'

'Yeah,' Soloman answered. 'More or less.'

Hawken laughed and Soloman waited in silence as the general took a heavier sip, warming to it. And as they stood so close a comparison was too obvious to overlook. Hawken was beefy with a thick truck-tire gut, his face pudgy around the edges. He had the body of a professional wrestler gone soft, the body of a man who possessed obvious physical strength but who'd forgone conditioning for too long. It was a dramatic physical contrast to Soloman, who'd been burned down and rebuilt by seven hard years of severe conditioning.

'Death Valley has been good for you, Sol,' Hawken grunted, nodding with what appeared to be genuine admiration. 'Maybe I should get a home here myself. Right now I'm about *ready* to retire.'

Soloman didn't reply. Drops of water fell from the slowly heating glass of Scotch held in his hand as Hawken continued to palaver about the medicinal benefits of living in Death Valley. And while the general talked he began to stroll casually about the room, apparently relaxing. But Soloman knew what Ben was truly doing; he was trying to get a feel for whatever kind of life it was that he lived in the desert.

There was little to see.

Spartan to the extreme, the humble stucco desert house was filled with cheap, impersonal furniture that revealed little or nothing about the man who inhabited it. There was a large wooden table and four sturdy chairs in a clean, practical kitchen that had few modern conveniences. The walls were bare and off-white, and there was no phone, no television or radio or communication equipment of any kind.

A large oak desk commanded a significant section of the room, seeming to be the heart of everything, as if the house had been expressly designed to accommodate it.

Then, behind, were deep rows of books, their spines imprinted with archaic Latin and Greek and a host of modern languages. Placed with obvious care on the shelves, the volumes were surrounded by other books, newer and in better condition, with everything carefully positioned for easy access. And there were entire sets of reference manuals, twenty and thirty volumes apiece, all organized with care. And last, there were heavy manuals on art and literature, plus references on intelligence work. Clearly, it was the library of a scholar, or the repository of a man searching for something.

Staring at a photograph of a young girl, a child ten years old with laughing eyes and an angelic face framed by chestnut hair, Hawken became morose. His voice was reminiscent. 'You know, that was probably the best picture you or Marilyn ever took of Lisa.'

Soloman frowned, silent. He stared down at the Scotch and his silence seemed to solidify, as if the frown would last forever, or had. After a long moment he took a heavy swallow.

Tilting his head to notice the somber action, Hawken cleared his throat. He turned to the books. 'Anyway,' he said, a little louder, 'I see you've continued your studies.'

'Keeps me busy,' Soloman answered, frowning into his glass.

'Yeah, I'll bet it does. So what are you studying now? Philosophy? Archeology?'

'Philo.'

'Hmm?'

'Philo. I'm studying Philo.'

Hawken nodded, appreciating it in silence.

Soloman sighed. 'Philo was an ancient Jewish philosopher, Ben. I'm comparing his logic of rhetoric to Aristotle's. And the Hebrew-Greek context is a fascinating study, in case you want to get into it.'

'That's … that's good, Sol. It's good that you're keeping busy.' He waited at that, tensing. 'But, tell me, have you finished with the Latin? Do you, uh, understand it pretty well?'

Soloman couldn't tell if the question meant anything or not. He hesitated a moment. 'Latin is a lifelong endeavor, Ben. I'll be studying it a few more years before I'm proficient.'

Hawken turned from the window to study Soloman's unexpressive face. Then the general took another sip. A big one, like he needed it. 'But you understand Latin, right?' he asked. 'I mean, if somebody dog-cussed me in Latin, you could tell me what they said?'

Soloman smiled faintly. 'Ben, I don't think anybody's

going to be dog-cussing you in Latin whether you deserve it or not. Which I'm sure you would.' He stared without friendship. 'Why don't you just tell me why you're here?'

A wave of genuine fear floated beneath General Benjamin Hawken's face as he gathered himself. 'We've got a situation, Sol. A situation that's ... out of hand.'

In military jargon, that meant that the security of the nation was in immediate peril and nobody at the Pentagon or the White House or even Langley had the faintest idea of what to do about it. And although Soloman had worked with Hawken three years in a secret program that utilized the best field operatives from Marine Force Recon and Army Special Forces to hunt rogue intelligence agents, he had never heard Hawken use the words.

Soloman, a marine lieutenant colonel at the time, had been second in command under Ben, an army general. But the blacked-out program had been far more counterintelligence than military, so rank or branch had been essentially insignificant.

For a moment Soloman was still, his lips tight. Then, relaxing, he walked slowly to the front window. He took a small sip from his glass and lowered it in a dead-cold hand, inspecting the Loach and the contingent of Delta commandos.

'I'm retired, Ben.'

Hawken grunted, and with peripheral vision Soloman saw him glance down at his glass. He opened his eyes to find it surprisingly empty before he walked to the cabinet, pouring himself another. He muttered hollowly, 'Yeah, Sol. I figured you'd say that.'

Soloman shifted, feeling something stir. He knew that this might be what he had sought in the long years of loneliness and that he didn't want, truly, to walk away from it, even as another part of him rose against it.

'It's probably best, anyway,' Hawken grunted, frowning into his drink. 'I mean, after what they did to Marilyn ... and Lisa.'

Soloman turned and his face sharpened around the dark glasses. He stood unmoving, his eyes hidden. Something within him – his essence – suddenly hardened, intensified. His stillness was now frightening.

Hawken sensed the change and quickly raised a hand. 'I know, Sol, I know. And any of us would have done the same thing. That is, if we *could* have. And I don't blame you for it. I never did. Never will. And, believe me, between the two of us I even admired you for it.'

'Is that why you didn't defend me at the hearing, Ben? Because you admired me?'

Hawken's face registered shock, disbelief. 'Nobody could have defended you, Sol! You crossed too many lines! Big time! And the heat that came down was too much for any of us to stand! They couldn't let you go public but they couldn't let you walk away untouched, either. Your promise of silence and resignation was the only reason those goons in Washington didn't sanction you! And that's the truth! It was best for everybody if you and the military just parted ways!'

Not responding, Soloman swirled the melting ice and Scotch. He gazed down, as if he wasn't sure what he saw in it.

'Tell me about your situation, Ben.'

Hawken hesitated. 'All right,' he began tiredly, 'I'll brief you. But, first, let me tell you that we've got almost two thousand men on this and I'm not sure we can't handle it ourselves. But certain people are ... *alarmed*. And they're ready to bring an ending to this thing by any means necessary.'

Soloman laughed. 'By any means necessary? You must be getting dramatic in your old age, Ben. We've been in hot zones all over the world and I've never heard you say that.'

There was a stoic pause before the barrel-chested general set his drink on the desk, crossing arms over his chest. His crew-cut black hair, heavily colored with gray, framed a commanding demeanor.

'Listen, Sol, something has happened. It's a hot situation and I'd just like you to look at some evidence. 'Cause we've got a rogue agent loose and, believe me, he's dangerous. More dangerous than anybody you've ever seen. More dangerous than anybody *any* of us have ever seen. And I don't have the foggiest where to start looking. So I need you to come in and study something and tell me what you think. That's all. Just take a look at something and tell me what you think.'

Soloman smiled. 'It always amuses me, Ben, that you can seem to say so much and so little at the same time. What are the orders?'

'The operation orders are to find this guy pronto and we've got people working on it full-tilt boogie.' Hawken nodded. 'We've got four wings of fully armed AH-64s and six platoons of Pathfinders tracking him. We've also mobilized the 101st out of Bragg and they've air-dropped into an area southeast of Albuquerque, 'cause we know this guy is moving north. There's ten Force Recon platoons in the woods and we've activated SEAL Team One. And, so far, we've passed it off as a training exercise, but the truth is that we're hunting this guy with our best people.'

'Any engagement so far?'

'Yeah,' Ben frowned. 'Two platoons of the Eagles stumbled over him. We loaded their dead bodies in a slick.'

Soloman stared. 'That's impossible.'

'No,' Ben shook his head. 'It's possible, and it happened. That's why we're not using civilian police. I don't want the guilt and complications of a lot of dead cops.'

Soloman knew from commanding a Marine Corps

Force Recon team, fast-attack supergrunts skilled in covert warfare, that no man could be that good. And the 101st, the Screaming Eagles, were the pride of the United States Army, the best infantrymen in the world. But Hawken communicated with his tone alone that that was, indeed, the case. After a moment Soloman asked, 'Where did this guy escape from, Ben?'

'From White Sands.'

'The missile range?'

'No. From an underground facility where they –' The general abruptly halted, raising his hands. 'Look, Sol, I can't tell you any more right now. Not unless you want to get into it. But this guy is moving north fast and we need to anticipate where he's going so we can triangulate on him and take him out. Big time. With a howitzer.'

Soloman was openly curious. After a moment he set his glass on a table. 'All right, Ben, I'll take a look at what you've got. I might be able to help you and I might not. I'm not making any promises.'

'Good, Sol. That's good enough.'

'Let me change into some yoots and boots and we'll get airborne in the Loach.' He moved from the room, walking smoothly until Hawken called to him: 'Hey, Sol.'

Soloman turned, motionless.

'Look, this is just between the two of us.' Hawken's eyes were hesitant, a shade of fear. 'But tell me the truth, 'cause we've known each other almost fifteen years, right? Why did you come out here? I mean, why'd you choose to live in the middle of nowhere?' He shook his head. 'Sol, there ain't nothing out here but death.'

Stoic, Soloman revealed nothing.

'Death isn't so bad, Ben,' he said, glancing at the picture of his dead child before he focused again on the general. 'I guess it all depends on what you've got to live for.'

CHAPTER 2

I t was incredible.
   Absolutely incredible.

Soloman watched the videotape for the third time in the underground bunker at White Sands, the Air Force base buried deep in the south of New Mexico. Concentrating to remember every detail, he saw the man – a man well above six feet tall and weighing perhaps two hundred and fifty pounds – sit violently upright on an autopsy table.

The man tore his wrist free from a steel manacle to snatch the scientist by the neck. Then he killed him with a flick of his wrist before effortlessly shattering steel brackets holding his other arm and legs. Fearless and with amazing calm, he rose and walked to a vault.

Soloman was stunned to hear his own voice so subdued: 'What's this man's name, Ben?'

Ben expelled a thick cloud of cigar smoke. 'His name was Roth Tiberius Cain.'

'Was?'

'Just watch it again.'

Soloman looked at the screen to see Cain standing before the vault. Then Cain reached out to brutally rip away the steel cover plate from the control box before rewiring it with superhuman efficiency. Seconds later the vault slid open and he emerged naked into the corridor, bold and challenging in the fluorescent light.

His head was bald and his entire body was massively

muscular with a deep chest, broad shoulders, and tremendously heavy arms and legs. It was a body gained from decades of dedicated weightlifting and enhanced with a dozen synthetic stimulants and steroids. Yet despite his incredible bulk he moved with a catlike step, inhumanly poised.

He walked purposefully down the hall, and here the camera angle switched to a Special Forces platoon. Over thirty heavily armed soldiers charged around a corner to come almost face-to-face with the giant before they leaped back, firing frantically.

Cain roared as he was hit, taking over a dozen rounds into his chest, arms, and legs, and then his face twisted in rage before he charged, moving too quickly to follow.

'We've slowed down this part of the video.' Hawken's breathing was a bit heavy. He reached out to hit a small button and then the figures were moving in slow motion. The conflict was deeply reflected, like fire, in Soloman's black glasses as he leaned forward, watching intently as the first soldier died.

Enraged by his wounds, Cain shouted something – Soloman couldn't be sure what it was – and fell upon the point man. His right hand struck like an ax to viciously split the ballistic vest, and Cain roared as he ripped the man's spine out of his chest. Hawken shook his head as he viciously blew out a haze of cigar smoke.

Soloman spoke. 'What did they do to this man, Ben?'

'It's too complicated to explain,' Hawken grunted. 'I couldn't explain it to you even if I wanted to. It's … scientific. Just keep watching.'

In the next second Cain spun, still moving fast though his movements were being replayed in slow motion. He laid hands on a rifle, firing. And from that moment it was a pure and simple point-blank shootout with the surviving Special Forces members.

Cain moved so quickly that the others seemed not to

be moving at all, killing and killing before he dropped the empty clip and tore another magazine from a massacred soldier, receiving even more wounds in his back and chest. He moved forward as he reloaded with the wholesale carnage continuing. And then it was over, dead men littering the corridor with walls painted in blood. Remorseless, Cain contemptuously hurled the rifle aside.

Walked away.

Cameras automatically followed him as he made a violent path through the laboratory, randomly encountering soldiers and killing them all with masterful skill, almost without effort. He was forced on two more occasions to defeat vaults and then he reached the last barrier to freedom: a thick cage of steel bars like those used in maximum-security prisons.

Covered in the blood that ran from countless bullet wounds that were healing even as they watched, Cain flung another rifle aside and reached up to grasp the bars with hands of frightening size and power. With a violent twist he shattered the lock.

Sliding the door open, he leaped forward and entered an elevator, rising to the surface of the facility. Seconds passed and the cameras picked him up as he exited the elevator, coming into the lobby. Through a holocaust of rifle fire he ran quickly across the long entrance, finally leaping through a plate-glass window to descend twenty feet to the cement lot where he landed lightly as a deer, continuing with amazing agility and strength.

Despite his wounds, Cain covered a quarter mile in less than thirty seconds to vanish into the woods. Exterior cameras followed him until he was lost to the dark.

Expelling a gloomy cloud of cigar smoke, Hawken leaned forward and lifted a trembling hand, shutting off the video. He turned grimly to Soloman. Said nothing.

Soloman folded his hands in front of his face, elbows

on the table. He tried to concentrate on what he had seen, tried to believe it. But it was beyond belief; it was impossible. From a distance he heard Hawken speaking, carefully separating each word.

'Well, Sol, what do you think?'

Soloman was expressionless. 'Have your people done cryptoanalysis on what Cain said?'

'Yeah.'

'Let's hear it.'

Hawken hit a button and the screen was once again alive. 'We had a naval guy, a submarine tech, do the sonic. He had to filter out the rifle fire and the rest in order to isolate the words.'

With an intentness that separated him from where he was, Soloman heard the sound of rifle fire diminishing degree by degree until the singularly terrifying image of Cain was on the screen. The deep voice was lordly and volcanic.

Killing with demoniacal purity, he lowered his head like a lion as he shouted, *'Di liberatus!'* Then as he tore the soldier's spine from his chest he surged through the rest of them, thundering in rage, *'Adversarius devicit leonem de tribu Juda!'*

Soloman's eyes narrowed.

Killing ... killing ...

Unstoppable.

Hawken spoke. 'We haven't translated it yet, Sol. I didn't think it was an appropriate security measure. But I think I caught some things in it. Because I wasn't born yesterday. It's Latin, I think. And I thought that maybe you could tell me what it means.'

'You're right, Ben. It's Latin. When Cain killed the first soldier he said, "I will be free." '

' "I will be free"?' Hawken stared. 'That's what he said?'

'Yeah. "I will be free." '

'Well ... what the hell does that mean, Sol? I mean,

23

Cain couldn't speak Latin when he died. He was a dangerous guy, even a brilliant guy. He was probably even insane. And he spoke German and French and Spanish. But he couldn't speak *Latin*.'

'Get me everything you have on Cain,' Soloman said, his face hardening. 'I want his 201. What was he? CI-2?'

'CI-1. The best killer the CIA had.'

'I want his psychological profile. And get me everything you have on this experiment. Then I want to talk to the scientist who headed this thing up. Send some people to bring him in. I don't care what he's doing. And secure me billeting at the base with video equipment where I can work undisturbed. I want the floor cleared. Assign a couple of Delta commandos to work rotating eight-hour, two-man shifts for detail.'

'You've got it.' Hawken turned in his chair. 'Are you going to take this thing on, Sol?'

'Maybe. But right now I need to get some chow and think it over. I'm too tired to make a decision.' Soloman walked toward the door and as he reached it he heard Hawken call, 'Hey, Sol, wait ... wait a second. You're not telling me everything.'

Soloman turned, expressionless.

'Cain said something else, didn't he? Something you're not telling me?' Hawken trembled slightly. 'Come on, buddy, don't hold out on me. What else was there?'

Raising narrow eyes, recalling the unearthly supremacy captured on Cain's face, Soloman was silent. When he finally spoke his voice was subdued, uncertain.

'He said, *"Adversarius devicit leonem de tribu Juda."* ' He paused. 'That's exactly what he said, Ben. As Cain killed that second man he said. "The Adversary has conquered the Lion of the Tribe of Judah." '

'Well, Sol, what does that mean?' Hawken was pale. 'I mean, what are we getting into here?'

After a long silence, Soloman replied, 'I'm not sure, Ben. But I know the only man ever known as the Lion of the Tribe of Judah died almost two thousand years ago.'

◆ ◆ ◆

After Soloman's departure, General Benjamin Hawken entered a soundproof, electronically swept room located at the back of the bunker and activated a SATCOM access code that engaged the National Defense Secondary Imaging System. Screens came alive in three other offices located in distant sections of the nation.

He knew one screen was hooked into Langley and recognized the haggard countenance of Winston Archette, the CIA's Assistant Director of Covert Operations. Another was linked with the Pentagon and Army Brigadier General Arthur Thompson, Chairman of the Joint Chiefs of Staff. And then the last screen blinked abruptly to lock on the face of Blake Hollman, Deputy Director of the National Security Agency.

Carefully, Ben typed: *Genocide One: Trinity Failsafe, Code: K-101-G-101. Authorization: General Benjamin Hawken-PKA.472.89.*

The nondisplayed characters were immediately routed through the Unified National Security Index Center, a highly classified complex buried in the hills of West Virginia that monitored all governmental transmissions color-coded RED or above.

General Thompson was the first to speak. 'Have you completed your analysis, Ben?'

'Yes, sir, General.'

'What is the operative's status?'

'Upon my judgment,' Ben answered, 'I believe we can grant full authority and command. Ghost is in operational condition and acquisition of the target is highly probable. He has competently translated messages left by target but has not completed evaluation. I believe we should authorize a green light and proceed with the Trinity Failsafe.'

Archette broke in. 'Are you certain of your analysis, General? If you don't mind, I would like for you to explain to me the grounds of your primary analysis.'

'Ghost is mentally sound and has retained optimum weapons skills required for this operation,' Ben answered, his voice flat. 'There is no indication of debilitating habit. His mental acuity is superior, consistent with past operational levels, and he has adapted to civilian life without any untoward signs of delayed stress. So, in my judgment, we are operational.'

'I see,' Archette replied. 'However ...' He hesitated. 'I urge you to use caution, General. Ten hours may not be sufficient for this analysis. Especially since you are evaluating an extremely complex individual.'

'I am familiar with this individual, Professor.'

'Of course you are, General. And make no mistake: I also believe that Ghost is an excellent selection to fulfill the Trinity Failsafe, insofar as his mind is now sound. I only want us to be as certain as possible because Ghost's past is ... discomforting.'

'I'm aware of that, sir.' Ben stared, holding his ground. 'But I believe my judgment is sound.'

'We all do, General.' Archette smiled briefly. 'I have full faith in your judgment. I only wanted to remind you of the time constraints which we may confront, according to the latest reports on the experiment. As you know, there will be no time for reorganization once Trinity is dispatched.'

Ben frowned, professional. 'I can stress to this council, based on my long association with this operative, that he is stable. Further, that he remains loyal to his country. He also seems to have overcome past revenge motivations and appears highly capable of termination orders. I judge him militarily capable and physically and intellectually superior. And, most importantly, he has retained his most salient skill: intuitive evaluation. Therefore I deem him to be the candidate best qualified to fulfill the mission.'

A hardened silence followed.

General Thompson stared for a long time, then reached out to touch a switch. 'We'll make a JCS decision by 1200 hours tomorrow, Ben.' He gave no indication of direction. 'Continue briefing. This communication is terminated.'

Silence blanketed the bunker, and Ben didn't move for a long moment, staring at the blank screen. He felt he'd betrayed his friend yet he knew he hadn't betrayed him. Because betrayal came from impure motivations and his motivations, he knew, were pure. Just as he knew that he was over his head in this, and he needed him … one last time.

He only hoped, in the end, that it would be enough.

CHAPTER 3

It took less time than he had feared to blend into the world, running without fatigue through the scorched desert. He was amazed that it required less than two days to escape the huge shifting dunes of White Sands, the endless sandstone mounds so fine that the granules swirled like dust.

Now the long gliding red hills of the San Andres Mountains swept up at slow angles on either side of him, only to descend into jagged ravines and chasms that provided excellent cover from his hunters.

It was late fall but the heat was greater than he'd anticipated, perhaps because of the severe physical exertion required for moving ahead of the all-too-frequent formations of aircraft, or perhaps it was because he was not killing frequently enough; he did not know. He would adjust day by day because he was determined to win, his phenomenal sense of anticipation lending him a tactical edge these humans would forever lack.

He skirted the Valley of Death – it would have exposed him to aerial or ground sighting – and proceeded through the broken crags until he rose on the steep slopes of the Salinas, quickly changing direction to move west.

Life was scarce in the colder heights and he was forced to follow ledges and rarely used animal paths where he found little to sustain him. But he survived, feasting on rattlesnakes that he detected and snatched from beneath stones. It was here he killed a cougar with a single backhanded blow, ferociously hurling it from the ledge where it was poised to leap. Then feasted on it.

But he needed more blood, for what was harbored within his colossal form was destabilizing faster than he'd anticipated.

As the days wore, he began to move with more economy, always selecting the least difficult route that still provided concealment, conserving his strength. And then he descended the mountains toward a wide river flanked by towering red cliffs.

Yes!

The Rio Grande!

He smiled.

Now he would simply follow the river north into Albuquerque, and along its water he would find the blood he needed to consummate his strength. It would be necessary to hide the bodies in order to conceal his direction of travel, but he knew he could accomplish the task. Then, when he reached the city, the real game would begin.

As he eased cautiously down the mountain he laughed at his almost effortless success, feeling more and more of his cosmic mind return, shadow upon shadow, until he could almost remember so much ...

But the true scope of his galactic knowledge would come slowly, he knew. It would take years to become what he had been, bringing all of that majestic might into this world, unless he could obtain the child.

For now, he only remembered specific things he had fiercely retained during the terrific seizure of this form, and even that much was uncertain. He could not remember his full plan, only faint shadows, ideas, the name and the locations of the documents.

Yes, he had retained knowledge of language and

culture and law and the locations of those things he must acquire, but he couldn't remember well enough why he must acquire them. There was the castle, yes, the castle where he would … *organize?*

No … that was not the reason. There was something else, something the castle held. It was coming to him slowly as the moments passed, but then … there was more, something he couldn't yet remember. He only sensed that it would give him the power he needed to overcome his most hated enemy.

In time, he told himself.

Yes, in time …

Yes, he would remember in time. And then, he knew, he would destroy them. He would decimate these sheep, would rule them, bring them into his fold; all of them together. Because they were merely mortal and he was far, far more than they could imagine.

Their faint lives, fading fast in the scope of this universe, were as chaff compared to the overcoming ecstasy of the vision and knowledge and insight that was his essence. No, he could never be less than they, and they could never raise themselves to overcome his place as lord and master, as he had almost been but for the wrath flung forth from that hateful arm …

Moving with the deadly poise of a lion seeking prey, he entered Albuquerque, descending from the hills. With superhuman strength that seemed all but inexhaustible, he found the Luna exchange and moved immediately east, staying on the outskirts of the city to remain far from heavily patrolled roads, continuing his search.

His clothes were insufficient now. He needed new garments unstained by blood and untorn by combat. And then he saw it: a massive two-story military surplus building that stood vague and alone in the dry dirt between a deserted saloon and hotel.

He raised his eyes to the sun, frowning at the light, knowing he could not move until darkness. So he searched till he found a low hollow filled with crusted gray dirt and sage, and lay down. Concealed from view, he would wait until it was safely dusk and then he would descend to take what he needed: food, clothing, a vehicle, and possibly weapons.

In the distance he heard low-flying helicopters, and he laughed. No, they were not wise enough to anticipate his movements. Because he knew their methods and technology, just as he knew that the wider the search perimeter became, the wider would be the gaps.

He had already fed, and even though he did not feel the burning deep thirst that drove him mad he knew he would have to feed again, and soon, because he had exhausted too much strength in killing the random soldiers who'd stumbled over him.

Yes, in time.

His joy, rising against the dying sun, was bestial.

Yes ...

In time.

◆ ◆ ◆

After finishing a meal prepared by the general's staff Soloman listened as Ben described how scientists at White Sands had taken Cain's body and rebuilt it piece by piece to make it superhuman, indestructible, immortal.

With distinct nervousness Ben recounted how Cain had died by electrocution in an apparent accident, even though the circumstances of the event were classified above Ben's 'need to know.'

Dead for more than fifteen minutes before his body

reached a military hospital, Cain was quickly declared legally deceased and, through the intervention of unknown forces, immediately placed on life-support. Machines kept oxygenated blood circulating in his system, apparently to preserve the body as much as possible in preparation for this strange experiment.

'What was the stated purpose of Genocide One?' asked Soloman, referring to the experiment by its cryptonym. 'Why did they want to take a man and make him unkillable?'

Ben released a heavy breath. 'The purpose of Genocide One was to create a ... Sol, they wanted to create a supersoldier.'

Soloman's mouth gaped. 'Jesus Christ, Ben.'

'Not hardly, Sol.'

Silence.

'All right,' Soloman said. 'Tell me about it.'

Ben shook his head. 'I don't know everything, Sol. To tell you the truth, I wasn't even in on the get-go. I was brought in just before you as part of the containment plan. But I figure it's because these CIA morons wanted to genetically alter a soldier so he could travel a hundred damn miles in a day. I guess us regular grunts weren't good enough for them. They wanted a freak strong enough to carry armor and weapons that a normal man couldn't even lift.'

Soloman noticed that Ben kept shifting as he continued. 'But, damn it, Sol, these people were messing with Mother Nature! It makes me nervous as hell and that's why I need you. Think about it: Cain was graveyard dead! It ... I mean, it isn't like they took a warm body and rebuilt it, Six Million Dollar Man and all that. No! This guy was *dead!* How could they have brought him back to life?'

'I understand, Ben.' Soloman was hit with a rush of compassion for his old friend. 'Answer this: Just how were these supermen supposed to be controlled? We have enough trouble controlling regular soldiers, but superior ability breeds superior ambition.'

'According to the specs,' Ben answered, 'there was supposed to be a device implanted inside their cerebrum so the white-coats and the commanders could track their monsters. They go off the reservation and you can tell them to self-destruct. Just a pinprick explosion, but it would cause instant edema. They'd be dead in three seconds.'

'A device that was never implanted in Cain.'

'Right. From what I understand, they never expected him to get up from the table.'

Soloman pursed his lips in thought.

'The future of warfare,' he said.

There was no true means of measuring the silence that followed. It was the kind of silence that a man holds when he anticipates horrible news. But the news had already been delivered so it reached beyond that.

'Ben,' Soloman said, his eyes hidden behind dark glasses. 'What do you really think we're dealing with?'

Ben frowned, clearly disturbed. 'I don't know,' he answered finally. 'Just ... some kind of freakin' Frankenstein or Dracula or something. Honest to God, I don't know. 'Cause I ain't no scientist. But one thing is for sure, Sol, even to a scientific flunky like me.'

'What's that?'

'It sure as hell ain't Cain.'

◆ ◆ ◆

The large edifice was silent in gray light.

Dark, in shadows.

Somberly the priest inside St Michael's Cathedral in Los Angeles removed the unfinished chalice of wine. Yet as he held the bowl he stared a moment, hesitating, before he drank what remained. Then he gazed downward, frowning.

A thunderous voice rumbled behind him.

'Sin is a beautiful thing.'

The priest gasped as he whirled.

Seated in shadow upon the shadowed altar-throne, the bald man laughed. Seemingly gigantic in the gloom, his strength was obvious even in stillness. Then he moved a massive hand lazily through the darkness as if to caress it, or command. The gesture was vaguely ominous, threatening.

'Father Lanester,' he whispered, 'your sins … precede you.'

'Wh-wh-wh … who are you?' the priest whispered.

Silence.

'Your friend.'

'Yes … yes of course. But the church is closing.'

'As always.' The man laughed again. 'Long overdue, I assure you.' Colossal, he rose smoothly and took a terrifying step forward. 'You have sins, Father,' he continued. 'Yes, many, many sins. For I know of your fondness for the fruit of the vine. I know of your fondness for women. Sins you hide because they belong only … to me.'

The priest staggered back.

'O my *God!*'

Scowling, the giant bent his head.

'No,' he growled. 'Not yet.'

◆ ◆ ◆

Soloman revealed no surprise but he was, indeed, surprised as the conference room doors opened and she entered. Dark brown hair fell over slender shoulders as Dr Martha Milton set a large black briefcase on the table and opened it with a curt smile.

'Good evening, gentlemen.' She nodded to them.

Her face was angular and smooth. Her neck was also lean and strong and she moved like an athlete. She obviously kept herself in shape. Though she appeared to be no more than thirty, Soloman suspected she was slightly older, maybe thirty-five.

'I'm sorry I'm late,' she continued. 'Shall we begin?'

Ben blinked. 'Of course,' he said abruptly. 'Yes, of course we should. Can I get you anything? Coffee?'

'Thank you. Black.'

Ben retrieved a cup and Soloman politely removed his glasses. His eyes, the pale blue of the sea surrounding a Mediterranean island, narrowed at the room's bright fluorescent light.

Dr Milton smiled faintly, glancing at the small round lenses laid on the table. Her own eyes were jade-green and clear. 'I'm pleased to meet you, Colonel,' she said with respect. 'But please feel free to wear your glasses, if you wish. I won't consider it impolite. You're obviously sensitive to light.'

'A little,' Soloman conceded.

'How good is your night vision?'

'I'm at a Minus 4.'

'That's as good as a cat,' she said without expression. 'But Cain's better. In fact, he's a lot better. His diopter reading is almost off the scale.'

The sudden change in conversation startled Ben and he sloshed the coffee, scalding his hand. He didn't seem to notice. He came back quickly to the table.

She had gone into it so smoothly, Soloman thought. If I don't get geared up fast, she's going to leave me in the dust. He tried not to reveal that he was already intimidated. 'Just what exactly are we dealing with, Doctor?' he asked.

She handed each of them black files stamped TOP SECRET/BIOLOGICAL WARFARE. 'Take a look at these, gentlemen, and you'll begin to understand that we are in a mortal situation. It is far more serious than anyone has told you.'

General Hawken grunted at that, let it go.

Studying the file, it only took Soloman a moment to understand the medical jargon. Concentrating, he studied Cain's chart to determine what they had done to the man. He singled out factors that seemed particularly disturbing: anterior spinal cord amplifiers, orthopedic transplants, bio-polymar subcutaneous coating for titanium-reinforced bones, interior titanium implants and immunity-acceptance levels with a breakdown of projected HyMar viral layers on secondary stratum corneum –

HyMar viral layers?

His attention was suddenly captured by a grisly color photograph of Cain on an operating table. Large metal plates of a strange curving design were carefully positioned on an instrument tray.

A team of surgeons bent over him. His chest and arms were laid open to the core as they apparently removed bones. Another surgeon worked on one of his knees, implanting what appeared to be a small titanium plate over the patella, or kneecap.

'That's a photo of the surgery where we implanted armor plating in Cain's chest,' she said. 'We also replaced his humerus, radius and ulna, and secondary skeletal appendages with cobalt-chromium-alloy bones. Something like the artificial titanium sockets used for contemporary joint replacements but light-years ahead in design. They have a projected use expectancy of more than a hundred years instead of ten. Plus, we placed curving niobium-titanium shields between his pectoralis major and all the internal organs, armoring him between the clavicle and the eighth rib.'

'Sounds complicated,' Soloman said, studying her eyes.

'That's nothing,' she replied evenly. 'Cain has recumbent anabolic steroid reserve cells, internal carpal and forearm titanium bosses, and organic modifiers that hyperconcentrate viral-induced muscle fibers. He could punch a hole through a steel door. And, to top it off, his outer stratum corneum is infected with a multiviral factor, specifically an altered strain of the Marburg virus. It's something we call HyMar. And that virus, gentlemen, makes Cain a walking time bomb.'

Soloman understood the ramifications because he had dealt with the destruction and theft of biological weaponry before. What he knew was that Marburg was the one that even scared the biowarfare specialists. No one knew where it came from, its vector, or a cure. They just knew it killed 99 percent of the people it touched and it did it ugly.

Ben leaned back, his cigar dead-cold. Clearly, shock had removed him from the conversation. Perhaps because he couldn't trust himself to speak. But Soloman was concentrating furiously: 'Why did you infect Cain with a strain of the Marburg virus, Doctor?'

'Because the Central Intelligence Agency and the Pentagon gave me a mandate to create the ultimate soldier, Colonel. And the funds to do it.'

'And ... did you do it?'

'Yes,' she said quietly. 'And then some.'

'How long do we have to find Cain, Doctor?'

'Ten days' was her answer, and genuine fear, for the first time, entered her voice.

'And if we don't?'

'Then,' she replied, 'Cain will be able to walk through the largest city in the world, Colonel, and kill everyone in it.'

◆ ◆ ◆

'Ah, so pleasant,' the giant murmured. 'I love cathedrals. They remind me so much ... of home.'

Seated in the half-light of the edifice, the towering image of the Crucifixion dominating a far wall, he rested before he continued, smiling faintly: 'Yes, such an aroma of death.'

He lifted a hand, slowly flexing it into a massive squared fist of incalculable power, power obvious even with the simple contraction. Staring, the trembling priest watched the movement, trying not to reveal his fear. But clearly, the strength in that taloned hand could kill without effort. The giant laughed again and tenderly reached out to turn the priest's head, staring into his face.

Terror, pure and concentrated, burned vividly in Father Lanester's face as he looked into the giant's horrific countenance. Then the priest closed his eyes, as if he could not endure what he saw.

There was a rumble, like an approaching storm, and then the giant murmured, *'Feoh othila ansux, os geo mannz kano?'*

Father Lanester violently shook his head, 'No, no, please, I –'

'Oh, I am so sorry,' he whispered. 'You do not understand Runic? No … of course not. Hmmm. Perhaps we should try Latin? Do you understand Latin? *Cognovi te a facie inimici?'*

'Yes!' Father Lanester shouted, eyes tight. 'I know you are the enemy! *Esto mihi, Domine, turris fortitudinis!'*

The giant frowned, menacing. 'Yes, Father. I am sure that … *he* … will be your strength. But times change. Believe me.' He smiled. 'Then again, perhaps we should leave Latin. Such dreadful repetition. We can speak any language you wish. I know them all. Of course, I would prefer to avoid Aramaic. I had a terrible experience with it … once.' His horrific face lightened in humor. 'Why don't we try German? *Kannst du nicht treu sein?'*

'Yes! I can be faithful to God!'

'No,' the giant said soothingly, gently caressing the priest's head as he would caress a lost dog. *'Meine Handpuppe profane, du hast nicht treu sein können.'*

'Yes!' the priest said, fear choking his throat. 'Yes! I *have* been faithful! I do not know you! I do not know you! You have no part of me! I am a priest of Deus et Dominus –'

Clamping his hand over the priest's face, the giant shut the words. Anger hardened his brow and his aspect was suddenly darker, violently intensifying the surrounding shadows. 'Please do not speak that name again in Latin, Father. It disturbs me ... somewhat. And if you insist, I shall remove you of the burden of your tongue, to ensure your silence. I would not mind. I am quite famished.'

Carefully he removed his hand from the priest, a massive hand that easily covered the face and forehead. And for a moment the priest stared fearfully up into the horrific countenance.

'You ... you cannot speak the name,' he whispered.

'The name?' the giant rumbled. 'Yes. In this form, Father, I can indeed speak the name. Yes, I can speak the name of ... of ... of *Dominus.*' His teeth gritted before he smiled again, more an illusion than the truth. 'For in this form I am more human than not. As you can see. But the verging of life and death has always been closer than any of you knew.' He laughed at the priest's terrified gaze. 'Just like a miracle.'

'What ... what do you want?'

'I want a document sealed in the Secret Archives hidden in the sub-basement, beneath the cellar. A document entombed in the vault with the seal of Archbishop Markus in 1936. I want the document for the Castle of Calistro ... which belongs to me.'

'B-but why ... why do you need it?' The priest was shaking so violently he almost fell from the steps. 'It is sealed! It is cursed! If you are really *him* then you would not need it!'

'Ah,' the giant answered, 'but I am not what I was, Father. Being human ... has its limitations. Even now, my mind, or what survived the merging, is childlike and diluted from my truly glorious state, though I continue to grow moment by moment. I remember little of what I knew, so I need time to acclimate myself to this form. And, to make it even worse, I have discovered that I cannot contact my flock. I am severed from my world.' He laughed. 'Yes, Father, my mind is broken and ragged, still healing from the merging. Some things I remember in full, but they are not the things I need. Though I can still speak to you of so much you do not know. So much that, when I leave you, will never bless you with sleep.'

The priest paled as the giant smiled.

'I can tell you of my poor, pathetic Pazuzzu's long flight through that hateful void to light upon the gate of Babylon, inspiring the fools to destroy the Hebrews,' he added casually. 'I can tell you how my servant, Belial, soared on wings beneath the moon as he laughed at the funeral pyres of Tel-Engedi, where those hundreds of thousands were burned alive, father and son, mother and daughter holding each other in their arms as they delivered their lives to a cloud that took the sun from the earth for a year. Yes ... and what a lovely aroma it was.' He laughed. 'I can describe those last, singing screams of children thrown into the burning belly of Moloch in the dying days of Carthage before that effete snob, Scipio, brought down one of the walls for the glory of expendable Rome. And I can tell you more than that. I can tell you of those fools, Paul and Peter, who are not what you think, even though –'

'But the *Nazarene* defeated you!' the priest shouted.

Silence.

Long ...

Longer.

'So and so,' the giant finally mused, 'the Nazarene.' A rage beyond hell glazed his eyes. His voice was a voice of caverns consuming the dead. 'Yes, unconquerable to the very end. And wiser than a serpent. Deceiving … deceiving even *me* … with the fate of the universe in the balance. A singularly horrific experience, I assure you. But then the Nazarene and I are fated to war again, Father, so let us speak of more pleasant things.' He laughed, diabolical music. 'Let me tell you of those glorious celebrations orchestrated by my faithful children Lilith, Incubus, and Succubus. Let me tell you of the exquisite carnal pleasures they inspired upon Sodom and Egypt and Askalon, unimaginable pleasures that put the Romans to shame. Pleasures that shamed even the sheer animal ecstasies of the slave barracoons of my servile Thoth-Amon, who made the prideful mistake of slaying Saul only to be eaten … by worms. Yes, and there is so much more. More than you mortals could ever –'

A grimace.

With a bestial growl of pain the giant bowed his head, appearing to fight a ravaging injury. His eyes were closed tight as he slowly reached out, grasping the priest by the arm as if he could crush the bones with effortless strength. Then he lifted him from the ground.

'Come, Father,' he whispered. 'I need my pretties.'

◆　◆　◆

'This doesn't make sense,' Soloman said, tossing the file onto the table. His eyes were flat. 'You people were keeping oxygenated blood circulating in what, in essence, was a dead man.'

'I'm not sure that I follow you, Colonel.'

'Call me Soloman.'

'Thank you. Call me Maggie.'

'My point,' Soloman continued, 'is that Cain – or whatever made Cain what he was – was no longer in that body.'

'But his brain wasn't damaged.'

'No, his brain wasn't damaged. Not the neurons. But a man is more than the base electrical synapse of ten billion neurons.' Soloman paused, frowning. 'Tell me something,' he continued, 'where does thought come from?'

From her face, he knew she had no answer. 'I know where you're going with this,' she answered. 'But I don't think a philosophical direction is going to help us.'

'Let me decide that.'

Hesitation.

'All right,' she said, finally. 'Nobody's able to localize the portion of the brain that originates thought. All we know is that "thought" is inserted into the electrochemical flow of ions at some point in the axon. That's a long nerve tendril leading out of a neuron that communicates to other neurons. Are you theorizing that Cain's mind is gone?'

'I don't know what I'm saying. But something doesn't add up. Because you can't bring anyone back to life. It's impossible.'

'But we did it, Colonel.'

'You don't know *what* you did, Maggie.' He didn't make his tone friendly. 'All you know is that you took a dead man and made him some kind of Frankenstein. But now it's loose and those morons that you work for expect Ben and me to stop it.' He shook his head. 'Why won't this HyMar virus kill him?' he continued. 'Is Cain immune to the virus like he's immune to everything else?'

She was affected by his criticism but recovered quickly. 'Cain is only immune to the mutated HyMar virus that we used to alter his genetic code. He's not immune to the original Marburg. The term for it is Viral-Engineering Manipulation.'

'Sounds very benign.' Soloman stared at her.

She blinked. 'The … the main DNA segment of the Marburg virus – the single most deadly virus on the planet – is about two thousand base pairs long. The rest of the strand is devoted to replication, direction, anaphase, whatever. But the main two-thousand-base-pair strand defines the characteristics of the virus. For instance, what the virus is going to do to the cells of its host. What it will give the cells. Now, in the telephase stage of mitosis there is a point called specialization. That's where a cell says to itself, "I'm going to be a muscle cell." Or, "I'm going to be a white blood cell to promote healing." And because the mutated Marburg, or HyMar, has human DNA buffers in it, the main strand has been redesigned and resegmented into the virus to promote *healing* instead of *cell destruction*. That's why Cain heals up almost instantly from any wound. HyMar is constantly promoting to a state of hypermitosis.'

'That accounts for his healing factor,' Soloman said. 'What accounts for his strength? I've read this man's 201. Cain was strong before he died, but he wasn't this strong. Nobody is this strong.'

'Cain's strength was developed through the use of the Sulijuki Forest virus. It's taken from the western forests of Uganda.' Her mouth tightened as she collected her thoughts. 'To truly grasp this phenomenon, you have to understand that Cain was a freak of nature even before we altered his chromosomes.'

'Why?'

'It's not in his file, but he had an exceedingly rare XYY coding.'

'What's that?'

'That's what's known in science as the "superman" trait,' she said. 'It's almost impossible for a male to possess two of the same chromosomes, but Cain did. That's why he was so strong in life, and the main reason he was selected for this experiment. But with the

43

Sulijuki Forest virus we managed to denature a part of the second Y chromosome and bond it strand-sight onto chromosome 14, which hyperconcentrates muscle cells. Plus, to make him strong enough to rip a car door off its hinges, we inserted anabolic steroid reserve cells inside his thorax and upper arms.'

Ben looked glumly away. 'Damn,' he muttered, 'just when you thought it couldn't get any worse.'

Soloman expressed nothing. 'All right, Maggie,' he replied, softening a bit. 'Explain to me why he's so fast.'

She ran a hand through her hair; Soloman saw faint beads of sweat on her forehead. 'That was fundamentally a chemical alteration,' she said. 'Sodium and potassium and magnesium regulate the speed of synapses. What we did with him was simply increase the chemical levels until there was virtually no waiting period.'

'But you never tested him, right?'

'No, we never had a chance.'

'Then give me your best guess,' Soloman concentrated. 'How fast is he? What're his limitations?'

Her face froze as she gazed to the side, calculating. 'He doesn't have cheetah speed. But maybe … a lion.' She leaned back. 'It would be eyes, hands, everything. He's probably at the level of someone when they touch a hot stove. Their hand is moving even before their nerves have identified why. It only lasts a tenth of a second with normal people, but Cain is at that speed constantly. He moves so fast that even he wouldn't know what he was doing if we hadn't modified his central nervous system with electrical enhancements. Of course, we had to provide a niobium-titanium skull shield to protect his brain from the overflow of magnesium and potassium that might have caused cerebral edema. The skull shield also protects his brain against traumatic impact.'

She leaned forward, jaw tight. 'Understand me,

Soloman. Cain does have a weakness: it's the original Marburg virus. If you could reinsert the missing DNA strands in the HyMar virus hosted in his system, it would promote him to full-blown hemorrhagic fever in seconds. In other words, it would take away his power on a molecular level.'

Soloman almost laughed. 'Well, Maggie, I don't think Cain is going to sit still while I give him an injection of the Marburg virus. And I'm not going to take a shot at him. What happens if I miss? What happens if the original Marburg is released in this ecosystem?'

She was silent, pursing her lips.

'If Marburg were inserted into this environment it would become an airborne disease a hundred times more infectious than the common cold.' Her words were slow, as if she were thinking of the very real possibility. 'Within two hours it would kill anyone who contracted it. On a geometric curve it would wipe out a city with the population and density of New York within twenty-four hours. Within forty-eight hours it would be in another half-dozen states and within a week there would be nothing living on this continent. A month after that, if it crosses the ocean on flights before this nation is quarantined, it could conceivably kill everything on the face of the earth.'

General Hawken's hand was trembling violently as he raised his cigar for a vicious drag. He cursed aloud as he expelled the smoke, massaging a sweat-slick forehead.

Soloman took a deep breath. 'I see. Well, then, let's move on. Does Cain have any *other* weaknesses?'

'Yes. There's one. And you might be able to exploit it if you're very, very careful.'

Ben spat out a piece of tobacco. 'Doc,' he growled, 'we passed "careful" about five hundred miles back.'

'What is Cain's other weakness?' Soloman asked.

Pain shut her eyes before she clenched her teeth.

'It … it came out of a severe miscalculation,' she answered. 'The takeover of Cain's DNA by the HyMar virus led to something we didn't want to do. And I want you to know that I consider what we did a very, very tragic mistake. It was something we did only because we thought Cain would only be turned loose in times of war. And in that scenario the enemy would have been the only one … the only one … consumed.'

Soloman's eyes narrowed. Her face was so tragic that Ben just bowed his head and shut his eyes, as if he knew something horrible was about to be said.

'We never anticipated it,' she said more softly. 'We never anticipated that Cain's DNA would be so heavily damaged by the virus. We thought there would be a backflow, a point where the damaged DNA would recover. But it never did. His ribosomal RNA went into a downward spiral that we couldn't reverse, so we had to find a way to replace it in a battlefield situation. And we came up with a method but … but … '

'What are you saying, Maggie?'

She sighed. 'I'm saying that Cain has to constantly replenish his human DNA. I'm saying that he has to –' She caught her breath, grimacing. 'Dear God, forgive me … but … but Cain has to have fresh … he has to have fresh human blood … every day. And if, for some reason, he can't get fresh blood, he'll starve.' The guilt in her voice was tragic but Soloman revealed no shock, somehow knew.

'How does Cain get blood, Maggie?' he asked coldly.

'We … modified him for it.'

'How?'

She closed her eyes, bowing her head.

'With fangs.'

◆ ◆ ◆

An indestructible vault that not even the giant could have torn from the wall was opened and the priest collapsed to the ground, trembling. Deep beneath the cathedral, in the Secret Archives of the cathedral, they were surrounded by ancient texts, artifacts, letters, and long-hidden documents. It was a place of dark secrets, hidden power.

'I need the documents that give ownership to the Castle of Calistro in England,' the giant murmured, staggering. He studied the shelves a long time, confused, for there was no filing system in the archives. Documents and testimonies were laid one upon the other, no numbering, no lettering to mark the sides. It was a wall of white and yellowed parchment in every direction, everything hidden in plain sight.

The giant stood poised in the room and his brow hardened, anger making the red eyes narrow and menacing as Father Lanester stared up, enraptured by the solemn stance.

'What is your name?' the priest asked, regretfully remembering the admonition to never, never ... no, *never* engage them in conversation. But at the words the man simply looked down, a faint smile.

'Cain,' he said. 'My name is Cain.'

'Cain,' the priest repeated. 'The first murderer.'

'And the last,' Cain said coldly. 'Now, where is the document I seek, priest? Where is my document?' His face twisted in a bolt of savage pain. 'I ... cannot remember.'

With a groan he fell to his knees, clutching his head. So close to him, the priest stared, mesmerized at the gigantic suffering that burned in the imperial face. It was the kind of pain that could drive a man insane, but the priest knew in his heart that this was no man.

'Tell me,' the giant mumbled, falling heavily on a hand, holding his head with the other. 'Tell me ... *quickly!*'

Inspired by desperate hope the priest shouted, 'No! ... No! I won't tell you!'

A slow shake of the horrific head and the giant reached out to settle his clawed left hand on the priest's knee. 'Foolish ... foolish mortal,' he moaned, head bowed. 'What makes you think you can contend ... with a god?'

The taloned hand closed to crush the bones of the leg to powder. Blood spiraled from ruptured skin to spray ancient documents. After the priest's hideous, rhythmic screams no longer reverberated from the walls of the subterranean chamber, the giant gazed at him again. He was breathing heavily, as if he were on the verge of death.

'Where ... is the document?'

The priest pointed with a high-pitched scream. 'There! On the shelf! Take it! Take it! Take ... ahhhh ... '

Staggering, Cain rose only to fall heavily against the shelves. He reached up, fumbling, pulling a handful of documents that fell to the floor. Roughly he rummaged, searching until he lifted a thick, ancient, leatherbound document, holding it in his unbloodied hand. He swayed as he turned to the horrified priest of St Michael's, still sprawled in blood.

Grimacing in pain, Cain walked forward, strength failing until he stood over Father Lanester, staring down with eyes as dead-opaque as those of a leopard crouching before a kill.

A violent fear overcame the priest's pain. For there was no pain here, no, not here. Here was the place where fear died. Here was the place of horror, of oncoming death. Then he screamed for the last time in his life as Cain's mouth gaped and fangs violently exploded from his upper and lower ridge, fangs as sharp and savage as a saber-toothed tiger's.

With a godlike hand Cain reached down, lifting the

priest cleanly from the floor. The giant's eyes glowed blood-red as he held him close, whispering over the glistening white tusks.

'Time to feed.'

◆ ◆ ◆

'It's all right, Maggie,' Soloman said, waiting. 'I'm a soldier, and I know what it's like. We both do our jobs. But right now we have to figure out how to stop this monster. Are you able to continue?'

She wiped her face, focusing almost immediately. Obviously, despite the guilt she felt, she possessed remarkable intelligence and control. 'I'm ... fine, Colonel.' She nodded to Ben. 'I'm just fine. Let's get on with it.'

Soloman's eyes softened in respect. 'Good. Thank you.' He took a moment. 'All right, why do we have only ten days before this HyMar virus becomes contagious? You said it wouldn't cause hemorrhagic fever.'

'The HyMar won't cause the fever in Cain, Soloman, but it's still mutating. That's what viruses do. That's *all* they do. I'd hoped that I altered the DL-3 and DL-4 strands to make it nonpathogenic, but I think I failed.'

'Why do you think that?'

Sighing, she seemed to be tiring quickly.

'Because, when I was completing bloodwork on Cain a couple of days ago I saw the virus undergoing silent mutations, or mutations that reveal no phenotypic effects. The mutagens that are still building up in the cell vacuoles are causing a concentration differential to accent pathogenesis. And very soon it's going to achieve a threshold effect.'

Soloman blinked. 'What's a threshold effect?'

'That's the point where a virus becomes lethal. It's ... like this: a Ping-Pong ball going five miles an hour doesn't hurt you. Even if it's going fifty miles an hour it probably won't hurt you. But at some specific point, at maybe eighty or a hundred miles an hour, that Ping-Pong ball reaches a level where it can kill you. HyMar is the same way. There will be a level where the HyMar cytoplasm and mutagens acquire enough host cells to promote the virus to a T-4 bacteriophage. And at that point it will become the most deadly organism this planet has ever seen.'

'And then?'

'And then,' she answered, eyes flashing, 'Cain will be a walking bubonic plague. Anyone who has atmosphere-to-atmosphere contact with him will instantly contract it. And the virus itself will be more resilient than any other Class Four organism ever seen, capable of surviving on a nonorganic surface for as long as two months. Anyone can catch it, and they will infect anyone who has atmospheric contact.'

Finally, Soloman shook his head and rose.

'All right,' he said. 'We're too tired to deal with this now. Let's hit the rack. We'll start again at 0500 but we'll eat chow in here because we've got a lot to do. We've got to find some means of locating this thing.'

'Yeah,' Ben growled. 'Like yesterday.'

Maggie wearily wiped sweat from her forehead. 'Thank you. That ... that *stupid* F-14 flight really took it out of me. Fool of a pilot.' She leaned on the table as she stood. 'I threw up so many times I lost count. Vomit was ... everywhere.'

Soloman smiled, understanding, before he turned to the general. 'Have you secured billeting for her, Ben?'

'Huh?' Ben stared a moment. 'There's no need for that, Sol. She's been living on and off the base for more than three months.' He took a drag, released it slowly. 'You're forgetting, son, that everything was done right here at White Sands, down in J-3. She only had to fly back because she was helping design emergency search-and-destroy procedures for the Seals. When she's here, she lives in the house of an 06 who's been reassigned to Quantico.'

Bowing his head, Soloman cursed himself for not thinking of that. It even scared him a little, making him suspect he'd lost an edge. 'All right, but I want you to change her quarters,' he said. 'Put Maggie on the same floor that I'm on in the administrative building. And I want you to double the Delta guys for added security.'

'Why, Sol? She's already got –'

'Just trust me, Ben. I think I'm right on this.'

Ben's face was emotionless; he nodded. 'All right, Sol. Whatever you want.'

Maggie was watching carefully when Soloman looked back. She stared at him in faint concern, as if her preternatural intelligence had caught something said only by his tone.

'Why should I be afraid, Soloman?' she asked, motionless. 'Cain doesn't know me. He's never … he's never even seen me.'

Whatever was hooded within Soloman's eyes would remain there. Without emotion he turned away.

'I wouldn't bet on it, Maggie.'

CHAPTER 4

A child knew death.
 Terrified eyes searched for the father she could
not find and would never find, no, not ever. And she
slowly turned, staring at the tall man who came for her,
the man that hurt her mother only to chase her so far
and so long.

She had tried to hide but he had found her over and
over, forcing her to run again, always run. But she was
tired of running, her legs heavy and numb, and she
knew that she could run no more.

She watched him come close.

Closer.

Then the tall man reached out to her as ... as *Daddy*
had so often reached out to her.

His hands opened.

A smile.

Death.

All she knew.

◆ ◆ ◆

Soloman let the killer's body fall to the ground.

He had hunted the man down, had hunted almost *all*
of them down and killed them with his own hands.
Because he would have it no other way. Because he had
to kill them all with his hands for what they had done.
Because he had to feel them die in his hands, had to

stare them in the eyes and know *they* knew they were dying ... in his hands.

But now the dark deed was done.

But not so dark, no, not so dark as ...

Her face as it must have been.

'Daddy!'

Soloman roared, awakening.

Too much.

His angry gaze scanned all there was in the room to acclimate himself to where he was. Then he sat upright in the chair where he'd fallen asleep, and with a deeper breath tried not to think that she was gone. Frowning and sweating, he tried to lose the pain but knew he couldn't.

No, he could never lose the pain.

Her blood ...

His guilt, because he had not been there to protect her ...

She was gone. All he had ever loved was gone, the only two people ever to love and trust him were gone. His *child*, murdered when she was so very, very weak by those so cruel, who died in return.

Silent, scowling, Soloman knew the loss and guilt as he knew it every night in the desert with the darkness and silence and cold, alone and lonely. Then he felt his face tighten in pain and tried to resist but knew in the moment that he could never resist.

He bowed his head.

Wept.

◆ ◆ ◆

'Can you stop this guy, Sol?'

Stoic, Soloman watched Cain kill the scientist again. He had watched the film twenty times since he had awoken and something continued to bother him, something he couldn't place. He felt it was there, knew it was there, but whatever it was, it was still eluding him.

Ben had staggered to Soloman's room at four in the morning, knocking sharply on the door, obnoxiously demanding entrance. After Soloman opened the door the general came in with a half-gone bottle of Glenlivet, joyfully lifting it for display.

'I liked this stuff so much that I got a bottle for myself!' he laughed. 'I had to haul old K.C. out of bed, kicking and screaming, to make him open the package store, but a general can do that kind of thing, long as it don't get around.' He swayed, staring at the bottle. 'Old son, this is stout stuff! It's just what I needed! But, good lord, Sol, who *wouldn't!* A freakin' Frankenstein with fangs and superhuman strength running loose? And we're supposed to stop his unkillable ass in ten days or he'll destroy the *world?*'

Soloman shook his head. He knew Ben was riding a deserved wild rapids on the glorious river of booze. He wondered how long it would be before the drop was over, and the calm came.

'Have a seat, Ben,' he muttered. 'That is, if you can.'

Ben collapsed with surprising control into a chair, belching with a slow nodding of his head that continued for a long time. Then his face became abruptly morose, as if he'd drunk himself past happy and into sad. He said nothing, stared at nothing.

'Are you all right, Ben?'

'Fine.' Ben slurred the word impressively. 'Just fine.' He was silent before he looked at Soloman, then smiled. ''Cause I got *you*, old buddy. And you're gonna catch this guy! Yeah, you're gonna catch him,' he nodded to it. 'Then we're gonna kill him. Then we're gonna drive a stake through his heart!' There was a solemn stare; Ben's emotions were changing direction like the wind. 'Do you know why they gave me this assignment, old buddy?'

Soloman laughed. 'Why no, Ben. Tell me about it.'

"Cause they wanted *you!*' he winked, or seemed to; Soloman couldn't be sure. 'Yeah, they wanted you … to come back. They wanted you –' He pointed the uncapped bottle toward the window, spilling a precious amount. 'Wanted you to come out of that *desert!* Because they knew nobody else could pull this off! They wanted the best butcher in the world and they came to me because I was the only one who could bring you out!' He took another swig, a slightly lesser amount to back off.

'Yeah,' he grimaced, 'they gave it to me because they knew nobody else could bring you out of that … Death Valley death house. I don't know what you were doing out there anyway, Sol. Looking to die, waiting to die, tryin' to die. Whatever. But it wasn't … a good place to be.'

Soloman was grim. 'Just staying in shape, Ben. Studying. That's all there is, really.'

'Yeah.' Ben lowered his voice. 'That's why they wanted you. And they used me to do it. I … I could have refused, Sol.' He bowed his head, closing his eyes. 'I could have. I'm only two years out, and they can't touch me. But I knew that you needed it. 'Cause I could see you out there. Remembering. Dreaming. And … and I thought I might bring you back.'

Soloman's lips pursed. He didn't look up.

Shaking his head, Ben continued, 'What was it, Sol?' He paused, staring ahead. 'I mean, what was it? You killed all of 'em deader'n a wedge. But it's like … it's like it ain't finished. Like it never was.'

Soloman frowned. 'One survived, Ben.'

Slowly, Ben nodded. 'Yeah, Sol. He probably did.' There was a moment of unspoken regret as Ben continued. 'Sol, you were the best warrior I ever saw … until you let guilt over Marilyn and Lisa … eat you alive.' His face flinched. 'But they're gone, Sol! And there … there ain't nothin' you can do about it! You did your best! *You're* not the one who gave away the safehouse! We don't know *who* did it! So I don't see how you can consider it your fault, especially since you were out doing your damned job!'

'I should have been there for them, Ben.' Soloman frowned, closing his eyes. 'They trusted me … they trusted me, and they needed me. And I wasn't there … when they needed me most.'

Ben fell silent, as if he'd passed the raging river of booze to fall into a dead and saddened calm.

'Death for death,' he whispered, nodding. 'Death for death.'

◆ ◆ ◆

Somewhere near dawn Ben's amazing vitality and intelligence reasserted itself and he sternly ordered the Delta soldiers to bring two pots of coffee from the mess hall, saying the words just steadily enough to conceal his condition. But then he didn't stand long in the doorway, either, obviously not trusting himself to hold balance for more than a moment. Afterwards he collapsed in a chair beside Soloman, trying to focus as Soloman watched the first scientist die for what may have been the hundredth time. Neither of them had slept after he'd arrived in the room.

Soloman concentrated on the screen as Ben put the cap on an empty bottle of Scotch. The general reached up, gently touching his head. 'I have … a very serious headache. I think this is what they call penance.'

'No, Ben. This is what they call sobering up.'

'Yeah.'

Catching a movement on the screen, Soloman's eyes narrowed.

He saw Cain kill the scientist again before shattering steel shackles holding him to an operating table. Then in the next split-second Cain snatched a coded security card from the scientist's side pocket, moving to the vault door. Moments later he confronted the Special Forces unit in an intersection of hallways, moving toward an unmarked elevator.

Di liberatus!

To be free!

'That's it!' Soloman shouted, stopping the video.

'What!'

'That! That's it!'

'That's *what?*'

Soloman rewound the tape, then froze the picture as Cain bent to take the card. He pointed to the screen. 'Did you see that? Did you see how Cain took the scientist's key card without searching for it? Do you see how he selected the right hallway for the elevator even though it was unmarked?'

'Yeah, yeah. I can see it.'

'Cain couldn't have known something like that! He could have known how to hotwire the vault or the rest of it, but there was no way he could have known that scientist's card was in the inside pocket of his coat. He should have been forced to search for it. And he shouldn't have known which hallway led to the elevator. He should have been forced to search for that, too.'

'And?'

'And so something is *wrong*, Ben.' Soloman rose. 'Did Cain ever meet that scientist before he died? Had Cain ever been inside this facility to learn the architecture?'

'No, no. Cain was *dead* when he got to the laboratory, Sol. His meetin' days were over.'

Soloman replayed the tape again and was certain. He forwarded it to where Cain killed the first unit of men and saw it happen again and knew it was there. And yet, still, it gave no real answers. It only opened up another level of mystery.

Soloman frowned. 'Ben, I think we're dealing with

something that's come back from the dead knowing things no one should know. And I don't know how that could happen.'

'But you can stop him, right?' Ben whispered, trembling. 'You can find this guy and stop him inside ten days? Because if you can't, then you know we're history.'

'I know already, Ben. I know.'

Soloman again beheld the lordly image of rage captured on the screen. It was the roaring height of bestial power, of galactic might as immeasurable and pure and far beyond the Earth as the stars.

'Soloman?' Ben whispered. 'What do you say, buddy? Can you take this guy down?'

Silence dominated as Soloman measured the river of blood already shed by this thing. He saw the lives lost, thought of the families destroyed. And he knew what he had to do.

His jaw tightened.

'I guess we're gonna find out,' he said.

◆ ◆ ◆

Archette's cadaverous face, skin stretched like parchment across haggard features, stared at Ben from the screen of the imaging system. The Chairman of the Joint Chiefs, General Arthur 'Bull' Thompson, spoke in a voice of weighty authority. 'So, Ben, what do you have for us? What's the result of the latest analysis?'

'I am convinced that we can reactivate him, sir,' Ben said, holding his line. 'He is utterly in control. And with respect, General, I think further evaluation is a good waste of time.'

'Good,' growled Bull, looking like a Roman centurion with his big square head and gray flattop. He added, 'How soon can you get this thing off the ground, Ben?'

'Airborne, sir.' Ben nodded. 'We're hot.'

'You've completed a Gittenger Analysis?' Archette asked from nowhere, staring at Ben over his beaklike nose. His face was analytical, the consummate CIA psychiatrist.

Ben turned to him, impassive. 'What?'

He knew better than to match psycho-jargon with the professor. Archette was an expert at picking the scabs of operatives and enemies alike. His almost preternatural keenness in detecting the weakness of foreign agents by using a complex series of Gittenger tests and subtests was legendary. Ben stalled to craft a reply.

'Have you completed the Gittenger Analysis?' Archette repeated, slightly perturbed. 'Certainly, General, you used the Gittenger Analysis, the most reliable means of detecting weakness in –'

'Oh, yeah.' Ben gave an apologetic wave. 'Sorry, doc, I didn't hear you. There's some static on your line. Yeah, I did it, start to finish. For sure, Ghost is sharp. Ready. Primed. We're wasting daylight in this.'

Archette lowered his face.

'Really,' he said.

'Good job, Ben,' Bull rumbled. 'Activate backstopping for the Trinity Mandate. Secure the safehouses you may need. Double the usual allowance. And get outfitted. It's coming to the wire.'

When the Trinity Failsafe was activated and Soloman's name was kicked out by the computer as the best field operative available, Ben had anticipated that Archette wouldn't want him dispatched because of their twisted past. But the hard truth was that there were only a handful of agents capable of dealing with the military and civilian complications of the mission, and Archette had been forced to shelve his personal reservations.

Still, Ben had expected a little more of the professor's

verbal judo when Soloman was contacted, was surprised that the CIA man had remained for the most part silent. He had wondered if Archette was simply biding his time to do a headcut.

General Thompson recounted the latest developments. 'We've got a media frenzy, Ben,' he said with an air of gloom. 'I know you've been busy, but the reports have been faxed to you on the JCIIS. Have your Com officers briefed you this morning?'

Ben knew it was a violation of procedure, even a serious violation of procedure during a crisis not to make morning briefings. But he'd been occupied, so he'd delayed it by a half hour. 'Not at this time, sir,' he replied. 'Can you tell me?'

'Cain crossed the Oscura Mountains south of Albuquerque yesterday,' Thompson said, revealing no disappointment at Ben's lack of procedure; he obviously understood that complications arose in the field. 'He killed at least seven residents of the Chipeqo Sioux Reservation and the place is in an uproar. They're claiming that "white men" are covertly invading reservation land, and the local guard is on full alert because we don't want another Wounded Knee.' He shook his head, angry. 'It's just another very serious complication caused by this ... this *thing*, and it's starting to add up.'

'I understand, sir.' Ben knew the conversation had just moved out of Archette's advisory level and into a military mode. Clearly, Thompson was contemplating action and so Ben pressed further. 'Are we still moving with an unlimited budget and full recertification?'

'I'm not certain of that,' Thompson replied with a hard stare. The question seemed to disturb him. 'But, to tell you the truth, Ben, I don't think we can do it without full recertification for authority and command.' He pondered it, finally reaching out to shut down the communications link. 'Keep an officer on watch. I'll let you know.'

'Communication terminated,' Ben said as he flicked off the Defense Secondary Imaging System. Then, rising, he moved through the electronically sealed safe-room, sensing his own hesitation.

He had seen war before, had commanded battalions and regiments almost all his life, and knew death, and sacrifice. But there was something uncanny and disturbing about this mission that felt like ...

Sheep at a slaughter.

◆ ◆ ◆

His thirst was quenched.

Yet it returned, always returned.

He awoke and swore he would suffer no more. With a growl he rose from his rest to see the dead, white-faced priest beside him. And for a moment he stared down, resting on colossal arms before noticing bloodied fang marks in the man's neck.

Father Lanester.

Such a fool, yes, such a fool to think his god would save him. The priest's own flesh had been his doom, as it was for all of them. For flesh had its ground, but it was ground that could be taken by force of will, or mind, or the sheer force of flesh itself.

A circle, a travesty forever and ever and more.

Yes, fools, all of them; locked in this world not knowing where true power resided or how to use it. They died for lack of knowledge, had always died for lack of knowledge.

The Nazarene won the battle, even the war. Had won by superior strength and the strength of a superior realm. Had won because he never surrendered to the temptation and pain, though he had bled with it.

Yes, the Nazarene had won.

But *vengeance* ...

He smiled over fangs.
Vengeance would be his.

CHAPTER 5

His somberness spoke for him, though the authoritative poise of his sixty-three years spoke far more. His forehead was high with his short white hair sweeping smoothly back from a thin, pale face, the face of a man who had spent his entire life in the intimate closure of dark confessionals and shadowed altars. His solid shoulders were slightly bent and his black frock was immaculately starched and pressed.

Moving slowly, he reached the wooden doors of the cathedral, gravely approaching two uniformed Los Angeles County sheriff's deputies, who stepped forward.

'I'm sorry, sir, but you can't –'

'I am Father William Barth,' the old man said. 'I have been summoned by your captain.' And then he moved through the wide double doors, shutting them quietly.

He was sighted immediately by a short man with a large gut, who raised an arm. And Father Barth walked forward, his face calm. The man who approached looked nervous, his face glistening with sweat.

His hand shook slightly as he extended it. The badge prominently displayed upon his belt indicated that he was a captain with the Los Angeles County Sheriff's Department.

Father Barth shook the hand as introductions were made. His voice was serene and deep. 'What has happened, Captain Wescott?'

'I don't know how to tell you this, Father, but … uh … '

'Please speak. I am old but I am not delicate. Has there been a desecration? Has one of the Church been injured?' After a moment Wescott shook his head: 'No. No one is injured, Father. We've got a murder.'

In a heartbeat Father Barth's face was severe. 'Who?'

'It's Father Lanester. He's in the rectory. He's been … uh … '

'Please, take me to him.'

'It's too late for Last Rites, Father.' Wescott was galvanized to significant fluency with the request. 'And I don't think that you want to see the crime scene. It's the most, and forgive me for saying this, Father, the most horrific crime scene I've ever seen in twenty-eight years on the force. Believe me, it's more gruesome than anything you've ever –'

'You'd be surprised at what I've seen in my lifetime, Captain. Now, please take me to the body of Father Lanester.'

Wescott hesitated. 'All right, Father, I'll take you to the scene. I called you here for some questions, but you might be able to tell us even more if you see the body. But, please be aware, this is going to be unpleasant. Even our uniform guys got sick when they arrived.'

'Who discovered the body?'

'Two of the young nuns from the convent. Sister Theresa and Sister Michelle.'

Father Barth bent his head, immediately concerned. 'I see. And what prompted Sister Theresa and Sister Michelle to search for Father Lanester in the rectory?'

'They were sent to look for him because he didn't arrive to supervise morning mass. They found him … or what was left of him … in his room. They're in pretty bad shape. Hysterical, in shock. We're trying to calm them down but we've been unsuccessful.' Wescott looked shocked himself. 'But, then, anybody would be hysterical after finding the … uh … '

'Where is the Mother Superior?'

'I … I don't know, Father. I haven't thought to ask about –'

Barth turned sharply to a young Hispanic altar boy standing close to the side. Barely twelve years old, the boy was holding both hands tightly in front of his chest. 'Miguel, come here.'

Instantly the boy ran forward as if he felt safer beside the old priest. He was trembling and nervous as Barth wrapped a long arm around his shoulders. 'Can you find the Mother Superior, Miguel? I believe she is busy at the hospital supervising morning prayers.'

'Yes, Father!' he said, trembling. 'I know I can!'

'Good, child, then find her quickly!' Father Barth gently slapped him on the back to hustle him away before he turned back to Wescott, his face becoming severe and grim.

'Now, Captain, please take me to my son.'

◆ ◆ ◆

Cries of two hysterical young nuns met Father Barth as he mounted the third-story steps to Father Lanester's room. As he came past the corner he saw them sitting in chairs, weeping uncontrollably, nervously moving rosary beads and crucifixes in trembling hands.

Ambulance personnel were trying without success to calm the two nuns, who appeared almost identical with dark skin and olive eyes swollen with tears. Hands were raised over their faces and plainclothes police officers stood behind the EMTs, waiting to ask questions.

Father Barth took a moment to try to soothe their nerves but realized quickly he would not succeed, so he patted their shoulders gently, concerned at the shock evident in their cries.

'It's this way, Father,' said Captain Wescott. 'They're about to remove … what's left of the body. You might want to take a look at it before they do.'

Steadily, Father William Barth turned his head. 'Yes, of course.' He moved for the door.

'Watch your step, Father.'

The old man stared down. 'Why?'

'Because … well … you'll see.'

With a dark frown, the priest entered the room.

◆ ◆ ◆

'We just received A-Classification orders on the Defense Imaging System,' Ben said. 'We've got a standing green light and an unlimited budget. And the Corps has recertified you, Sol. Back to your former rank of Lieutenant Colonel, with no time loss. They're giving you one hour to sign or decline.'

Soloman made an expression, a smile or frown. 'The JCS is requiring full recertification?'

'Yeah, Sol. They want a light colonel running this show since we're using fully armed gunships. They're not going to settle for an independent operative. So, you're either completely in or completely out. But if you do come in, you'll have full authority and command, just like the old days. My guys will take your orders just like the SEALs or your supergrunts.'

'Who's running the show?'

'Bull Thompson. The old man.'

'Does the JCS retain jurisdiction?'

'Yeah, the JCS. But there's … ' Ben hesitated. 'There's a few goons involved. The CIA. NSA. They said security was compromised so they had some kinda jurisdictional interest. They didn't get all the cards, but they're on the Trinity Council as advisers.'

'Who's the point man for the CIA?'

Ben was up-front; old times behind it.

'Archette,' he said, low.

Leaning back, Soloman was silent.

Then he saw again the blood-drenched moment when he had come to take the life of the CIA psychiatrist, again beheld Ben squared off before him, intent to defend the life of the man most responsible for the death of Soloman's wife and child …

◆ ◆ ◆

The storm-torn night roared with vengeance.

Soloman staggered forward in blood, having traveled so far to finish the life of the man who, according to the dying gasp of the last terrorist, had compromised the location of his family. And Soloman had believed the words; had believed them because no man suffering the kind of hideous pain Soloman had inflicted could have lied.

He had narrowly threaded his way through Customs and New York police to track the revered Dr Winston Archette, gentleman, scholar, Deputy Director of Covert Operations for the Central Intelligence Agency, and traitor, to his retreat on Martha's Vineyard. Then Soloman had crawled slowly and painfully through the tight CIA perimeter for half a night, defeating security with the assistance of a thundering rainstorm to enter, dying on his feet, the back of the cottage.

To find Ben waiting for him.

The general didn't even have a gun, had chosen not to wear one. No, his trust and friendship had been his only weapon, and Soloman would never forget the conversation.

'Get out of the way, Ben,' he said, staring darkly at the professor's cringing form, bleeding slowly onto the wooden floor. 'I mean it,' he added. 'I'll kill you if I have to.'

'No,' Ben responded flatly. 'It's over, Sol. You did 'em all.'

'Not this one.'

Soloman remembered how he went light in the moment, swaying as he lifted the Colt. But Ben didn't move, stood solidly in front of the trembling shape. 'Think about it, Ben!' Soloman fought for consciousness. 'If Archette isn't guilty, how did he know I was coming for him?'

'There'll be an investigation,' Ben responded firmly. 'But you can't just kill him, Sol. It'd be murder, and you're not a murderer. You got the rest of 'em. Screw 'em. They deserved it. But Archette works for us and you've got to have proof before you take him 'round the corner. That's just the way it is.' He paused. 'I can't back down from this.'

They stood in silence before Ben added, 'You can kill me if you want, Sol. I ain't gonna raise a weapon against you. But if you back down, I guarantee you that Archette will stand trial. And you can believe me on that: I guarantee it.'

Remembering the scene, Soloman grunted.

A trial.

What a joke.

It had been a mockery with uncertifiable testimony from double-agents, triple-agents, shades of secret alliances and betrayals that laid such a convoluted network of lies that not even a military tribunal combined with a Senate Intelligence Subcommittee hearing could discover anything except that Soloman had, indeed, vengefully sanctioned every member of the elite terrorist team that had murdered his family.

In the end, the truth had been buried with his wife and child, and Archette walked cleanly away but for the tarnish of Soloman's accusations, which carried little weight inside the agency.

Butcher, they'd called him.

But he was no butcher. He had avenged what was sacred, had known from the first that, if it ever happened, he would avenge them. And now it had all come home again, and he felt it again. Maybe, he thought, things just had a way of coming around, of bringing you back home.

After a moment he shook his head, his mind returning to the desert. He had sought something there for so many years in the silent dark that would close the memories and ghosts and regrets. And now he'd been brought back to what haunted him … most of all.

◆ ◆ ◆

Make a decision.

Soloman bowed his head.

'Tell them I'm in,' he said.

'It's done.'

Suddenly the door opened and Maggie Milton entered, looking far better than she had on the previous night. Her hair was fresh and she appeared striking in a businesslike black pants suit. She nodded cordially as she came close and sat down, opening a file.

'Good morning, Maggie,' Soloman said pleasantly. 'You look refreshed.'

'I am,' she smiled. 'Shall we get started?'

'Let's,' he said.

It took most of the day for Maggie to explain fully the complex alterations she'd made to Cain's body. Soloman compared the endless scientific data with Cain's extensive military 201 file, searching to find any clue that might enable him to anticipate Cain's next move, to discover some small weakness. But he found nothing because there was simply nothing there. And, even as he sat there, dozens of agents were busy in the field, checking Cain's comrades and contacts. As Soloman had predicted, Cain had made no contact with any of them. It was infinitely frustrating, and at day's end all three were fatigued at finding nothing.

Shaking his head angrily, Soloman leaned back from the table, eyes dry. Then he began replaying the video in his mind, again and again seeing a dead man brought to life by this strange, occult experiment, once more walking the world of the living to – *Di liberatus!*

I will be free!

Soloman shot to his feet, staring.

'Damn!' Ben hurled a file aside. 'What is it?'

Soloman focused on Maggie, then his watch.

'What *is* it, Sol!' Ben staggered.

Soloman leaned hard over the conference table, unable to contain the intensity of his voice as he asked, 'Maggie, in this mutated form, what is Cain's anticipated life period?'

'It's unknown.' She seemed to catch something in his tone, became vaguely alarmed. 'Maybe … maybe a few years. But his DNA is suffering too much damage, so it won't be longer than that.'

'You're certain?'

'Yes. As certain as I can be. According to enzyme tests, Cain's DNA can only hold the HyMar in check for three years. Then there will be a backflow that will be too much for him to counter.'

But Soloman knew something else was there. It had come to him again and again as he had watched Cain on the screen, a thought driven into him by that roaring white threat: *I will be free!*

'This is very important, Maggie,' he continued, watching her for the faintest flicker of doubt. 'Could the blood of the donor that was used to alter the DNA code of the original Marburg virus be used to reinstate the machine language for Cain's mutated DNA, thereby correcting his genetic imbalance? Could the original donor's blood be used to negate any further mutation of the HyMar virus?'

One of her hands clenched involuntarily.

'It's … possible. The bottom line is that the ribosomal RNA in each cell is the … uh, the genetic guardian of the process. It makes sure that every replication of each individual cell is genetically perfect. If Cain could acquire the molecular guardians of the blood used to alter the virus that altered him, he might reverse the backflow and cancel further mutation. In fact, we considered that a while back, but it wasn't an option. At all.'

Ben joined in. 'Well, forgive me for saying it, Doctor, because I might be stupid – I certainly *feel* stupid – but why didn't your people just normalize this thing's DNA in the beginning instead of turning him into some sort of blood-sucking freak?'

'One reason,' she answered, hard. 'The donor, who was the only perfect genetic match for Cain, is too small. She's only six years old and she couldn't sacrifice enough blood to correct Cain's instability.'

'And why is that?'

'Because … ' She hesitated. 'Because of Cain's proportions it would take an explosive infusion of all her enzymes and blood serum at once, something done within minutes. Either that, or he would just burn it up, drop by drop. Which means, General, that it would take all the blood in her body, given all at once. And I wouldn't allow that. I would never allow that.'

'Well, Doc, why did you let them use her blood to alter this Marburg virus in the first place?'

'Modifying the Marburg virus only required a few milliliters of blood, General. That's nothing! That's far less than a blood test. But to give Cain enough blood to correct his genetic spiral would have required a simultaneous infusion of every drop of blood that she has in her body. And that was *not* going to happen.' She shook her head. 'It's *never* going to happen!'

Cigar smoking in his hand, Ben leaned back. Then his jaw tightened as he scowled, studying her.

'Listen, gentlemen,' Maggie continued, spreading her fingers flat on the table, 'please understand me; I agree that this experiment could have been coordinated much more effectively, but I did not have full authority. The Central Intelligence Agency had full authority. Basically I never liked any of the containment measures, and I'm repeatedly on record about it. I wasn't even in the facility when Cain achieved resurrection. If I had been, I would have seen the EEG activity and heavily sedated him before he reached this unexpected resuscitation. As it is, I'm as stunned as you are.'

Ben grunted. 'I doubt that, Doctor.'

'Maggie,' Soloman asked gently, 'who donated the human DNA that was used to alter the original Marburg?'

She briefly closed her eyes, raising her hands a moment as she took a deep breath. 'There was only one choice,' she answered, 'but they were an almost perfect match.'

Soloman sensed it somehow, but heard himself ask, 'Who?'

Her face paled in a quickening fear.

'My daughter.'

Trembling at the carnage despite his control, Father Barth left Father Lanester's room. Weak-kneed, he heard an angry debate in the hallway. A harsh old voice rose strangely over both the demands of police and the hysterical cries of nuns, and he knew she had finally arrived.

He entered the corridor to see the standoff.

Mother Superior Mary Francis was short and stooped

and implacable as she stood between police and the shocked nuns. Her wrinkled old face of sixty-seven years was set like flint, mouth locked in a grim line as she stared up at the angry, frustrated investigators.

'Look, Sister, I'm *serious* about this!' shouted Wescott, appearing to at least *attempt* to be diplomatic. 'We need to ask these nuns some questions! And we can't let them leave!'

'And how will you question children who can share words only with tears?' Mother Superior Mary Francis asked, evenly holding his glare. Her pale gray eyes didn't blink at all.

Wescott didn't respond but he didn't move, either. So Mother Superior Mary Francis moved for him. She turned and reached out to roughly shake each nun by the shoulder. 'Hush!' she shouted. 'Hush now! You are bent! Not broken!'

Startled by the implacable authority, the nuns looked up through tears, and Father Barth glimpsed the thin hidden smile of the Mother Superior. There was a moment of intimate eye contact, and then she hugged each of them fearlessly with an old, strong arm.

'God alone can hear what your heart speaks,' she whispered to their faces. 'So you will speak with God, first. Then you will share a cup of hot tea with your friends to remind you of how wonderful is your own strength!'

Grimacing in tears, they nodded, slowly composing themselves. Then the old nun released them, turning without hesitation to the investigator. Her stern face would accept no protest. 'When they are ready, they will send for you,' she said, her world and life behind her. 'But you can do nothing for them now, Captain, and they can do nothing for you.'

Not waiting for agreement she turned and shooed the young nuns away as other, older nuns took them inside protective arms, escorting them down the hallway like a black-cloaked cadre of bodyguards. Then she gazed with a suddenly demure aspect at Father Barth.

'Have they removed the body of poor Father Lanester?' she asked gently, folding her wrinkled hands.

'Yes, Sister,' he replied, trembling. 'They have collected their evidence. And they have said that we can clean the room whenever … whenever we are prepared to do it!' Abruptly he blessed himself and the Mother Superior. *Ecce Crux Domini. Fugite, partes adversae!*

Mary Francis silently blessed herself.

But Father Barth could not prevent himself from repeating the blessing in English, turning to slash the cross in the air over police officers who stared wide-eyed at the gesture. All of them took off their caps at the movement and the great enraged voice.

'Behold the cross of the Lord!' the priest thundered, raising his hand again. 'Begone, ye hostile powers!'

Then the old man lowered his gray head, perilously exhausted. He was breathing heavily as he lifted a slender hand over his heart. 'Yes, Sister Mary Francis, the police have said we can clean the room whenever we are prepared … to do it … '

Mother Superior Mary Francis nodded mournfully and moved to the door of Father Lanester's hauntingly empty, silent room. Yet when she reached the doorway, she paused. Without expression she stared at the hideous, wholesale carnage.

Old eyes looked over the bloody marks scarred in the walls, marks left by monstrous taloned hands raking in infinite rage to claw unspeakable curses in ancient Hebrew and Latin. And beneath the thin wooden crucifix hung above the bed, where the whiteness was stained a deep black-red, two horrific words were scrawled.

TYRANT!

And beneath that …

SPITE!

Her aspect hardened as she seemed to see something else clawed into the wall, raked into the plaster by razor-sharp talons that knew no resistance in earthly substance.

'So and so,' she said, 'it has come ... '

Silence fell like a thunderclap in the corridor.

Police, involuntarily, stepped back together.

'Tell the others to abandon this floor,' she whispered, frowning. 'I will do this alone.'

And, blessing herself, she went in.

CHAPTER 6

'This is a matter of grave concern, Father.'

Father Jacob Marcelle sat with his usual lack of ceremony in the imperial office of Father William Barth, positioned before the glistening oak desk and a photograph of Pope John Paul II.

With his immaculate black cassock and nicotine-stained fingers, Marcelle was a study in almost laughable contrasts. Though he carried himself with humility, he had the physique of one who worked with his hands – short and hairy with a solid torso and thick arms – and he clearly commanded a measure of strength that could intimidate larger men.

His face was shadowed with a beard only six hours after he had shaved and the backs of his hands were obscured with black hair. The thick hair on his head was short-cut and also utterly black, while his eyebrows seemed a solid bar on his heavy forehead.

Father William Barth stared across his desk with commiseration, as if he had true sympathy for the slightly younger man seated before him.

Marcelle shifted. 'Yes, Father?'

'There has been a dark deed committed,' the old man said, as if no more would be welcomed.

'I am … very sorry,' Marcelle responded, unshaken. 'May I inquire?'

'Father Lanester was killed this morning, Marcelle. He was murdered in his room at the rectory.'

'I see,' said Marcelle, eyes glinting. 'And how was Father Lanester killed?'

Remorse masked the older priest's face as he shook his head once more. He struggled before he spoke. 'As I said, it was a dark deed. For Father Lanester was not merely ... not merely *murdered*. That would have been merciful. No, he was murdered and mutilated, his bones torn out one by one and driven like nails through the walls. He was also disemboweled, his entrails laid in obscene signs on the floor.'

Marcelle bowed his head as Barth continued. 'Yes, Marcelle, and all done within easy listening distance of others living on the third floor. Moreover, it was clearly an act of malice because Father Lanester was already dead at the time. Or so the police tell me.'

Pausing respectfully, Marcelle replied in a low voice, 'I am ... deeply grieved, Father.'

'Yes, Marcelle. As are all of us, I assure you.' Barth paused. 'But we have a situation that, perhaps, requires your attention. Because there were two words written on the wall.'

'What are the words?'

' "Spite," ' Barth said with a bend of his head. 'Yes, "Spite." And below that the word "Tyrant." '

'I see.' Marcelle's thick black brow seemed to become more solid. His voice was measured. 'And do the police have this murderer in custody?'

'No,' Barth answered. 'They are interviewing the list of habitual desecrators and psychomaniacal attackers of the evangelical community. But I do not think they will find ... this one.'

'And why is that?'

Barth seemed suddenly older. 'Tell me, Marcelle, what kind of unnatural strength would enable a man to dismember another man using nothing but his own hands? What kind of power could give a man the strength to drive a human rib through stone?'

Marcelle did not blink. 'There are certain mental illnesses which could conceivably provide sufficient epiphenomenalism,' he answered finally. 'This deed, while incredible, is not necessarily an occult act. And intellectual credulity, as we both know, is a sin.'

'Yes, Marcelle, I know it is an intellectual sin to believe too readily in occult phenomena. But nevertheless, what we have confronted must be investigated.'

Marcelle said nothing. Educated at Fordham University in New York City, he had been a Jesuit since he had joined the order at seventeen, enduring the long fifteen-year tenure of training in philosophy and theology only to find that he had come to love rigorous thought.

After completing the courses he continued to quench his enormous intellectual appetite by acquiring dual doctorates in archeology and clinical psychology, consequently spending three years in Israel where he excavated the ruined Temples of Dagon.

At present, however, his primary responsibilities were as priest of Antiguis Cathedral in San Francisco and as Professor Emeritus of Aberrant Psychology at the Jesuit-controlled University of San Francisco. For, despite his revered reputation as an archeologist and psychologist, he was also regarded as a devoted pastor and an accomplished speaker.

'Yes,' repeated Father Barth, 'I am quite aware, Marcelle, that being too willing to believe in occult phenomena is an intellectual sin. But the sum of this phenomenon is indicative of such, so we must examine the event and strive to answer the mystery.'

'And what mystery do you perceive, Father?'

'The first mystery, Marcelle, is this: Why was it Father Lanester who was murdered? Why Father Lanester and not I? Or even Sister Mary Francis? Yes, that is the question. And then we must ask whether the words written upon the wall are simply the deluded ravings of human evil, or whether it is the work of ... of a more sinister force.'

Jesuit intelligence, twisting in endless gliding circles, glinted in Marcelle's narrow black eyes. 'You ask these questions because you wish to know if someone within the Church is subjugated.'

As it was said, it was not a question.

Father Barth's hands rested on the desk. 'It is a premise that I harbor, Marcelle. I will not deny my solicitude, nor should I. The skepticism of intelligent men is both the shield and sword of evil, and evil flourishes nowhere so strongly as where men refuse to believe that evil itself exists. For there, where it is unsuspected, it walks among us protected by our arrogance, laughing as it feasts on our pride.'

Marcelle concentrated. 'If you don't mind my asking, Father, why did you send specifically for me?'

'Because you are revered for your understanding of these things, Marcelle. Because you have worked with the Behavioral Science and Research unit in Quantico, and have been an adviser to the FBI on ritual crimes. And, known only to a few, because you are the senior member of Eradicare In Carne.'

With a frown Barth blessed himself at the mention of the Jesuit Society's secret, official group of exorcists, and Marcelle respectfully repeated the gesture.

Marcelle was without expression. 'As you know, Father, I am under formal restraint not to speak openly of these things. There is a necessity ... for discretion. And you must know that for years I have been more of an academic than a participating member of the Order.'

'And yet, in your experience, would this murder not seem to qualify as satanic?' Barth pressed.

'Perhaps,' Marcelle replied steadily. 'But you must remember that even the terms "satanic" and "ritualistic" can be confusing and counterproductive.' He paused. 'I stress, Father, that an investigation of this nature is best left to the police. Ritual murder, if this qualifies as such, can stem as easily from psychotic hallucinations and delusions as from true subjugation which, I add, is exceedingly rare. And to make it even more confusing there are emotional, religious, sexual, and psychological rituals that can overlap. Often these situations have more than a single root cause. They are not necessarily … evil.'

Absorbing the words, Barth said, 'But there are clearly elements of satanism, Marcelle. Certainly enough to provoke concern.'

'Yes,' Marcelle slowly agreed. 'Yes, there appear to be satanic elements. But you must remember that the bizarreness or cruelty does not automatically make it such. Forgive me for seeming callous, but not all who commit "ritualistic" crimes practice satanism. Nor are activities such as Santeria, grave robbing, or even human sacrifice necessarily satanic. It depends on a combination of elements. The only true criterion for qualifying a crime as satanic is the motivation of the perpetrator.'

'And what motivation do you perceive in this?'

Marcelle shook his head, pausing a long time. 'In all honesty, Father, I see certain elements which could contribute to your premise. But in these situations it is easy to become irrational, so perspective must be maintained. As difficult as it may be, we must separate the religious and psychological aspects.'

Barth was silent a moment. 'I see,' he said, with an air of disappointment. 'And yet, Marcelle, you have not yet investigated the situation, so you cannot confirm that there are not more … substantial elements at work.'

Marcelle's eyes hardened. 'As I said, Father, I have not investigated these matters for many years. I am primarily in supervision now. I am not certain how well I would coordinate a field inquiry.'

A smile came to Father Barth slowly. 'You would do

well, Marcelle. I am certain that you have not lost that fearless stoutness of character for which you were ... once lauded.'

Marcelle's face tightened, as if he had been stung by the words. His tone deepened. 'There are seasons in a man's life, Father,' he replied. 'And what you ask requires ... great faith.'

'That is true, Marcelle.' The older priest was unfazed, and released a compassionate smile. 'And I know that I cannot persuade one of your august wisdom. I only ask you to once again defend those who are not capable of defending themselves.' He paused. 'It is a simple request from a simple man, my son. But you alone must decide whether the winter has ended ... or whether it shall continue.'

Marcelle stared down, and a slow grimness emerged from behind his face that could not be concealed any more than the stout development of his frame. His eyes were hidden by shadow as he reached into a pocket. Then he shook his head, letting his hand fall away.

'Please, Marcelle,' said the old man in a gesture of courtesy, 'we are not constrained by customary practices of court. No, certainly not now. Please consider yourself free ... to smoke.'

Slowly and without demurring Marcelle withdrew an unfiltered Camel. And an instant later he lit, expelling an amazingly thick cloud of smoke. His head was bowed, degree by degree building into a remorseless concentration. The air about him seemed to fall still, and there was no expression as he blinked once and sighed.

'The mercy of God,' he said softly. 'So severe.'

'It wounds, Marcelle. And it heals.'

'Very well, Father,' he added. 'I am not convinced by any means that elemental forces are at work in this incident. There are essential and exacting criteria which must be met, as you well know. But I will examine the facts.' His black eyes focused. 'First, tell me: What were Father Lanester's duties in the Church?'

The old priest released a long-withheld breath, openly pleased, before he considered an answer. 'Do you, uh, not wish to first study photographs of the crime scene, Marcelle?' he questioned. 'Do you not wish to study the scene of the murder?'

'In time,' Marcelle responded, utterly cold and scientific. 'But not at this moment. First we will explore the preliminaries. What were Father Lanester's duties in the Church?'

Barth's eyes roamed the desk. 'He, ah … he supervised morning mass. Usually he gave simple homilies on everyday life, means by which we sin and should repent. And he was basically inoffensive. Not a dramatic orator. But he was a good pastor, and well-respected. Then, after mass, he received confessions until noon. And in the afternoon he assisted me in visitation and other scheduled services.'

Waiting another moment, Marcelle said, 'And is that all?'

'Yes, yes, most assuredly.' Father Barth seemed amazed. 'Why do you ask?'

'Because there is nothing unusual in those duties,' replied Marcelle, releasing another heavy breath of blue smoke. 'What has happened to Father Lanester is out of the ordinary, so there must be something out of the ordinary about his responsibilities. What else did Father Lanester do? What duties was Father Lanester, alone, assigned?'

Barth waited a long time. His face was vaguely frightened.

'Father Lanester was keeper of the Secret Archives, Marcelle,' he said finally.

Marcelle's face was that of a man who had long ago regarded surprise as a luxury that he could not afford.

He didn't blink as he held the old man's gaze. 'Where are the Secret Archives located?'

'In a secret vault in a hidden sub-basement,' answered the older priest. Clearly, he had not expected to reveal the location of that highly secretive library of manuscripts, letters, concealed documents, and controversial confessions of dark deeds. He continued, 'Good God, Marcelle! We have approximately forty-five thousand documents in the vault! Its very existence is our most closely guarded secret! How could it be involved?'

Marcelle said nothing as he lowered his head. He slowly released a thick cloud of cigarette smoke.

'Has anyone checked the vault?' he asked somberly.

◆ ◆ ◆

Maggie Milton slammed a hand on the table.

'That's *impossible*, Soloman! Cain doesn't even know who any of us are!' She stepped away before turning back to point hard at the files. 'This man was dead, Soloman! *Dead!* He never saw any of us and never saw any information on this experiment! How can my daughter be in danger? How can Cain even know who my daughter *is?*'

Soloman wasn't certain of anything but knew that he wasn't going to take the chance because the words kept coming to him again and again: *Di liberatus! I will be free!* He tried to keep his voice calm and confident, nor was it as difficult as he anticipated as he asked, 'Where is your daughter now, Maggie?'

'At home. With a babysitter.'

'Where's home?'

'It's in Fallbrook. South of L.A.'

Soloman turned to Hawken. 'Ben, notify the Los Angeles FBI Watch Commander and tell him to get a dozen agents to Maggie's house right now. Tell them to relocate the child and babysitter in a fortified safehouse until we arrive. Then fire up a Nightcat and scramble me some backup. Tell them we're airborne in thirty minutes! No more!'

Soloman went for the door as Hawken picked up the phone, speaking quickly as he fed a report into the Joint Defense Intelligence Imaging System, routed automatically to the Pentagon. But Maggie approached Soloman as he moved, her face calm as her phenomenal intelligence asserted itself to overcome her emotions, even her love for her child.

'Where are you going?' she asked.

'To the armory.' He paused in the open door. 'Get your files together, Maggie. Forget what's in your room. Your things will be packed and sent to you.'

'Soloman.' She stared. 'Do you really think ... '

Both of them controlled the moment with disciplined hearts. But Soloman caught a faint flicker of fear behind her jade-green eyes and felt a wave of compassion.

'I could be wrong, Maggie,' he said. 'I've been wrong before. And in any case the FBI will be guarding your daughter within a half hour. But I'm not taking any chances.'

'But ... but do you really think Cain will come for my daughter?' The love of a wounded mother burned in the question, and Soloman strangely felt his compassion warm. She repeated, 'Do you really think Amy's in danger?'

Soloman was still.

'We're all in danger, Maggie. You know that already.'

◆ ◆ ◆

A colossal gloom, gothic and surreal, cloaked the atmosphere with a black cloud that smelled dusty and metallic as Marcelle descended the last steps of the long stone stairway that vanished into the dark of the sub-basement.

Holding a flashlight because the light switch, oddly, did not work, Marcelle cautiously stood in the gloom, searching. The room was intimidatingly silent, echoing with the sound of suppressed breath. There was none of the sanctuary's opulence in evidence here. There was a spartan rectangular table surrounded by a dozen tall wooden chairs, and in the distance a large vault stood open, darkness within it utterly impenetrable. Marcelle sensed Barth suppressing a gasp, heard the old man's hands tighten on the staircase railing.

Peering into the shadows, Marcelle stepped down. He shone the light upward to the light socket and saw that the bulb was shattered, turned to the other priest. 'We can fix the light easily,' he said, attempting to strengthen the old man's nerve. 'Please retrieve another bulb, Father, and a bar of soap to remove the shattered remnants of the broken one.'

'Yes, yes,' said Barth as he turned quickly.

As he moved away Marcelle walked cautiously forward.

Having made the grim decision to once more assume the mantle of Eradicare In Carne, he wanted to approach the vault alone, knowing what he might encounter if the old man was right. Just as he knew that the electrifying confrontation could cause even the stoutest hearts to fail by quickly escalating into a horrifying conflict of competing will and faith, of life and death; a war waged in a world that was not this.

Marcelle's dead-steady hand came from his cloak holding a large silver crucifix. His other hand held the flashlight as he stared into the gloom of the cavernous chamber, the vault thrown widely open. And what he saw was made even more haunting by the surreal silence, the stench of ancient things, of dead things, of curses hidden and dark deeds buried in religious lies.

Frightening sheets of blackened blood coated the floor where the carnage had occurred, but Marcelle held his place, not revealing the fear he felt inside. For he had learned long ago, before he turned his back on what he had been, never to reveal fear. Yes, fear was a weapon that could be used against him, and he could not let his fear be used against him.

The Enemy had weapons enough.

With determination, he was silent. Nor did he whirl, as his racing heart demanded, to cast the light back across the room. His keen intellect assured him that the sub-basement was empty. Fear could be ignored.

Then he heard steps descending and turned calmly as Barth entered the room holding a flashlight and a chair. Seconds later they shoved a bar of soap into the shattered metal remnant of the bulb to extract it easily. Then, after inserting a new bulb, Marcelle pulled the chain and turned to the vault in the glaring light.

Yes, it was there.

Blood was drawn across the floor, but not so much as it seemed in the dim cast of the flashlight. And Marcelle was confident that this was where Father Lanester's true death had occurred, and not in the rectory. Whatever happened there was mere bestial exultation. And as he stared down, he perceived that this was something more.

Yes, he thought, this was something more. This was the work of precious blood; blood that was treasured, and not to be spilt. He tried to ignore the faint words of Father Barth as he knelt, studying the pattern.

There was not much to discern, but he saw the indiscriminate blackened drops spread in a strange circular pattern, as if a terrible wound had been struck while a heart beat in fierce fear.

'Was he tortured?' Father Barth raised his voice. 'Was poor Father Lanester tortured?'

'Tortured,' Marcelle repeated coldly, sensing a path back to a life of horror he had left behind long ago, to preserve himself. 'Yes,' he added. 'He was tortured.'

The old man groaned, blessing himself. *'Sed libera nos a malo. Exaudi orationem meam.'*

Grimly, Marcelle stood up at those words. As he stared across the vault he could see purpose here, purpose malevolent and cunning and bestial. Whatever had done this would leave no living thing in its wake if it could not be destroyed.

In a grave tone Marcelle repeated the old man's blessing.

'Yes, O God, deliver us ... from this Evil.'

◆　◆　◆

Two uniformed guards approached Soloman as he advanced through the star-shrouded heat of White Sands to reach the Armory. Three hundred feet in the distance a Humvee with engine roaring and lights glaring approached and Soloman measured its arrival with an enlivened mechanical skill of the Marine colonel he'd once been: thirty seconds.

'Halt!' one of the MPs shouted at port arms. 'Who goes there!'

Soloman replied boldly to indicate his position in the dark.

'Colonel James L. Soloman!'

Both soldiers stepped forward. 'Advance to be recognized!'

Preliminaries completed according to regulation, Soloman approached quickly but cautiously, knowing the drill. 'I'm Colonel Soloman, Private!' he shouted. 'I'm under General Hawken's command! I need access!'

Nervous glances were exchanged between the guards and Soloman suddenly remembered that he hadn't been issued his credentials yet. This, he realized, might become a problem because he didn't have any time to waste. Then, engine straining to the last moment, the Humvee arrived at the door and Soloman turned.

A square-jawed figure clambered from it and came forward without any announcement, as though he'd kick serious ass if *he* were challenged. Built wide and low and solid – like a human bison – the man walked with a slight limp as he saluted sharply and spoke in a southern accent faded from too many years in foreign fields. 'I'm here to assist you, Colonel. I'm Sergeant Chatwell.'

'Can you open this door, Sergeant?'

Chatwell was already moving for the steel panel. 'Yes, sir, you bet I can. General Hawken briefed me.' He shouldered the guards aside. 'Move aside, boys. He said you needed a sidearm with ammo and a carry, Colonel. What do you prefer? We've got some .45s, we've got a wheelbarrow load of Berettas, and they just sent us a shipment of them brand-new Sig Sauers.'

'I'll take a .45 if you've got one in good shape, Sergeant.'

Laughing, Chatwell opened the door and hit the light as he moved forward, clearly amused. 'Yes sir, we've got a .45 you might have some fun with.'

Already they had reached the internal security gate and in another second Chatwell was inside the vault, laying the massive lock aside. Soloman glanced back to see the other two MPs stationed at port arms on either side of the doorway, staring out.

'Try this one, sir.'

Chatwell handed a black-matte semiautomatic to Soloman, who reflexively ejected the empty magazine and pulled back the slide to lock. It was incredible, he thought, how in the space of three seconds he handled the gun as well as he ever had, though it had been seven years. He heard himself speak as he worked, enjoying Chatwell's old Army attitude.

'You coming with us, Chatwell?'

'Airborne, sir.'

'You bringing shake-and-bakes?'

'Negative, sir. Delta's been scrambled. They're on the deck right now wearing Air Force gloves.'

Soloman smiled at that. 'Air Force gloves' meant the soldiers were standing around with their hands in their pockets, waiting for something to happen. But Soloman knew it was also a euphemism because Delta commandos never stood around waiting for anything. They prepared.

'Good enough,' he replied.

The port was unloaded and Soloman dropped the slide to feel a solid hit. Then he checked the spring and, peripherally, felt the slightly wider grip. Instantly he knew it wasn't a Colt and looked at the imprint on the slide: *Para-Ordinance P-13*, a single-action .45 with a double-stacked magazine that gave it thirteen rounds instead of the usual seven.

A formidable weapon; it looked brand-new.

'Has this thing been broken in?' Soloman asked as he disassembled it, ejecting the loading lock and removing the slide and barrel. He knew that any pistol had to have at least five hundred rounds through it before it could be relied upon not to jam.

'We put seven hundred rounds through it in the last two days, Colonel. But the boys cleaned it up real good after we fired it on the –'

'Load me some magazines,' Soloman interrupted. 'What kind of ammo do you have?'

'Hydro-shock 148 grain full metal jacket.' Chatwell broke open a locker. 'Velocity is nine hundred feet per second at twenty feet and it'll give you six hundred pounds-per-square-inch knockdown with a one-inch drop at twenty-five. Just tell me how many clips you want, sir.'

'Load five magazines at full capacity and give me two boxes in a pouch. Then give me two of those double Safariland magazine holders and a pocket-sized cleaning kit with a perpendicular shoulder holster. And I need a pair of infrared night-vision Blackwing goggles.'

'Yes, sir.' Chatwell began loading clips with expert efficiency, slamming in the .45-caliber bullets as quickly as he could depress the spring. 'Is there anything else, Colonel?'

'Yeah,' Soloman frowned. 'Give me an out-of-the-box Mylar vest with wraparound rib protection and a steel shock plate. Make sure it's less than two years old. Break out a SPAS-12 that works on semiautomatic or pump and give me five boxes of double-ought buck. Then open the munitions locker and issue me two dozen antipersonnel grenades.'

Chatwell laid the shotgun and magazines on the table.

'We goin' for bear, Colonel?'

Soloman didn't look up as he sharply dropped the slide, not chambering a round because it was against regulations to chamber a round inside the Armory or on a flight.

As the steel shut, he stared somberly at the weapon. 'I wish.'

◆ ◆ ◆

Maggie slid her encryption card through a magnetic lock and a thermal imaging screen glowed sea-green. Glancing to either side, she assured herself that the underground laboratory was abandoned and placed her hand against the thermal imaging screen that read the track of major veins inside her palm. The vault slid open.

Quickly donning a bacterial isolation suit, she entered the primary laboratory where they had created Cain. A containment cell where they created the bacteria was at the rear.

It had been simple to bypass the guards after she

convinced General Hawken that if she were leaving she *had* to ensure that the viruses were properly secured. A mistake in this lab, she explained, would wipe out all the NASA personnel and the military and every civilian within a one-hundred-mile radius. Cain wasn't the only killer they'd created here.

Ben shook his head morosely. 'You cold-blooded scientists … '

He ordered every guard in the compound to stand down and inside fifteen minutes she was in the lab. But, struck by guilt and unaccustomed to stealth, she was unable to keep herself from continually searching for anyone who might be watching.

Above the door of the containment cell was printed in bold red letters: GENOCIDE ONE, MI-MV, HyMar-I.

Without hesitation she opened the freezer and entered to close it more quietly than necessary. And for the briefest moment she stared down, hand tightening on the panel, wondering if she were right. Then love for her child flared and she walked without remorse down the aisle to a row of small bags marked MI, MII, MIII, MIV, MV, HyMar-I. She reached up slowly to remove the first and turned to a table, careful to keep the biosuit's airhose close and untangled.

In seconds she removed a stainless-steel syringe from a gray row and with clinical skill inserted the needle into the bag's nodule. Slowly she extracted two hundred cc's of the original Marburg virus, removing the needle. Then she turned and placed an air-sealing cap on the hypodermic, laying it carefully on the counter. Replacing the MI toxin on the shelf, she opened another freezer to remove a fist-sized liquid nitrogen container.

It was less than six inches long, slate gray and cylindrical, and could easily be concealed in her purse. She placed the unbreakable steel syringe within the niobium-titanium transportation unit and closed the container with an airtight latch, measuring the nitrogen level.

There was enough in the container to keep the syringe at 32 degrees Fahrenheit for twelve days. Staring down, she watched the red needle holding steady. Then she had another moment of guilt and wondered if she were truly right, or even responsible, in what she was doing. But as she paused she recalled the horrific videotape of Cain escaping and somehow knew that, in the end, the virus would be their only chance.

Concentrating, she reviewed all the safety factors; the Marburg virus was housed in an unbreakable steel syringe sealed with a safe-locked airtight cap; the syringe was housed in another airtight, almost indestructible niobium-titanium transportation unit that held enough liquid nitrogen to keep the virus frozen for twelve days, and she knew that, if necessary, she could destroy it at any time with an injection of mercury. With that thought she reached up and lifted a small vial of mercury, another syringe for insertion.

Sweating heavily inside her suit despite the chill of the freezer, she tried not to think about the enormity of the risk. She was not only violating federal laws and ethics and international treaties that prohibited the transportation of Class IV viruses, she was conceivably endangering the entire world. But then the world was already in danger and she was certain that conventional military weapons would never finish Cain. Yes, she'd been certain of that single horrifying fact since the day they finished rebuilding him and his traumatic incisions had healed without scars within an hour.

And, most of all, there was Amy.

Maggie grimaced: No! Cain could not have her child. He would *never* have her child!

She was certain that if she could hit Cain for even a tenth of a second with the needle he would be as dead as he'd been before. And in her soul she knew she was more responsible than anyone for starting this; she was willing to give her life to finish it; a penance well-deserved.

Face hardening in determination, she lifted the mercury and the nitrogen unit, holding it in a tight fist, and left the laboratory.

◆ ◆ ◆

Soloman hit the deck at the Lear before Chatwell could even stop the Jeep. He saw Ben boarding the hatch of the jet beside a somber Maggie. At his arrival, Ben turned and gave him the thumbs-up.

Soloman was sweating heavily in the night heat and nodded as he moved toward a fiercely armed Delta contingent: twelve men wearing full body armor and bearing an intimidating array of weapons.

He was on top of them in seconds, commanding like the colonel he'd once been and felt himself becoming again – mean, disciplined, and advising by sheer attitude that he wouldn't take any crap or excuse for failure. These were men who were best led from the front – and that was where he planned to be.

'School circle on me!' he called out, and the men were instantly around him. 'Who's the XO?'

'Here, sir!' A big Mexican stepped up.

Soloman saw that the Mexican was much larger than he was, even larger than Chatwell. He wasn't muscular in the contemporary sense, but he held the aura of a deep and natural animal power; something that was hard the day he was born and hardened more by a life of hardship. His bearded face – bearded because Delta commandos were often required to work in foreign countries under civilian cover – made him look like a Cuban drug runner. His eyes were black and implacable with only the faintest crescent moons and Soloman reflexively knew him for what he was: a professional soldier, someone who lived to fight and fought well.

Thoroughly prepared, he was armed with a backslung eight-shot Remington 870 shotgun and an MP-5 – a compact 9-mm submachine gun that had a nine-hundred-round-per-minute cycling rate. A Colt .45 was on his hip with extra ammo and a large bowie knife. He carried the load as if it were weightless.

'What's your name, lieutenant?' Soloman squared off, settling up front who was in charge, knowing that he had to do it now or never.

'Lieutenant Garcia, sir.'

A snappy reply.

Soloman nodded: Good, there wouldn't be any problems with these guys because they were the real thing. Not shake-and-bakes with a green M-16 that they couldn't use effectively if you gave them a truckload of ammo.

'Lieutenant,' Soloman said sternly, 'we go locked and cocked when we hit the deck at Fallbrook.'

'Is this a drop, sir?'

'Negative.' Soloman had come to it, feeling alive as the words gave something back to him. 'We've got two slicks standing hot in a pick-up zone to deliver us for a snatch-and-grab. When we get the objective safely airborne we'll have two gunships as escorts. But if things go bad, and they might, we have a naval sanction to use deadly force in civilian territory. You'll be issued a briefing file when we close the hatch.'

'We're hot, sir.'

'Good. I'm Apache One and Chatwell is Apache Two. What's your designation?'

Garcia smiled, teeth gleaming in a harsh Mexican face that you wouldn't want to meet anywhere but in a church, and even then not to hear his confession. He spoke distinctly.

'*Malo Hombre.*'

Soloman couldn't help smiling as he turned away.
Yeah, he probably was as bad as bad gets.

CHAPTER 7

Night, yes.

Night ... so nice.

It was so much more pleasant than the hateful light of day that tormented him with so much he could not fully remember.

He stood a time in the concealing dark, beneath the trees, sensing dimly that this paleness was as nothing compared to the stygian fire of his half-forgotten world. Yes, for in that place even the shadows burned with cold flame that scorched his soul and scarred his mind moment by moment with the awakening of pain, pain, too much pain to torment him for eternity because it would never leave his blackened heart in peace.

He growled, raising eyes against the stars where he had risen to cast down his throne. 'Almost,' he whispered balefully. 'I almost brought down that holy pride.'

He waited long, and longer, but only silence answered, as the wind fell still. Frowning, a brooding beast in the gloom, he stared over the house, knowing so well that the seed of his life was inside, protected now by men who surrounded the structure with weapons that could never destroy this fantastic form he inhabited.

It was the FBI, he knew. But they could not stop him. Nothing on Earth could stop him because he was more than all the Earth. He was the destroyer of worlds, had always been the destroyer of worlds though this world had been taken from him, until now. But now, yes, here and now he could again become the god he had been.

He was dressed in a black shirt with black pants and boots that he'd stolen from the military surplus store, with a vehicle. Afterwards he had traveled northward, driving along the vast forest roads that twisted through Colorado. It had been easier than he'd anticipated because the military perimeter had finally yielded to the awkwardness of distance, becoming widely gapped at two hundred miles.

Now he was free from the search party, though the physical limitations imposed by this form continued to irritate. And for a moment he cursed the restraints forced on him by seizing this humanity, lamenting the phenomenon that had caused him to forget so much, remembering so little. Yet he knew that the temporary loss of memory was the horrific price paid to cross the void, the price to gain control over this splendid flesh that rendered him impervious to attack and even pain.

He was surprised at first when he had suffered such grievous wounds inside the laboratory at White Sands only to return the force and more, killing easily as his heart gloried in the blood he shed. For he had never expected it to be so easy, had expected more resistance even as he had been resisted when he'd been *struck down* so horribly and cast out to –

Falling.

Days … darkness …

Floating on stygian fire.

Floating … awakening …

He closed his eyes.

Enough, he thought, *I am not what I was. I cannot remember what I was. But I will always be more … than they*.

It was of no matter. For the agony of this world, and even the agony of the Abyss, were mere glory compared

to the cursed and hated presence of that musical light
that he himself had created so long ago to glorify what
he would never glorify again.

Glorify?

Eyes glowing red, he snarled as fangs emerged.

No, he would never glorify anything but himself.

◆ ◆ ◆

'Okay, Amy, let's play a game!'

Sitting on the floor of the den, sunlight-blond hair
falling over her face to frame angelic blue eyes that
were both intelligent and innocent, Amy Milton looked
up and saw the kind of vivid fear that adults can never
hide.

She saw her babysitter, Kathy, smiling too much and
talking too fast and acting as if there were nothing to
fear, and Amy knew clearly that there was something to
fear. 'What's happening, Kathy?' she asked, in a soft
voice. 'Who are all those men outside? Why do they
have guns?'

'Nothing's happening, Amy!' Kathy smiled disarm-
ingly. 'There's just a bunch of policemen outside.
They're making sure that we're safe.'

'Safe from what?'

Kathy paused. 'Just … safe.'

But her reply couldn't conceal her fear and then she
blinked, as if realizing she'd failed. Slowly she reached
out with a gentle hand. 'I don't know, Amy,' she said,
reality there. 'I wish I did, kiddo. But I don't.'

A moment passed and then the babysitter leaned
forward to hug the six-year-old, already dressed in her
pajamas. Eye to eye, holding the child's tiny shoulders,
Kathy added, 'But you know I'm gonna stay with you.
We're in it together.' She winked, smiled. 'And your
mom's gonna be home soon. She'll tell you.'

'Those people aren't going to hurt us?'

'No,' Kathy whispered, openly amazed at the question. 'These men aren't going to hurt us, Amy. They're the FBI.'

'What's the FBI?'

'They're good people, Amy. They're our friends.'

Amy's eyes gleamed with a perception rare for her age; it was the kind of intelligence adults feared because it told a child what they really thought. She said nothing as she gazed at the older girl.

'It's going to be all right, kid,' Kathy said, smiling. 'Like I said, we're in it together. These people will protect us.'

Amy lowered her head, blond hair falling over soft blue eyes.

'But … from what?'

◆ ◆ ◆

Screaming in at two hundred miles an hour, the Nightcat burned a black trail on the tarmac of Fallbrook National Airport.

Soloman glared out the window to see emergency vehicles racing alongside, yellow lights flashing, and in a hot combat mode unbuckled his belt. He stood as the pilot lifted the horizontal flaps to aid the brakes and then he was leaning over the squared face of Chatwell, yelling above the roar of reversing engines.

'Lock and cock when we hit the deck and remind Malo that he's got a standing green light to fire on acquisition of this *thing!* I want six men per slick and tell that police chopper we're going in full-tilt boogie! Make sure you put Maggie with the wingman!'

'Yes, sir!' Chatwell obeyed without hesitation. He unfastened his belt and staggered toward the rear of the jet where the twelve-man Delta squad was already on their feet, loading.

Soloman moved across the aisle. 'Ben!'

'Yeah!'

'Tell the FBI we're coming in hot! If they haven't moved her yet, tell 'em to hold their ground!'

'Are you sure about this, Sol?' Ben's eyes gleamed with excitement. 'You're sure we're not wasting our time?'

Soloman sharply shook his head. 'There's no way to be sure! But I'm not taking the chance! After we get the girl relocated we'll get down to tracking this thing!'

'Good enough!' Ben reached up and snatched a plane phone off the hook. He was speaking in seconds, shouting over the twin engines as the Lear slowed hard, wheels almost skidding on the tarmac. Bracing himself, Soloman snatched up the black bag of shells and the SPAS-12 shotgun before turning to stare at Maggie. 'You're getting in the secondary chopper!' he shouted. 'Just do as you're told, Maggie!'

Her eyes were blazing with concentration, catching every detail second by second with amazing speed. She wasn't intimidated by any of it, Soloman could see clearly, and her grim frown revealed that she'd caught a measure of his combat heat. She grabbed his arm strongly as he turned away.

'Soloman! Listen to me for a second!'

He stared down.

A measured breath and she continued, 'Listen! If Cain comes for Amy and you have to fight, then you have to hit him *dead-center* in the chest and keep hitting until he falls! The only chance you'll have is to cause a shock trauma to his heart because conventional weapons won't penetrate the internal plates! Do you understand what I'm saying?'

'Yeah, Maggie.' He nodded. 'I think so.'

She repeated it, screaming over the chaos of the jet. 'It's all *psychological!* I saw it on the tape. Everyone hits Cain hard but then they hesitate because they expect him to fall! And Cain uses that moment of hesitation to launch a counterattack! The only chance you have in a stand-up fight is to hit him *repeatedly* in the chest! That might cause his heart to skip or even stop and could put him down for a few seconds until HyMar gets his heart back on line!'

Soloman had already thought of that because it was the classic mistake of a soldier. They hit hard but then hesitated to see what kind of effect the blow had, and that's what got them killed. He'd seen it over and over in his career. He was genuinely impressed that she'd perceived it on her own, and so quickly. He realized that her intelligence was astounding, and it wasn't limited to the laboratory.

'Thanks, Maggie,' he said curtly. 'You can count on it.'

He turned away as the emergency vehicles pulled up and he saw that some had red-blue code equipment; civilian police, federal agents only used blue. Then the door was yanked open and he was the first man off, Delta commandos close.

In seconds they reached their two Hueys. The rotor blades were already spinning lazily. They split into squads, Soloman leading Squad One, Malo leading Squad Two. Soloman turned as he heard a police officer frantically hailing Ben.

Running quickly to the patrol car, Ben spoke over the whining engines as Soloman placed Maggie on the wingman's chopper, the blades roaring feet above their heads. Then above the din he heard Ben screaming and spun.

And knew.

The general's voice was barely audible above the ungodly roar.

'They've lost her!'

◆ ◆ ◆

Night echoed with the howls of dying men as Amy Milton ran quickly through the woods at the back of her house, for she'd seen the giant charging through the white flashing maze of gunfire, had seen him hurt the other men, the FBI men who were there to protect her. Then she saw the monstrosity on the front steps and was backing into the kitchen as *it* hit the door, smashing the wood into sections.

Standing dark in the door, he was drenched in blood. His shirt was smoking as his head turned until he sighted her and then the terrible face split in a horrible grin and Amy knew *she* was the one he truly wanted.

With a scream she fled, glimpsing Kathy as she wildly threw herself in the giant's path. Then Amy heard Kathy's scream die to nothing as she frantically jerked open the back door where wounded men crawled and limped across the backyard. Raising hands to the screams she ran through them, knowing somehow that they couldn't save her, and then she was beyond the grass, legs flashing white in the moonlight.

She whirled back as she cleared the yard to see the giant following, always following, down the steps. Then deafening gunfire erupted in the night as the FBI also saw him and began firing.

It was a war face-to-face and Amy staggered, seeing the thing fall backward at the assault before he rose with a vicious roar. He leaped over the hood of a car to hit a man hard in the chest and then the rest of them were on top of him, firing, firing, always firing.

It wasn't enough.

The monster went through them, bloodied and ugly and horrible, and as the red eyes saw her again he howled in laughter, leaping forward only to be engaged by other FBI men who never stopped firing and then they were all fighting together in a haze of blinding noise.

So loud, before silence.

Amy was deep inside the treeline as a horrible roar followed her into the darkness.

'*Aaaaaaamy!*'

◆ ◆ ◆

Like gleaming black dragonflies the Hueys swept in over Amy's house, turbos straining. But they saw nothing except ambulances and police cars and innumerable infrared signatures. Soloman ordered a tight circular pattern at two hundred feet.

'Infrared is *useless*, Colonel!'

Soloman cursed, expecting it. He'd hoped that the infrared signature of Cain would be colder or somehow different than the rest, but it was obviously the same, if it was there at all. He searched for another tactic, thinking furiously.

'What do you want to do, Colonel?' the pilot shouted.

'Use air to ground lighting!' Soloman yelled. 'Put those quasars at ten million candlepower and light this place up!' He turned to the six Delta commandos. 'Visual search! Find the girl or find Cain! One or the other *I don't give a damn!*'

Dividing three by three – each man already belted to his seat – the teams instantly leaned out the open hatches. They pointed weapons downward ready to open fire on sight as the massive searchlight beam descended from the belly of the Huey.

'Colonel!' the pilot shouted.

'What!'

'They've got a report from a wounded FBI agent that the girl was running in a northeast direction with Cain in foot pursuit! They say she ran into an eighty-acre section of woods!'

A Delta commando pointed sharply. 'There it is,

Colonel! Right behind the house! It leads to that water treatment plant at two o'clock!'

'Set this bird down on the north side of the treatment plant!' Soloman shouted. 'Relay the command and tell the other slick to land south! Advise Malo to initiate a three-by-three pattern on infrared for a blood trail! Then I want both of these birds lighting up the forest in a holding pattern until we locate Cain or the girl!'

'Aye, sir,' the pilot said as Soloman hefted the SPAS-12. The murderously heavy shotgun was already chambered because, by training and experience, he never went into battle with an unchambered weapon. The .45 on his hip was also cocked and locked, ready to fire the instant he flicked off the safety.

As they hit the ground they were on night vision and Soloman divided Squad Two into three-man teams, one moving east, one west. Then with Chatwell behind him he stood in the middle of the field, studying the situation, the lay of the land. He knew the girl would be frightened and tired, moving as quickly as she could because she would want to put distance on Cain, to outrun him even though there would be no chance of outrunning him.

Then the chopper was airborne again, carefully trying to keep the harsh spotlight off them and on the woods. And Soloman vaguely admired the pilot for his presence of mind, because he hadn't reminded him to do it. Obviously the kid was a smart flyer, someone he would have taken on any high-risk mission.

Angry, drenched in sweat, Soloman stared fiercely over the terrain, trying to slow his thoughts to cold logic and reason. He held the shotgun hard and close and crouched dead-silent and dangerous in the middle of the field, desperately trying to find the mind of a child.

The field was ringed with illuminated trees that seemed suddenly safe in the lamps of the Hueys but

Soloman knew the forest had been black as pitch when Amy had fled through here. And, like any other child, she would be instinctively scared of the dark. She would have stayed as close to the light as possible, falsely comforted by the sense of safety.

Soloman began to sense her probable direction but it was a desperate idea and he didn't have time to waste, not if Squad Two had found any track at all. He touched his neck microphone.

'Apache One to Malo.'

A pause.

'Malo,' was the whispered reply.

'Anything?'

'Negative. We're moving three by three in a path-finder spread. We haven't found anything.'

'Copy. Out.'

Twisting his head, Soloman gazed up. A full moon was visible in the night sky and he knew that the blaze would have made this long oval field seem like broad daylight only a few minutes ago. It would have looked like a heaven of light through a blackened forest.

Intuition; the path a child would take ...

Soloman grimaced.

Intuition! The path a child would take!

It was all he had.

Come on! Move!

Without hesitation he low-ran the center of the waist-high delta, moving in a serpentine pattern. He switched the Nightwing goggles to dual infrared-starlight imaging and tried not to break a leg with the sudden lack of depth perception. Increasingly desperate with each second, he fiercely hunted the blood trail in the dark but continued to see nothing and began wondering if Cain had been hit at all by the FBI agents.

Moving, moving, legs strong in a crouch.

Moments passed and Soloman savagely fought the panic.

No, no, she had to come this —

As he saw it.

He'd almost crossed over again before he realized what it was; a faint red glow on the side of a small shrub, something picked out by the thermal enhancement of the goggles. Not much, but enough. And with the sign Soloman spun to Chatwell, raising a fist.

Chatwell full-stopped at the gesture, crouching and raising his weapon. But Soloman shook his head, pointed to the bush. Then he was moving forward fast as Chatwell raised the radio, speaking quickly, and Soloman knew that within minutes the commandos would be converging on this zone to pick up the sign. But he didn't have time to wait for them.

He ran low and cautious, holding the heavy SPAS more easily than he'd ever held it before, and he knew the rush of adrenaline was giving his strength a quick edge. Slowing only slightly as the dense woods loomed before him, Soloman followed the trail into the maze.

Through the wall of trees he could see nothing – the goggles couldn't read heat through solid wood or metal – and he knew that if Cain were inside the woodline he could walk straight into the giant's arms: instant death. But Soloman didn't think Amy had stopped running, just as he didn't think Cain had stopped pursuing.

If Chatwell was close behind Soloman couldn't hear it because his hearing had instinctively modified itself to mid-tone ranges, his vision tunneling more and more as he got closer and closer to the conflict. And although he hadn't felt the sensation in a long time, he found himself acclimating quickly, at home.

Placing his back against a tree, he took a moment, breathing deeply, trying to slow his thoughts and lock out narrow vision until the confrontation. But it was impossible to ignore the possibility that Cain could be upon him in seconds.

Then in that strange and uncanny moment that often

comes over men in combat, his mind turned to something that has nothing at all to do with the battle itself. It was the kind of phenomenon that you couldn't avoid and often got you killed. And, for the space of a breath, Soloman was shocked that he cared at all about dying.

No! No time for thought!

Find her! Find her! Find her!

Knowing that almost every untrained person moved angularly in the forest, disoriented by the lack of reference, Soloman selected the course Amy probably would have followed, taking it in a heartbeat. He moved quietly downhill where the brush was thinnest and in moments picked up Cain's blood trail again.

Smiling savagely, Soloman moved over it, sweat burning his eyes that narrowed more and more in an unquenchable rage that reached back to a place he couldn't even remember in the darkness that had become his life.

◆ ◆ ◆

Amy ran to the large water tunnel that bordered the woods, looking up as she came to the entrance. She had played here so many times that she knew these tunnels by heart, but that had been in the day.

Now the tunnel was deep in blackness, and frightening. She felt her legs tremble, couldn't catch her breath.

No, maybe … another place.

She turned to see something terrible in the far darkness and then she heard the horrible voice roaring.

'Come to me, child! Come to me!'

Crying out, she ran into the tunnel.

◆ ◆ ◆

Soloman held the SPAS close, using its weight for

balance the same as a tightrope walker uses a pole. Following Maggie's advice, he'd set the massive shotgun on semiautomatic so it would fire its full arsenal of twelve double-ought buck rounds as fast as he could pull the trigger.

Each round contained eight balls of lead, impacting into the target like eight nine-millimeter rounds fired at once. At close-range, he knew from experience, a single shot would vaporize a man's torso. It was one of the most effective weapons ever made.

Soloman saw the tunnel looming up and glimpsed – or thought he glimpsed – the surreal image of Cain moving into the blackness, and he raised the SPAS for a shot. But the darkness caused him to shift the sights, searching, and then he knew Cain had entered the inky blackness of the huge drainage pipe.

Behind, Soloman heard steps and turned to see Chatwell coming through the woodline, staggering with fatigue. Soloman motioned silently for him to hurry and Chatwell was heaving like a racehorse as he reached the entrance, falling against the side with a Remington 870 shotgun held low in his hands. His face was weary, drenched in sweat from running through the humid woods. 'Did you … did you get a visual, Colonel?' he gasped.

'Yeah, I got one,' Soloman said steadily, enraged and livid with combat acuity. He had found his way back to this world without even trying; everything seemed twice as sharp, his mind already at computer speed. 'Wait here for Delta and then follow the blood trail!'

He moved on it.

'Colonel!' Chatwell grabbed at him. 'Wait for Delta!'

'No time!' Soloman tore his arm free and went quickly forward. He stalked into the gigantic tunnel as fast as caution allowed and glared down to see the mud marred by footprints. But the blood was a better trail, painting the circular floor in red heat.

Chatwell was far behind him giving frantic radio instructions to the Delta soldiers who were converging at the entrance.

As a little girl screamed.

CHAPTER 8

Soloman flicked off the safety and was charging before Chatwell could even yell for backup. Moving quickly, he sought face-to-face battle, all caution forgotten as the horrified cries of the child flooded over him.

Screaming, screaming that was hideous and haunting; a child's scream.

He smoothly leaped a small ravine and hit running, his mind at combat speed.

Faint mist raised from his heated breath fogged the goggles in the increasing humidity of the pipeline as he followed the glowing red blood. And very, very quickly he was both amazed and terrified at the thought of how Amy could have found her way through this frightening maze without any light at all. Then the goggles were lit with white and he squinted up to see a surface grate.

He bent his head and realized that this was where the underground facility could be accessed from the ground. High above he heard the faint sound of a passing vehicle and realized he was beneath a road, past the interstate.

As the screaming stopped.

Clenching his teeth Soloman turned into a tunnel where the screams still echoed, something rising inside him to overcome his fear with a purpose pure and vengeful, seeking deliverance.

◆ ◆ ◆

Blinded by tears, Amy looked up.

Bloodied, the giant stood over her, staring down.

Cowering against the wall, able to see him only in the dim light of the grate above them, Amy hugged her shoulders and cried uncontrollably. She'd come to this place because it was so deep inside the tunnels and she could easily climb the ladder to get back out and she had never guessed that he could find her here because no one had ever found her here, not ever. But he had found her and now he stood over her like death, black and silent and infinitely frightening.

Even in her fear Amy knew the giant should be dead because the FBI men had shot him again and again. But he wasn't dead; he was a monster, a monster and he was alive and he was with her in the dark, staring down, glowering, and she knew with all that a child could know that she was about to die.

Silence.

Then, suddenly, he staggered, lowering his head to lean against a wall. He grimaced in pain, shaking his face. Then his fangs – fangs incredibly long and sharp – gleamed frighteningly in the faint light as she heard his words.

'How horrible,' he rasped, 'that this frail blood … could be my life.' He swayed. 'One who made the nations tremble has fallen … to this inglorious state.'

He almost collapsed and Amy thought she heard the cave growl of a beast as he bent his head even lower. And in that moment of skin-crawling threat she would have fled farther if it were possible, but they had reached a ledge where a raging river of water swept beneath.

In the light of the grate Amy could see the current carried into a nearby tunnel, dark and roaring. She crouched fearfully at the edge before the man suddenly turned his head. He stared long into the water as if listening … or remembering.

Time passed.

'Yes,' he whispered finally, 'of course, that is why I seek it. The castle is the place of power … that is why I sought it.' A pause. 'Yes, now I remember the … *Grimorium Verum.*'

His smile was metallic and Amy saw more clearly the sharp fangs gleaming. And then she truly wanted to scream but couldn't scream so that the silent cry erupted inside her, overflowing into horror.

'Underworld,' the man whispered, staring down with glowing red eyes. 'Skyworld, earthworld, and ground that holds copper … to strengthen the spell. And deep water that hides … yes … that hides the treasure that I need to destroy … the millennium.'

Silence struck like thunder as he smiled slowly. The smile grew moment by moment until he threw back his head to laugh, a roar with tiger fangs flashing in the light. And the horrific black mirth continued long until the giant released a deep breath, exhaling slowly. His voice was distant and satisfied.

'No … no force could equal my pride,' he said. 'But I need neither pride nor force to kindle rebellion on this loathsome sphere … this loathsome sphere that harbors that most cherished flesh of your flesh.'

He smiled hatefully.

'Hell hath not my equal, you know,' he spoke. 'Not Hell, or Earth, or even Heaven. Together, the dimensions behold my pride with amazement and horror. Not even baneful Moloch, warring with me eternally even as you, can match the height and depth and breadth of my spite, and my wrath is a curse to him as long as fear shall last. But hear me, Old One, hear the words sworn on the secret name you have taken from my mind lest I mock you, that all war before this was only a parade to the war now raised, for my banner is hate, and is uplifted. And you yourself shall curse the day you withheld your arm from delivering my destruction.

'From the graveyard of your celestial might I will watch your wind scatter the flesh and bones of your beloved dead, and I will laugh. Because I am among the sheep you adore so foolishly, and they shall not last the conflict.' He snarled. 'And because you will not dishonor yourself by undoing the folly these fools have wrought, you will be destroyed with them. For not even you can violate your ... your *justice*.'

Silence and darkness descended, breathing.

Amy stared. 'Wh-wh-who are you?' she whispered. 'Why ... why do you want to hurt me?'

The man lifted his head, as if he'd forgotten her in remembering so much else. Then he smiled, standing away from the wall to step closer. His voice rumbled past the grating fangs.

'Don't be afraid, child,' he said, and Amy saw the fangs slowly, silently sliding back into his jaws. 'Now I remember ... and remember well.' He paused. 'We must travel far from here. But when we reach the place of power you will see such a world that mortals dream of, yet never know. And when the moon is aligned with Saturn and Mars, I will reclaim all that was mine. I will once again be what I was; Lord of the Earth.'

She couldn't contain her tears.

'What ... what are you going to do to me?'

'Yours shall be the denouement, Amy,' he smiled. 'You will give me eternal life, and the blood you shed will resurrect a kingdom lost so long that not even I remember the glory of it.'

Amy brought her knees higher, pleading. And, ignoring her cries, the giant raised his face to stare upward. White moonlight spilled through the metal cage that separated them from the world.

'*Du rosa raziel nopa padous*,' he murmured. 'The second pentacle of Saturn and Mars against the water of the moon to give strength … against the greatest of adversaries.' Frowning or smiling, he lowered his head, staring slowly over her. His eyes gleamed, malicious and evil.

He laughed as he bent to –

'*Cain!*'

Cain whirled as the man leaped into the tunnel, and then the cavern exploded as Cain roared and staggered back. Instantly the intruder fired again and Amy was screaming and screaming, endlessly screaming as she raised hands over her head.

◆ ◆ ◆

Livid with rage, Malo whirled as distant gunfire reverberated through the tunnels. He searched frantically but couldn't pinpoint a direction and spun toward Chatwell. 'Chatwell! Where did the colonel go!'

'I don't know!' the sergeant gasped, staggering with fatigue as he glared into the spotlit darkness. 'He just vanished! He said he couldn't wait for backup!'

Malo whirled back as sounds of shotgun fire and a wild animal roar collided. 'Spread out and find the colonel!' he shouted to all of them as he ran forward. '*Come on, come on, come on! We're out of time!*'

◆ ◆ ◆

Soloman fired point-blank into Cain's chest and Cain fully took the blast, staggering. He hovered on the edge of the ledge and Soloman advanced as he fired again and again, impacts of the SPAS-12 shredding the giant's torso in violent concussions that painted the white walls red, but Cain didn't drop so Soloman kept firing.

Then with a galactic scream Cain staggered forward, lifting taloned hands to grapple and Soloman roared in rage as he stepped into it, the SPAS ejecting spent rounds as quick as he could pull the trigger.

Taking five blasts dead-center to the chest Cain was moved back again by the onslaught to hover on the edge of the ledge. Then his face twisted with pain and fangs exploded from his jaws in a thundering god-roar as Soloman fired the twelfth and last round from the SPAS, instantly dropping the shotgun to fast-draw the .45.

Before the shotgun struck the ground Soloman fired to hit Cain in the forehead only to hear the .45 round ricochet into the dark, defeated by the titanium skull. He fired five, ten, twelve rounds point-blank into Cain's head and chest and then the giant swayed on the edge of the abyss, his body hovering above the river. Soloman shouted as he sighted between Cain's eyes.

Fired his last shot.

The bullet hit Cain's forehead center-mass and, like a mountain, the giant fell from the ledge, bellowing in rage. He hit the river hard where the impact was lost to the deafening roar of the river itself and then he was gone, taken by the current.

Sweating in the mist, Soloman stared angrily from the edge of the river as he dropped the empty magazine. He slammed in another to instantly chamber a round and searched a long moment but saw nothing and realized Cain had been defeated by the river. He was gone. Gone into the darkness of the connecting pipeline.

Grave, breathing hard and heavy, Soloman turned to stare down at the little girl, searching and concerned. But he saw she was unharmed as she whispered fearfully, 'Did you ... did you kill it?'

Soloman was silent a long time, compassion and control giving tone to his eventual words.

'No, Amy. I don't think I did.'

◆ ◆ ◆

Marcelle gently touched the wall, feeling the deep talon marks torn in the plaster of Father Lanester's room. The monstrous claws had raked with phenomenal power to tear furrows as wide and deep as his fingernail, clearly the work of inhuman strength.

The room had been almost cleaned by a single old nun, who labored yet. Working on her knees with a scrub brush, she stubbornly struggled to remove blood stains from the glossy wood.

She had looked up, unsurprised, as Marcelle emerged to stand silently in the door frame. Her wrinkled face was implacable, mouth set in a grim line. As one deeply inured to the secret ways of the Church, she seemed to know why he had come. Silently she nodded, closing her eyes, and Marcelle gravely returned the gesture, also wordless, understanding.

Then she went back to her cleaning, tirelessly trying to defeat the blood as Marcelle fully entered the room, his quiet footsteps overcome by the sound of determined brushing. Ten minutes later Father Barth also appeared in the doorway. Although the old man spoke loudly and boldly to Marcelle, he did not enter the room.

'We have begun to catalogue the Archives against the last list of interred documents,' he said. 'The Archbishop has called Rome for assistance, and they are flying in the Librarian Superior and Superior General Aveling forthwith. He will be here by late tonight to assist us.'

Marcelle indicated that he understood, not wishing to speak against the silence of the room – a silence broken only by the dogged work of the old nun so intent on her task. He was amazed that the walls had already been cleaned, for the chamber was not small. She had obviously begun at the top and worked her way down, where the blood had pooled. He could not even imagine how many buckets of blood she had already carried from the room, just as he knew that it had been a horrifying task. Though the horror of it seemed only to enhance, rather than dilute, her iron will.

He looked at the bed to see more talon markings deeply torn in the plaster, scratches that began low and rose to descend again, writing ... something. He studied it to translate and almost with the first letter, he knew. His mouth opened in a shock that even he could not conceal, and then he sadly shook his head as he finished, knowing what he had long feared had finally come, as he always knew it would come.

'What is it?' asked Barth, noticing the change.

Marcelle's mouth tightened.

'Marcelle!' the old man repeated. 'What do you see? Can you not tell me?'

'A word,' Marcelle replied, teeth clenched. 'A single word.'

Braced by the presence of others, the old man walked into the room. Even though he was of strong fortitude, the event, so horrible and in his own parish, had shaken his constitution. He stared at the wall, reading the scrawl left by the claws. His voice was quieter when he spoke.

'Neshamah,' he murmured, squinting a moment as if searching across a great gray distance, perceiving an enemy there. 'It was written beneath the blood. That's why I didn't see it.'

'Yes,' Marcelle agreed coldly. 'Always beneath the blood.'

Barth could almost be seen searching his mind, the definition of the word coming to him slowly. 'Yes, Neshamah. I know this word. It is old Hebrew, used to identify ... yes, to identify the soul proper. It is meant to identify the essence of what is true being, of what is truly man. But what does it mean here?' He turned to

Marcelle. 'Why would it be torn into the wall beneath Father Lanester's blood, Marcelle?'

'Jealousy,' Marcelle replied. 'Jealousy for what it cannot have.'

'And … what does that mean? Are my suspicions correct? Is someone subjugated?' Barth waited, staring hard. 'What does it *mean*, Marcelle?'

Marcelle bowed his head. Then without hesitating in her work at all and without looking up, the old nun spoke from the floor. Her voice was defiant and unflinching. 'Golem,' she said quietly.

Father Barth gazed at her.

No wind moved the air that moved.

'Golem?' he repeated. 'What is this, Sister? I am not familiar with this word.'

Mary Francis respectfully waited for Marcelle to deliver an answer to the question, but Marcelle held his silence. After a moment she spoke while working, always working.

'Golem is a man that is not man,' she said, dipping the blood into the bucket. 'Golem is a man created … by man.' She began brushing again. 'The Golem is a dead man that lives. A dead man inhabited by Satan because he has no soul.'

Barth was clearly shaken by the words, spoken with such a lack of emotion that the calm greatly enhanced the horror. 'Can it be true, Marcelle?' he asked, trembling. 'Can such a thing be true?'

Marcelle was deliberate. 'Yes, Father, it can be true. The Golem is a man that lives unnaturally. A man that has no neshamah, consequently leaving the mind empty for possession by the *mazzikim*, the angels of destruction. The ancients record as early as the Mosaic period that a Golem could be created by old masters of sorcery. Then, after the Golem entered the world of men, its soulless void could be filled by the most powerful of demons.'

'But is this not mere superstition?' Barth gasped. 'A dead man living? Inhabited by Satan? You are a man of science, Marcelle! Tell me! Is it possible that something so terrible could come into our world?'

'Thousands of years ago men believed so,' Marcelle said. 'And in many ways the ancients remain wiser than us, despite our science. The Golem is even mentioned in the Scriptures, in Psalm 139, verse sixteen. It is a passage that refers to a man that is imperfectly and improperly formed. It's an obscure passage, and confusing to many. But it is there. It has always … been there.'

Father Barth blessed himself and leaned against the wall.

Then, as if struck by something beyond them all, Sister Mary Francis suddenly ceased her labor, raising her face to look curiously upon Marcelle. It was a curiosity that passed beneath old eyes and slowly faded at Marcelle's grim countenance until it was gone completely to be replaced with a deep and sincere compassion. Then, almost without expression, the old nun slowly crossed herself, slowly lifted her rosary beads to move them in silence, finally resting her hands on her knees in prayer.

But Marcelle knew it wasn't for herself.

With a frown he raised his eyes to the wall.

To see death, there.

◆ ◆ ◆

Soloman gently cradled Amy in his arms as he made his way through the hazardous tunnel, using the throat mike to communicate with Delta commandos who were still trying to find them in the underground labyrinth. The child was trembling violently from shock, murmuring over and over about the monster, the monster, the monster …

Touched despite the cold nothingness that he had

come to know as life, Soloman paused to gaze down, his face slowly softening. Moment by moment his warlike fierceness faded to a gentle, tender aspect. 'It's over, Amy,' he said. 'Rest easy. It's over.'

'But ... ,' she whispered. 'But you didn't kill him. And he'll come back for me. He'll come back ... ' Soloman felt one of her small hands clutching his with all the strength a child could possess.

'Don't worry about it, Amy,' he said strongly. 'I'm going to stay with you. No matter what.'

Blinking, she gazed up. 'But he ... he's *evil*. He said he was going to hurt me.' Fatigue washed across her eyes, half-closing them. 'He said he was going ... to kill me.'

'Nobody's going to hurt you, darlin'. I'll protect you.'

'You'll ... protect me ... from him?'

Soloman hesitated. 'Yeah, darlin'. I'll protect you from him.'

She faded with each word. 'Are you ... FBI?'

'No, honey. I'm just a soldier. My name is Soloman.'

Silence, a long stare.

'Thank you, Soloman,' she said, and reached up so tenderly, touching his face. 'Thank you ... for saving me.'

Then she rolled herself into Soloman's chest knowing that she was, at last, safe in the arms of someone who would protect her. Little by little her trembling slowed, stilled.

She whispered, 'Thank you ... for saving me,' and surrendered to sleep.

Soloman stood a long time in the darkness. Then he gently tightened his arms to hold her even closer, warming her. And as he gazed into the angelic face he remembered the last time he'd cradled a still, silent child, a child who'd died only because he hadn't been there for her.

With a frown Soloman bowed his head, wondering at

it. Wondering how love for a child had destroyed him, how love for a child had resurrected him, how death itself had brought him back to life.

He gazed into her face, spoke softly.

'I was about to tell you the same thing, Amy.'

◆ ◆ ◆

Maggie was pacing nervously at the entrance of the tunnel, both Hueys decked in the field behind her, when Soloman emerged from the darkness holding Amy tight to his chest. Malo and Chatwell and the Delta squad were close behind him and as they cleared the entrance they flared out to either side, effectively securing the area.

Maggie ran forward and Soloman stopped in place as she settled a soft hand on Amy's face, reflexively feeling. Despite overwhelming emotions, she controlled herself with remarkable will and determination. But as they stood close Soloman could all too easily read the pain expressed by her tight mouth, the tears standing on the edges of her eyes.

'She's all right, Maggie,' he said calmly. 'She's in light shock but she'll be fine once we get her warm. Right now we have to get you and her to a place where she'll be secure.'

Maggie looked up, searching.

'No,' Soloman shook his head. 'Cain's not dead.'

Maggie reached out to take Amy from his arms, but he didn't comply. 'She's heavy, Maggie, and it's a forty-minute flight. You'd better let me hold her on the bird.'

She bit her lip, nodded once. 'All right,' she whispered. 'But I'm not leaving her side.'

Together they walked toward the Huey and the pilot heated the turbos at their approach. Then as they reached the bay Soloman settled into a seat, cradling the sleeping child in his arms. Maggie sat next to him as Malo suddenly came near the hatch, leaning in.

'Negative on a perimeter search, Colonel!'

Soloman's eyes narrowed. He nodded, 'All right. Then put every bird the local police have in the air for a zone search. But *you* take charge of any assault if Cain is sighted! Continue until you determine whether Cain has broken clear of zones, then meet me at the safehouse.'

'Aye, sir,' Malo replied and solidly shut the hatch, distancing them from the thunderous sound of rotors and turbos. 'Let's go!' Soloman shouted to the pilot and Maggie clutched Amy's hand tightly as the Huey ascended sharply from the field, angling to clear trees as they flew high and hard into a night that had already lasted too long.

◆ ◆ ◆

After twenty minutes in the air, monitoring Amy's pulse and respiration, Maggie was content that her child was uninjured and was glad Soloman had chosen to hold her for the flight, because it had to be exhausting. Yet his arms were almost motionless as he cradled Amy's blanketed form, seemingly unaffected by fatigue as they sailed through the dark.

Finally Maggie leaned back, wiping wet bangs from her sweat-streaked face. Then she released a deep breath and glanced around at the sophisticated and confusing military equipment, neither intimidated nor impressed. She blinked slowly as she looked once more at Soloman's silent silhouette.

Neither of them had said ten words since they left the ground, each preferring the respite.

Now, though, she saw Soloman's head bent, his face hidden in shadow as he gazed at Amy. And Maggie caught a somberness in the bend of his brow that seemed sadder than anything motion could ever capture; it was a stillness that seemed to reveal a hint of hidden pain, of tragic regret, or haunting loss.

She watched him a long time and he seemed to have forgotten her presence as he bent to Amy's angelic face. Then he did something almost too small to observe. But she knew it was there as his fingers curled closely on the blanket, holding as if to comfort … or ask forgiveness.

She hoped her curiosity wouldn't draw his attention but as he leaned back again she felt the hard impact of his eyes, implacable once more, staring over her. She opened her mouth. Didn't know what to say.

Finally he gazed away.

Silent.

CHAPTER 9

A dark, dismal, soundless night haunted the aftermath of the battle, shrouding the safehouse where they secured Amy. There was no triumph in their countenance, no words spoken to alleviate their mutual despair. A family in their fear, it was as if they knew together that hopeful words would not only be futile but despised. What they faced, they knew, was too profound for anything but the horrible truth, so they said nothing at all.

Soloman sat in silence, his gaze narrow and set against a window, watching a gathering storm. His face was distinctly bitter as if, even now, he could not re-envision what he had witnessed. Even the implacable fire of his eyes seemed shaken and dimmed, as if he had measured his own meager strength against a superhuman force he could never approach.

His head had the hated bend of defeat and, inside his shocked mind, Soloman could see only one thing over and over again: the face of the child, the child with desperate, terrified eyes staring up at *him*.

It had moved him in a way he never thought he could ever be moved again because he had long ago reckoned that part of himself as dead. Now, though, with a child's single pleading gaze, he'd been roused from a dead man's desert grave to find himself reluctantly return to something he had fled for so long. With a disturbed frown he stared into the dark, wondering how it could have happened to a heart gone so long.

◆ ◆ ◆

Secured deeply within the windswept, scattered green birch and evergreen woodlands of San Bernardino National Forest, the safehouse was reinforced with steel walls, steel doors, and lead windows.

But none of them felt any comfort at its strength; they had seen already that nothing they carried could truly stop the virtual force of nature that had come against them. Only the fact that they were well hidden gave them temporary peace, for not even Cain could kill what he could not find.

Amy had fallen into blissful sleep with the help of a sedative, and Soloman heard Maggie quietly exit the bedroom, entering the den where he sat isolated. Ben had secured himself in the communications room to conference with the Trinity Council.

The big general had already been in there a long time, and Soloman knew he was probably having a difficult conference on the imaging system. But there was nothing he could do to help, so he turned his mind to security.

All the Delta commandos were outside with Chatwell, ensuring that the perimeter of the four-bedroom structure was covered. They were setting a wide array of heat and motion sensors to detect an approach.

Gazing quietly at Soloman, Maggie leaned against a wall. 'She's going to be okay. Her shock was psychological. But I gave her some Valium, so she should sleep soundly until morning.' She paused. 'Amy told me you hit him with a lot of rounds. How badly did you wound him?'

Soloman was amazed that she seemed even less shaken than he was, and he wrote it off as a measure of her phenomenal mind. Then with a grimace he took a deep breath, as if resurrecting a determination that had faded in the savage confrontation. He wasn't sure what made him evade her question. Perhaps it was because he feared his own answer. 'Maggie,' he began, 'could Cain have drowned in that tunnel?'

'It's possible, Soloman. Cain can drown just like anyone else. But he's not anyone else. If there was any way at all out of that tunnel, he found it. Even in pitch-black he can see where to go.'

'But there's no light,' Soloman countered.

'He registers light at two-thousandths lux or less and translates it to a range of twenty-five thousand,' she said, as if reading from a chart. 'To Cain, the absolute dark of a cave would just be shades of gray. Even your guys' starlight scopes can't approach it. It's possible, even likely, that he's already found a way out.'

With a supreme effort of will Soloman shook his head, as if to flame the stunned fire of his will, and Maggie was silent as he did. He had no doubt now that whatever horrific force delivered an ending to this conflict would take his life with it; knew somehow that victory, if it was to be bought, would be bought with the blood of everyone who stood in the gap.

He only regretted it because he had just discovered, to his surprise, a faint interest in living again. But in the end, he knew, he had a duty to do; a duty he would do even if he had to shed his very last drop of blood ...

◆ ◆ ◆

Ben reluctantly recognized that he was retreating, reading the lay of the land as it seemed to change before him in a political earthquake. After more than seven minutes of continuous questioning, he was becoming more and more certain that Archette was playing a carefully crafted game.

'If you will, General, allow me to ask another question,' the professor continued, ultimately controlled. 'Why did Ghost not earlier anticipate this direction of Genocide One? Was that not his responsibility? Such a lack of anticipation, a quality for which this operative is so highly vaunted, almost led to this child's death and provided Genocide One with a cure for his abnormalities. And did, indeed, result in the deaths of eight federal agents.'

Ben really didn't feel like dancing over this.

'Well, Doc, I think he *did* do his job.' Ben gave all of himself to the tone. 'Ghost figured this out before the rest of us. Even before the researchers. It was *our* man, Professor, I stress, who got to the girl before Genocide One could kill her. Without Ghost's intuition and judgment, she'd be dead.'

'But his actions were decidedly not fully preemptive,' Archette stressed, leaning forward as if Ben lay on a couch. 'That is what you must understand, General. If we –'

'Look, Doc.' Ben returned the posture. 'You're not a professional soldier. I don't know what the hell you are. But I know you're not qualified to judge how fast we figured this out. No, we didn't completely second-guess Genocide One. That's obvious. But with the help of this operative we're beginning to anticipate this guy. And I'm convinced that pretty soon we'll be a step ahead of him. Plus, you have to remember that we're still early in this game. I'll say again that Ghost's success tonight demonstrates, indeed, that he can anticipate the moves of this target.'

From the screen located in the Pentagon, Brigadier General 'Bull' Thompson seemed to concur and turned to the NSA assistant director. 'Well, Mr Hollman, what is your perspective?'

Inured to the complexities of catastrophes, Blake Hollman was quiet a moment. His face was bland but also faintly dismal. 'I don't know military procedures, General. It's not my place to second-guess professional soldiers who should be doing a professional job. But I do know we're getting heat from the Hill.' He emphasized the threat with perfect timing. 'Significant heat.'

Releasing a slow drag of his cigar, Ben tried to reveal that he didn't give a damn. Which he didn't.

'Heat about what?' he asked.

'About the deaths of eight federal agents in a public place, and about the fact that we've got to put a credible spin on this disaster,' Hollman responded, unaffected. 'About the fact that we've got a madman walking around infected with a virus that could go supra-epidemic in a week. About the fact that internal antagonists of this experiment – an experiment which could be interpreted to violate international treaties prohibiting germ warfare – may eventually leak it to the media, if they anticipate imminent failure. About the fact that any subsequent global disasters will be construed as our fault.' He hesitated. 'And that, gentlemen, even if Genocide One is ultimately found and destroyed before Class Four mortality rates are achieved, will injure our position. Conceivably, it could change the scope of our influence.'

As usual, General Thompson revealed nothing at hearing this threat. He stared at Hollman's screen and Ben could see the NSA's solidity. He also knew the tension wouldn't fade because Bull was a fighter. In the silence that followed, he thought of Soloman and regretted bringing him into it.

'Well,' General Thompson said flatly to Hollman, 'I think we need to stand behind this team a little longer before we initiate more comprehensive means of containing Genocide One, sir, because if General Hawken and his men are successful, there will be a minimal loss of life. And in military jargon that's called "accuracy."'

You kill the target without excessive collateral damage. And you can remind the President that the next-in-line failsafe, which entails dropping a bomb on whatever area Cain is located, is decidedly worse than giving this team another few days.'

Hollman was thoughtful. 'Very well, General. I'll relay the –'

'I concur with General Thompson,' interrupted Archette. 'I am not sure what measure of collateral damage must be acquired before we terminate this exercise, but backup failsafes are decidedly worse than our current plan. But I would like to make a suggestion: If we meet in person to discuss the situation we may be able to articulate our views more adequately and design superior strategy. General Hawken, I would like to meet with you at the safehouse.'

Ben was ignited at the suggestion. He didn't like it at all. 'The location of the safehouse is classified beyond your need to know, Professor. I have no intention of allowing you or anyone else inside my perimeter.'

'General.' Archette shook his head. 'Do you recall our collective clearances?'

'Doctor, not even the President of the United States has the clearance to approach this safehouse.' Ben was inspired by his own anger as he continued. 'Your suggestion is out of bounds. Further, if you attempt to –'

'That's enough, Ben,' said General Thompson, turning to stare at Archette's screen. 'Archette, even *I* do not know the location of the safehouse that General Hawken, in his tactical judgment, has selected. That is under the Trinity Mandate. You are well aware that this was to be a closed operation of a single field operative, a scientist, and a military commander. Your request is outside parameters. Nor do I want to hear it forwarded again.'

'Of course,' said Archette, with a slight nod. 'I merely

meant that, as unexpected threats have complicated this mission, specifically the threat of a profound security breach, that we should confer to discuss alternate tactics. And I wished to do it without inconveniencing General Hawken. But since my … suggestion … is deemed unsuitable, General Hawken can meet us in New York or Washington.'

Ben cursed under his breath. The last thing he wanted was to sit in a room with Archette and Hollman. But, then again, Bull would be present and the old man would assure a purposeful approach, shutting the lid on anything that even hinted of self-aggrandizement. Unless, of course, things got too out of hand in Los Angeles, and, in that situation, the fighting had just begun. There was no telling how bad it was going to get.

'Very well,' said Thompson finally. 'Ben, can you fly to New York and convene here if necessary?'

'Yes, sir. If it's necessary.'

'Good. Then we'll schedule a meeting tomorrow night or the following day, depending on developments. But if things get too hot, we have to come to you. Understood?'

'Yes, sir.'

'Good,' Thompson said. 'Until then, gentlemen, we will allow Trinity to reacquire the target and complete their assignment, although we will be perilously close to a deadline if Trinity fails. This transmission is terminated.' He cut the display without further words.

Ben released a deep breath. He debated what he had heard and knew he had perceived a slight tightening of the bolts from Archette. Not enough to make him suspect, but there was an intensity of tone, as if the CIA man were beginning to lay groundwork, preparing for something.

Ben knew it could simply be the fact that Archette was covering his butt, putting himself on record to question Soloman's judgment at the same time that he stood behind Trinity; it would be the best of both worlds. But Archette's sudden change of direction at this moment, authorizing Soloman a few more days even though they would be running out of time fast if they were forced to derail the team and select another failsafe, was curious.

It didn't make sense, and Ben stared at the screen a long time, searching it out. Some things made sense and some didn't, and finally he shelved it. He was too old for this, he knew. Too old by half.

He should have retired a long time ago, along with Soloman. But he was in it now, up to his neck, and he would finish it. He scowled at the blank screen that had held Archette's haggard face, and remembered the night he'd saved him from Soloman's wrath.

Even now, so many years later, it felt wrong. But it had been regulation and law, and Ben had moved on what he knew. He had regretted it at the time, had regretted even more the travesty of a trial that ended with Archette walking away clean, Soloman broken from the ranks.

And, damn it, here he was again.

The cigar hung forgotten in his hand.

◆ ◆ ◆

Ben exited the communications room to find Maggie and Soloman deep in a conversation that seemed more personal than professional. It wasn't because of what they were saying; he could plainly hear Soloman explaining his interest in languages and philosophy. No, he thought, it seemed personal because of the way Soloman was relaxing and gesturing. He even smiled once; something that hit quick and was gone just as quick, but it was there. Then Ben thought that he hadn't seen his old buddy's face so devoid of bitterness and anger since … since *before*.

Strolling about the kitchen, he took his time to make a martini, searching for something else to do, leaving them alone.

◆ ◆ ◆

'That's fascinating,' Maggie said, grateful for a respite. 'You know, I never figured you to be so scholarly, Sol. I mean, I knew you were smart. That was obvious. I just thought of you more as a soldier.'

Soloman shrugged. 'Well, you know, I'm a soldier. I think.' He laughed. 'I guess I'm just a grunt, basically.'

'Oh, you're more than that.'

Her eyes gleamed with amusement as he suddenly shifted, uncomfortable. 'You're sort of like the classical warrior-philosopher, you know? Like Lancelot. You've got this highly developed code of honor, but you can be vicious when you have to be. And deep down you're really a sensitive person. Sort of like you live in the best of both worlds.'

'Or the worst.'

She regarded him in silence. 'Do you get burned out?'

He smiled, shook his head. 'Sometimes.'

'Do you trust anyone?'

Soloman didn't answer; she didn't blink.

'Yeah,' he said finally. 'There's been a few I trusted. A few that I trusted … a lot.' His jaw tightened, control solidifying in seconds. 'But trust can be pretty dangerous, too.'

She knew, but asked, 'Why's that?'

He smiled, half-sad, half-bitter. 'Everybody's got the story. The clock strikes and nothing happens. The bell tolls, and you're the one to answer.' His pause was long. 'Trust is something we have to do, to live.'

Something in the way he stated the words, so plain and simple, caused her an intuitive impulse of pain. Her green eyes narrowed and she thought of asking him about the moment on the Huey; it was in her mouth and face, borne from the center of her body, but she held back.

No, she knew it would be too early.

She bit her lip, silent.

Soloman stared at his coffee, then took a deep breath and leaned back, as if expectant. He was gazing patiently at a corner of the kitchen as Ben came around it five seconds later, a king-sized martini in his hand. His face was void of pleasant thought as he sat down in a recliner, sipping. After a time he shook his head, as if amazed.

'The executive branch is scrambling big-time to put a halfway credible spin on the deaths of eight federal agents,' he growled. 'Not an easy thing, mind you, even for those liars. And the President, in turn, is putting serious heat on the Joint Chiefs before someone leaks that we were stupid enough to create a freakin' Frankenstein or Dracula or whatever the hell this thing is.' He looked at Soloman. 'They want an ending, buddy. And they want it *now.*'

Soloman's aspect hardened almost imperceptibly at first but became more and more visible with a gathering will. He pondered it a long time and finally shook his head, rising to walk to the darkness of a leaded window.

The three-inch-thick glass mercifully silenced the roar of an oncoming north wind that bent shadowed woods. In the distance, under the dome of a dark moon, the towering cliff edges of the national forest were littered with windtorn trees.

When they'd arrived at the safehouse, Soloman had been vaguely surprised at the crisp cleanness of the air. Compared to the dead-air heat of Los Angeles that seemed to hover even in winter, this place was like paradise, a radical contrast in so short a distance. Nor, at this elevation, was the dust chalky, as it was in the city. It still lifted at footfalls but was also heavier, thicker, and more solid. It was a good place to be ... at peace.

Enough. He shook his head.

Concentrate on what you have to do.

With a frown he turned his mind to tactics.

'All we need,' he said, 'is a break. We need to be able to anticipate where Cain is going so we can set up noncollateral countermeasures for free fire. Because we'll never beat him in a standup fight. He's too fast and too strong.' He turned to Ben. 'Are the FBI guys checking all murders in the greater Los Angeles area for anything that resembles Cain's methods?'

'Yeah. They're on it. *Been* on it.'

'Nothing?'

'Well, Sol, there's a ton of casualties. A bunch of dead bodies with the blood drained, but no clues of where he's going.'

'They know to contact us, right?'

'Yeah. They're gonna get with us on the imaging system as soon as they have something. And they will. They're pissed. They want this guy as bad as we do.'

'I figure.' Soloman turned away again. 'Maggie, how long before Cain recovers from what I did to him?'

Her eyes narrowed. 'You haven't told me how badly you injured him, Sol. First you need to tell me what you did. Where'd you hit him?'

Soloman again recalled the horrific face-to-face standoff. 'I hit him point-blank in the chest with twelve rounds of double ought buck. It staggered him, did a lot of damage. He tried to come at me but the rounds held him back. Then I put thirteen .45-caliber rounds into his face and chest, and the last shot sent him off the ledge and into the current.'

She was analytical. 'Then you did a lot of superficial

damage. The serratus magnus and intercostals, and probably even the axillary thoracics, were severed by the shotgun. But the coracoid process, the internal fascia located behind the chest muscles in the thorax, is fully sheathed in a curved niobium-titanium plate. It's virtually impenetrable, so it would have protected every organ between the clavicle and eighth rib. And unless your facial shots penetrated an occipital, the titanium skullplates would have defeated the pistol. I think it's safe to say that he's pretty badly hurt, but he'll heal back fast.'

'Why is that?'

'Because all the injuries are to large, fast-healing muscle groups,' she answered. 'I told you before, Sol, Cain can survive almost any kind of conventional small-arms fire. But … ' She paused as if to allow Soloman a small measure of victory. 'He's still going to have a lot of tissue damage, a lot of muscle damage. And he's going to need more human DNA so HyMar can heal his wounds without sending the unstable DNA into a backflow that will destroy him. He'll have to kill about a dozen people to acquire sufficient ribosomes for molecular synthesis and white-cell replacement.'

She stared, blinked sadly.

'The killing in this is just starting, Sol.'

◆ ◆ ◆

Marcelle didn't move as he stared at the hideous pictures of the scene in Father Lanester's chamber. The color photographs were so graphic that they seemed surreal, passing horror to become almost sterile.

Enough blood, Marcelle thought, *and blood becomes meaningless.*

He didn't even try to appreciate the immense strength required to literally tear the dead priest limb from limb and then drive his bones with such vicious force into the walls like spikes. He only knew that whatever had done this was strong beyond belief, beyond the reach of man.

And yet he didn't want to become distracted by the fear of it, so he concentrated on the words that had been written in blood across the four walls of the room, words that held ancient and fully frightening meanings that were all but lost to time.

Because he was almost as much a man of psychology as of the Church, he was still somewhat reluctant to believe without reservation that this was the work of demonic possession. And the accumulated fear and horror interred within his soul from past encounters made him even more reluctant to accept the horror of another exorcism.

But then there was the desert ...

He knew that shadowed hour held a fear he had evaded for long years, drowning the memory in academic discipline and intellectual coldness. And even now he could not fully contemplate what might have occurred when he broke the seal on that cursed tomb. But he could never lose the suspicion.

Skeletal eyes burning in darkness ...

Golem ...

Marcelle shut his eyes, jaw tightening.

I WILL BE FREE!

He released a tired sigh and concentrated, focusing again on the situation. From hard Jesuit training he knew that three of the five criteria used to define demonic possession were fulfilled.

There was superhuman strength, an inexplicable command of ancient languages, and knowledge of things that should not have been known – primarily the location and existence of the Secret Archives. Other qualifying signs included telekinesis and the ability to communicate with the dead. Those had not yet been demonstrated but enough was present, for certain, to warrant an exorcism. Still, though, there was something that disturbed him about the writing, something he couldn't place.

As he bent over the photographs he remembered the words of his mentor, Anton Aveling, the man who had taught him the reality of spiritual warfare: 'When a person is convinced that he is possessed by the devil,' Aveling had said so often, 'then you can be sure that there is no devil. The devil, when he is there, does everything possible to mask his presence.'

Marcelle knew it, all at once.

There was too much to understand; yes, far, far too much. The words too easily revealed themselves, leaving nothing hidden. It was as if the creature were challenging him, and Marcelle knew from experience that a demonic force would avoid a confrontation with an exorcist at any cost.

An exorcism was a conflict that neither antagonist sought because by nature it was a grueling ordeal, testing the endurance of the possessed, the exorcist, and even the demon itself. No, it was not something the devil invited, as it seemed to be doing now, so this was something different. With a frown Marcelle pondered it, becoming more and more certain that this was no ordinary act of possession. No, this was something far different, something …

More sinister.

Together the words scrawled in blood upon the walls had different shades of the same meaning. But Marcelle realized that all of them were meant to signify a single image, an image heated and deepened level by level to plummet into a black and terrible abyss.

Moving soundlessly from the darkness, Father Barth entered the shadowed room. And behind him, emerging from the portal, framed by the light of the fireplace, Marcelle saw another figure dressed in imperial white and priestly purple with an ecclesiastical cloak descending from his shoulders. Immediately Marcelle recognized the tall balding figure and rose to walk quickly forward, falling to one knee to kiss the ring of the Jesuit Superior General, Father Anton Aveling.

'Arise, old friend,' said the eighty-year-old Aveling, with a slight bow. 'I bring encouragement from Rome.'

Marcelle nodded gravely as he rose, stepping back so that the superior priest could seat himself in an opulent red leather chair positioned in front of Father Barth.

Barth himself sat back solemnly behind the desk, hands in view. And last, as protocol demanded, Marcelle sat opposite Aveling to feel the powerful impact of the old man's steady gray eyes.

'As I said,' Aveling continued in a slightly fatigued voice, 'I bring encouragement from the Dome of Michelangelo, Marcelle. Words of greeting from our brother, the Archbishop of Rome.'

Marcelle nodded at once, pausing. 'I am humbled, Father, that the Archbishop would consider me worthy of a personal message, especially one delivered by so noble an emissary.'

There was no pause as the older priest spoke with a smile of familiarity and friendship. 'There is much appreciation, my son, for your courage in taking on this investigation. I know that there are few more qualified to deal with the terrible task which may be before us.'

Marcelle was silent.

'Have you something to say, Marcelle?' the old man asked gently, with a becoming smile. 'You have never hesitated to deliver your august mind to my understanding. Just as you have never been short for courage. Or even sheer determination.'

Marcelle did not look up as he spoke. 'How can I be of assistance to you, Superior General? It has always been my sacred mission to serve, as you know from my actions, and not my words.'

For a time, the aged priest stared. 'We have entered an evil time, Marcelle,' he said finally. 'A time when those of us who dare must stand alone on this battlefield. You, a man who battled to exorcise the demon Raphael from an innocent woman, a revered member of Eradicare In Carne, know that we have no surety that the Church will outlive us. We have no certainty, even, that those who have held up our arms for four hundred years will agree with what we must do. Yet, in the end, we have no choice. For this is the hour of darkness, when we must enter the dangerous arena of what is ultimately good and ultimately evil. It is not a task fit for man, but for God. But it is a burden man must bear if we are to eradicate this evil from the world. It is a battle which must be fought in secret, and yet it must be fought, with no one but our brotherhood to mark our graves should we fall in the fight. Our toil must be in secret, and our blood shed in darkness with only God as our reward. But from this battle, as you know from the past, there can be no withdrawal. The present, if we are to survive at all, must mirror the oncoming final conflict between God and Satan.'

Marcelle was stoic at the words. Yet when the old man fell silent he looked up. 'Were these the words you have brought to me from Rome, noble Aveling?'

'Yes, Marcelle, and more than these. For I have seen the photos of the crime scene, just as you have. I have studied the names scratched into the wall – Mawet, Resheph, Ashtaroth, and Beliyy'al.' He paused. 'Mawet, whom the ancients teach us made a covenant with Death, then Resheph, the great and unconquerable demon-lord forever at war with the one who cursed him. Ashtaroth, the angel of death who brings about the end of the world. And finally … Beliyy'al, the dark angel who lords over all other fallen angels and brings them into subjection by the strength that is his, and his alone.'

'Yes,' agreed Marcelle, 'I have seen these things, also.'

'And so … ' Aveling paused, frowning suddenly. 'Yes, and so here we stand, Marcelle. And I must ask you this last discriminating question. Who is it, my son, that we face in battle a final time?'

A moment passed in dark silence. Marcelle finally stood and walked slowly to the fireplace. He waited a long time, his face grim while the merciless holocaust rose before him, consuming all that could be consumed. He stared into the flames, and none could say what he saw there.

His voice was hushed.

'One who was once a prince,' he said.

◆ ◆ ◆

His iron hand gripped the steel rung on the ladder as the water cascaded past him and he roared as his strength endured. Then, groaning inch by inch, he overcame the flooding force and began to haul himself from the flowing power of the underground river. The rusted rung bent at the combined pressure of his great weight and the torrent, but his hand would not release, was locked solidly as death.

Ancient curses twisted his face as he brought himself to air, fighting to find breath and life in this cursed tomb of dark and cold that had carried him so helplessly. Yet the deep steel of the rung held this time and he shouted, viciously lashing up to find purchase, hauling his chest from the flow.

Grimacing, growling, he climbed foot by foot to claim a hateful escape, ascending to the slender shadow of false light that haloed the manhole cover above him.

His wounds were agony, even worse than the wounds he'd suffered in the battle at White Sands where he'd escaped into the night to kill, and kill, and kill. He didn't know the man that had attacked him – he'd only glimpsed the face in the chaotic eruption of light that threw him back, blasting him into the river – but he knew he would find him one day, yes, he would find him and then he would deliver terror seen only once since the beginning of all things.

In time, yes, if I can only claim the blood of the child!

He gazed up at the manhole cover.

Light!

How he'd hated it! And now it was *life!*

He laughed as his feet cleared the river and then he was in the cold misty haze, climbing quickly upward. He hesitated briefly as he reached the last rung, poising close to the steel cover, listening. But he heard no traffic, saw no shadows passing overhead.

Silence was all.

He knew the Army could not have foretold his destination, for they couldn't have known where he would finally find a grip to climb from this sewer. But he did not want any witnesses that could attest to his emerging from the pipe, witnesses that might in turn report to the police who could create another secured perimeter. No, he needed time to heal, needed time to overcome the grievous injuries inflicted upon him by this unknown attacker who had come to defend the child.

With a single titanic blow he shattered asphalt cementing the manhole cover to the road. Then he hurled the heavy steel plate aside and climbed from the underworld like a blood-drenched gargoyle emerging from a bone-littered tomb, raising black-taloned hands to embrace the glorious night.

Recovering, drawing hot breath, he searched for witnesses and saw only one: a lonely figure silhouetted on the sidewalk beneath the light of a lamp. The figure had a grocery cart in front of him. His mouth hung open in shock.

Cain smiled as he turned and walked quickly forward. For at the sight, he knew …

He needed his blood.

◆ ◆ ◆

'And, now, what will the Golem do, my son?' Aveling's bald head glistened in the somber light with his question. He repeated it again as if he knew there could be no answer. 'Yes … that is the question we must answer. What will the Golem do?'

Marcelle was seated again and his face hardened as the moments passed. 'Did the Librarian Superior of the Archives come with you from Rome, Aveling? Is he in the Archives as we speak?'

There was assent.

Marcelle nodded, turning his mind with an effort to analysis. 'Yes, that is the place to begin. For Father Lanester was probably slain only because he held the combination to the vault. Surely, whatever this fiend desired was sealed within its walls.'

'But you forget that I also hold the combination to the vault, Marcelle,' Barth interrupted. 'I also have means of entering the Archives.'

With the words Marcelle stared, his brow hardening like flint. Then he rose, striding again before the fire. He turned back sharply. 'And where were you at the time of Father Lanester's murder?'

Barth shook his head, searching his memory. 'I … ah … I was at Imperial Funeral Home to conduct an all-night vigil for the death of a beloved donor to the Church. I did not arrive again at the cathedral until this morning, after I had been summoned by the police.'

Marcelle nodded with each word. 'Yes … yes … '

'What is it, Marcelle?' Aveling asked. 'What do you perceive?'

Moving away quickly with a single stride Marcelle

spoke. 'Yes! I should have thought of it before! Did you not even ask the question yourself, Father Barth? Of course that is it!'

'What?' gasped Barth. 'What are you saying?'

Crossing an arm over his chest, Marcelle marched like a soldier before the flames. 'Our enemy is too wise not to know he must do us harm at every opportunity! And is it not better to strike at the head than the body? Yes, surely. So, if this beast could have, he would have waited for Father Barth to return so that he could have taken a general instead of a captain! But he could not! So this tells us much! Our enemy fears something!'

Aveling's gray eyes narrowed. 'Yes, Marcelle, I follow your reasoning, but what is it that he fears?'

'He fears *time*,' Marcelle replied as he leaned suddenly upon the fireplace, becoming utterly still with concentration. 'The Golem's needs could not be delayed. He fears that, for some reason, his time is short, and so he hurries, forsaking the blood of the master for the servant. Yes! Father Lanester's death was a victory for him! But it was a far lesser victory than he would have preferred!'

Barth shook his head. 'I would have had it another way.'

'We know that you would,' Marcelle said without hesitation, 'because you are a father of the Church, and a noble man. But the battle that has been joined is in the hands of God, and we have no time, nor should we have compulsion, for regret. We must continue the struggle with courage and strength and whatever meager means we have at our disposal because the price of defeat may be greater than the value of all our lives combined.'

At the words Barth rose from his seat. 'And what is before us now, Marcelle? You, better than anyone, understand the mind of this evil. You say that time is not on his side? Is it on ours?'

Marcelle turned to gaze dismally into the flames. He shook his head and without permission withdrew a cigarette. Once it was lit, he expelled a thick, meditative cloud of smoke. The gathering silence in the room seemed to hang on his unspoken words.

'I do not know,' he said, implacable once more. 'But there is nothing we can do, yet. Because we do not yet know this monster's intentions. We must give Father James, the Librarian Superior, time to complete his search.'

'And then?' Barth asked as Aveling released a faint smile.

'Then we will see how wise and strong our enemy truly is,' Marcelle said, utterly calm. 'We will see how great is this strength he so cruelly used against a gentle man of peace.'

There was an ominous tone to the words.

'But are we not all men of peace, Marcelle?' Barth asked. 'How can mortal men defy immortal force?'

Marcelle took another long breath and released smoke in a cloud that, rising before the fire's light, covered him in a haunting white haze. He stood utterly alone and somber, as if he were surrounded by the ghosts of ancient battle, spectral faces of defeated heroes.

'Peace, Father?' he answered. 'There has never been peace in this world. It has been war since the Beast was created. Now, the only life we have is to fight … to fight until we die.'

CHAPTER 10

Chatwell wandered in at 11:00 p.m., gazing about the room until he sighted Malo's heavy BDU jacket laid across a chair. He winked at Soloman and Maggie as he limped over, carefully searching the pockets. Then from the front right he took a long black cigar that looked to be the finest Cuban and slipped it quickly into his shirt.

Turning back, he said, 'We'll have everything secured in a few minutes, Colonel.' Then he smiled, clearly glad to be back in the field. 'Malo was smoking one of these, so I thought I'd try one. God bless his miserable, crooked black heart.'

Soloman laughed. '*Semper fi*, sarge?'

Thumbs up. '*Semper fi*, Colonel,' he smiled, exiting.

Maggie smiled, amused. 'He obviously stole that cigar from Malo.' She laughed. 'What does *semper fi* mean?'

Soloman shook his head at Chatwell's antics, taking a sip of coffee before answering. '*Semper Fidelis*. Always faithful. It's a code of honor, the motto of the Corps. I'm Marine and Chatwell's Army, but everyone understands that it really means we take care of each other. We fight together until we win or die. And there can be even more to it than that.'

'Like?'

'Well,' Soloman took a deep breath, 'it's military, but it's more than military. It's … like, when you make a commitment to someone, you're there to the end, life or death. You never leave them alone, no matter what. If you've got food or ammo or cigarettes, you share it. What's yours is theirs. And as long as they're alive … you never leave their side … when they need you.'

He bent his head with the words, clearing his throat, and she saw that something about the statement troubled him. She let it go.

'I understand,' she said. 'It's in everything you do, Sol. In everything you say and don't say. And the rest have it, too, to a degree. They show it by how they fight. Like the way Malo was searching for you in the tunnel. He was absolutely frantic.'

Soloman cast her a glance.

'Yeah,' she nodded, taking a moment. 'I heard all of it. I was listening in on the chopper headset. Malo, as mean and uncaring as he seems to be, would have gone through Hell itself to find you, even though he knew what you were up against.'

'Malo's a brave man,' Soloman said, grimacing. 'He isn't half as cold as he acts. But it's his way of dealing with things.' He paused. 'Yeah, he'd stand behind me, no matter what.'

Smiling slightly, she was suddenly more beautiful. And as Soloman stared at her he began to warm to her. This woman, he knew, was unique. Perhaps she was the kind of woman a man would die for. He had only known one other like that.

Strange, he realized, how quickly friendships were forged in the heat of conflict when people had to find what was truly important to them. Wondering at it, he gazed again at his coffee. He wanted to say something meaningful but he'd built such a huge wall between himself and his feelings that he had no clue what to say. Yet inside, he knew, a part of that wall was crumbling.

They turned together as Malo stalked in the door. He moved with his MP-5 slung over his back, not even looking at them. 'We got heat sensors in a crossover pattern, Colonel,' he said absently as he reached his coat, searching the front right pocket. 'Got motion detectors set five feet off the ground to avoid trippin' 'em on bear, but I still got to –'

He frowned, abruptly removing all his cigars from the pocket, counting with severe displeasure. He counted them again as Soloman watched from the corner of his eyes. Then the big Delta commando turned to both of them. 'Who took one of my cigars?' he asked.

'Huh?' replied Soloman, raising his face.

Maggie shook her head, raising hands. 'I didn't see a thing, Malo. I was in the kitchen making a pot of coffee.'

Malo's black eyes narrowed in suspicion. He shook the black cigars. 'Uh-huh,' he nodded. 'Well, I'll find out who it was. 'Cause if they took it, they're gonna *smoke* it.' He stuffed the rest in the leg pocket of his BDUs. 'Let's see 'em take one out of here!'

Soloman was smiling openly as Malo stalked out of the house and Maggie joined him, her open laughter the most beautiful music Soloman had heard in a long, long time.

◆　◆　◆

Archette's black limousine delivered him to the isolated Long Island manor at midnight and a wordless servant, tall and gaunt, opened the oak doors to grant his expected entrance.

Head bowed, Archette stepped into the expansive foyer crowned by majestic high ceilings and a winding staircase that ascended to a walkway shrouded in darkness. Beyond him, surrounding chambers were also shadowed, as if to conceal things he was not meant to know.

He waited, not raising his eyes to search the rooms until a tall black man dressed in a long, flowing black robe approached. The man's head was hooded, his pale face barely visible. His waist was tied with a stout rope, and a polished, short sword with Hebrew inscriptions burned cryptically into the blade hung from his left side.

Muscular and intimidating, the man stood in silence, as if his unspoken command should be understood. And Archette moved quietly forward, resisting the impulse to wipe beads of sweat from his brow. In seconds he passed through the long corridors to finally arrive at a subterranean chamber that was almost void of decoration.

There was a large round table comprising thick oak planks, and seven chairs, now empty. Built with rough-hewn wood, the table was Celtic or Roman in design; it had the aura of great age.

A large fire roared in a hearth, and before it a single man stood in silence, resting an arm on the mantel. His face was turned away and his white hair flamed out in a crescent from his bald head, shaved in a dome, according to his custom. He wore a black shirt of loose-sleeved, fourteenth-century glamour. His loose black pants were crafted from leather that appeared soft and comfortable. He did not move.

Archette waited, and sensed rather than saw the cloaked servant moving silently into the shadows, though he knew the bodyguard would not venture far. For this was a place of power, and secrets, and was heavily guarded.

'Things have not gone according to our plans,' the man said finally, still unmoving. There was an impatient intonation to the words.

'No, they have not,' Archette replied, holding place. 'There were too many complications, I believe. And the outcome of the … the experiment … remains in doubt.

We are not sure yet, Lazarus, whether we have actually succeeded.'

'We have succeeded,' Lazarus spoke, convinced. 'That is not my concern. But … he … is out there, Professor. He is out there, and he is apparently confused. Or he would have already come to us.' A pause. 'Do you have any idea what price you will pay for failure?'

'I believe, yes, I believe … that I do.' Archette hesitated. 'But there … there are, indeed, great complications. Because we cannot find him. He is here, yes, among us. But … but where?'

'That is for you to discover.' Lazarus frowned. 'But tell me of Soloman. Does he again imperil us?'

'Soloman will be eliminated,' Archette answered. 'I must move carefully but, yes, Soloman will be eliminated. He will not endanger our plans as … as before. Perhaps it would have been wiser if we had killed him in the past, Lazarus. Instead of his family.'

The man known as Lazarus turned fully at the words and Archette once again beheld the commanding face, diamond-black eyes set deep in a saturnine countenance that seemed to know neither mercy nor weakness. His high cheekbones, sharp and intelligent, accented a face and jaw that were almost perfect in strength. His frown was terrifying.

'If we had killed Soloman, then he would only have been reborn, Archette,' he rasped. 'I am an Overlord. Do you think that I do not understand the power of martyrdom?'

'No, no, of course not,' Archette swayed. 'I only meant that –'

'I will not have Soloman reborn to exact vengeance upon either me or the Family,' he said, black eyes blazing. 'The death of Soloman's wife and child broke his mind, as it does with all the chattel. And that was sufficient. Because he no longer pursued those we recruited to serve us within The Circle. But to kill an enemy as powerful as Soloman ... can be a dangerous thing.' He turned again to the flames. 'Unless we had utterly destroyed his body, it would have made him even more powerful ... in his next life. Then one day, many years from now, he would have again threatened us.'

Archette stood in silence, hands clasped.

'No,' Lazarus continued, vaguely disturbed. 'We will only kill Soloman at the Master's words. For ... *he* is the God who would be, and cannot be threatened by flesh. Not even ... by Soloman.'

'Yes, of course. It will be as you say.'

'The Family is displeased, Professor,' he said with colder emotion. 'We have cultivated you. We have trained you. We have given you what you could never have gained for yourself. Then we asked for this, for you to bring the Master to us. And you failed. But you will fail no more. You *will* find him. And then you will assist him in whatever he requires. Or there will be no forgiveness. Or future.'

'I will not fail,' Archette whispered. 'I will not fail.'

'Do not.' Lazarus turned back again. 'Or you will hear serpents hissing in the halls of your house.'

Suppressing a trembling he had known only rarely in this place – trembling excited by the sacrifices and the dark blood running into water that washed it from the altar – Archette crept away, hoping no more words would be said. Then he heard the soft voice call after him.

He paused. 'Yes?'

The man was concentrated.

'If the Master comes, remember that you must not tremble.'

Archette suppressed his racing breath.

'I would never tremble.'

Lazarus laughed.

'We will see.'

◆　◆　◆

'Damn!' Ben shouted as he tore off a report from the JDIIS telefax, abruptly handing it to Soloman.

Sipping a cold cup, Soloman took the message and responded wearily, 'What the hell is this, Ben?'

'It's from the FBI!' Ben answered, swaying. 'They've got a wheelbarrow-load of dead bodies with the blood drained but this is something different! I think he finally made a mistake!'

Soloman quickly filtered out pertinent facts and he saw that a priest, Father Lanester, had been murdered in a cathedral. It was a particularly bloody killing that amazed even veteran homicide investigators. No autopsy had been ordered because virtually nothing remained of the body.

Soloman's eyes narrowed as he read the report, translating ancient words that had been written in the priest's blood. And he knew somehow that the killing was related. Not just because of the phenomenal strength required for such wholesale murder but because of the malevolent meaning contained in the words themselves.

He stood quickly, walking and speaking, 'Have the county homicide units color-fax photos of the crime scene, Ben. Do it now. I want to make sure they've got this stuff right. Then heat up the Loach and arrange for a car to meet me at LAX. I'm going to this cathedral.'

Clenching his teeth as he stood, Soloman felt something awaken violently, something that told him he might not be facing an indomitable foe. For if Cain had made a mistake, even a single mistake, then he could make two. And a second mistake could put him in a killing field.

He turned with new energy to Maggie, suddenly

remembering that they hadn't yet spoken about what Cain had said to Amy in the tunnel. The shock of combat had driven the thought from Soloman's head but it was back and wide awake now.

'Maggie,' he began, 'we haven't talked about what happened with Amy in the tunnel before I arrived. Did Cain say anything to her? Did she repeat anything that Cain said?'

'Amy said he was going to kill her,' she said quietly. 'She said that he talked about the moon and water. And maybe some planets. She couldn't remember which ones. Then she said that he mentioned something that sounded like ... verus, or verum ... or grim verum.' She paused. 'I don't know what it means, Sol, and I didn't question her too hard.'

Soloman was still as stone, searching his memory for anything that sounded like *grim verum*.

For a long moment he concentrated but nothing came. He shook his head; there was no way to know. But he had a suspicion about the planets, the moon, and the water. Studies he'd done on the Dark Ages made him suspect it was probably a spell and maybe even related to satanism, which led him deeper and deeper into a hypothesis that he hadn't spoken aloud to anyone. Nor would he, unless he was sure, because it was too fantastic.

'All right,' he said, staring into the composed green eyes. 'I appreciate everything you did. I know it wasn't easy.'

She nodded, smiling faintly. And something inside Soloman responded to it. Feelings, need rose within him with volcanic intensity. He hardened himself against them. This was not the time.

◆ ◆ ◆

The telefax began printing photographs of remarkable

clarity and Soloman studied them as they emerged. He'd braced himself to ignore the carnage, concentrating on clues, but even though he was long ago inured to the sight of blood and slain men, he was shocked at the mutilation. He read the words scrawled in the walls and sensed that this was, indeed, what they had needed: a chance to move ahead of the game. Yeah, now he had something to work with, a place to begin the hunt. He moved for the door.

'I'll be back by morning,' he said. 'Tell Malo to stay in condition red until I return.'

Ben was following. 'Why would Cain kill a priest, Sol?'

'I don't know,' Soloman responded, lifting the shotgun as he snapped the hammer back on the .45, placing it on safety. 'But Cain doesn't do anything without a reason. At least he hasn't yet. There was probably something he wanted at the cathedral and the priest got in the way.'

'But what would Cain want at a cathedral?'

'There's no way to know. That's why I'm going to church.' Soloman was at the door before turning back. 'Ben, don't let Cain get to Amy. That's everything right now. Don't let him get to the girl, no matter what. If he wants a fight, you make sure that you give more than you get.'

Ben licked his lips. 'Sol, look, Cain ain't even human. Fact is, I don't think anything can stop this guy.'

'Look, Ben,' Soloman said sternly, silhouetted alone against the darkness. 'I felt beaten before but now I think that Cain can make mistakes. And if he makes mistakes at all, then he might make a mistake that'll let us anticipate him and triangulate.'

'What are you gonna do?'

Soloman's eyes reflected the rage that was deep and haunting and permanent. As he walked away he said, 'I'm gonna see if a dead man can die.'

◆ ◆ ◆

Soloman reached the cathedral at midnight. He left the shotgun in the trunk of the black Cavalier that met him at the airport and moved to the wide wooden doors, which he found locked.

Bending, he picked the bolt in seconds – always one of his best skills – before moving silently inside to see only the altar lit by a ghostly white glow. Staring up, he saw a gigantic, crucified Christ commanding the cathedral, staring with deep shadowed eyes.

Soloman stared for a long moment at the cold bronze silhouette with its crown of blood-washed black thorns before he finally moved past it. He was haunted by the ancient pain and the current unearthly conflict, and it took all his control to shut down the surreal sensation that caused his hairs to stand on end, the skin to crawl along his back.

It was less difficult than he had anticipated to stalk silently through the wintry corridors. And despite the surety that Cain was no longer in the cathedral, he couldn't prevent himself from searching every shadow, every corner, moving with supreme tactical caution.

Within ten minutes, following the detailed description of the reports, he found the priest's room on the third floor. The door was closed with crime-scene tape. He reached out to turn the knob.

'There is no need,' a voice said behind him.

Soloman drew and whirled before he realized he'd dropped the safety of the .45. With clenched teeth he focused hard on the figure and his finger tightened on the trigger before he identified the threat as a nun.

A breath came from him slowly as he stared at the old nun hidden in the gloom of an alcove. Soloman didn't understand how he could have missed her but there she was, utterly motionless in a straight-backed chair, hidden in the shadows. Slowly he lowered the pistol to his side, staring until he saw more clearly the white and black habit.

'I'm sorry to disturb you, Sister.' His voice sounded rude and intrusive in the gloom of the hall. 'I'm Colonel James L. Soloman. I'm ... I'm looking for the man who committed this crime.'

'He is not here,' she responded cryptically. 'And we have washed away the blood that glorified him. So, Colonel, you will find nothing within the chamber of Father Lanester. He ... is gone.'

Soloman knew she wasn't speaking of the priest. He stepped toward her, concentrated, for some reason not holstering the .45.

'Do you know what this is about, Sister?' he asked.

'Yes.'

'Then ... ' He hesitated. 'You know what I'm looking for? Have you seen him?'

A pause.

'I have seen him in many forms, Colonel,' she whispered, moving rosary beads in pale, slender fingers. 'I have seen him in the eyes of the children he has left without a father or mother ... or love. I have seen his face mirrored in the blood his hate has shed, and in the lives he has stolen.' She paused. 'Yes, I have seen him, Colonel. I have seen him many times.'

Soloman didn't know how to respond in the heavy silence that followed. Then the nun, seemingly ancient in the gray half-light, rose and walked slowly forward, holding the rosary and crucifix in her hands as if she would never release them. Fearless, she stared up into his face a long time, old eyes narrow and penetrating, piercing. Soloman coldly returned the glare until she was finished, and seemed to nod.

'Yes,' she murmured. 'Now you, too ... have been joined in the battle.' Her face was certain, no surprise. 'There are others, Colonel, who are like you. Those who fight, and may yet destroy him.' Bending her head, she walked past him. 'Come, and I will take you.'

Staring, Soloman felt the cathedral's haunting atmosphere of age-old conflict, of evil and good, and things that should be feared. He hesitated, then, with a frown, gripped the pistol more tightly, and followed her into darkness.

◆ ◆ ◆

Introductions were almost wordless, done more by one man sensing the other than speaking. Soloman settled into a red leather chair in the office of the priest, Father Marcelle, who sat before the fireplace in a dark chamber. He regarded Soloman with unrevealing black eyes.

It had taken Soloman a few minutes to get accustomed to the priest's unconventional appearance. Looking more like a small gorilla than a priest, Marcelle sat beside an ashtray filled with unfiltered cigarette butts and ash, and even now calmly smoked another.

Soloman didn't want to reveal too much with his questions, but somehow knew he couldn't approach this man without alerting the obviously formidable intellect glinting in the obsidian eyes. Also he assumed that the priest, too, was somehow involved in this situation. He guessed that Marcelle was some kind of investigator, or troubleshooter, for the Pope. He was probably a man of extraordinary power, a man of unique power, who feared nothing at all.

Settled in with a glass of red wine beside him, Soloman turned to gaze at the venerable old nun who stood with infinite patience beside the door, perpetually ready to serve. Marcelle noticed the glance and spoke with a single nod.

'That will be all, Sister Mary Francis.' He focused on

Soloman with the next words. 'I'm sure the colonel and I will need no further assistance. You may retire.'

Sister Mary Francis nodded and turned, hovering for a heartbeat on the edge of darkness, until with ghostly silence and ghostly poise she was gone. Soloman watched her leave and hesitated, staring into the stone-gray gloom before turning back to Marcelle.

The priest's dark face was almost perfectly expressionless but Soloman detected a faint grimness in his eyes, in the reclining posture. It was as if Marcelle had both dreaded and somehow expected Soloman's presence. He took a long draw on the cigarette before speaking.

'Sister Mary Francis has been assigned to assist me in exploring the reasons for Father Lanester's murder, Colonel. She is quite a remarkable woman. Of the old school. You may find her somewhat discomforting, but I find her steadiness encouraging.' He paused. 'There are few of her kind remaining in this age of ... expendable faith. But then, I distract you; let us proceed. Please, tell me how I can be of assistance.'

Soloman's eyes narrowed, and he knew that the man knew far more than he could ever reveal. A man of highly developed intellect and responsibility, who bore a heavy mantle. As he measured the priest, something told him there was nothing to be gained by games.

'I won't insult your intelligence, Father. I think you know who I'm looking for. What can you tell me?'

Marcelle was silent as he took another long breath of smoke, which spiraled up lazily from his stout, square face. His response came slowly, as if he were carefully weighing each word. 'I can tell you some things, Colonel. And, not to your surprise, there will be things I cannot.'

'That's not much of an answer, Marcelle.' Soloman purposely dropped the 'Father,' hoping to communicate with the priest man to man.

Marcelle understood what this soldier was doing and thought that it had been far too long since anyone outside the Church had done so. Slowly he stubbed out the cigarette, took a sip of wine. He set the glass down carefully, running a finger gently over the lip. His tone revealed quiet amusement: 'Tell me, Colonel. How can you know that the man you seek is guilty of the murder of Father Lanester?'

'It's a suspicion. I've seen photos of the crime scene, and this man for whom killing isn't enough. He wants his horror show. Plus, he speaks, or in this case writes, in dead languages. It's one of his signatures.'

'And who is this man?'

'His name is Cain.'

Marcelle's finger froze on the edge of the glass, as if he'd been cut. He nodded after a moment. 'And now you want to discover what I know about Father Lanester so that you may track this man, Cain, and kill him?' He looked up with a world of experience hard-gained at the price of Jesuit pain. 'Is that not true, Colonel?'

Soloman detected no surprise and no judgment.

'Yes,' he answered.

Marcelle responded with a somewhat bitter smile. 'Killing Cain may be more difficult than you presume.'

'There's much here I don't know, but I do know there may be unexplainable forces at work.'

'Satanic forces, Colonel?' the priest asked without any hesitation at all, as if he'd been waiting for the time. 'Is that what you're alluding to?'

'That's … that's unlikely.' Soloman paused. 'I just meant that there were certain things happening that are hard to explain.'

Marcelle's quiet smile masked something else. 'Did you know,' he began simply enough, 'that satanism is no more illegal than Catholicism? Though the acts of satanists do tend to gravitate to the illegal. That's why the FBI has trained a handful of experts. I have consulted with them on several publications which explored the herd mentality of what is true satanism.'

Blinking, Soloman asked, 'And what is true satanism?'

'True satanism,' Marcelle said, 'is not the worship of lunar gods or pedestrian witchcraft or even Santeria, which is only a combination of Catholicism and Haitian paganism. True satanism is the singular worship of Lucifer, the supposed fallen angel, as the one true God of this universe. True satanism does not entail the worship of nature, or fortune-telling, or Tarot reading, or horoscopes. True satanism is a highly systematic act of worshipping Satan as singularly eminent to the Hebrew God, Yahweh. It is self-contained, and though there may be vagaries from cult to cult, which can itself be a misleading term, true satanism is very narrowly defined.'

Soloman stared in silence.

With a faintly amused expression, the priest bent his head. 'What do you fear to tell me, Colonel? Because in this … inferno … where we have been hurled, I fear that fear gives us no advantage. Believe me when I tell you that I have been here before, and it can be an apocalyptic ordeal.'

Soloman knew that the priest had just issued a warning, but he didn't understand what it was. He also realized that whatever he himself said about the experiment at White Sands could be construed as a breach of national security, landing him in prison. But his bones told him that the man had knowledge that he needed, and badly.

Making a deadly decision, Soloman told him of Cain's bizarre resurrection and escape, proceeding into the last days of the chase when Cain slaughtered the FBI agents, only to escape again. Yet he purposely omitted the phenomenon of the HyMar virus and the pending plague.

Never before had Soloman used actual truth to persuade cooperation; always it had been mixed with lies. But now, seated among the cathedral shadows, surrounded by secrets he could never imagine, he knew there was no other course. And at the end of it Marcelle sat in silence, staring with a slightly bent head into the fire. He spoke with a sense of melancholy, almost amused.

'What beasts men have made of men,' he commented. 'A dead man who lives ... and yet it is not a new thing.'

Soloman scowled. 'What do you mean?'

'It has been done before, Colonel.'

'When?'

'Many centuries ago.'

'This science wasn't available then, Marcelle. I don't think that you fully understand what I'm telling you. I'm saying that this man is scientifically enhanced to be, for all practical purposes, unkillable.' Soloman shook his head. 'What I'm trying to tell you is that this guy was dead and that now he's alive. And he is *not* human.'

A bitter laugh escaped Marcelle. 'None of them were, Colonel. No ... none of them.'

Something about the priest's enigmatic turn gave Soloman pause. He stared for a long time until Marcelle spoke again, as if reminiscing.

'Tell me, Colonel,' he began. 'What part of a man must die before he is truly dead? Does death come with the death of the body or the brain? Or does death come with the destruction of something more than the brain?' His expression was wistful. 'Descartes taught that all things not man were automata which obey sensory and mechanical laws that regulate Nature. But in man the automata were infused with psycho-physical parallelism, a symbiosis that could only be severed by the death of the soul. And this, my friend, was the birth of modern psychology. A revelation that Descartes and Locke first posited on the dualism of man.'

Soloman said nothing. His eyes narrowed.

'Hebrew legend holds that the ancients knew the secrets of human resurrection because they understood the dualism of man far better than we,' Marcelle continued. 'And I have, perhaps, seen evidence of it. So, although your people may have done it without that occult knowledge, it is not a new thing. What has been done … has been done before.'

Silence darkened the room.

'Did you know, Colonel,' he continued, 'that Augustine designated the will as the force that moves both intellect and inner sense to action, the will itself ethically and psychologically free?' The priest laughed. *'Homo corpore utitur.'*

'Man making use of a body,' Soloman said.

Marcelle raised his eyes, genuinely impressed. 'You understand Latin?'

'Latin. German. French. A few more. Why don't you just say what you mean to say?'

Leaning back, the priest continued. 'Man acts upon a body, but is not acted upon by it. That is what I mean to say. These elemental forces are not easily understood or controlled. Like imagination and memory, understanding and intellect, all of them dominated by a force that is classified so vaguely as "will." Surely an inadequate term for whatever, in the end, defines the true essence, or soul, of man.'

Soloman pursed his lips, concentrating. 'I've thought a little about that, Marcelle. And you might be onto something. But right now I need to know what you know. I need some answers.'

Unfazed, the priest withdrew another cigarette,

speaking without hesitation. 'Proceed with your questions, Colonel. I will withhold virtually nothing. Measure for measure, just as you have done.'

Concentrating, Soloman's mind kept returning to the words Maggie had spoken after exiting Amy's room. He didn't understand them but knew they were somehow important. 'Tell me, have you ever heard the term *'grim verum'*?'

Frozen in waving shadow, Marcelle took a long time to reply. 'Yes, Colonel, I believe that I know the term. Is that what Cain said to the child before your confrontation in the tunnel?'

'Yes.'

'So ... yes.' Marcelle stared away, expelling a breath toward the hearth. 'Yes ... what Cain spoke of was very likely the *Grimorium Verum*. It is a book, a centuries-old book, and a cursed work. It was never reprinted for the masses because the fear of what it contained was too great, even to those who did not believe. The only surviving copies are in Hebrew and Latin, and sealed in three places.'

'What places?'

'One copy is sealed in the Los Angeles Museum of Natural History,' Marcelle answered, eyes narrowing with what appeared to be a sudden suspicion. 'Another is sealed in New York's Museum of Natural History, and the last is secured in Rome, in the Secret Archives of the Vatican. They are very ancient and fragile, and not available for reading.'

'Why would Cain want it?'

The priest shook his head. 'Who can be certain, Colonel? All that is known is that the *Grimorium Verum* is the ultimate encyclopedia of Black Magic. According to accumulated legend and superstition, and what I know personally, men can supposedly use it to access powers as mysterious to modern man as electricity was to ancient Romans.'

'That doesn't answer my question,' Soloman said. 'Why, exactly, would Cain risk exposure to actually *possess* this book? Can't he obtain whatever information it contains from another source?'

'No, Colonel. The spells contained within the *Grimorium Verum* are vastly complicated and intricate, and unknown. Some of the incantations require ancient names and spectacular combinations of elements.' He gestured vaguely. 'Some must be performed in specific locations with fresh water or salt water, or different types of blood dried for an exact number of days on a sword or knife that is polished at an ordained hour of a certain day. Some require detailed diagrams or pentacles and signs, or elements even more complicated. And everything must be done in exacting sequence. If one does not go step by step with each conjuration, then the spell, according to legend, is useless. And as I said, there is no other source but these three copies. So, I surmise, this is why Cain would risk much to possess one of them. In his mind, it can provide the meticulous incantation he wishes to evoke. At least, that seems a logical deduction.'

Soloman nodded slowly to indicate his agreement. 'Have you ever read this book? Do you know what Cain might want it for?'

'I have examined it upon occasion,' the priest replied quietly; he obviously didn't want to remember the experience. 'But it is a vast work. There are any number of things Cain may desire. Right now we don't have enough information to even couch the question.'

Studious, Soloman turned it in his mind, thinking half-aloud. 'So … Cain apparently needs this book to ensure that he correctly evokes some sort of spell, or the spell is useless …'

'It would seem so,' the priest said, expelling a long stream of smoke, 'but no living man can say with absolute certainty whether there is any truth to it. All we can say is that Cain apparently believes that it contains something he seeks. That is why he so mindlessly mentioned it in front of the child; a mistake born from obsession. Though ... I *can* say that whatever the purpose, it will probably involve a sacrifice of human blood.'

Soloman started. 'Why do you say that?'

'Because virtually every page of the manuscript contains such an incantation.' Marcelle bowed his head with the reply. 'There is human sacrifice for the gain of wealth, for knowledge, for the death of an enemy. And it was for that reason, more than any other, that the book was archived by Pope Innocent III. You can certainly understand that there are deranged persons who would have taken it and committed atrocities that have been easily avoided by its suppression.'

Soloman sensed his heartbeat quicken. It was the first moment of encouragement that he'd felt in the hard battle to bring Cain to the ground. And in the moment he considered the priest as a colleague, compelling him to ask, 'Who are you, Marcelle? I mean ... really.'

Marcelle's faint smile faded to nothing, then a frown, and he leaned back more deeply in the opulent chair. Smoke from the cigarette floated up to cast a thin white veil between them.

'You're an exorcist,' Soloman said.

There was another long cloud of smoke released. 'I am a priest, Colonel,' Marcelle answered calmly. 'And I serve the Church in many capacities that I am not at liberty to discuss, even though I should feel inclined. I hope that is sufficient. But, to add, I will say that there are probably few who understand Cain as well as I.'

'And what do you understand?'

'I understand that, because of what your people have done, Cain may be the purest of his kind.' He concentrated his tone. 'He is undead, and yet unliving. And although I have dealt with occult phenomena, I have never confronted anything like this. Regrettably, we are both cast into a strange and unknown arena. And, to be honest, I do not know if my faith or skills will avail us anything at all. In fact, I doubt it.'

'Still, maybe we can help each other,' Soloman said. 'You seem to have insight that I could use.'

'Perhaps,' Marcelle paused. 'But I am not under military command, Colonel. My jurisdiction is delivered by the strong right hand ... of a superior realm.'

Soloman nodded with respect. 'As it should be, Marcelle. But that doesn't change the fact that you do have insight into Cain. You might even be able to understand him better than me because you understand the occult better than I do. And if you can stay current on information.'

Marcelle took a long drag on the cigarette, eventually turned his shadowed face to the flames. His brow hardened in concentration. 'I can say, Colonel, that it would be an unusual alliance.'

'It would be a *useful* alliance, Marcelle. Because I have access to everything that can track Cain. And you have the psychological insight that I need to predict his moves. Together, we might stand a chance of hunting him down before ... '

Marcelle gazed back. 'Before, Colonel?'

Without moving at all, Soloman said, 'You'll have to trust me. Right now I want your best guess on Cain's next move.'

A concentration as impregnable as a fortress solidified the priest's face. His black eyes gleamed, reflecting shadow and flame together, and his frown became deeper, the cigarette burning forgotten in his fingers. 'Cain has lost the child,' he said finally, 'so he will attempt to claim a copy of the *Grimorium Verum*. Then he would logically attempt to obtain knowledge of the child's whereabouts, and come for her once more.'

'Why will he immediately attempt to obtain this book?'

'Because he fears time.'

'How do you know that?'

'Because of things I have not yet told you.' Marcelle's confidence was contagious. 'But have no doubt, Soloman, Cain indeed fears time. And so he will come for the book. Perhaps even tonight.'

With an angry aspect Soloman glanced at his watch; six hours remained until daylight. He hesitated a single breath before he rose, staring down at the priest.

'Let's go to the museum,' he said.

CHAPTER II

A night of shadow surrounded Soloman as far as he could see or sense. It was an azure haze of streetlight that cast a dead-air atmosphere over the Los Angeles Museum of Natural History. And the building was Soloman's focus; one of the three surviving copies of the *Grimorium Verum* was secured inside the steel doors.

Leaning against a wall on the opposite side of the rear parking lot, Marcelle at his side, Soloman surveyed the back of the monolith, lamenting the fact that they were so far away. There was probably three hundred feet between them and the building, but Soloman's night vision was adequate for the task; he could see clearly enough.

Traffic had thinned on surrounding side streets but heat hovered, carried through the night to smother them in fumes. And Soloman remembered that he had always hated this city with the traffic and traffic and traffic, the noise and pollution and five seasons of Hell. Even Death Valley or White Sands was better than this. Then he shook his head at the thought, amazed that it occurred to him in this perilous situation. He concentrated again on the building.

Cain would attempt to make entry as covertly as possible, taking all precautions against another confrontation. And not because he couldn't easily kill whoever came against him; it was because he didn't want the complications of another escape.

Soloman grimaced, remembering how he'd only narrowly defeated the monstrosity in the tunnel. And at the thought he lifted the heavy shotgun beneath Marcelle's frowning gaze, sliding back the ejection shield to ensure that a round was chambered; it was. He was glad that he'd exchanged the .00 rounds with Malo for exploding .12 gauge three-inch slugs.

Filled with mercury and a small measure of C-4, the magnum rounds impacted with the force of a small grenade. Capable of blowing a wooden door in half, they were only issued to elite counterterrorist teams like Force Recon or Seal Team One. Soloman was mercilessly determined to see how Cain could survive one of them.

Glancing at his watch, he saw that only four hours remained until daylight, and shook his head with fatigue. Then he cast a glance to see Marcelle so stoic, so infinitely patient as he calmly smoked another cigarette, and felt a measure of respect at the composure. Truly, the priest was an exceptional man. He had not even shown fear when, an hour ago, a trio of street thugs wearing red bandannas stalked down a nearby alley. Immediately threatening, they had retreated quickly when Soloman casually raised the SPAS from behind his back, saying in a deathly cold voice, 'I'm busy. Maybe later.'

They never came back.

Since then, he and Marcelle had been quiet together, each understanding and respecting the other's discipline and patience. But the combined silence also seemed to reinforce to both of them that the darkness was lending cold reality to their fears.

Slowly, night became deeper, morning stars sliding slowly across the sky. And Soloman still didn't move, hoping to find the hated silhouette of Cain against a wall. But there was nothing.

Eventually the night lessened, a distant dawn hazing the horizon beyond the glaring streetlights. Yet Soloman continued to see nothing but shadows, as day crept closer. And despite his previous convictions he began to doubt, wondering if … maybe they were wrong …

Movement.

A faint shadowing of dark within dark. It was all there was, but it was what Soloman had been awaiting. He locked on it instantly as he heard Marcelle's composed whisper, 'There.'

'I see it,' Soloman said, and suddenly felt the kind of respect for the priest that comes only when one man has finally measured the other in the field. With one word Marcelle had suddenly come to a new level of regard, as far as Soloman was concerned.

Soloman focused keenly on the darkness and then, again, saw the shadowy outline; a gigantic human form highlighted by streetlight against a slate-gray wall. It was there in the distant sound of rending steel for the briefest moment and then not even Soloman's superior night vision could find it again. It was gone as cleanly as the wind; nothing at all.

Marcelle didn't move.

Soloman shifted, reaching back to grasp the shotgun. And, very slowly, brought the weapon in front, holding it close as he stared without breath into the blackness.

No, nothing.

Marcelle stood away from the wall, squinting, and Soloman could tell from the priest's frustrated face that he also saw nothing. The priest scowled, staring, but he was obviously confused, as if he had seen an apparition appear and disappear in the same breath. After a moment he shook his head. 'I see nothing, Colonel.'

Frowning in gathering anger, Soloman withdrew a

cellular phone and dialed Malo, giving terse instructions to descend on the parking lot. Then he turned to Marcelle. 'Stay here,' he said. 'I'm going in.'

Marcelle gripped his arm. 'Perhaps we should wait for more men, Soloman.' He spoke with concern. 'We know he is inside the building and, in this situation, time is to our advantage.'

Soloman pulled away. 'This is personal, Marcelle,' he rasped. 'That thing has killed a lot of good men and tried to kill a little girl that I happen to care for. I'm not going to give it another chance to escape.'

Marcelle stared as Soloman ran in a loping combat crouch, closing on the building. He crossed the empty parking lot as covertly as possible, using separated shrubbery and largely decorative trees, and then he was at the door Cain had compromised.

Looking down at the portal, Soloman saw that the stainless-steel knob had been sheared away like wet paper. Ragged threads were all that was visible where the lock had been, and Soloman knew from the absence of an alarm that it had been disabled.

Bending, he went through the exit and melted instantly into the dark. Sliding against a wall he listened, hushing his breathing as he searched the faint gray light of the museum, but he detected nothing.

Soloman's racing heart and almost silent breath sounded terrifyingly loud to him in the gloom, but he knew that was a fear-generated illusion, for not even Cain could hear his pounding heart.

Soloman held the SPAS close as he moved carefully down the hallway, knowing the giant would be involved in searching for the book. But Soloman had no idea where it was either, so he was forced into a random search-and-destroy.

When he found Cain he knew it would hit like lightning and escalate into a raging battle that would likely leave this building on fire. But Soloman knew he was ready for it; he had the grenades and the .45 and was wearing a vest with a steel shockplate reinforcing his chest.

He was heavily armored enough to last for a few moments before either he or Cain went down. And even if he did go down, he was hatefully determined to injure Cain badly enough to slow him down. Something was driving Soloman that he didn't understand and didn't try to understand, sensing only that it was something deep and quick and becoming more and more alive ...

Silently he crept through the museum, turning his head minutely to detect movement or sound, but there was only silence. Cain, wherever he was, was working quiet as a ghost in the gloom to find the –

Blood.

A rivulet of red moved slowly over the marble floor.

Soloman turned his head to glimpse a gray uniform extending beyond a corner; the legs of a doomed security guard who had obviously happened upon Cain when he entered the building. But Soloman didn't take time to examine the body; it didn't matter how the man died. He was simply dead, another life taken by this thing that should have never seen the world.

Death after death after death; it was all there was.

He stalked forward, using solid cover. He searched the wide square balcony above lit with faint light but he saw nothing, heard nothing, detected nothing, was becoming increasingly frustrated. He knew that he had to hit Cain while he was preoccupied with the theft. He had to hit him from behind and continue to hit until he fell. Then he would hurl one of the antipersonnel grenades secured on his belt, which he hoped would separate Cain's head from his shoulders.

Sweating furiously, swiping perspiration from his face with a free hand, Soloman walked along a rear wall, his combat boots making no sound on the marble floor. He was tempted to leave the shadows and then it occurred to him that not even Cain could have *perfect* night vision, especially if he were standing in light, because his eyes would be apertured to the greater light instead of the lesser. And it was something that not even Cain could undo because it was an optic reflex no more changeable than unconscious breath. The more light, the more effective the shadows.

Soloman had taken a dozen more steps when he suddenly halted, not knowing why. It had seldom happened without any visible or audible warning, but over the years he had come to trust it. Something dangerous was close beside him, he realized. Something unseen, and silent.

The last time the instinct had struck had been in Beirut when Soloman was tracking down a senior member of the jihad. Not even knowing why, Soloman had halted in an alley and dropped fast to the ground as an AK-47 opened up from a darkened window less than ten feet away.

He had never been able to determine what made him stop and fall to the ground a split-second before the bullets passed over his head; he had simply done it. Nor did he know why he stopped now, it simply happened. Alarmed, he turned his head minutely to detect anything as –

Cain.

Emerged from the darkness.

In a rumble of haunting thunder Cain stepped from the deepest shadow, less than ten feet away. Galactic and gigantic and ultimately menacing, the beast took a single slow stride into the light. His smile was malevolent, mocking. His red gaze fixed on Soloman with baleful intensity.

He was dressed utterly in black, his head already covered with thick dark hair that descended to his massive shoulders, sweeping back from the broad, fearless forehead. And he had acquired a long cloak that made him seem even more mammoth. His long fingers tapered to wicked black talons.

A bright-white flood of horror and adrenaline had rushed from the center of Soloman, and he couldn't catch his breath as he backed up, matching Cain slow step for slow step. He knew his heart had somehow skipped a beat, and he had to glance down to ensure that the SPAS was centered on the giant's chest.

Soloman retreated another stride and didn't know why he hadn't fired the shotgun. It was as if they were both awaiting some unknown signal to initiate the oncoming battle. Then Soloman realized the entire confrontation was shockingly wild and uncanny, a spellbinding battle to the death that had begun without a single blow being thrown.

With a warlike glance Cain regarded the SPAS as nothing, his dark face distorted by a contemptuous frown. Then he stopped in place, poised as powerful as death. And Soloman saw an ancient manuscript clutched in his right hand: the *Grimorium Verum*. The book was bound with a thick wooden latch, the spine comprising a row of wide leather straps.

Soloman realized with spiraling horror that Cain had probably seen them watching outside, had known what they were planning to do. That's why he'd made himself visible; he'd wanted Soloman to follow him into the museum, playing them perfectly.

With a slight tilt of his head Cain regarded Soloman and his weapons as if, together, they posed no more threat than a child. Then he spoke in the volcanic voice Soloman had heard on the tape, a voice that gods would envy. It was human thunder rumbling with power never used and never needed, fearing nothing. On the tape it had been enraged and lordly and imperious. Now it was cold and contemptuous.

'So,' Cain said with an indulgent smile, '... you are

my great adversary. The one who wounded me.' He laughed. 'That was a blow well dealt ... *butcher*. You enjoy the blood as much as I.'

Frowning, Soloman moved to the side, knowing Cain's superhuman speed could close the gap between them in the blink of an eye, also knowing that with his first shot an all-out war to the death would erupt. He froze his finger tightly around the trigger of the shotgun.

He didn't want to engage Cain in battle like this because if the first shot didn't kill then Cain would be all over him raging and rending, finishing him in seconds.

An amused smile crept over the fiendish face as Soloman shifted, sweating and glaring and watching with hair-trigger alertness. 'You came for the child,' he rumbled. 'Yes, you came for *her*.'

Playing for time so that Malo and the Delta commandos could close on the museum with the two choppers, Soloman frowned. He tried to keep the fear out of his voice as he said, 'Yeah ... and for you.'

Cain smiled, lifting heavy hands to the side.

'I am here.'

Soloman shifted, his hand tightening on the trigger of the SPAS until no slack at all remained in the trigger; a half-ounce more pressure and the weapon would discharge. Then Cain bent, laying the manuscript on a small mahogany table. He murmured something in Latin, something that held a deathly intonation. And as the taloned fingers lifted, it happened.

That fast.

Cain was nearly motionless and in the next second was roaring forward in a wave and Soloman fired blind as a fist smashed into his chest. He bellowed as he flew back, the shotgun somehow torn from his hands, then hit the floor hard and rolled back and up, drawing the .45 to fire instantly. He saw Cain coming over him and a half-dozen rounds thundered bright into the air, a boom-blinding strobe in the room.

Cain took the rounds to the chest and arm as he closed and then he struck the pistol aside and hit Soloman again, blasting him back. Brutally stunned, Soloman was thrown hard from a wall and hurled a wild blow that Cain deflected with contempt, returning his own.

Cast into another world by the murderous impacts of the blows, Soloman bent and staggered. It was like getting hit by a cannon, and in a breathless red haze he struggled for air and life, knowing somehow that the steel shockplate was dented, and something else didn't feel right in his chest and leg but he had no time to contemplate it.

In the next breath Cain threw him aside and Soloman crashed into a marble statue that he grabbed wildly from the pedestal, shattering both of them. Struggling violently to reorient himself, Soloman rolled over white shards, groaning.

No time for this!
Get up, damn it!
Get up!

Staggering numbly to his feet, he whirled as Cain closed again like a panther playing with a dog and he knew the monstrosity was going to kill him slowly, just as he realized that any of the blows would have already killed if Cain had used even slightly more force.

Cain laughed as Soloman rose shocked and breathless and drenched in wild sweat, searching desperately for anything that could give him a faint fighting chance. He moaned in pain as he clutched his chest, dimly realizing that the ballistic vest had been shredded.

He knew that in normal combat the sheer concussion of the blows would have rendered him unconscious, but a fantastic survival base was in command now, a part of his mind that compelled him to survive on instinct and training because courage had fled.

No, he told himself, *I won't fall.*

Stumbling, he cursed savagely as he tripped backwards over a small golden couch. And Cain roared in laughter, horrific bestial fangs violently exploding from his jaws like prehistoric tusks. The hellish mirth made his face fiendish, fangs hurling back the light with an ultimate killing wrath.

Shocked at the sight, Soloman rose again and angled to the side, gasping. Then in a rumbling storm Cain came closer and he found the strength to focus, recovering. Committed to taking Cain with him, he reached up to curl a finger tightly through the pin of a grenade strapped to his chest.

Eyes narrowing suddenly, Cain halted in place. He glanced at the grenade clutched in Soloman's trembling hand and a smile came to him slowly. 'Ah ... a sacrificial move,' he growled, clearly amused. 'How frightening. Should I ... flee from you?'

Soloman frowned.

'I'm the last, Cain. Not even you will survive this.'

Cain laughed, taking his time. His bloodthirsty joy was unforced and unconcealed. 'You pleasure me,' he smiled. 'Before I take your life, I want to know your name. You are ... worth remembering.'

Soloman tightened his finger even more in the ring. 'It's Soloman. You've got three seconds ... to remember it.'

With ghastly mirth Cain laughed again, throwing back his head. Soloman was confused for a moment and then *knew* what the giant was planning to do, and he pulled the grenade pin with the thought, hurling himself aside before –

It was too quick.

In a black roar Cain's forearm caught him viciously across the neck, clotheslining him. Then a taloned hand lashed out like lightning to tear the grenade from his vest and Cain whirled in the same heartbeat, hurling the grenade away across the room where it detonated in a deafening explosion that brought down marble and ceiling and plaster, sending a superheated shockwave to the cavernous walls.

Lost in rage, Soloman shouted in pain as he staggered up, fumbling frantically for another grenade and then Cain was *there*, a human lion roaring with the strength of twenty men. Soloman never even saw the arm that lashed out to somersault him and then he was being raised to his feet again, lifted cleanly from the floor. The remaining three grenades were instantly torn from his vest and hurled to the side.

Red eyes …

Snarling fangs …

Cain growled before him.

Cain's scarlet glare was narrow with wrath, unconquerable, and Soloman knew it was over. There was nothing left to do. He frowned at the breath that flowed from the fangs, breath hot with the stench of a world of blood and death and the grave.

'Yes,' Cain whispered as Soloman's head rolled in half-consciousness, 'you were, indeed, a worthy opponent. But, no, not my last victim.' He leaned forward as the fangs touched the skin of Soloman's neck to –

'*Adjuro vos. Fugite, partes adversae!*'

Soloman never knew where he landed at the words but even in his shock he recognized the voice, and knew Cain had hurled him aside to confront the Exorcist. In seconds he rolled to a knee to see Marcelle standing alone in the middle of the room.

The priest stood grim and enraged in defiance. He held a large silver crucifix extended in a single hand and then Soloman stumbled weakly to the side, fumbling, finally finding a single grenade. He clipped it reflexively to his waist and staggered up as Cain walked slowly toward the priest, his head tilted as if he could not believe the futile challenge.

His face distorted with horrible courage, Marcelle slashed the crucifix in the air as he thundered, *'Begone ye hostile powers!* Depart thou infernal creation! And do not think to despise the words of this sinner who dost serve the Lord of Hosts who *Himself* hurled ye headlong from the heights to thine infernal reckoning!'

Another cross was cut with violent wrath. 'Yield to God!' the Jesuit shouted. 'Yield to the Lord of Hosts before whose countenance thou dost eternally tremble! *Discedite ergo nunc!* Begone! Begone I say! *Ecce Crux Domini, fugite, partes adversae! Vincit leo de tribu Juda, radix David!'*

Cain halted in place for a frozen moment, as if he expected something to happen at the words. Then with a smile that reflected the purest bloodthirst he laughed.

Moving forward.

Without any indication of fear Marcelle boldly stepped into the confrontation, slashing a terrific image of the cross in the face of the beast. 'Begone thou seducer!' he raged. 'In the name of Jesus of Nazareth who *Himself* hurled thee down to the dwelling of the Serpent, I cast thee *out!* Begone I say! Begone! The blood of Christ compels thee! The blood of Christ compels thee! The blood of Christ compels thee!'

With a growl that came from an intensifying black animal center, Cain snatched the priest by the vestment and pulled him close to the monstrous fangs. And Marcelle's hand instantly gripped the giant's wrist as they strained. Then the priest's teeth clenched in the fiendish test of strength and a breath exploded from him. Cain's horrific face split in a jagged smile and Marcelle gasped, overwhelmed.

As Soloman lifted the shotgun from the floor.

'Cain!'

Spitefully, Cain spun his head.

Soloman centered the shotgun on the copy of the *Grimorium Verum*, still lying on the small table. 'Let him go!' he gasped. 'Let him go now or I'll destroy the book!'

Cain snarled, frowning.

Taking a single step forward, Soloman raised the shotgun to his shoulder to lock a solid aim. 'Let him go *now*, Cain! This'll vaporize that thing! You've got two seconds!'

Cain let Marcelle fall to the ground and for a moment seemed to grow even larger and more terrifying in his wrath. With a narrow glance he measured the distance, determining whether he could leap between Soloman and the book before Soloman made the shot.

'You'll never make it,' Soloman whispered, concentrated. Not even Cain was that fast, and they both realized it. If the giant moved at all, if he even flinched, Soloman could make the shot.

Frustration blazed on Cain's vicious countenance as Marcelle gained solid footing at last. And the priest still held the crucifix in his hand, as if he could never release it. Nor did he appear shocked at the savage encounter. In seconds he once more held his grim countenance, casting a grateful nod to Soloman.

Smoke and spiraling flames rose along the museum walls to cast the cavernous chamber in an infernal light, a gathering roar.

Cain shook his head, smoldering. The hair along his head rose like the hackles of a wolf and his entire essence seemed electrified with fiendish rage. Then, slowly, a shadow of defeat fell across the dark countenance. His growl thundered beneath the room, despising all strength but his own.

'Fools!' he snarled, glaring wrathfully at Soloman. 'You dare to challenge *me?*' He frowned with contempt. 'You are *nothing!* Flesh and blood and bone! Don't you know me yet, Soloman? Don't you know who you've challenged? I ruled this world before you were even born!' He shook his head. 'It was mine! All mine! And taken from me only because I dared to raise my throne against the Most High! You think you can defeat one who warred with *God?* You think you can defeat one who struck down great Michael to the Earth? *Do you?*' His eyes blazed. '*You* with your meaningless weapons! Can you name the nations I've destroyed? No! You know nothing! And that is your doom! You challenge one who made the continents tremble! One who reduced the proudest empires of this world to ruin! You think you have won but you have won nothing! I shall take my revenge on you and it shall be sweet! You think to defend the girl? Bah! She is already mine! I will take her and all you love and before you die you yourself will belong to *me!*' He cast a glance at the manuscript, raised an embered glare. 'You will know death a thousand times, Soloman. You and all you love. For there is nothing that can defeat me! You wish to know me? Then know *this!* I am the beast that feasts on your children in the night! Yes! Your children! Know all you have ever loved and lost and you will know *me!* Then know your own death! For it is all *mine!*'

Cain took a stride.

Soloman's voice trembled and he centered the shotgun, speaking low, 'Take one more step, Cain, and I'll blast that manuscript into dust. This is the last time I'll warn you.'

'Destroy it!' Fangs grated as the monstrous form continued to advance. 'Play your meaningless role in this act! For in time I will remember all it contains because I am its author! Then it will mean nothing! Yes! Its author! I am the one who opened the gateway! The one who crossed that hateful void to *conquer this world!*'

Soloman tried to steel his nerves again but he was shaken to his bones by the otherworldly rage and tone.

Then Marcelle stepped forward to cut the cross, shouting, *'Dicas mihi nomen tuum –'*

Cain whirled, livid.

'I will tell you *nothing*, priest!' he bellowed. 'Not in this lifeless flesh!' He pointed at Soloman. *'They* have done this, priest! Not me! *They* resurrected this flesh to live in death as Aaron's staff! It was *man* who violated nature! Yes! Man! Not me! So there is no soul within this body to save!' He started toward the priest. 'This flesh is rightfully mine! All mine! And your rituals can go with you to the grave!'

Marcelle thundered with biblical wrath, 'You cannot prevail, beast! Is *this* the one who made the nations tremble? *Tell me!* Oh, how fallen! How changed! How horrible that such glory is brought to such ruin!'

At the defiant challenge Cain's fangs extended sharply, eyes burning in narrow embers. Then, the jaws unhinged even further and he took a maddened step, moving toward the priest. His snarl was inhabited storm.

'You will be *defeated!*' Marcelle shouted, his face white with the stress of the conflict. He pointed violently with the crucifix. 'Man may have opened this gateway but God shall close it!'

Cain roared like a lion as he leaped and Soloman spun to fire from the hip, the slug hitting dead-center, hurling the goliath back wildly. The impact was powerful and ravaging enough to slam Cain against a marble column but he came off it like a hound of hell, lifting razored talons, and Soloman realized it wasn't enough, *that nothing would be enough!*

The giant hit the floor in a red blaze and Soloman fired as fast as he could pull the trigger until Cain twisted behind another column, evading the horrific onslaught. Then from somewhere behind him Soloman heard a heated command and whirled to see Malo and the Delta commandos running forward.

And Cain charged.

Closing with the sinuous speed of a panther he was among them, whirling and striking as Soloman twisted down and away with a fist thundering over his head. It was a frantic fight with bullets hitting commando and foe, and Cain howled with pain as he laid hands on a rifle, instantly turning to fire. Soloman leaped forward as he killed the first man.

'Cain!' he bellowed, leaping.

Ablaze with fury Cain whirled into the challenge as Soloman fired dead-on, the explosive slugs impacting into the massive chest. A violent eruption of red lava showered all of them at the blast and as Soloman hit the ground he screamed, firing again and again and again to finally send Cain to the ground.

As the giant crashed thunderously to his back Soloman dove cleanly over him to hit the marble floor hard, rolling to his feet with the shotgun high, jacking a round.

'Kill him!' he roared.

All of them opened up and the museum thundered in automatic rifle fire. But as Soloman managed an emergency reload he saw Cain erupt once more to his feet, taking the horrendous damage only to tear out a throat, a heart, and then shatter a neck like a rotten branch before charging full-force, taking a soldier down in a tumbling heap.

Hurling the unconscious commando over a shoulder like a child, he bellowed a curse and surged toward a plate-glass window. Only at the last second did he lash out to snatch the *Grimorium Verum* from the table as Malo frantically raised a fist. 'Cease fire! Cease fire!' he screamed over the deafening din of battle and flame. 'Cease fire or we'll hit our own man!'

With the force of a freight train Cain smashed through the window, landing far on the sidewalk to stagger into the street where he turned, the soldier held effortlessly. Pausing in darkness and blood he glared with hellish wrath at Soloman.

'In *time*, Soloman!' he raged.

Soloman charged. *'Let's do it now, Cain!'*

With a curse, Cain ran.

Was lost.

'Three by three in sectors!' Malo shouted, hurling the MP-5 aside to haul his shotgun from his back. 'Bravo one! Charlie two! Delta three! Echo four! Initiate! Initiate! Initiate!'

Everyone leaped together to disintegrate what remained of the glass in a shower of shards, fearlessly pursuing Cain into the night as Malo bellowed over and over: *'Kill him, kill him, kill him!'*

Soloman hit the street in a rush, mind moving like lightning. Even as he landed, he slammed more rounds into the SPAS and visualized an overview of the surrounding alleys and roads, trying to anticipate where Cain would go. Decision made instantly, he whirled at Malo.

'There's no way out of here!' he shouted. 'Cain's got to steal transportation!'

Malo lifted the radio, and Soloman heard the sounds of police and military choppers closing on the building. 'Cain's last known direction of travel was northeast!' the lieutenant shouted. 'I repeat! Cain's last direction of travel was northeast! Triangulate on him! Triangulate! If he doesn't have our man with him I'm authorizing cannons! I repeat! I'm authorizing cannons!'

Soloman was already running, passing several Delta commandos as he heard the chopper pilot on the radio. 'I've got visual acquisition of the target! He's moving north! He's going for Drake and Cloverdale!'

Soloman cursed.

No way to make it!

He knew it in a heartbeat.

Because in the last few seconds Cain had covered

almost a quarter mile and Soloman couldn't match the giant's speed. But he also knew that Cain was badly wounded and had to be tiring, and fast, so he would have to find a vehicle. It was his only chance for escape.

Soloman remembered that Drake and Cloverdale was an overpass, and he slammed another round hard into the SPAS, running instantly toward the tunnel that connected the streets to the interstate. It was a battle decision and it could have been dead-wrong but Soloman knew from experience that that was all there was in true war, instant decisions that won the battle or lost it.

He ran in an all-out sprint and then heard the chopper pilot on the radio: 'Cain has stolen a dark blue four-door at Drake and Cloverdale! He's dropped the prisoner and he's moving for the tunnel! I repeat! Cain dropped our man! He's moving for the tunnel!'

Focusing on the radio traffic Soloman heard Malo shouting, 'Take the shot! Take the shot! Take the shot!'

'Negative, sir!' the pilot screamed back. 'I'll hit civilian vehicles!'

Using a field and then a dry drainage ditch to cover the distance with surprising speed, Soloman reached the overpass as the chopper came up the roadway in a white haze, the spotlight highlighting a dark blue four-door that weaved frantically in and out of traffic. Threading a reckless path, the vehicle closed on the tunnel and Soloman knew there was no way to fire without hitting surrounding cars.

He quickly unslung the shotgun and whirled, focusing for a wild split-second on a bus slowed by traffic. There was an instant spent on careful aim and he shot out tires on the left side, the exploding shells demolishing rim and rubber together as the bus driver desperately tried to pull away.

It stalled in the intersection, backpiling traffic.

Timing it as he ran forward, Soloman knew that Cain

would already be halfway through the tunnel. He dove far from the concrete walkway with the shotgun slung across his back and hit the ground rolling, coming instantly to his feet from the terrific momentum, running. And as he reached the exit of the tunnel in a sprint he saw Cain smashing his way through the deadlock, forcing a path to freedom.

Caught in a breathless commitment to carry this fight to the death, Soloman hurled the shotgun aside and shouted as he snatched the tanto from his waist, diving forward to land on the trunk of the car, all fear forgotten in the fatal decision.

As he crashed against the vehicle he stabbed downward, ferociously impaling the blade in the thick steel of the truck. Then Cain found a path and surged forward, blasting a smaller car from his escape route.

Soloman rose to a knee and lashed out to shatter the rear window. He didn't even feel the pain though he knew he was injured. He barely held balance as Cain hotly accelerated, the spotlight of the chopper glaring, blinding all of them.

Soloman snatched a grenade from his waist as Cain accelerated even more, approaching a bridge over a river and raising an MP-5, firing back blindly over his shoulder.

Seeing the weapon raised, Soloman rolled away as the blast tore a jagged steel path across the trunk and with the slow-motion acuity that comes only in combat *knew* everything in a vivid second, desperately pulling the grenade pin with his teeth as the car hit the bridge at a hundred miles an hour.

White water flashed past in freezing wind as Soloman cast a wild glance toward the guardrail and moved on it, twisting back to smash the grenade through the window. Then in the next second he slammed his foot violently on the edge of the trunk, hurling himself into the night.

Soloman sailed over the side, narrowly missing a girder to be engulfed by cold. Then he was falling through endless dark as the night behind him exploded in a roaring white light and he spun to see a fantastic circle of fire pinwheeling down the bridge.

With a vengeful scream, he hurled up a fist.

Struck the water hard.

CHAPTER 12

Blood seeped slowly through gauze binding the wound in Soloman's forearm. He didn't remember being hit by a round as Cain fired the MP-5 through the window, but a single bullet had indeed caught him, cutting a narrow hole through muscle and skin.

But the bleeding had almost already stopped and no bones were broken, no nerves cut. And he felt the quickly administered morphine injection freeing his mind from the pain as he analyzed the situation.

Cain's car had been demolished by the grenade, cartwheeling down the bridge before spectacularly striking the guardrail and going over the edge in a mushrooming firestorm. It descended over 150 feet to collide like a meteor with the river where it slowly vanished in a hissing holocaust of steam and flame, leaving a superheated fog on the waves.

It was the last thing Soloman saw before being savagely pulled down by the undercurrent, a drowning deliverance that tumbled him over and over through deep moving water until he frantically tore off the heavy vest and equipment belt and fought clear of the suction. Without hesitation he threw over two thousand dollars' worth of equipment into the brink, but that was the price of war. Equipment was expendable, men who could effectively use the equipment weren't. It was a fundamental part of elite commando training to sacrifice money and equipment for lives.

Straining to the last moment to hold exploding lungs, Soloman inhaled violently as he reached the surface, finding himself a hundred yards downriver, and amphibious assault training took over once more. Fighting the current, he made it to the shore.

The surviving Delta soldiers quickly lifted him from the water and as Soloman saw their shocked expressions he knew that they held him in new respect, as always happened when soldiers witnessed another soldier do something so daring in the field.

They weren't men who impressed easily, he knew, but they regarded him with something like holiness as he sat silent and bleeding, having paid the price for his true authority. And he knew that it would last; they had seen him in the field now, knew he was for real.

All of the commandos were Navy-trained as corpsmen and a few minutes after they'd lifted him from the water his wounds had been completely tended, his hand being the most seriously injured with glass embedded in the skin. Even the bullet wound wasn't as serious because a through-and-through hit to an extremity almost always caused less damage than people anticipated, and rarely prevented a soldier from fighting. But if a man's hands were injured, then his ability to return force was instantly and severely limited, which could lead to far more serious complications – like death.

Questions began immediately by confused police, and the Los Angeles Watch Commander dealt with Ben personally, backing down because he'd been briefed by higher-ups – men of cautious political instincts who knew this involved national security. No one with rank objected to surrendering authority of the situation to the major general. But angry street officers, reflexively antagonistic to federal agents of any kind, were openly resentful that they had to clean up a situation they hadn't created.

Ben came up to Soloman as a commando finished

bandaging his hand, and Soloman gazed up like a man too exhausted to be angry. He was trembling violently from adrenaline and cold, and a wool blanket had been draped over his shoulders. Abruptly he noticed that he was holding a hot tin of coffee; he had no idea who'd given it to him.

'Well,' the general began, morose, 'we lost six men. They're dead. And Chatwell's leg is broken, but he'll live. He wanted to stay but he's a liability now. So after they fix him up I'm sending him back to Bragg. And I've called for the county rescue boys to start dragging.' He stared, licked his lips nervously. 'Sol, do you think ...'

Knowing what it was as the question faded, Soloman shook his head. 'There's no way to know whether I finished him or not.' He took a deep breath. 'He was hit hard, but he's been hit hard before. I'm not going to believe he's dead until I see it.'

Rising slowly, Soloman began a weary path up the rocks. 'Let's get back to the safehouse,' he added. 'And have somebody get back to the museum to pick up the priest. I need to talk to him some more.'

'What?' Ben's eyes hardened. 'You're not going to bring a priest to the safehouse, are you? C'mon, Sol, you can't do that. If the JCS finds out, they'll have both our heads on a stick.'

'Just trust me on this,' Soloman said as they reached the chopper. 'He's got information that we need. I'll take a stint at Leavenworth if it burns down.'

'That happens,' Ben muttered, 'we'll be sharing a cell.'

◆ ◆ ◆

Enraged, Malo stalked the floor.

'As God is my witness, I'm gonna kill that thing,' he growled over and over. His swarthy beard virtually stood on end, and his fists clenched and unclenched as he added, 'He killed six of my men, and nobody kills my men and lives. Nobody.'

It had only been an hour but members of the Los Angeles County Rescue Team were already searching the river. Yet Soloman, shocked by Cain's display of superhuman strength, feared they would find nothing but the scorched vehicle itself.

He had simply witnessed too much. Had seen Cain survive almost measureless damage only to counter-attack like a force of Nature, killing and killing and killing, then escaping again. He was beginning to fear that nothing could destroy whatever it was that Cain had become.

It was rare that Delta commandos showed emotion in combat; they were trained to subdue it. But the superhuman strength and sheer animal brutality that Cain had displayed had shaken all of them, even the normally implacable Malo. And now, because blood had been shed, the game had forever changed and Soloman wasn't sure how solidly he could control either Malo or the rest of the Delta unit.

Soloman knew it was almost impossible to keep a hard hand on soldiers who were taking and returning fire, men more concerned about staying alive than following a bellowed command. And, as it was in this situation, a chaotic battle with high casualties left the survivors superheated for vengeance.

Standing dark and menacing before the lead-reinforced window, Malo had already hotly disputed Soloman's recommendation to reconstitute the team with new men. Turning to stare down, the lieutenant persuasively argued that this … this *thing* was outside the parameters of any combat training they'd ever received, so what was the use of getting more men?

'They don't exactly train us to fight *monsters*, Colonel,' he growled. 'At least *we've* seen what this thing can do. And we won't be taken by surprise again. But if you bring in more men who can be taken off guard by that thing's speed or strength, maybe even guys who've never seen *any* combat, then you're going to have a lot of dead soldiers on your conscience.'

Soloman understood the reasoning, and in truth half-agreed with it. He also knew that Malo and the remaining commandos, knowing what they did and as heated as they were about putting Cain in the ground, were probably worth three or four fresh squads.

It was one thing to see Cain's inhuman power on tape; it was another to narrowly evade those talons and fangs while frantically tracking for a shot. That kind of combat experience couldn't be replaced.

Yeah, Soloman thought after a moment, with good luck and a good plan they might neutralize at least a measure of Cain's inhuman superiority. And, for certain, none of them would ever underestimate the terrific scope of that bestial force again. When they hit him the next time they would hit him together and wouldn't stop firing until every round and RPG was spent.

Lighting a cigar and listening closely, General Hawken wisely let the debate reverberate between Soloman and the Delta lieutenant, although he could have pulled his formidable rank. And Soloman respected him for it, knowing it wasn't something a lot of generals would have done. Out of sheer pride they would have thrown in their considerable weight, taking charge over those who knew far better than they. But Ben was from the old school, the old Army, and had long ago learned that in the field you had to trust those who knew the true nuts and bolts of combat.

Finally Soloman agreed to proceed with a single unit of seven men, and Malo stared down a moment, seething. 'I'm going to kill that monster, Colonel. As God is my witness, I'm going to kill it.'

Father Marcelle, sitting silently across the room, smiled slightly. And as Malo lifted the MP-5 he cast a glance at the priest. Then Malo crossed himself before dropping his hand over the hilt of a wicked-looking bowie knife strapped to his gunbelt.

'Pray for us, Father,' he said coldly.

Marcelle nodded without expression to gently cut the blessing in the air. '*Dominus vobiscum coram inimico vestro.*'

Malo, as fierce and warlike as any soldier Soloman had ever seen, bowed his head a moment to bless himself again and repeated, 'In the Name of the Father, the Son, and the Holy Spirit. Amen.' Then with a frown he vanished through the darkened door, head bent like a medieval warrior casting himself upon some doomed quest.

Ben turned and picked up the phone as it rang. When he laid it down he stared at Soloman, gloomy. 'Cain ain't in the car,' he said. 'They found it, and he ain't in it. They're gonna drag the river for his body but ... but I wouldn't hold out hope.'

'I don't,' Soloman mumbled, lifting a hand to his head. Somewhere in the chaos his face had been cut and he couldn't even remember how. A slender gash ran from the corner of his eye to his mouth. 'This guy is going down hard, Ben. As hard as it gets.'

'Well,' Ben began, 'let's talk truth, old son. You already gave it to him hard. If you can't put him down with that much ordnance, you probably can't put him down at all.'

'He died once. He can die again,' Soloman said simply. 'We've just been playing the wrong game.' He shook his head. 'We've been playing *his* game. Fighting him with brute force. But that's ... that's not going to work. We have to neutralize his advantages, somehow. Have to put him in a position where he can't use that strength and speed. We have to ... put him on a human level.'

A heavy silence held, endured.

'Cain ain't human, Sol.' The general's voice was flat with conviction. 'I don't know what the hell he is. But he ain't human.'

'He's an animal.' Soloman closed his eyes, released a tired sigh. 'He's an animal. And that's how I'm gonna hunt him. That's how I'm gonna hunt him. That's how I'm gonna kill him.'

◆ ◆ ◆

'Your analogy of an animal may be quite accurate,' Marcelle said after he'd retrieved another hot cup of coffee for Soloman. The priest walked slowly away, thoughtful. 'Cain may, indeed, be an animal. But, to your distinct advantage, he may also be a confused animal. I believe you possess more advantages than you realize.'

Finishing a slow sip, Soloman set the cup down on a table, staring for a moment. 'There's always advantages, Marcelle. The difficult part is rationally implementing them in a condition of pure terror. That's why so few plans survive the first thirty seconds of combat.'

The priest walked forward. 'Yes, I agree. But I believe that Cain revealed a weakness tonight. Nor do I think that it was a ruse. It was something he did out of pride as … as always.'

Casting a glance to see Ben's scowl, Soloman was glad that the general didn't fully understand the true nature of the discussion. Ben was a good man, and he had his own suspicions, but the last thing he needed right now was yet another debate about supernatural forces at work. Marcelle apparently also realized it, tempering his terminology.

'Expatiate,' Soloman said.

'It was expressed by Cain himself, Colonel.' Marcelle was eminently priestly, standing without moving. 'Cain said that he *would* remember all that he knew. Which means he does not remember everything at this moment. And that may be the key.'

'Yeah,' Soloman agreed. 'Cain said he *would* remember. But remember what?'

'There is no way to be certain. This concupiscent misuse of Nature creates too many unknowns. Even Cain, who is more aware of his power than' – he glanced at the general – 'any other, has no certainty. But he is definitely frightened of something.'

'Earlier you said that he fears time.'

'Time is only a measure of what he fears. There is something *within* time that he fears.'

'How can you know that?'

'Because Cain's unnatural strength, within itself, has virtually no limitations. He can kill and kill and kill almost without limit and could be, for all practical purposes, immortal. Even these men surrounding you possess only a slight chance for success if they again engage him in combat. And your narrow victory tonight may or may not be repeatable. You injured Cain primarily because you retained the remarkable presence of mind to tactically outthink him. But it is not a feat you are likely to repeat. Neither you, nor any other. Because no measure of human will and skill, or even courage, can match the force of Nature that Cain has become, and is continuing to become.'

There was a dead silence before Soloman replied, 'All right, Marcelle, you're saying that Cain is afraid of something in time. Some kind of event that he has a limited window to meet. What would that be?'

Marcelle frowned. 'You told me that Cain said something mysterious and confusing when he was in the water treatment plant.' He began to stroll, lighting a cigarette. 'Perhaps the answer lies within those words. Can you tell me what Amy – is that her name?'

'Yeah. Amy Milton. She's asleep in one of the bedrooms. Her mother is in there with her.'

'Yes, I thought so. In any case,' the priest continued, 'can you tell me what Amy repeated? Can you tell me what Cain said to her before you engaged him in battle?'

'She said Cain talked about the moon and planets. It sounds like some kind of Black Magic, or something. And since Cain says he can't remember everything he needs to remember, that fits with our theory on the *Grimorium Verum.*'

'I agree.' Marcelle concentrated. 'And I believe that there is one within the city who may throw even more light on this mystery. A man of great learning, and great wisdom.'

'Who?'

'The Archbishop of the Jesuit Order, Superior General Anton Aveling. He is knowledgeable about all things occultic, ritualistic and demonic. More knowledgeable than I or any other.' Glancing down at his watch, the priest added, 'In a few hours the child will awaken. Then, with your permission, I could ask her a few simple questions. I believe I can accomplish the task without undue disturbance, and perhaps overturn a stone. If we are fortunate, the answer may reveal something of merit.'

Soloman waited a moment before he nodded. 'All right. We'll do it after Amy's good and awake.' Bowing his head, he rubbed his eyes. 'Right now ... I've got to get some rest. While we've still got time.'

Feeling the numbness of the morphine taking an edge off his concentration, Soloman picked up his shotgun and walked to the door, opening it to step into the cold heart of an utterly shadowed and dooming night.

◆　◆　◆

It was frosty on the porch, and Soloman zipped up his

jacket as he moved outside. Malo, motionless, was close beside the door, leaning on a rail. He'd lit a long cigar, smoked meditatively.

Soloman mirrored the lieutenant, leaning against the opposite post. He didn't especially want to talk to Malo right now, but there was no place else to go. None of them were straying very far from the safehouse.

Four of the Delta unit were snatching sleep and one was in the front yard, roving. A sixth was out back, and the seventh was monitoring an array of starlight and infrared cameras in the attic that covered every approach to the house, providing them with a small sense of safety.

Finally Malo looked over, chewing what looked like a Cuban cigar. Then the big Delta commando silently took another one from his jacket, offering. Soloman stared a moment into the impassive face and cigar and accepted with a grateful nod.

He also took a lighter from the lieutenant that had the lightning bolt of the 101st Infantry emblazoned on the side. After a brief silence Malo exhaled and spoke, his voice remarkably subdued considering the short period that had passed since his outburst.

'So, Colonel, where to now?'

Soloman continued to light. 'Not sure, Lieutenant. Maybe New York. It's too early to tell.'

'Huh. Been there.'

'Yeah, I figure you have.' Soloman blew out a long stream of smoke, felt a faint buzz from the cigar mingling with the morphine in his veins. *Yeah, it was Cuban.*

'How did you get this thing?' he gazed down.

'Got a buddy in Miami. Customs.' Malo stared into the faraway morning light that vaguely articulated skeletal trees against a cobalt-blue sky. 'He comes in handy sometimes.'

'Is that where you grew up? Miami?'

'No,' Malo responded distantly. 'Monterrey. The Chipinque Mesa, beneath the saddle. Left when I was six, after my folks died in that cement shack, and made my way north. 'Bout like everybody else. I crossed the Rio up around San Diego back when the PD was running BARF squads through the night, trying to catch the bandits terrorizing the immigrants. It was a real serious experience. For a kid.'

Scowling, Malo shook his bearded head, and Soloman knew he was remembering the horrific confrontation with Cain. 'But that was *nuthin'* compared to this, Colonel. Even Delta qualifications seem like a keg party compared to huntin' this guy. The general's right about one thing, for sure. This don't belong to the military. It belongs to God, or something.'

Soloman decided not to fuel the fire. Let some silence pass. 'So who took care of you after you reached the States?' he asked.

'An uncle in Miami. He's history now.' The reply held deep emotion calloused by time. 'Yeah, they're all history. Been dead awhile.' He paused. 'Anyway, when I was eighteen I got my GED and put my mark on the line.' He moved his mouth around the cigar. 'Been in since.'

'It worked out good for you.'

Malo laughed – an unusual expression for such an impassive face. 'Yeah. I figured shootin' and lootin' was all I was good at, so I might as well get paid for it. And it went better than I anticipated. Eventually got myself a college degree to qualify for OCS, made light lieutenant. Got recruited for Delta a few years back, and it's been good work, good pay. I ain't got no complaints.'

'You're a good soldier,' Soloman said. 'And I know, 'cause I've seen a few.'

'Yeah, I figure you have.' Malo turned his head to meet Soloman's gaze. 'Colonel James L. Soloman.

Annapolis graduate. Former commander of Force Recon. Supposed to be a supergrunt with the mind of a scholar. A Renaissance Man. Soldier. Philosopher. Killer. Speaks German and French and Spanish and a couple more. Commanded at Albany. Lejeune. Okinawa. You were being groomed for a post in the Pentagon but passed it over to run a top-secret program to hunt rogue counterintelligence agents. Worked in a blacked-out unit of SEALs and Special Forces and Force Recon with full authority and command. All of 'em elite hunters. And, word is, you were the keenest hound to ever run in the pack. Could track a ghost through a fog, a fish through water.' He placed the cigar back in his mouth, looked out. 'Yeah, everybody who's a stud knows who you are, Colonel. You're something like a legend, I guess. Just like we all know why you got out ... I'm sorry about your family.'

Soloman revealed nothing. 'It's in the past, Malo. Right now we need to stay centered.'

'Yeah, for sure.' He grunted. 'We're in badass Indian territory on this one.'

Indian territory: *hostile ground.*

Soloman smiled; it'd been awhile since he'd heard that one. 'Well, we're down but we're not out. I think we might turn the tables on this guy if we get the chance. War can ... bring out the best in people.'

'Think so?' Malo was keen to it, as if he'd seen too much of the bad. 'Why do you say that?'

'Well, Winston Churchill said it best,' Soloman continued, quoting. ' "War opens the most fruitful field to all human virtues, for at every moment constancy, pity, magnanimity, heroism, and mercy shine forth in it, and every moment offers an opportunity to exercise one of these virtues." '

There was silence as Malo considered it. 'Colonel, that's almost poetic.'

Soloman laughed and thought of the Delta commando's curious exchange with Marcelle. 'I didn't know you were Catholic,' he said quietly.

Malo spat out a sliver of tobacco. 'I ain't, really. I grew up Catholic 'cause my mama was Catholic, God bless her heart. I know the rules, the prayers, when to stand and kneel, all that. But I don't do it no more. I just don't care anything for it, I guess. But you know what they say: There ain't no atheists on a battlefield. And, anyway, it's best to cover yourself. Can't lose nothin', for sure.' They were silent a long moment until he said, more morosely, 'You really think we can take him?'

There was a faint disturbance in the question, a cold realization that they might not, in the end, have what it took to finish this fight. It was something Soloman had expected to hear eventually after Malo calmed down from the initial adrenaline rush.

'Yeah, Malo,' Soloman said, steady. 'I think we can take him.'

Malo didn't look back.

'We'll see,' he whispered, black eyes narrowing to subdue a shadow of true fear. 'We'll see.'

◆ ◆ ◆

Reptilian sounds, sounds of slow water and subterranean life, moved over him *so loud* in the gloom that concealed his form, and he heard his burned tendons grating against blackened bones.

He moved slightly, growling at the agony of such horrible searing wounds, and snaked a ravaged arm over his body, finally finding purchase. Then he began to crawl deeper into the darkness.

He knew that he should be dead, for surely nothing could have survived what he had somehow survived. But he had, indeed, survived, he realized with vengeful glee, as he crawled slowly, so slowly ...

Darkness caressed him and the shadows seemed very much like the home he'd forgotten in the flaming trauma of his defeat ...

What defeat?

In the depth of his wounds, he could not remember. He only remembered the dark flaming current, being swept along in blazing pain as he tumbled alive in the dark-light that hurled him into the sea ...

The sea?

No ... no ...

Not the sea ...

With a severe act of will, he opened his eyes.

No, he knew, not the sea; he was far from that sea where he had been hurled and where he would one day rise again, the apocalyptic image of pain and death and a long-awaited bloody deliverance. Yes, he was still far from that, though he knew it was coming ... one day.

Moving, he tensed his ravaged muscles in a fantastic sphere of agony that would have made him scream, had he been less. But he would not scream, no, he would never scream because that would acknowledge his defeat. So in order to mock it he would feast on the pain, despising what was his only claim, his only take, from this hated loss.

Air flowed over him, cool and chilling, and he remembered where he was, how he had come to it. He saw the darkness of the tunnel again as he tumbled beneath the water of the river, once again knew the fiendish struggle to gain the underwater entrance in the cascading current as his fingers locked desperately on the iron grate. Then he remembered swimming through the hideous burning, the breathless race to find a place to hide before the pain would be too great to overcome, and he would collapse.

And he had claimed his victory, finally raising himself

above the water level where he had fallen on his face in the slime, slithering as a serpent, moaning and rolling in the tormenting prison of his pain until, exhausted, he fled into sleep, escaping the agony. And now he must feast, he knew, for this body, tremendous and magnificent though it was, could not overcome the damage ... without more blood.

Yes, Soloman was skilled and savage, a superior fighter from a superior realm lost to the world for so long that even he could not remember the true greatness of it.

Growling, he remembered facing only one other – *the son of Jesse* – who fought with such will. One who never retreated, knowing only attack with such purity of purpose. He closed his eyes as he remembered the sweeping black blade weaving a wheel of steel before him.

He'd sought to escape the wrath of the warrior-king, but he had failed and finally turned on the rampart, each challenging the other as the Temple of Dagon burned down around them. Sword in hand, ignoring the flaming timbers that crashed like trees, the Hebrew had advanced like a sea-king of old, unyielding and unconquerable to the last to claim a victory that was not of this world.

Their swords met, fire flying from the clash.

Iron against iron ...

David roaring before him.

Blow after blow ...

David spinning, whirling the great black blade.

Such strength ...

Attacking, attacking.

Fire and sword ...

A blow struck true, drawn.

Agony!

A blazing bearded image of righteous rage.

Retreat ...

The black sword rose high, a kingly roar descending as it fell to –

Darkness.

He shook his head, snarling.

No!

Enough!

I will not be defeated again!

It cursed him that he remembered so well how it came to pass. For the body of the gigantic Gadite, resurrected from death by Egyptian sorcery in the sacred ritual of Saturn and Mars, had been the single physical form he'd managed to possess during the long ages. And he had wreaked havoc on the Hebrews with that almost unkillable strength, defeating great Benaiah, Abishai, and even the legendary Jashobeam, who once slew eight hundred men in a day's fighting, in single combat.

Yes, he had scattered Israel's strongest warriors like chaff until David, their anointed king, had come to understand what cosmic force was ravaging his mighty army.

And then the Hebrew had risen from his throne, taken up the sword of Goliath and hunted him down, angrily challenging him in the Temple of Dagon where the last, savage battle ensued, a merciless mortal conflict that left the temple shattered and aflame. But it was not enough for the King of Israel to claim mere victory; he had felt it necessary to rid the Earth of his presence forever, if possible. So with kingly vengeance he ordered the Gadite body buried in a subterranean chamber far beneath the disintegrating walls, daring the wrath of a white sandstorm approaching from the east.

David himself had sealed the tomb with a sword, driving it through the stone sheath before shattering the blade. Then, at his own peril, as flames rose on all sides, took precious seconds to chisel those hated words above the grave, casting a curse on all who would dare open the gateway.

So many years …

Yes, for so many years he had been imprisoned within those stone walls, for he was not beyond the limitations of space and time and light. No, he was a prisoner, too, of nature, as much as lightning or even man. His essence was different from flesh, but he was not as the Old One. He could not transcend the physical. He was a created being and could not be omnipresent, nor could he cross the void, or even the Earth, without a portal.

He had lain within the tomb for so many dark years, dreaming dreams of revenge. And then the priest – he could not remember the face or name – had come to set him free, the priest who defied the curse and opened the portal that loosened him once more upon the world.

At last!

Yes, free at last to deliver his vengeance upon the world, because the Hebrew King had long ago returned to dust, lost to ages. And now he inhabited another superhuman form, a form far, far more marvelous than the first; a form that he had never beheld even among the Nephilim who ruled the land before David's hated sword drove them into ravines and valleys where they were slaughtered by that scornful strength.

But now was the hour of his revenge, and he laughed.

He moved inch by slow inch, crawling through the dark to find the first faint tendril of light, a spectral white that cut through the grate above. Then he raised his scarred head, gazing up to see a blue sliver of moon. And with the sight he moved more quickly, finding what he had to find, the dark, rising with final fierceness until he was climbing. As he reached the surface he shattered the steel cover with a fast fading strength, and after insuring that the street was empty, emerged.

Yes, he needed time ... to heal.

Rolling in infinite agony, he gazed about and saw the glistening wet streets. Then he rolled again and saw the October moon low in the sky like a grinning skull, brooding over a building that hunched black and wide on a shrouded hill, surrounding trees swayed by nightwind. Massive and ponderous, the building commanded the small knoll, a thick iron gate surrounding it with pikes articulated against a storm-clouded sky. He squinted through gathering wind and abandoned air to read the sign: *Halcrouth Sanitorium.*

He laughed.

Yes, of course; it would be the perfect place to hide while his wounds healed, the perfect place to recover before he once again waged war with this soldier who had so foolishly defied him.

Rising with effort, he stumbled forward, hesitating only at the last moment to prevent himself from shattering the chain on the isolated rear entrance. No, no, he remembered, he must leave no careless clues that might lead these mortals to him. He must be cunning.

Grimacing in agony, he climbed the pikes, quickly finding himself in the bright moonlit sheen of grass. Then he walked through the dark mossy silence, a ravaged humanlike thing emerging silently from shadow. And in the far night he saw the front gate, a guard reading.

He found a door and effortlessly shattered the lock, for there was no manner of penetrating the building without causing some measure of damage. But by the time it was discovered in the morning, he knew he would be so well hidden inside the walls that they would never find him.

He moved in an aura of rumbling death down the now-haunted corridors to find where he could feed. Then he forced another door without hesitation and opened it to enter the room of ... a woman.

She lay upon the bed, her face bandaged to cover the incisions of the surgeon. Yes, she had been healed – healed by the healing that came from a realm that was not this, as all their healing came. And she was so happy with it, he knew. Yes, so happy that her disfigurement was corrected, making her as beautiful as the rest.

Staggering, he approached the bed to stand, gazing down with black eyes that cast no reflection. He smiled softly as his charred hand reached out, caressing the face, touching the incisions. And then he laughed, a cut of hideous intent in darkened air. He ripped the gauze from her face and she opened her eyes instantly, awakening and turning to him in shock.

He smothered her scream.

CHAPTER 13

Amy was amazingly bright and alert as she sat in a plush white recliner, light blond hair spilling like sunlight over pale blue eyes. Her gaze was intently focused on Marcelle as he sat before her, an encouraging smile. But her body revealed the slightest measure of tension, as if she knew the priest was about to approach something dreadful, something that should be feared.

Then, with a slight bend of his head, Marcelle casually intensified his benevolence, seemingly summoning a faint measure of confidence from within her. When he spoke it was with the full measure of that masterful confidence that Soloman had come to know so well: the tone of a man who had suffered much, and was eminently qualified to speak with those who had endured the same.

'Hello, Amy,' he began slowly. 'I am Father Jacob Marcelle. I am happy to see that you are well.'

There was silence as she seemed to measure him. 'I'm fine,' she replied carefully.

'Yes, my dear, of course you are.' Marcelle's familiarity was respectfully distant; no, he would not attempt to presume. 'I have spoken with your mother, and she has told me that you slept well last night, resting better than anyone anticipated amidst these annoying circumstances.' He smiled. 'Your mother was happy to see you get some rest, as all of us were, I assure you. And, in fact, that is why we are here. We want to ensure that you remain safe.' Marcelle leaned closer with the words, hovering majestically on an invisible line. 'You see, we want to help you, Amy. Do you think, if it is no trouble, that you might also help us?'

A moment.

Faintly, she nodded.

'Yes.' Marcelle laughed easily. 'Yes, I was certain that you would be willing to help us, as well as yourself. And it will be no trouble for you, I assure you.'

Amy shifted. 'What do you want me to do?'

'Oh, only a simple thing,' he continued with consummate composure, his face comforting. 'I need only to ask a few small questions, and the answers will be simple enough, I promise. But you don't have to answer at all if you don't want to. Whatever you wish is fine.'

He smiled expectantly.

'All right,' she said, but the words came slowly, as if she remained uncertain.

'Good,' Marcelle replied and for a split-second carefully paused, his aspect telegraphing that he was about to approach a subject that might be painful. But with another alteration he seemed to acknowledge her courage.

Amy blinked, her mouth tightening.

'Yes, well,' he continued, settling hands on his knees, 'I only want to ask you one or two questions, and I'm sure that whatever you say will be fine. Then we will not need to speak again.'

She bit her lip, nodded.

'Good,' Marcelle smiled encouragingly, his eyes kind and gentle as he leaned comfortably forward. 'So, let us begin. Now, this man, this criminal who chased you, he said something about the stars and the moon and planets, things like that. And I want to repeat to you something that may have sounded like what he said. Only a few words, mind you, and you can tell me whether I am correct or not. Can you listen to me while I do that?'

Another nod, stronger this time.

Soloman glanced to the side to see Maggie Milton nervously chewing a fingernail. Her stance was tense, faintly trembling. He looked back at Marcelle as he continued. 'It, perhaps, sounded like this. This man was probably not speaking to you. He was … uh, perhaps speaking to himself. But he might have said something to the effect of the moon, or the power of the moon, or, uh, the blood of the moon. Was it something like that?'

'Yes.'

Soloman frowned. He had already told Marcelle that much; the priest wasn't covering any new ground. But Amy seemed to lighten in aspect as Marcelle nodded his square head, openly pleased. 'Ah, yes,' he said, a good smile, 'yes, I knew that would be it. I was certain that it would be the *power* of the moon.'

Silence.

'No,' Amy replied, pausing. 'That's not what he said. He said, "the *water* of the moon." '

A hidden shudder went through Soloman at the repetition of what Cain said in that horrible moment, extracted so easily by Marcelle's subtle skills of interrogation. Or, rather, skills that seemed subtle but which had been gained by a lifetime of delving into the darkest heart of man.

Soloman knew from years of counterintelligence work that interrogation was an exceedingly difficult skill that required extensive experience and training. For not only did the questioner have to remain far, far ahead of those being questioned, he had to reveal nothing – no excitement, no interest – when he finally approached the true target of his quest. If he did, then those being interrogated could be spooked into a dozen lines of manipulation or retreat, or even reconsideration. It was an exacting science, and Soloman was respectfully amazed as Marcelle proceeded.

'Ah, yes,' he repeated. 'Yes, well, that is such an old saying, Amy, the *water* of the moon.' He laughed. 'But, of course, we both know there is no water on the *moon*.'

Her head tilted. 'What about the other part?'

'Oh, yes, the part about planets,' Marcelle said as he cupped his chin for a moment, apparently confused. 'I'm sorry, but for some reason I can't remember the other part.' Then he nodded, convinced. 'Ah, yes, now I remember. It was about Venus and Saturn.' A laugh. 'Such an old wives' tale. But they are all old wives' tales, you know.'

'But you don't have it right.' Amy leaned slightly forward. 'It was about Mars.'

'Mars?' Marcelle looked crestfallen, feigning disappointment in his inability to remember something so simple. 'Mars is it? Are you certain? I, ah … perhaps I'm getting too old for these games.' He stared away, studious. 'I was certain that it was Venus and Saturn.'

'No.' She shook her head solidly. 'It was Saturn and Mars.' She leaned even farther forward. 'It was like … like something about Saturn and Mars and the water of the moon!' At the words she seemed pleased, as if she'd defeated the priest in a word game.

'Hmm.' Marcelle frowned. 'You know, now that you say it, my dear, I think you may be right.' He made a circular gesture in the air, amazed at his sudden recall. 'Yes, yes, something about all of them being together, all in a line, or something like that.'

She stared at him, nodded more easily.

A pause, and Marcelle suddenly released a deep breath, slapping both hands on his knees. 'Well, Amy, I guess we should forget all those questions I was going to ask. I seem to be forgetting everything today.' He smiled. 'Why don't you just enjoy your day? I shan't trouble you anymore.'

He rose with a kindly nod and turned, taking a single step.

'But what about the man?' Amy asked after him and Marcelle hesitated, gazing back patiently. She was suddenly and openly frightened. 'Will he try to hurt me again?'

Marcelle did not move but his aspect changed, solidifying and strengthening. 'We will never let him hurt you, Amy,' he said.

'Well … did I help you?'

Marcelle smiled benevolently.

'Yes, child,' he said. 'More than enough.'

◆ ◆ ◆

The priest leaned on a rail, smoking his habitual cigarette, when Soloman emerged a few minutes later. He waited in silence as Marcelle expelled a slow breath, and clearly read the severe hardness of his face. Knew the priest had discovered something unsettling.

There was another long breath and Marcelle sniffed, frowning as his cigarette spiraled purest white in the early morning light. A lengthy space grew between them.

'So,' Soloman said finally, 'what was all that about, Marcelle?'

'About a dark and disbelieved god that lives,' the priest replied, glancing at the sun. 'About one whose name means "Who is like God upon the Earth." And before whom the world once trembled." He grimaced. 'It was about one who, for a while in these last years of my life, I ceased to believe was an actual force in this old, cursed world of ours.'

Still for a moment, Soloman cast a slight glance to ensure they were alone and unheard. 'Look, Marcelle, just tell me what the hell we're dealing with here. I'm tired of games, tired of riddles, tired of spells and things that go bump in the night. I want to know exactly what you think we're up against.'

'You already have your suspicions.'

Soloman stepped closer. 'I want to know what you're thinking.'

With a bitter gaze the priest continued, 'Cain was correct, Soloman. We do not know him. I know more than almost any other, and yet I know nothing at all, really. It is a mystery, in the end.'

'Try and explain it.'

Marcelle seemed to settle. Not physically, but with an invisible, internal gravity that made him somehow more substantial. A solemn certainty creased the lines of his face.

'It is the oldest theme of man,' he said slowly, 'and the most mysterious. Shakespeare approached it again and again and never managed to reveal more than a dim reflection. Milton strongly challenged it and failed to lift it above the level of romantic ideal. Yet it is a fear that inhabits the deepest instinct of man. Something that has dominated literature and art for six centuries.' He gestured. 'Theramo wrote of it in *Belial*. Sprenger and Institoris approached it in the epic *Malleu Maleficarum*.' He blew out a slow stream. '*Doomsday* by Alexanderus, *La battaglia celeste tra Michele e Lucifero* by Alfano, *El Adversae* by Rolf of Alexandria. It has always been an obsession of man to understand what place … he … once held in this universe.'

Soloman knew, but he asked the question anyway. 'What are you talking about?'

The priest paused, steady. 'I speak of Satan, Colonel.'

As it was said, Soloman heard himself deny it. 'That's impossible.' He shook his head, leaning forward. 'Satan is a mythological concept, Marcelle. I mean, there might be such a thing as supernatural evil – I tend to believe that there is – but you're talking about the *Devil*.'

'Oh, I'm speaking about far more than "the Devil," '
Marcelle replied evenly. 'I'm speaking of a cosmic being
so powerful, and so deceived by his own great fierceness, that he threatened to tread underfoot the Throne
of God. I'm speaking of a celestial entity that was once
the greatest heavenly force, and even dared to wage war
with the Creator of the Universe. Yes, Colonel, a being
that makes the blackest of all human sins seem as
nothing when measured against the purity of his evil.'

Soloman wasn't sure how to receive it. He tried to
contain his shock and amazement. 'Look, Marcelle,' he
began, 'I believe that a man is more than a bunch of
electrical neurons, but I'm not sure if I can believe in
what theologians call "Satan." '

'But is there anything else that would more appropriately define this adversary?' Marcelle waited patiently,
almost challenging; Soloman didn't reply. 'Do you not
remember what Cain spoke of in the museum, Colonel?' he continued. 'Did he not reveal himself? And the
elements of this spell hold the purest satanic characteristics.'

'Yeah, I remember what Cain said in the museum,'
Soloman conceded. 'I'm just not sure what it means. Or
what all this means about the moon and planets. I agree
that it sounds like some kind of Black Magic, but that
could just be superstition. Some of it could have some
substance, I don't know. But I don't know that it does,
either. There's no way to know whether any of this is
real.'

Marcelle spoke with certainty. 'Black Magic, or
superstition as you term it, has endured so many
centuries because there is something true and real at the
heart of it. And, if it will ease your mind, I have learned
that belief in a supremely evil, supernatural being who
wars with God is a dominant theme among all the
world's people and religions. Everyone, it seems, tends
to believe in Satan, even though they may not believe in

God. But, then, as Milton demonstrated, the Devil is more interesting.'

Soloman glanced behind himself; yeah, good, they were alone, though he knew they could switch to German or French if someone approached. He turned back with a whisper: 'Marcelle, if anybody knew we were talking about this, they'd lock us up.'

'And yet this theme dominates the earliest sacred writings of man, Colonel. It was held sacred by the Celts, the Druids, and even the Norsemen. And since the beginning of recorded history it has been explored by every nation and tribe, submerged within the varying mythologies. Just as it is a dominant theme of the Church. Yes, history alone grants substantial weight and substance to what intelligent men, in their prideful arrogance and ignorance, tend to ridicule. But what the centuries have held to be preeminent must be respected, regardless of our prejudices.'

For a while Soloman said nothing. 'I don't know if I can agree with you on this, Marcelle. I mean, it's obvious that Cain isn't human. That much is clear. But this is a stretch that I'm not sure I can make. There's not enough evidence. And just to be safe I don't think we should mention it to anyone. We'd lose credibility, and they wouldn't believe us anyway.'

Marcelle stared with a faint gleam. 'Indulge me for a moment, Soloman,' he said finally, 'and I will explain my perspective. And you can accept it or not. For you are correct; I have no means of proving anything. Just as you would have no means of disproving. Logic is merely the beginning in the search for truth, but logic, forever, will end at faith.'

Soloman glanced around. 'All right,' he said slowly, 'but switch to another language if someone approaches us.'

They began to stroll along the porch, shoulder to shoulder. 'Man's concept of Satan has changed greatly through the ages,' Marcelle continued. 'And the Enlightenment fundamentally altered the manner in which modern man looks upon him. From Calvin to Luther and the contemplative mystics, to Augustine, Milton –' He waved. 'All of them were involved. Even Voltaire and Rousseau, fathers of modern existentialism, influenced our current concept of what is, and always has been, known as Lucifer.

'It was during the sixteenth century, during the last gasp of the Reformation, that the traditional concept of Satan was absorbed by materialism, making evil simply an opposing force of good; a dualism of force that kept the universe in balance. Psychologists have a term for it; it is called "splitting." In scientific terms, it is the means by which men defensively divide the universe into cohabitating halves; good and evil, harmful and helpful, friendly and unfriendly. And many social mores, if you will, were born from that psychological development. There was the death of the witch craze, the removal of a tyrannical Church, the upheaval of social structures in England and the Continent. And it was an appropriate maturation, I believe; an advance long overdue. But there was also, to our detriment, a distancing from a belief that "Satan" himself exists, allowing Satan to become little more than an impersonal personification of universal evil, somewhat shuffled off to the realm of mythology like Loki or Set.' He paused, grunting at a sudden thought. 'But let me ask you a question, Soloman, since you were formerly a manhunter: If you wanted to hide and everyone were hunting you, what would be the wisest course of action?'

Soloman knew it by rote; it was a fundamental procedure of counterintelligence. 'If you want to go under and stay under, you make them think you're already dead.'

'Exactly,' Marcelle nodded. 'For if your enemy believes you are already dead, then they will not search

214

so ferociously for you. And what could be a greater victory for a presupreme being who may desire to design the destiny of every life on the Earth? If men believed in Satan, they would fear him. And then they would seek God for protection. But if men did not believe in Satan, then they would not need God. It is as simple as that. If there is no such thing as Satan, then ... ' He gestured vaguely.

Malo strolled toward them, patrolling the perimeter, and Marcelle switched effortlessly to French. *'Si on ne cherche pas le Diable, pourquoi cherche le Dieu? Maintenant, je pense qu'il n'y a personne qui cherche. Ils se sont tous égarés.'*

Closing, Malo cast a vaguely suspicious glance as Soloman switched over. *'Oui,'* he replied, *'je connais les mots. "Le serpent ancien, appelé le Diable et Satan, qui séduit tout le monde."'*

'Le même,' Marcelle replied pensively.

Malo passed and Marcelle switched again to English. 'Yes, Colonel, it would be the same: Satan, the Devil, who deceives the whole world. As you quoted from Revelations.' He paused. 'I didn't know you were familiar with the Scriptures.'

'I've read them,' Soloman said simply. 'I don't know what I believe, but I've read it cover to cover.'

'Good.' The priest frowned. 'No man is intelligent if he cannot speak thoroughly on the subject.'

'But what you said a few moments ago is something I've heard before, Marcelle. It's not a new thought.'

'Fundamental truths usually aren't, Colonel,' he agreed. 'The genius of a great thought ...'

'... is measured by its simplicity,' Soloman finished, and they fell silent together. Truly, Soloman didn't know what to believe, but the certainty in the priest's tone intimated that there could be something substantial to the theory. In addition, Soloman remembered that Marcelle was a man of science; he was not prone to mysticism.

'I believe,' Marcelle said with gravity, 'that there are forces in this universe not easily understood. Forces of incredible power. I believe, even, that you may be challenging ... a god.'

'Maybe.' Soloman shook his head. 'Whatever it is, I guess I've challenged him.'

Marcelle stopped, leaning on the rail. 'I gave up all I had for my faith,' he added, suddenly contemplative. 'And I've spent too many years forgetting it ... until now. It is a long journey, Soloman. I tell you the truth, from faith to faith. From believing to disbelieving, and believing again. From beginning in darkness to find your way through that labyrinth of lies and deceptions, the intentional misuse of truth. Separating the known from the unknowable, and accepting. It is a journey that has consumed my entire life and still, sometimes, I perceive that I know little more than when I began.'

'No,' Soloman said, 'you know a lot more, Marcelle. It's just that in the beginning you simply believed, so a prayer was just a prayer. But then you began to question. And, after a little while, a prayer wasn't just a prayer anymore. It was a mystery. Questions without answers. But after forty years of answering one question after another you learned that the mystery never ends, so you were back where you began. At simple faith.'

The priest glanced away and seemed to consider the truth of Soloman's words. 'Perhaps you're right. But now the circle is complete, I believe. And I do not know if faith shall be enough.'

'Why's that?'

The priest looked at the sun, frowning.

'Because no one has more faith in God,' he said, 'than Satan himself.'

◆ ◆ ◆

Soloman was both relieved and pleased when he re-entered the house and saw Amy sitting in front of a big-screen television, watching a video. She had a big bowl of popcorn, a strange meal for so early in the morning. But Soloman expected a lot of leeway would be given in the next few days.

It had been so long since Soloman had seen a movie that it actually distracted him. He stood a moment, staring at the screen. It was amazing how much things had changed in seven years. All of a sudden he felt seriously old and out of touch.

Wordless, Amy gazed up. She didn't say anything but Soloman suddenly felt the attention. He didn't care to talk about Cain anymore and he knew she didn't, either. He pointed vaguely to the screen. 'That looks like a pretty good movie.'

She looked back at the screen, munching a mouthful of popcorn. 'Yes, sir. I've seen it eight times.'

'Eight times?' Soloman was genuinely impressed. 'You've seen this thing eight times?'

'Yes, sir. Eight times, I think. Maybe more, though. Mommy's out of town a lot, so I stay with babysitters and they really don't know what to do with me. I like games, but they usually put in a movie and do their homework. Mommy says that one day she's not going to have to work so much.' She paused. 'I hope not. I get lonely … lots of times.'

Soloman wondered about her father, but discretion prevented him from asking. Still, he felt a wave of sincere compassion, knowing what it was like to be alone and lonely. It was something they had in common. 'Well,' he said, 'maybe we could play some games in a little while, Amy. Think you might like that?'

She opened her eyes wider. 'Monopoly?'

'Yeah,' he smiled, 'I'm sure we've got a set around here. If we don't, we can send somebody out to get it.'

The sweetness of Amy's smile broadened as he gazed into the blue eyes and then he laughed, turning away. 'Go ahead and enjoy your movie, and I'll see what I can do,' he added.

'Thanks, Soloman.' She stared after him. 'I think it would be fun.'

'I do, too.' He smiled. 'I do, too.'

Soloman understood as he moved that they were becoming comfortable with each other, and he enjoyed the feeling, knowing satisfaction for the first time in a long while.

It was an odd sensation for him because he'd reckoned his internal defenses as complete. And as he walked away he wondered vaguely how a small child could begin breaking down something a man had spent seven years building to such cold perfection.

◆ ◆ ◆

Malo was cleaning the MP-5, methodically executing every move with easy familiarity. And Soloman remembered that that was exactly how Delta commandos were trained to disassemble a weapon: start to finish in three seconds. If anybody needed more than five, they were considered a flunky or worse. Soloman had seen some of them simply slam the butt of an M-16 on a table, holding the rifle just so, and the thing would literally disintegrate, disassembled in the blink of an eye; it was incredible.

Without a glance Malo answered Soloman's oncoming question. 'I got Tony and Drake in the front listening posts, fifty yards out. Magic and Filo are in the back. They got all four angles covered. Gray and Hank and Chemo are getting some sleep.'

Soloman nodded, poured a cup of coffee. He'd need some sleep himself tonight, he knew. Or today. But he'd have to catch it in two-hour catnaps because he was in combat flow and he never truly slept because of the vivid alertness that caused. He would rise before sunrise, counting each of them, wondering how long the fight could continue, amazed that it did, and that he did.

Without turning his head Malo spoke. 'I was a little messed up last night, Colonel.' There was no remorse or apology. 'Just wanted to tell you that there was no disrespect intended. I was just ... pissed.'

Soloman slapped him on the shoulder as he moved out of the kitchen: 'Sorry, Malo. I can't remember a thing you said.'

The re-assembly halted.

'Colonel?'

Half-turning his head, Soloman hesitated.

'Appreciate it, sir.'

A curt nod, and Soloman stepped out the back door to reflexively search out and identify two highly concealed single-man listening posts set deep in the surrounding trees. The commandos were masterfully camouflaged but Soloman, from years of training, could perceive the leaflike gili suits prone in the forest floor. He knew that with their phenomenal discipline they could hold that position for days, using patience that would drive a normal man insane.

Maggie, sitting on the porch, looked up with a smile. A cup of coffee was beside her and a book was laid open, the cover not visible. She appeared tired of reading.

'What's the book?' he asked, sitting.

'*The New Face of War*. Found it on a shelf.'

'Yeah? How is it?'

She smiled. 'I wouldn't call it entertainment.'

Soloman laughed, leaning forward. It was one of the few restful moments they'd shared since they'd been joined in the underground bunker at White Sands. And Soloman thought, strangely, that it was the first time he'd laughed in a long time. Then he remembered

Amy, the transparent smile and light in her eyes. It seemed as if he was moving further with every moment he spent with the two of them, and he began to wonder where it would end.

'I can barely see those guys out there,' Maggie said. 'Those what-you-call-it suits really make them blend.'

'Yeah,' he replied. 'The suits help.' He took a sip. 'But those guys are good. They don't make too many mistakes.'

With a more tender expression she turned to him. 'I'm sorry about what happened to your guys last night, Sol. Cain took a lot, and I know you're hurt. I feel sorry for their families.'

He paused, frowning. 'They were good men, but they knew the risks. Just like the rest of us. They were willing to die for what they believed and they did. And I think that Cain – or whatever the hell he's become – remembers a lot about tactical response, counterattack, whatever. It's like some sort of reflex instinct that his brain retained, like muscle memory. He always does the right thing at the right time.'

She gazed at him a long time before she said quietly, 'I heard about what you did. Heard the Delta guys talking about it. They said it took a steel spine to pull a stunt like that.'

He shrugged. 'It happens, sometimes. You get caught up in the moment, do something stupid.' He smiled, winked. 'Just don't let your temper get you killed.'

She smiled wanly, turned to look out. 'I just wanted to thank you,' she continued, 'for spitting in Cain's face.'

'Yeah, well, I didn't finish the job. Next time I think it'll end differently.'

She seemed to absorb the thought. 'Have you always been a soldier?' she asked.

'Yeah, pretty much. I grew up in New York. My football prowess got me into Annapolis.'

'You played football? Really?'

'Yeah.'

'What position?'

'Quarterback,' he replied. 'I didn't have a cannon for an arm, but I was good at reading defenses, so it compensated. Ben's never forgiven me for beating Army my last two seasons.'

She laughed.

'Anyway,' he continued, 'after graduation I joined the Corps. Went for Force Recon, qualified. Made captain and major in record time, then commanded in Beirut, the Philippines, Panama. Ran a few companies after I made light colonel.'

'Why didn't you go ahead and make full colonel? Or even general or something?'

'Or something?' he laughed. 'Like President?'

'Okay, I got it.' She laughed, and Soloman felt that she was truly lowering her guard. But then, suddenly, he didn't really want to talk about his life. He turned to the trees, scanning by zone. He took another sip of coffee, cleared his throat.

'So?' She waited.

He shook his head, staring into the woods. 'So I didn't make full colonel because I took early retirement.'

She waited a long time before she followed up with, 'Am I pushing you?'

He didn't reply.

'That's okay,' she said dismissively. 'Everyone's got their secrets.'

'*You've* got secrets?' he said, with a slight smile. 'Miss Prodigal Genius with degrees out the wazoo has secrets?'

'Everybody's got secrets, Soloman,' she said, almost sad. 'Especially us goody-two-shoes doctors who act like we've got so much control. I knew girls in med school who hooked at night, just for a break. Then they'd go into the lab the next day like Einstein-come-again. They were as smart and sweet and gorgeous as could be and they had entire graveyards in their closets. Big surprise. But they had to get rid of that part of themselves that was so stifled, so dead, in the lab. You'd be surprised at the madness I've seen.'

Soloman revealed respect. 'No, Maggie, I don't think I would.' Then for a while they said nothing, and Soloman casually crossed a line. 'So, what does Amy's father do for a living?'

She became quiet, morose, and placed both hands under her chin as she answered, 'Dave, or Amy's father, left us to fend for ourselves a long time ago. Found fresher pastures, I guess.'

He grimaced, pausing. 'I'm sorry, Maggie. I didn't know.'

'That's all right,' she said. 'Dave was just a weak man. He supported us well enough, I suppose. But he didn't like being tied down. Didn't like the responsibilities.' She grimaced slightly. 'Or the same old thing every night. So I come home from med school one day and he meets me at the door, says he's leaving. Just sign the papers when you get 'em.' Her laugh was sad. 'Left me when Amy wasn't even a year old. She's never known a father.'

'You've done well with her.'

'Well, I think she's taken it harder than it looks. She's always wanted a father. And it's sad, really, because she's such a sweet kid. Never did go through the terrible twos. Went right over them.'

Soloman understood her pain, just as he understood Amy's. He wondered if Malo was watching and decided that he didn't care. Her next question was hesitant as she turned to him: 'And you?'

He looked slowly away. 'I, uh, had a little girl. A wife. We got married out of high school. And Marilyn ... she was a good woman. The best. Put up with me, put up with the Corps.' He paused. 'Yeah ... the best. But ... but they're gone now. They were killed when Lisa was only six years old.' He grimaced, hardening. 'Some people sanctioned them ... because of my job.'

'Oh, Sol,' she whispered, almost reaching out. 'I'm so sorry. What happened to the people that killed your family?'

Cold, he stared into the forest.

'They died.'

◆　◆　◆

Ben had expected this to be a ball-bashing fiasco.

After the disaster at the museum, the Trinity Council had been unable to contain the meetings to cold computer screens. So early this morning Archette had demanded a face-to-face evaluation of procedures and progress, and they had all flown to Los Angeles.

It was noon when they convened in the Los Angeles FBI field office, the largest law-enforcement office in the world, securing themselves in the soundproof communications chamber located in a third-level basement. After the meeting, Archette explained, he would take a Central Intelligence Agency jet to New York to prepare backup failsafes.

That had also been something Ben anticipated, reading that the psychiatrist had been laying careful groundwork. And now, finally, he understood that the CIA man had been covering all the bases so that no matter how things went down he would be on record as either an advocate or an opponent, following the wind.

'Foolish, foolish, foolish,' Archette continued. 'I vaguely perceived the dangers of allowing these two men, General Hawken and Colonel Soloman, to work together in a highly compromising covert mission, especially when their mutual history is so littered with scandal and –'

'Now wait just a minute, Professor,' Ben growled, eyes dangerous.

Patient and professional, Archette said, 'Emotions are out of place in a deliberate assembly, General, and are not conducive to –'

'Save it,' Ben said. 'The truth is, Archette, you don't know anything about the military. You don't have a clue about combat radius or maintainability or defense systems or strategic zones. So you're not qualified to tell me whether my tactical judgment was correct or not. My men used a secure fire zone until it was violated by the objective. We used closed communications and reconnaissance and backstopping – tell me if you know what any of this means – and air support and surveillance and highly trained commandos to execute a coordinated tactical assault. But this was a battlefield and a battlefield always contains vulnerability factors. Nobody in this room can guarantee the outcome of a conflict. That's the nature of war. And we *are* in a war. I'm not going to back down to you or anyone else who doesn't know the rules. Further, my personal feelings toward *my* men are none of your concern. I don't know what your agenda is, but if you try to debate the execution of my attack, you're going to lose.'

Archette was unfazed. 'General, as I said, please control yourself. We have a situation of compromised national security and a threat of global contamination. And we must decide whether the Trinity Failsafe is equal to the task of neutralizing the danger. I also state that Colonel Soloman is obviously inadequate for the assignment and should be replaced by a more proficient operative, someone who is not as impulsive or uncontrollable.'

Staring over a cigar, Ben was grim.

Bull, seated at the head of the table, frowned. And Ben decided to attack on a different angle, knowing he was losing the battle. He placed two burly forearms on the edge and stared at Archette. 'Dr Archette,' he began coolly, 'I want to ask you something.'

'Yes?'

'Who authorized the creation of Genocide One?'

Archette paused. 'Why, *I* did, of course. Genocide One was an Agency operation from the beginning.'

'And who authorized the Trinity Failsafe?'

A pause.

'I believe that is obvious,' Archette said. 'It was one of three failsafes designed by the Agency to contain the project should it violate a secure perimeter.'

'Correct,' Ben continued. 'You approved Trinity as a failsafe but Trinity has to be controlled by Pentagon command because it uses military hardware in populated areas. So don't complain about it. Plus, you knew from the beginning that this would be a search-and-destroy mission, just as you should know that search-and-destroy missions always involve risk. But now you're balking because of a personal grievance against Colonel Soloman and –'

Archette's tone unexpectedly sharpened. 'My personal feelings against Soloman have nothing to do with –'

'Military exercises always involve casualties,' Ben pressed. 'Even training. Because this is a dangerous business, and it requires men at home with danger. Colonel Soloman is an educated man, yes, but he is also a highly skilled professional soldier. And if this ... this *council* ... can agree to stay out of Colonel Soloman's way for another two or three days, I think he can reacquire the target and destroy it. But lamenting over collateral damage and media attention is only stalling this freakin' manhunt.'

Archette stared as other voices joined in. And, staring back, Ben saw that the CIA man was heading slowly but inexorably in a direction to make Trinity fail, and wondered why, couldn't conceive of a reason.

If Archette possessed such a secret grievance toward Soloman, why had he been so slow to stop Trinity? Why had he moved in such a zigzag pattern? It didn't make any sense because, as it was, Archette was going to waffle to the very end and then there would be no time left to initiate another failsafe; Cain would get away clean.

With a grimace Ben looked away and knew somehow in his soul that Archette was playing more cards than he revealed. He felt it come over him in a cloud, silencing the debate. And he knew something else, settling into it tightly as he hardened his fists.

This time, he was going to know the truth.

◆ ◆ ◆

Marcelle quickly gathered the sacred items he sought, relics that were blessed as sacred weapons. Then he made a studious visit to the archives and was told that they had yet another thirty thousand manuscripts to catalogue, and realized it might be days before they could conclude anything at all.

As he made his way back through the silent shrouded corridors he caught the austere sight of ancient Aveling leaning over a desk. A glass of red wine and an apple rested before him, and the old man's face revealed nothing as Marcelle came slowly forward, gently setting the bag on the table. At the sight, Aveling asked quietly, 'Artifacts?'

'Yes,' Marcelle replied. 'Artifacts that I fear will avail us nothing at all, Aveling. But they have been of use to me in the past, and might yet serve some purpose.' He paused, composing himself. 'And now I need something from you, my old friend.'

'Speak, Marcelle.' The old gray eyes gleamed with keen discernment and the faintest shade of humor, enlivened by the request. 'You know that you need not ask my permission.'

Moving quickly around the table, Marcelle glanced across the chamber to ensure their isolation. He continued in a colder tone, 'I confronted our adversary last night, Father.'

Aveling's eyes widened. 'And?'

'He is a formidable enemy.' Marcelle's teeth gleamed in a grimace. 'He is cunning. Strong beyond measure.' He shook his head, seemingly overcome. 'Many of the criteria have been met. His command of sacred language is complete, and he knows things no man should know. But he is also somehow … uh, confused, it seems. By some mysterious phenomenon he has lost a measure of what he was. He cannot remember all that he knew.'

'So, he was not destroyed?'

'No, Aveling. He escaped us.'

Aveling shook his head. 'He cannot escape us, Marcelle.'

'No,' Marcelle agreed. 'No, not forever. But I am certain now that it is in our enemy's mind to evoke some sort of incantation, for a purpose unknown. I know only that it has something to do with the water of the moon, Saturn, and Mars. I also believe that it has something to do with human sacrifice but I can find nothing in my reference materials. In truth, I do not even know where to begin, except to know that the spell is probably contained somewhere within the *Grimorium Verum*. Yet you have the benefit of greater years and experience, Aveling. Do these things mean anything to you?'

The old priest smiled, and he regarded Marcelle as if he were the returning Prodigal Son. He waited a long time to speak. 'You have come back, Marcelle,' he nodded with a kind smile. 'You have become, again, what you once were. Even your aspect is once again fierce and formidable.'

Marcelle paused grimly. 'I have found what I had lost, old friend.'

'And what is this thing, Marcelle? What is this thing that you had lost until now?'

'It is ... what I am.' Marcelle's face softened. 'I have once again found ... my faith.'

'And what is faith?' Aveling smiled as a father.

'Faith ... it is the substance of things hoped for, Aveling. The evidence of things unseen.'

'That is the biblical answer, and correct.' The old man's stare did not waver. 'But what is faith to you, my son? What is faith to the son I love more than all my others?'

The hard lines of Marcelle's face faded. 'I ... don't know, Aveling. It is my life. It is all I have. I cannot live without it, though I fall in it. But I continue to search, to hope, and to pray. Sometimes I do not know, and then, sometimes, it seems to come to me as ... as –'

'As God comes to you?' Aveling whispered with a compassionate gaze. Marcelle saw no condemnation – only the love and kindness of one who has been there, and knows.

'Yes, Aveling. As ... as God comes to me.'

The old man nodded. 'Then all is well,' he laughed lightly. 'You have been to the desert and returned, my son. As all of us must.' Then he closed his eyes, concentrating. 'Now,' he added, 'let us proceed with your mystery, so that we may unravel it. As we surely will.'

◆ ◆ ◆

Hidden in the basement dark, he gently felt his oozing wounds, wet to the touch. Needles pierced his skin at the soft pressure and he leaned his head back, teeth clenched, enduring what he was forced to endure before he could return to the hospital far above.

He had taken only enough blood to leave his victims unconscious. He had killed no one because he did not want attention drawn to the building. No, now he needed solitude so he had taken just enough to begin the transformation, the healing.

Doctors would be confused, he knew, and investigate. But they would probably not see the needlelike marks. And by routine procedure – so predictable – they would prescribe medication and transfusions and tests and wait until tonight to see the result of therapy.

Tonight, yes.

When he would emerge ...

Even in the ravaged aftermath of the battle he had known it was too early to battle again. First, he realized, he must reconstitute. He must enhance his strength through the long day, with the molecular synthesis. And then, tonight, he would kill them all one by one to regain strength and renew his battle with ... with ... *Soloman.*

Fangs emerged in a growl.

Somehow, despite his immeasurable rage, the name struck him with a fear he would never reveal. And his eyes glowed in the subterranean depths as he remembered the savage confrontation, seeing once again the fierceness of the warrior as they battled inside the museum.

Yes, in that moment he'd realized that there was no fear in this one; no, this one was different from the rest. He knew only attack, attack, attack, like the cursed desert king of old who struck and struck and refused to retreat until victory was finally won.

David ...

How he hated the name.

A warrior-poet, they called him; a warrior-poet who slew tens and tens of thousands; who wrote the Psalms; who conquered the most savage empires the world had ever seen and brought the tribes together at last to unite the priesthood and kingship upon a single throne, something not done since the days of Moses.

Lion of the Tribe of Judah.

His endless hate gave him strength as he clenched his fists, feeling skin splitting in blood. And he promised the pain to another, vowing it, feeling it already delivered. For David had returned to the dust from which he came, and was beyond even his reach. Yet here was another, an equal, to take his place. Yes, an equal who could receive the vengeance he'd failed to deliver against the Hebrew king's raging, defiant strength.

Volcanic pain made him twist, contorting him for a long, spellbinding moment, and he moaned as he endured. Then it lessened little by little and he finally rested, utterly still, and he was more certain that he would recover soon.

Yes, very, very soon.

Then he would ascend with the night to deliver his dark, fatal touch to those lying so helplessly above, to those who still had hope ...

Hope ...

It made him laugh.

No ... not tonight ...

Tonight there would be no hope.

◆ ◆ ◆

Marcelle went over the facts, leaving nothing out. He spoke quickly and Aveling's aged visage revealed that he followed. Sometimes the elder priest would nod to himself, discerning and sifting and eliminating what was irrelevant to the more important causes.

'Yes,' Aveling said finally. 'Yes, Marcelle, I know vaguely of this spell. It is something from the old country of the Druids. A place of new sorcery and old, where those forest priests still worship the world of the dead.'

'But what does it mean?' Marcelle pressed. 'I must know, Aveling. Why does our adversary seek to evoke this incantation?'

The old priest stared away. 'The scope of all possible universes must be remembered in this, Marcelle,' he said. 'Can you remember the cosmology?'

'Yes,' Marcelle replied without effort. 'The vastness of all conceivable universes is ten raised to the Antonian Abstract. Or ten to the fifteenth power raised to the two-hundredth pi with depth equal to the radius of the visible universe that we know as our own, or twenty billion light-years, with mass to the tenth power being the mass inside each sphere.'

'Succinctly put,' Aveling nodded. 'And you are familiar with the Omega Point Theory and the Quantum Mechanical Argument?'

For Marcelle, it was elemental. 'Yes. Omega Point Theory says that there is a place where all universes converge at the R-concept zone of alternating light and space. And the Quantum Mechanical Argument hypothesizes that it is possible for two molecules to be exchanged without untoward damage to either universe as long as the replacement molecules are noninjurious to the space-light continuum comprising each. It is a foundational tenet of physics.'

'Precisely,' the old man said, squinting. 'And what implications do the laws of the Omega Point and Quantum Mechanics have upon the theory of resurrection from the dead?'

Marcelle was stunned. 'It … it is uncertain what –'

'No,' the old man broke in sternly, 'the laws of physics are not uncertain, Marcelle. Reality is, and remains so. Physical laws are unchangeable. So what postulates rise from the certainty of the Omega Point and the possible quantum exchange of molecules from one universe to another?'

'I, ah, are we speaking of an actual, physical resurrection from death, Aveling?' Marcelle's tone was shocked. 'Are we speaking of the brute force resurrection of a human body? The actual resurrection of a human being who had died?'

With a laugh the old man answered, 'Why must everything relate to this physical universe, Marcelle? Why, when someone speaks of resurrection, must man relate it to flesh?' He laughed again. 'It is only the hubris of man that compels him to place himself at the center of the universe, my son.'

A pause.

'So,' Marcelle began, hesitating as he saw again the monstrous image of Cain growling before him, 'this exchange of molecules, or light, can occur between two dimensions that are unknown to us?'

'That is irrelevant, Marcelle.' The old gray eyes were as piercing as lasers. 'One dimension may be known. None may be known. The question is: Is it possible for this exchange to occur between two dimensions seen or unseen?'

Marcelle considered it against the backdrop of established physics. He pondered it quickly, his mind analyzing the concepts against mathematical laws. Finally he looked up. 'Yes, Aveling. I believe it is possible. But what are the implications of such a theory?'

'A single stride less than the infinite,' replied the old man. 'But it is a Rock of Gibraltar theory that these borders of parallel universes are filled with a kind of slashing tide of molecules, as the sea colliding with the shore. And we could even at this moment exchange atoms with other dimensions if we could somehow filter out the static that fills the void. But this is the crux, my son. This static, this roaring of colliding universes, fills the barrier so completely that an accidental exchange of molecules is impossible except when ...'

Silence.

'Except when, Aveling?'

'Except when the cosmos is in sufficient arrangement to dilute the static,' the old man said, bowing his head.

'For instance?'

'For instance, when Saturn and Mars are conjunct with the water, or the northern pole, of the moon. A time that comes only once a year.'

'When?'

'On Samhain.'

Darkness, silence.

'Samhain,' Marcelle repeated. 'Five days from now.'

'Yes.'

'But what does our enemy wish to gain in this?'

'There is no means of knowing, for certain. But did you not say that our adversary is somewhat, ah, confused? Did you not say that he cannot remember all that he knew?'

'Yes, Aveling. He cannot remember all that he knew.' Confusion was evident in Marcelle's eyes. 'But how could that be, Father? Why does Cain not remember all that he knew?'

Aveling laughed. 'It is simple, Marcelle. Because Cain, as you name him, has just opened his eyes to see.'

'What do you mean?'

'I mean that a man who has been blind since birth is sometimes healed by miracles of science. But upon seeing for the first time he does not know how to process information gained through his new-formed brain. He cannot see and identify what is "square," even though he knows what is square through his other senses. He cannot identify something so simple as a tree, or even himself. He knows what "square" feels like, but if you were to hold a "square" in front of his eyes, he will not be able to identify it. He must feel it with his hands, as you tell him that this is "square," and so he learns little by little. Yes, he learns as his brain discerns itself. Until his mind is accustomed to this flesh, and the gaining of it. Not a thing so difficult to understand, even to be anticipated. And Cain is obviously suffering a similar phenomenon. But he will learn, Marcelle. Yes, be certain, he will learn. He is too terribly intelligent to fail in his chosen task.'

'So you are saying that Cain is attempting to acclimate himself to this body? To this brain? Is this the singular reason for his confusion?'

'Nothing is singular, Marcelle,' Aveling whispered. 'We do not know what forces fight for us. No one does. But that is the essence of Cain's confusion, I believe. He is seeking to acclimate himself to this corporeal form, undead and yet unliving.'

Marcelle went into it, Jesuit intelligence flashing keen in his concentrated glare. 'Let us use sequential logic,' he said.

'Proceed.'

'Cain cannot remember all that he knew,' he began. 'He seeks the *Grimorium Verum*. But for what purpose? He also seeks the child. We know already that he needs her blood to correct his anomaly. But there must be another reason or he would have killed her in the tunnel before Soloman reached them. Why would he delay? Why did he hesitate? Tell me, old friend. What is the sum of these things?'

The old priest folded his hands before his severe face. His eyes narrowed, gazing forward as if reading an invisible page.

'Cain's pride reveals him, Marcelle. If he is, indeed, our adversary, if he is the Prince of the Air as we suspect, then he seeks to be worshipped even as God is worshipped. So we can logically deduce that he is trying to remember the names and locations of those who worship him. Yes, and so, he may be seeking to remember these and others. And to continue the line of logic to its end, as we must do to determine truth, he may be attempting to remember secret pacts with princes of the Earth, to remember those in power that he has cunningly won by deception. Or even the location of hidden treasures, or empires dedicated to serving his cause. For even our adversary, in this human form, will need vassals to execute his plans.'

'And the spell?' Marcelle asked. 'The *Grimorium Verum*?'

'May be the means of obtaining such lost memory.'

Marcelle stared. 'My God, Aveling. Is such a thing possible? Can … can *memory* be transferred from one universe to another? I hold you with the deepest respect, Father. But that seems impossible.'

An indulgent laugh. 'Remember, Marcelle, that ions and electric impulse, and thus memory, are as real as physical life or lightning itself. Soul cannot be defined, it's true. But the physics of memory are readily understood. And nothing physical is ever lost, even in death. It is only transferred, as science has indisputably proven.'

'And when Cain obtains this memory?'

'If Cain possessed such memory, his wisdom would be supreme. His purposes would be laid deep and pursued with the advantage of cosmic cunning that no mortal could overcome.' Aveling pondered the theory. 'That is, *if* he could remember. And that is apparently what he seeks through the spell. As I said, my son, his words reveal him. He *cannot* remember all that he knew but he *seeks* to remember, and I conjecture that he seeks the *Grimorium Verum* to assist him in this task. So, if you combine all hypotheses, then you have a logical conclusion. It is mathematical, a line that is not broken.' He paused. 'Cain seeks this child's blood to correct the strange disintegration of his own form. That is accepted as fact. But he also seeks to use her in this spell that will allow him to remember all that he knew. Thus he seeks to use her to obtain dominion over this world. Or destroy it.'

Marcelle was suddenly fierce. 'We don't have much time, Aveling. Cain must be destroyed. As quickly as possible. How prepared is Rome to stand behind what I must do? My terms may be extreme.'

Aveling nodded. 'With any means necessary.'

'Good. Then we must move with purpose. Will you use all your power to make arrangements for me as I describe them?'

The old man removed a sheet of paper from the desk.

'The weakest ink is better than the strongest memory,' he smiled.

◆ ◆ ◆

A silhouette in shadow awaited Marcelle as he exited the cathedral and he turned his head, immediately identifying the bent, cloaked form of Sister Mary Francis standing silent and shadowed in the foyer. She stood with centuries-old patience, unmoving. But he felt the impact of those hard eyes and knew she had been searching for him. Holding the artifacts in his hand, he approached her in grim silence.

She bent her head. 'The child lives?'

Marcelle stared. It was impossible that she could know anything of the situation outside these walls, and yet she seemed to know it all. He didn't know how to respond, finally decided to use the truth: 'Yes, Mother Superior. The child lives.' He paused. 'How can you know of this?'

'Always it is children,' she replied. 'Yes, he wars eternally against children. I have spent too many long nights nursing them to life, and praying with them until they passed, to know any less.' The lack of fear in her voice was inspiring. 'You must protect the child, Marcelle,' she continued. 'Is it ... a male child?'

'No,' he replied. 'It is a young girl. And our adversary, Cain, seeks to take her life to preserve his own.'

'He is too inhuman to do otherwise,' she answered simply. 'But you must not fear him.'

Marcelle's face tightened. 'But ... but I do fear him, Sister. I have met him. And I fear him.'

'Fear him not!' she said sternly. 'He will use your fear! He will defeat you by your fear! Remember that he is *not* omnipotent, Marcelle! He is only a creature! Like us!' She paused, slowly folding hands in her habit. 'The eyes of the children who died in my arms, and who understood the love of God with their last, blessed breath, feared him not ... in the end.' She turned her head to the side. 'We must have no less courage than them.'

For a moment they said nothing and then she angled her head, gently moving the rosary and crucifix. 'I humbly request permission to accompany you, Father,' she said. 'I perceive it ... as my duty. And I perceive more: I perceive that if we do not stand together in faith, and hope, and prayer, then we shall not stand at all.'

Marcelle debated, wondering and fearing what Soloman would say if he did not return alone; they were already on tenuous legal ground. But the decision took only a second as he sensed the old nun's formidable strength inspiring him with the will to carry on.

He nodded. 'I will await you outside,' he replied.

CHAPTER 14

Alone on the steps of the cathedral, waiting for Mother Superior Mary Francis to retrieve her things, Marcelle contemplated all he had heard. And it meant something to him.

It seemed so clear now that he had spent too many years isolated in cold academic thought; too many years acquiring a formidable intellect but somehow losing what had called him here, in the beginning.

Shadowed from within in the full light of day, he wondered how life had brought him to this place and where he'd lost the essence of what he truly was. It had been a terrific loss, he realized; a loss of years and love with so much time spent searching for a treasure that could not be found.

He felt foolish, as if he had wasted decades in abandoned, desolate places, digging with nothing more than rumors and legend to lead him, always disappointed when he could have been building a truer life for himself in a truer world.

Time that could not be redeemed.

He scanned the surrounding buildings as he listened to the distant traffic, the world of men. And it seemed suddenly meaningless to him, more meaningless than it had ever been.

He realized that the old nun knew more than he; knew that whatever was the heart of her faith was far simpler and easier to gain than the fantastic but meaningless disciplines he'd mastered, disciplines that could never build a tower to God. For somewhere in that simple faith lay a truth he had left far behind.

Wind moved over him and it seemed he had never felt it so clear, his skin so sensitive … to the touch. It was simple and natural and he knew it, yes, invisible but there, always there.

Wind, whispering.

Yes, the evidence of things unseen.

With a thin smile he would no longer search to understand what lay beyond, because he could never know what lay beyond. But he was struck at once with a memory of all the stars and all the nights he had ever seen; a starry host blazing and gazing, alive with life.

He took a deep breath.

Nodded.

It was enough.

◆ ◆ ◆

It was late afternoon when Soloman finally received a Monopoly game from a somewhat surly FBI agent and winked. 'Need some distraction.'

The agent didn't even reply as Soloman entered the kitchen to find Amy and Maggie sitting at the table. Malo was standing aside, rifle in hand with the stock set on his hip, chewing a cigar.

'Got it, Amy,' he said as he sat.

'Great!' She clapped her hands. 'I knew you'd do it!'

Soloman felt a rush that came through the small cracks of his internal armor and didn't try to stop the release – wind moaning from a tomb – as he laid out the game. Confused, he tried to remember how much money was involved but it had been so long that he couldn't recall the rules. Then Amy apparently sensed his confusion, reaching out.

'Here!' She laughed. 'Let me do it!'

Soloman smiled, leaning back. 'Go ahead, kid.'

He watched her work, and it was good. Clearing his throat, he narrowly studied the instructions to see where everything was laid. His face made it obvious that he had no idea.

'Let me help,' Maggie said, taking the rest from his hands. She began laying out pieces, glancing up with a smile. 'You play Monopoly a lot, Sol?'

Soloman scowled. 'Uh, no. Not really.'

'Well, then, I guess it's time to get back into it.' She grinned as she finished laying the pieces and leaned back, casting a challenging glance at Malo. 'Want to join in, Malo? See how tough you really are?'

Frowning, Malo shook his head. 'No, ma'am. I think this is gonna get too mean for me.' He chomped down hard on the cigar. 'I probably need to be ... doing something.'

Soloman cut him a glance as he walked away, muttering about checking heat sensors and motion ... whatever. He went through the kitchen, leaving Soloman with a very determined looking Amy and her openly amused mother. Soloman focused on the child.

'You sure you know how to play?' he asked, dismayed at how quickly she'd laid out the money. Something told him he was in trouble.

'Yeah!' She smiled. 'I play this a lot! I even beat Mommy most of the time!' Soloman looked up to see Maggie's laughing gaze and grimaced, clearing his throat. He began, 'Yeah, well, maybe we should play a little warmup game, or something, just so we can –'

'Oh, I already know all the rules.' Amy laughed and nodded curtly, suddenly serious. 'It's your move, Soloman.'

Soloman met the beaming gaze and glanced at the board. Felt a sense of doom.

'I was afraid of that,' he said.

◆ ◆ ◆

Ben wasn't certain if he'd prevailed or not. He perceived from the last few minutes that the team might receive more time, but the winds of the career-minded were blowing hot and hunting for heads.

Haggard and gaunt, Archette was constructing an elaborate argument to explain how Soloman's failure to conform to military norms, his disrespect of lawful behavior, and his unfortunate tendency to initiate overly aggressive procedures could be indicative of a dangerous antisocial disorder that might endanger the mission.

To a point, Ben couldn't dispute the accusation. Because, despite his earlier diatribe, Soloman had indeed gone outside regulations at the museum.

If the confrontation had ended in success, it could have been forgiven. But it hadn't. It had resulted in the deaths of six elite commandos, virtually destroyed a national monument, closed down a major thoroughfare, and initiated a massive mobilization of the entire Los Angeles Rescue Squad. Not to mention that virtually every news agency in the world was now scrambling to uncover anything on this very, very sensitive operation.

Tired, Ben muttered a curse. He wasn't sure how it could get any worse. Until it did.

'Is it not true,' Archette asked, almost painfully, 'that Colonel Soloman has actually violated the safehouse with unsecured personnel?'

Ben knew he couldn't hesitate at all. Nor could he reveal what Archette so quaintly referred to as 'micro-expressions,' which, in psychiatric circles, were identified as almost invisible physical tics that expressed emotion far better than words.

'That,' Ben said flatly, 'is a lie.'

Archette said nothing. Stared. 'I have received reports,' he continued slowly, 'that a priest is advising

Colonel Soloman in this mission. Can you confirm this?'

'The colonel is conducting a classified investigation,' Ben answered. 'I am not at liberty to discuss whom he has or has not contacted. That would be a breach of security.'

'Not if he has violated security parameters of the Trinity Mandate,' Archette replied steadily, and Ben knew he was right. He'd also known it would be Archette's next response, and he'd taken the moment to craft a carefully timed reply.

'Gentlemen,' he began, glancing at the frowning faces of Bull Thompson and Blake Hollman, both of whom had to catch flights to New York within an hour. 'I certainly know the security parameters. It is not a compromise of procedure for Soloman to confer, within limits, with anyone that he elects in order to facilitate the execution of this failsafe. I can assure you that there has been no violation of procedure.'

Bull took less time than Hollman. The NSA man, troubleshooter and general fixer for the State Department, stared at Ben as if he somehow harbingered a plague.

'I accept your assessment,' Bull said finally. 'And I trust that neither you nor your team have violated the security mandate. But, Ben, I'm not going to be able to give you more than another forty-eight hours. If you or your team haven't made significant progress within that time frame, the Trinity Failsafe will be dismantled.'

'I understand.' Ben nodded. 'Give us forty-eight hours.'

◆ ◆ ◆

A crimson sun colored tree-strewn cliffs when Marcelle returned in the late evening. It had taken him the last half of the day to reach the safehouse, where he found

Soloman and Maggie playing Monopoly with Amy, game pieces scattered across the kitchen table, an extensive display of money and houses and hotels and cards claimed by all. It looked like they'd been playing for most of the afternoon.

Soloman turned as Marcelle entered and saw the old nun, Mother Superior Mary Francis, walking beside the priest. Her hands were folded inside her habit, her head bowed to wordlessly ask his acceptance.

Rising instantly, Soloman walked forward, studying the situation. He wasn't surprised at how things kept getting away from regulation. After his discussion with Marcelle this morning, nothing could surprise him. He was aware of Malo's tilted grin at the development.

'Sister Mary Francis?' Soloman reminded himself aloud.

A demure nod. 'I do not know that it will avail you anything at all, Colonel,' she said quietly. 'But, with your permission, I would like to offer my assistance.'

Malo smiled – actually smiled – enjoying it. 'The general's gonna love this when he gets back,' he said.

'All right, Sister,' Soloman replied. 'I guess we can use all the help we can get. Why don't you fix us something to eat? You can ask Maggie and Amy if they want something special, but anything is fine for the rest of us.'

Mary Francis nodded and gave him a narrow smile. 'Thank you, Colonel. It would be my pleasure.' She moved past him.

Unfazed, Marcelle spoke as she entered the kitchen. 'You are a man of rare wisdom, Colonel. Sister Mary Francis may be of more use than it would seem.'

Not responding, Soloman headed for the door. 'Take over for me, Malo.'

'I don't think that I want to take over for you, Colonel,' the lieutenant replied. 'No disrespect intended, sir, but your position' – he glanced at Amy, tempering his language – 'isn't the best.'

Soloman turned to glare a *direct* order and Malo reluctantly laid his rifle on the counter. As he took Soloman's position he looked with open admiration at Amy and the large accumulation of money and houses, still chewing the unlit cigar. 'You ever done any money laundering, kid?' he asked. 'I think you got a real knack for it.'

With a smile Amy clapped her hands. 'You want to trade all four railroads for Boardwalk, Malo? I've got a hotel on it. And, by the way, Soloman just landed on Pennsylvania Avenue. You owe me two thousand dollars.'

Malo scowled at the board. 'Eh?'

Maggie laughed out loud and Soloman smiled as he reached the door, following Marcelle onto the porch. He'd commandeered yet another cigar from Malo and lit it before meeting the darkening air of the forest.

Carefully, Marcelle laid a small black bag of obvious quality and antiquity on a chair. Gold stitching sealed the seams and it was glossy in the dim light. As Soloman followed the stout priest from the door he spoke. 'So, Marcelle, what's in the bag?'

'Artifacts,' the priest answered vaguely. His head was bowed in thought. 'Holy artifacts that, quite probably, will avail us nothing.' He shrugged. 'But there is no reason not to hope. It is always better to hope than to despair, as Goethe would say.'

Soloman raised an eyebrow. 'The poet?'

'Yes. Who retold the legend of Faust, which dates from the sixteenth century. You, of course, know the story. Faust sold his soul to the Devil for the chance to achieve intellectual perfection. And, guided by Mephistopheles, a reflection of Satan, he moved from one realm of human experience to another without ever attaining the satisfaction he so desperately sought. For intellectual perfection is forever … ultimately unsatisfying.'

'Yeah, I've read it. Read it a couple of times, in fact.'

'I'm sure you would have.' Marcelle smiled. 'Because, even though you are a soldier, you are also a scholar. In fact I've pondered whether you missed your calling.' He laughed. 'You would have made an excellent priest, you know. You have a nature suited for the task.'

'I appreciate that.' Soloman gazed around by reflex. 'But Goethe's *Faust* is an interesting work for anyone. Satan loses a wager for Faust's soul because Faust sought only perfection, not pleasure. I've never been certain of the morality, or if there is any, really. I guess it's just a product of the Enlightenment, when everyone was rebelling against a tyrannical Church.'

Marcelle nodded. 'Yes. Tyrannical is the word, I believe.'

'A stout thing for a priest to say.'

'The Church is multifaceted,' Marcelle replied. 'There are priests who agree with the Curia, those who do not, and multitudinous positions spanning the extremes. But there was a time, indeed, when the Church was tyrannical. And in some respects remains so.'

'But you're not Catholic, right? You're a Jesuit.'

'Yes, I am a Jesuit and a Catholic. As much as we are independent of the Church hierarchy the Society of Jesus has been an ally of Rome since Pius VII removed the ban imposed in 1773. So our order is pledged to the Archbishop's authority, and many Jesuits have been canonized as saints. We take a lifelong vow of poverty and celibacy and undergo a fifteen-year training period. And our official elected leader, Superior General Anton Aveling, whom I told you of, holds a position of power over the Order.'

'That's interesting,' Soloman muttered, releasing a cloud of cigar smoke. 'I've never really studied it.' Then he proceeded to move on with the issue at hand. 'So, tell me, what'd you find out?'

'I believe,' Marcelle replied, 'that Cain intends to use Amy in some sort of occult ritual. A ritual that can only be evoked precisely on Samhain. It is apparently an exercise of sorcery in which he will use her to regain something he has lost, and something he cannot complete without a copy of the *Grimorium Verum*. We can only conjecture, but his intentions are surely fatal for the child. Aveling suspects that Cain may attempt to use her to regain some measure of lost knowledge.'

Soloman shook his head with a humorless smile as he blew out more smoke. 'You know, Marcelle, I thought you were going to say something like that.'

The priest did not reply for a long time. 'It was a suspicion that I harbored,' he said eventually. 'Whether there is anything real to it or not is of no matter. But Cain obviously believes, so he will be determined to obtain Amy before Samhain, which is only five days from now. That is why he fears time. Apparently, this spell means everything to him, and he will risk everything to claim Amy for the consummation.'

'Does Aveling feel certain?'

Marcelle nodded. 'Yes. And Aveling knows more than you or I will learn in a lifetime. So I believe his conclusions are correct. Amy's blood, as we already know, will cure the virus in Cain's system and grant him, for all practical purposes, immortality. But Cain wants more. He wants to sacrifice her and gain something through the sacrifice: his memory, and perhaps the names and places of his truest servants, so that he may build his empire. For even Cain, if he is who I believe him to be, cannot rule alone. He must have ambassadors, bodyguards, the vassals of a monarch. He is … limited.'

There was no true silence because the descending night rumbled with crickets and forest sounds. Wind moaned through surrounding trees, and Soloman studied the theory a long time before he continued. 'All right,' he began, 'let's assume for a moment that you're right. We already know that Cain wants Amy's blood to cure the virus, and we can propose that he wants her for this ritual. If that's correct, how can we use it to our advantage?'

'There is only one means,' Marcelle replied, and Soloman knew where he was going. 'We must use Cain's obsession with time and this ritual to lure him out of hiding. We must ... use Amy.'

Soloman didn't blink. 'I don't think I'm going to do that, Marcelle.'

Marcelle obviously didn't like the idea, either. He took a long drag on a cigarette, releasing smoke with each word. 'Remember, Soloman. Cain can wait for the child, if he must. But he cannot wait for the ritual. Samhain is only five days from now. And one day after that, if Maggie's calculations are correct, the virus will become supraepidemic. So if we are to prevent this plague we must use Cain's race against time to our advantage. We must use Amy herself to lure him out of hiding. It is ... desperate, I agree. But if you are willing to meet him once again in combat, it may be the means of destroying him.'

Turning to study the darkened treeline, Soloman was silent. He was glad that Maggie was inside playing Monopoly with Amy and Malo. She would be going ballistic at this. He also knew that a hard decision had to be made, and he was fighting at the tip of the wedge.

'Go on,' he said.

'We must play Cain's game,' the priest responded with the air of a soldier. 'We must use Cain's greatest weakness, his own hubris, against him. For Cain believes he can overcome any mortal force to claim the child. Therefore, you must challenge his pride.'

'And how do we do that?'

'Make a simple mistake. Do you remember the three locations I mentioned for the *Grimorium Verum*? They were Los Angeles, New York, and the Vatican. And in order to perform the ritual he must yet claim a copy of the book. So New York is his next destination. And if Amy is also in New York, Cain will come for her there. It would be a challenge he could not resist.'

'And how can we pull that off?' Soloman asked. 'If it looks like we've put out the information on purpose, Cain will suspect a trap.'

'He will suspect a trap in any case, Soloman, because he has great animal cunning, and his mind is growing day by day. He knows more tonight than he did this morning. That is why we must move quickly. In time we will not be able to confound him at all. A small measure of time is all we have on our side, so we must be as shrewd as serpents.'

Soloman didn't like any of it, but he knew the priest was onto something. 'All right, Marcelle,' he said. 'Spell it out.'

'Cain has failed in his chosen task to take the child,' the priest answered. 'Or so it seems. He has reached a point where he can do nothing more than attempt to take the second manuscript from the museum in New York and hope to obtain Amy at a later time. So we must do something there, within the museum, that will lead him to the child.'

'Why don't we just set up an ambush in the museum and forget about using Amy?'

'Because Cain can ultimately forsake the manuscript if the fighting becomes too fierce.' Marcelle spoke with conviction. 'But he certainly will not forsake the girl if he knows he might yet take her before Samhain.'

'Go on.'

'Cain realizes that the Church is somehow involved,' Marcelle continued. 'Just as he suspects that I am pursuing him because of what he took from St Michael's.'

'And just what was it that he took from St Michael's?' Soloman asked finally. It was a question that had been troubling him since the beginning, and Marcelle hesitated for only the briefest moment.

'He took a document that was secured in the Secret Archives, Soloman. It is a library locked inside a vault hidden beneath a sub-basement. Its very existence is a papal secret.'

'I thought the Secret Archives of the Catholic Church were located in Rome.'

'A portion of the Secret Archives are secured in Rome, for certain,' the priest replied, lighting another cigarette. 'And, in truth, Rome controls both libraries. Father James, Librarian Superior for the Vatican, has jurisdiction over all documents. But many acts and hidden pacts made between Church and State on this continent are secured on this continent by the order of Clement IX, for easier categorizing. The Archbishop, in his wisdom, wanted to keep matters relevant to America in America. It is an unspoken tradition spawned in the days when the Church so strongly settled the California coast. And they eventually selected St Michael's as the repository, though there are also documents deposited there involving European affairs.'

'Why?'

'Because,' Marcelle replied, 'the Archives are a peculiar phenomenon, Colonel. There is no means of indexing any materials, except the secret system invented by Innocent III. They are meant to be stored in such a way that only the Librarian Superior or the keeper at St Michael's could know the location of any item. And sometimes documents cross the Atlantic for purposes of further concealment. It is a ... diabolical ... manner of preservation. A man could walk through the Archives for a century and not find what he sought unless the Librarian Superior revealed it to him. Everything is hidden in plain sight.'

'All right,' Soloman said, catching on. 'But why don't you know what Cain took?'

'Because Father Lanester, keeper of the Archives at St Michael's, is dead. But Father James has arrived and the Jesuit Superior General, Anton Aveling, is personally overseeing the investigation, so I believe we shall know soon enough. And when we do, it will give us yet another advantage over this adversary.'

They walked in silence.

'Go back to the plan,' Soloman said finally.

'Very well,' the priest said with gravity. 'Cain will not be surprised if the Church were somehow working for the child. He would even anticipate it; a logical sequence of events. So, as a ruse, we can make it seem as if we are performing rituals of protection. Then inform Cain of Amy's location.'

'So we take Amy to New York,' Soloman finished. 'We somehow associate her with the location of the book and leave an open door for Cain. Then, when he comes for her, we take him down.'

'Yes. But make no mistake, Soloman: Cain is wise, and wiser by the moment. He will not launch an attack until he is certain. What I'm saying is that we cannot bluff. We must actually use the child. Without her actual presence, Cain will walk away from another encounter.'

Soloman stared, measuring the scope of it. He knew that the execution would be complicated, but that wasn't what bothered him most. Because in order to do this he would have to purposely place the life of a child in danger, a child who had no guilt and no responsibility.

Silence; a decision to make.
Finish it.
Save this kid.

His reply was slow.

'Where can we put her? If the Church is involved, then we need a place associated with the Church. But it has to be isolated because I want the freedom to use overwhelming force, Marcelle. I want the freedom to utilize fully armed gunships with a standing green light to fire on acquisition. And I don't want the complications of any collateral damage either. Understand me on that. I want a killing field.'

Marcelle didn't hesitate. 'There is an abandoned site, the Basilica of St Angela, located west of New York City in Warwick. It was built over one hundred years ago with three-foot-thick stone walls and is more fortress than church. The walls are impregnable, even to Cain. And there are only two means of egress, front and back, one of which Cain will surely be forced to use. Also, it is surrounded by a high wall that encloses an inner courtyard. With the skill of yourself and your men, you can trap him there in a, uh … as you say, a killing field. And to your further advantage it's surrounded by a mile of empty swamp. If Cain escapes the basilica and makes it into the field, as he escaped the museum, he will be an easy target for your gunships. They can open fire without any danger of collateral civilian damage. And not even Cain can flee quickly through the moor. No one can flee quickly when they are knee-deep in black water. If your gunships triangulate on him in the swamp, he will be torn limb from limb, finally destroyed.'

Soloman was silent.

On balance, it sounded like a good plan, just as long as they could triangulate on Cain as he approached the basilica. But the logistics and concealment and targeting procedures had to be perfect because Cain was too smart and fast for a stand-up fight. And, as Marcelle had stressed, he knew Cain would never walk into a confrontation unless he knew that his prey was obtainable, so Amy had to be there.

A multitude of factors blitzed through Soloman's mind: concealment, surveillance, a theater of fire, ambush tactics, pursuit restrictions, communications ... on and on.

Shaking his head, he suppressed a grunt. This would be close, he felt; as close as anything he'd ever done. Then he remembered the most important law of combat, the one that never failed: Murphy's.

'It's a ballsy plan, Marcelle,' he said. 'But the combat-issue version of Murphy's Law says that no plan survives the first thirty seconds of combat. It also says that perfect plans aren't. Are you willing to put the death of this child on your conscience?'

'If we cannot kill Cain, Soloman, then Amy's death will be on all consciences. For Cain will certainly claim her.' Marcelle's confidence was contagious, and Soloman knew he was right. 'Whether it takes Cain one year or two or three, he will ultimately kill her. You and your men cannot protect her forever and you know as much. No one can protect her forever. Nor can she hide. One day, and soon, Cain will find her. Because he will become wiser than all of us together. His intellect will be unsearchable. His heart, the throne of will. And his abilities will not be limited to the flesh.'

'You're forgetting about the virus, Marcelle.' Soloman stared at him. 'It's unlikely that any of us will be alive in a year. Or even six months. All of us, and most of the world, including Amy, will be in the graveyard. That is, if there's enough of the living left to bury the dead.'

'Perhaps,' Marcelle responded coolly. 'And if this epidemic is realized, then we will have no lives left to defend. But if this plague is not forthcoming, and there is no way to know for certain, then we will have given Cain time to locate the child. And if Cain takes her blood he will defeat this virus to ultimately gain immortality.' He waited. 'Time is not on his side, Soloman. Nor is it on ours. Cain is afraid that he will not claim the child by Samhain. And I believe he also fears that the true scope of his knowledge will never return. So he desires immortality, and whatever he gains in this ritual, to mature and execute the full scope of his plans. We must use these things against him.'

Soloman was grim as Marcelle stepped closer. 'Cain *can* be defeated, Colonel. His strength is not without limit. I believe that one similiar to Cain was defeated in the past.' He paused. 'Yes, I have seen evidence of it. He was defeated by fire and the sword of the greatest warrior ever to walk the face of the Earth. So if you are willing to match your strength and skill against him once more, you may yet destroy him.'

Soloman paused as a moaning wind moved through the surrounding forest and he lifted his eyes with a spectral gaze, watching it sway skeletal trees. His strength and skill and will stood balanced against death in the descending dark and he rose against it, summoning his heart, his life, all he was, for a final act. He bowed his head.

'Make arrangements for the church,' he said and turned to see Amy through a window, smiling, all fear forgotten. *Such a beautiful place to be.* He watched over her a long time, felt the smile on his face. But when he looked again at the priest his aspect altered instantly, frightening even Marcelle. His voice was deathly cold.

'You just make damn sure I've got room to kill that thing,' he said.

◆ ◆ ◆

Halcrouth Sanitorium was shrouded in a tenebrous, dreary, unnaturally still night as Dr Felix Dubin drove through the guarded front gate, rising along wet cobblestones to approach the rear of the building. He parked and exited, absently noticing an ominous fog moving slowly, coldly across the finely manicured lawn.

Low clouds and mist made the sanitorium seem isolated and alone in the world. And, despite being a man of science, Dr Dubin felt an icy, disturbing sensation, a chill that closed over him with an aspect at once desolate and terrible.

Watching over his shoulder, he unlocked the door and shut it fast against the night, staring with strange fear at the gathering. He could not understand his racing heart, the horror that had come so quickly.

But after a moment, with the door locked, he took a deeper breath that didn't disintegrate within him. Slowly feeling more like a scientist than a superstitious old man, he calmed himself measure by measure and walked down a shadowed hallway, attempting to ignore the fact that his hands were trembling.

Many patients were on his list tonight, all of them fortunate recipients of free plastic surgery from physicians who, out of compassion, had donated their time and skill to correct severe disfigurement. Most of them were battered women who had been horribly scarred by abusive husbands, women that had lived for years in hopeless pain. And Dubin felt great pleasure in his most benevolent enterprise, knowing it was rare that such a project was successfully undertaken.

And further, most of them were indigent – sad products of broken homes and dysfunctional families that married too early or wrongly. Fortunately, though, many of the broken cheeks and eye sockets, the sunken chins and dislocated jaws, had been repairable.

Yes, correcting the cruel disfigurements had been the most satisfying project of Dubin's life, for it provided him with the extreme pleasure of donating his extraordinary skills to help those who truly needed help, those who truly appreciated it. It was so much more satisfying than the narcissistic enhancement of wealthy patients who already possessed beauty but only wanted more, never finding in the flesh what their souls alone could provide. Smiling, he forgot the night as he moved down the hall where –

A wounded moan liquefied his heart, an instinctive fear that adrenalized his entire system at once, and he stared about himself, gazing numbly at dim shadows of carnage, unable to understand. It required a single, surreal moment for his mind to begin …

He saw mutilated patients in bloody gowns, their twisted bodies sprawled along an interior lobby. And for a moment he wondered if there had been a horrible accident before he knew somehow that it was something else, yes, something else that –

But what could have …

He couldn't understand and searched to see his last patient moaning in blinding pain, still conscious and knowing all too clearly what had happened to her. He groaned at the sight, for he had meticulously worked for seventeen hours to repair that jaw, now brutally shattered once more. He staggered in shock as he turned to see another, and another.

What remained of her cheek hung crooked on her face. Her eyes, so beautifully rebuilt to her tear-stained pleasure, were savagely gouged, leaving only bloody sockets. And then another was vividly before him, and another, piece by piece taken but still alive with the moaning horror of what had been stolen, cursed that for a few brief moments they had been beautiful as the rest.

Appalled, moaning, Dubin gazed at the horror, barely noticing the dead security guards, the unmoving forms of nightshift personnel. Then he shouted at a death-cold laugh and whirled to see a monstrous, manlike *thing* standing in shadow.

The gigantic shape did not move, and seemed

somehow disfigured. The head was bald, red in the faint light, and peeling. Its hands were like long black talons, curling with a slow, horrible pleasure.

'I have improved on your work, Doctor,' it laughed.

'What ... what have you done?' Dubin shouted, and this awakened screaming in the room from those who now realized he had come. They cried desperately to him as he tried to ignore the tragic chorus, knowing that the shape had caused this horror.

'You ruined what I created.' The thing smiled, shaking its bald head. 'Did you not respect my artistry? Did you not appreciate the beauty of my hands? How ... arrogant of you.'

'*Madman!*' Dubin shouted, instinctively backing. 'You ... *you would do this?* What kind of ... what kind of *beast* are you that you would do this!'

'Oh, Doctor, I am only ... a pilgrim.'

It stepped from the wall and Dubin saw a fire-scarred, cadaverous face with skin falling in blackened folds. Then another laugh rumbled forth and Dubin, struck with fear, backed away shocked that a man so severely injured could still be alive.

'Do not fear for me, Doctor,' the man whispered, seeing his expression. 'By morning, if I continue to feast upon this delicious sustenance that you have provided, I will be whole again. These' – he gestured vaguely to his face and chest – 'are only a nuisance. In the morning, yes, I shall leave your silent sanitorium to rest in peace.' He smiled. 'With you.'

Dubin screamed as he spun and ran with such speed that he startled even himself, sailing fast and low as he leaped frantically over broken bodies, fleeing toward the wide double doors of the lobby.

Wildly he glanced back and glimpsed his own shadow racing along the wall, horrified to madness as he saw the gigantic shadow already upon him in a roar of laughter, an arm raised high and descending toward his head to –

◆ ◆ ◆

'We're gonna trap Cain in a killing zone and cut him to pieces.' Soloman frowned, glaring viciously at a map. 'Nothing that ever lived could survive this. Nothing.'

Malo nodded with murderous pleasure. Clearly, the thought of trapping Cain in a swamp where two AH-64 Apache gunships could open up on him with mini-cannons, blasting him limb from limb in a merciless holocaust of flesh, had touched his heart.

They were in the soundproof interrogation room of the safehouse, having excused themselves from Maggie and Amy under the pretense of delayed after-incident paperwork.

'It looks like a good plan, Colonel,' Malo replied, stroking his black beard. 'But how do you know he'll come? This thing is smart. He might suspect a trap. And it ain't gonna be easy to conceal a couple of gunships at a church.' He grunted, leaning back. 'In fact, it's going to be impossible. We're gonna have to deck 'em in nearby fields and activate 'em when it hits the fan. And when they tilt, they'd better come in hot or they won't find anything at that basilica but a bunch of dead bodies.'

'That's ... a complication,' Soloman muttered. He had come fully into a fighting mode, committed and merciless, everything else forgotten. 'All right, to compensate we're going to need cloaked surveillance.' He looked up sharply. 'And I mean *cloaked*, Malo. Underground sniper bunkers close to the church or every man concealed behind stone with angled vision equipment. And I don't want anybody to even be *near* an entrance. I don't want Cain to catch any heat signatures.'

Still stroking his beard, Malo nodded.

'Another thing,' Soloman continued. 'I don't want snipers on regular issue Remingtons. I want 'em on Weatherby H and H .300 Magnums. I want 'em on elephant guns.' He frowned. 'A four-hundred-grain round going four thousand feet per second oughta take a little steam out of his stride.'

'And if we don't see him coming?' Malo leaned back. 'What if he steals an armored truck and just drives it through the front of the church? It's been done before, you know. And if that happens, Colonel, we're going to be fighting face-to-face with that thing.' His face revealed a reluctant fear. 'That's likely to be a situation, sir. Unless we just blow the whole building with a ton of C-4 and take him out with us.'

'That's always an option,' Soloman said without hesitation, glancing up as he sat. 'But we'll have to get Amy and Maggie airborne before we bring it down.'

'How are we gonna work that?'

Soloman took his time to reply. 'Like this. We'll have a Loach heated up in the front courtyard. Marcelle has drawn a blueprint.' He tossed it over. 'It's a good idea because Cain will expect to see a chopper. He'll probably be suspicious if he doesn't. Then, once we paint him with lasers, I want that kid airborne. Immediately.' His face reflected intense concentration. 'This is what I want you to do. Take one of the slicks to LAX and get airborne in the Nightcat. Have a dozen topographical maps of this quadrant teletyped to you in flight. And make sure you classify it by the Trinity Mandate. Use the code. You'll reach Bragg by 0300 and I'll cut orders to acquisition everything you'll need. You'll have flight command with nav-scan coordinates pre-programmed into a Jet Ranger. It has a top speed of 210, so you should get to the church inside an hour. Then, when you're on the ground, set up concealed heat sensors, motion detectors, everything you've got.

Two hundred yards out or better. I don't want a mouse to be able to get through. But don't set up claymores. This is an isolated civilian forest, but it's not uninhabited. And I don't want some kid wandering by to get his head blown off. Then design a field of fire. Assign each man a zone, crossing them in pipelines. After that, conceal the AH-64s. Hawken will authorize full arsenals. And last, wire the columns of the church with enough C-4 to make it distant history. Take five of the men, leave two with me. I'll meet you there at 1500 tomorrow with Amy, Maggie, the old nun, and the priest.'

Malo nodded. 'Like I said, it sounds like a good plan, Colonel. And no disrespect intended, sir, but this is going to be a ton of work. Why do you have to stay here? We got trouble?'

'Yeah,' Soloman muttered. 'A little, I think. Ben was called to an emergency meeting of the "curs." And I've got to stay here until he gets back. Then I'm gonna fly us to LAX and we'll catch a rented Lear to Bragg where I've acquisitioned a fully-armed Loach. It'll have a minigun and two air-to-ground ARMs. I'll drop Amy and Ben and Maggie off at the church at 1500 hours and get to the New York Museum of Natural History by tomorrow night to set up a trap for Cain. I've got to leave something with that second manuscript that will lead him to us. After I do that, I'll boogie back and we'll lay up for him.'

A grimace revealed what Malo thought. 'You're going up against him alone, Colonel? I don't think that's a good tactic, sir. No disrespect intended, but the last time you went up against this guy he almost tore off your head and shut down your –'

'I don't plan on a fight,' Soloman interrupted. 'I'm just going to set up a trap that will lead him to us.' He paused. 'Listen, Malo. We probably don't have much time. If my political ass-kissing instincts are correct,

Ben is taking a serious beating right now. There's too much collateral damage, which in this case means too much media attention. I know they're getting pieces of it, probably from the police, who know everything anyway. If I'm right, we're gonna have one more shot at this guy before they reassign us and we're history.'

'One more shot is all we should need, sir.'

Soloman took a moment to study the grim image of the Delta sergeant. 'You be careful, Malo,' he said. 'This is going to get hot. And I don't want to see any of my men killed.'

Malo glanced away, as if he could all too clearly envision the possibility. He said nothing as Soloman, frowning, abruptly rolled the maps, a subtle move that brought them back to familiar territory.

'Take all the C-4 Bragg has in stock,' Soloman said as he handed over the scrolls. 'And tell those Apache cowboys that I want them firing as soon as they get a visual.'

'Yes, sir.'

The Delta commando walked away.

'Hey, Malo.' The big man turned, waited. 'You think we've got everything covered?'

'As covered as it can get, Colonel.' Malo's voice was solemn. 'But this thing ain't human. It can't even spell human. And it's like an amateur; there's no way to anticipate a line of attack.'

A moment.

'What do you think our chances are?'

'What do I think?' The Delta sergeant returned the question, pausing. 'I think we're in for a hell of a fight, sir.'

◆ ◆ ◆

'You're crazy!' Maggie shouted, glaring at Soloman.

'You think I'm going to let them use my daughter as *bait!*'

Soloman raised his hands for calm. He was glad he'd waited for Amy to go to bed before he brought the plan to Maggie; the child couldn't hear a sound in the steel-reinforced bedroom.

Maggie paced violently, a hand held to her forehead as if she absolutely could not *believe* that he had presented the idea.

'Maggie,' he began, 'listen to me for a –'

'No!' She pressed a finger against his chest. 'No! You listen to me! I agreed to work with you to find and kill this thing! And I've done my job! But my daughter isn't part of it! And I'm *not* going to let her be used as some sort of … of *alligator* bait thrown into a swamp with a rope around her waist just so Cain can be lured out of hiding!'

Soloman shook his head as she stepped closer, speaking more deliberately. 'Just tell me something, Sol,' she continued. 'How close did Cain come to beating you last time?' She raised two fingers and held them slightly apart. 'This close, Sol. This close. You only beat him because Malo arrived with the team. If you hadn't been lucky, Cain would have torn you to shreds.'

'Maggie, I –'

'What?' She stared. 'What were you going to say? That this is the only way to lure Cain out of hiding?' Stoic, Soloman said nothing. 'Well, I don't think so!' she continued. 'There's got to be a better way than using a *six-year-old child* to –'

It was enough.

'Maggie!' Soloman grabbed her by the shoulders. 'Listen to me! Cain is going to find Amy! He *will* find her because we can't protect her forever! Do you want her to live in a prison the rest of her life? No! You don't! You want Cain dead and she's the only thing that will bring him out! Listen to me! I can kill him but you've got to go with my plan! You have to go with my plan if you want me to kill him!'

Her face went ice-cold.

Soloman was grim.

After a moment she shook her head, speaking softly. 'If you get my daughter killed, Sol, I'll die. I'll ... just die. She's all I've got in this life.' She began crying. 'She's all I've got ... '

He stared down. 'The only way Cain is getting to Amy is over both our dead bodies,' he said.

A long silence, a stare, joined them. Then she relaxed slightly, settling her face into Soloman's chest as he wrapped his arms around her. Gently, she placed a hand on his chest, breathing deeply, settling. And Soloman held her, waiting. When she finally spoke, he could barely hear it.

'I know I created this thing, Sol. I know that ... the guilt is mine. But she's all I've got. She's all I'll ever have.'

'There's no guilt, Maggie.' Soloman swayed gently. 'You did what they told you to do. It's not your fault.'

'It wasn't right,' she whispered.

'Just trust me,' Soloman said quietly to the side of her face. 'I'm not going to let him get to her. I promise.' He waited as the intimate closeness and silence and affection communicated what words never could. Her breath was warm on his chest.

Peace settled.

'You'll die for this?' she asked.

Gently, he lifted her face.

'I'll die for you,' he whispered. 'I'll die for Amy.'

CHAPTER 15

Maggie came into the room where Soloman was studying a blueprint of the basilica, waiting for Ben's return. She leaned against the wall, crossed her arms over her chest, and smiled. She had obviously recovered from their earlier confrontation.

'What?' said Soloman, feeling like he'd been caught doing something he shouldn't. But Maggie only continued to gaze in smiling silence as he repeated it: *'What?'*

'Amy wants you to put her to bed.' She laughed, jade-green eyes gleaming. She was clearly enjoying it. 'You want me to tell her that you're too busy?'

Blinking, Soloman looked at the maps but didn't see anything. He was a little amazed at how things were changing and, though he could have controlled the feeling, he was also somehow drawn to it. 'No,' he said. 'I'll do it. But it's been a long time.' He tried to remember. 'Does she say prayers? What's the routine?'

Maggie laughed again. 'She just wants you to put her to bed, Sol. It's not that complicated. Just go and tuck her in.'

'Yeah,' Soloman said, rising from the table. He walked past Maggie, sensing only the glowing face, the smiling eyes. Then he was at the room where Amy lay in bed, quilts already tucked tight. Uncomfortable, he stood for a moment in the doorway, staring until she silently raised her hand, motioning him to come forward. Approaching, he tried to have the composure of an adult.

'I thought you might want to say goodnight to me,' Amy said quietly.

'Why, of course I did.' He smiled, sitting with casual smoothness and adjusting the quilts, returning by long-unused reflex to another part of himself that had been utterly dead until now.

And in the moment it seemed as if he'd never been in the desert at all, as if he'd been right here through it all. 'Thanks for playing Monopoly with me,' Amy added, her face serious. 'That was nice.'

Soloman smiled warmly. 'Oh, I had fun, Amy.' He was surprisingly comfortable with closeness, leaning on an arm. But he wished he wasn't laden down with weapons. The pistol on his chest felt out of place and intrusive. 'We'll do it again,' he said. 'Maybe tomorrow.'

She said nothing for a long time, finally laying a hand on his.

'You know something?' she whispered.

'What?'

'I never ... had a daddy.'

Soloman didn't know what to say. He held her hand lightly. 'Yeah, well, you're gonna be just fine, kid,' he whispered, compassion compelling him to look her in the eyes; no matter his pain; it would have been cruel to do any less. 'I'm not going to let anybody hurt you. I'll be here all night, and I'll be here when you wake up in the morning.'

Suddenly a tear rolled down her face and she became infinitely, infinitely sad. It was a moment that changed everything. Soloman leaned forward, gently wiping it from her face. He hovered close.

'Don't worry about it, darlin',' he said softly. 'He's not going to get to you. I'll protect you.'

'I hope so,' she whispered.

Another tear fell as she closed her eyes and whimpered.

Soloman's teeth clenched and before he knew what he was doing he'd lifted her, holding her tightly as she cried into his chest, so afraid. Silent, he wrapped his arms around her to comfort her. Then he laid her down, everything slow and natural, both of them comfortable. After a moment she closed her eyes and rolled to the side, relaxing.

Like that, it was over.

Soloman sat beside her to let her know he was going to be close, resting a hand on her shoulder. Then he lowered it to the bed as he realized that life, as he had known it for so long, would never be the same. There had been something shared, and it couldn't be taken back.

When her breaths were deep and rhythmic – the breaths of a child who'd finally fallen asleep – he rose, careful not to disturb her, and moved toward the door. He paused to glance at her once more, assuring himself that she was fast asleep. He was careful to leave a light on, should she awaken.

◆ ◆ ◆

Deep beneath the Earth, they convened.

Archette waited at the foot of the table, beholding each pale countenance. Six wore the rich scarlet robes that signified their exalted rank. But Lazarus wore a robe of the purest white with a single gold eye intricately embroidered on the chest.

Moving his arms to adjust the luxurious folds, Lazarus lowered his head at Archette, who had come as soon as he had returned from Los Angeles because Lazarus despised impersonal communication. Furtive for a moment, Archette glanced about and saw none of the black-cloaked bodyguards, but the shadows were thick in the far reaches of the cavern.

'And?' Lazarus asked in a threatening tone.

'And, so, it is almost finished,' Archette replied steadily, gathering himself before the feel of such power. 'Soloman has only forty-eight hours to complete the mission. But he cannot complete it in so short a time, I assure you. He has been eliminated, as I promised.'

Nothing could be read in Lazarus's burning black eyes, and the rest of the Family turned to gaze at the inhuman, coldly composed figure. For a long time there was silence, and then a reply.

'Remember ... ,' he said. 'Remember whom you serve, Archette. Your earlier errors were grave, but redeemable.' He paused. 'We are not as the rest, my son. We do not dream empty dreams. Our power is real. Our purposes are laid deep, and brought to substance. And our will is the stuff of life. We have held the secrets, and the power, within the Family for five hundred years, building empire upon empire. And we share our knowledge only with a cherished few. You are welcome ... once more.'

The torches crackled. 'Come closer,' Lazarus said.

Nervously relieved, Archette moved closer, glancing at the surrounding faces, feeling himself forgiven. He had failed in the experiment, yes, failed by releasing the Master before the transformation was complete. Before they could prepare him and the way. But he had justified himself by also eliminating Soloman, so ... perhaps ...

Lazarus continued in a low voice.

'Your redemption is almost complete.' He folded hands before his face, contemplative. 'But now you must find our Lord. Or he must somehow remember, and find us.'

'Of course,' Archette said, and began to thirst ...

'You will be rewarded,' Lazarus said with no tone. And as he rose Archette could taste the delicious pleasure, the rapturous night that had vividly emerged before him. Just as he knew that the power long cultivated would not be taken from him.

Lazarus gestured, turning into the darkness.

'Tonight you shall possess your dreams,' he murmured.

◆ ◆ ◆

At midnight Ben returned. He appeared disheveled and pale and surprisingly haggard for someone of such prosperous proportions. He also appeared to have suffered distinctly unsettling stress, his sweat-slick forehead glistening in the light of the kitchen.

As he passed Soloman and Maggie he waved dismissively, in no mood to speak. Then, with the direct purpose of a man who seriously needs a drink but has held off too long, he headed for the cabinet above the sink.

'Is Amy asleep?' he whispered, opening the cabinet.

Soloman smiled. 'Yeah, Ben, she's asleep. Go ahead and pour yourself one.' He looked at Maggie and she nodded, pushed back her bangs. 'And pour one for each of us.'

Ben mixed a small pitcher of vodka martinis, poured three glasses, and collapsed in a chair. He leaned back, loosening his tie with a fatigue that almost made Soloman laugh out loud. He waited until Ben took a heavy hit, watched while he shook his head slightly, as if he could still hear a host of attacking voices. Ben's mouth moved in a silent, obviously obscene reply to someone who was not there.

'So.' Soloman smiled. 'It went well?'

Ben muttered, 'But this is what happens when you work with a bunch of boot-licking pencil-pushers. Old

Bull, warrior that he is, stood like the Rock of Gibraltar. But he can't keep it up. That wreck on the bridge really set 'em off, boy. And that fiasco at the museum was almost too much, what with the destruction of twenty-five million dollars in irreplaceable art.' He was staggered. 'God Almighty, it was like the Inquisition. You should have heard Blake Hollman, the NSA guy.' He attempted a broad imitation, ' "Who the hell's gonna pay for it? The city? No! The Army? Hell, no! The State Department? Good luck!" ' He paused. 'I told him that I didn't know and I didn't care but it sure as hell wasn't gonna be me. Then they started in on the rest of it. Seven dead soldiers, each with a million dollars' worth of training, a seriously pissed off Los Angeles Police Department which, by the way, can kiss my freckled butt. And the fact that this wholesale media orgy over a bunch of mutilated bodies is about to reach an orgasm that's gonna make blood run out their ears and curl their toes up over their knees.'

'You're going to be all right, Ben,' Solomon said, winking. 'I think we've come up with a plan to lure Cain out of hiding. With any luck, we'll get him trapped in a free-fire zone with two AH-64s that'll open up on him with miniguns. We'll pump the cycle to four thousand rounds a minute and just let 'em go.' He raised his glass in a toast. 'Fire at will, boys.'

'Are you kidding?' Ben stared.

'Nope.'

'You're serious?'

'Yep.'

'You really think you can kill him with this?'

'Yeah.'

'Jesus.'

Soloman laughed.

'But,' Ben stammered, '… but when did you come up with it? Why didn't you tell me about –'

'We didn't come up with it until after you left,'

Soloman answered. 'But it's a good plan. Malo and five of the men are in Warwick, New York. It's about sixty miles from the city. There's an abandoned basilica there surrounded by about two thousand feet of swamp. When Cain comes for the manuscript at the Museum of Natural History, which he will, we're going to leave him clues as to the location of Amy. Then, I think, he'll come for her.' Soloman paused at Ben's abruptly deadened gaze. 'We're going to use Amy as bait, Ben.'

Ben looked at Maggie Milton. She nodded, cupping the martini tightly in her hands. And when he regarded Soloman again he seemed to have trouble coming to terms with the concept.

'Sol, maybe we ought to think about this.'

'It's a good plan, Ben.'

'Well, maybe. But they think you've already pushed this thing too far into the daylight. And ... and I'm not sure that I disagree with them. That stunt at the museum ...'

'I know,' Soloman agreed. 'I pushed it. But this is a solid plan, Ben. We can catch this guy in the open and liquefy him. And Amy's not even going to be there when the shooting starts.'

Only silence answered, a sea of silence that no one seemed eager to break. Ben stared at his already empty glass, unhesitatingly poured himself another. 'You really think it'll work? I mean, this SOB ... he ain't human, Sol. Jesus, I don't know what he is. And if there's more collateral damage, we're finished. As it is, they're only giving us forty-eight hours to take our best shot.'

With a weary sigh Soloman lowered his eyes. He had expected that. 'Yeah, there's some unknowns. But there's always going to be unknowns. Only one thing is certain. Cain won't stop looking for Amy, and he's not indestructible. Nothing is indestructible.' He took a slow sip. 'I'm gonna find how much the boy can take. Right down his throat.'

'Are we gonna stick with the team?'

'Yeah.'

'And the priest?'

'Is cover. The only complication is that we have to let Cain get to the second manuscript in the museum without getting anybody killed. We have to devise a way to associate her with it without arousing Cain's suspicions. 'Cause I want Cain to think he's got the advantage of surprise.' He grunted. 'Then I'm gonna give him the last surprise of his life.'

Ben warmed to the idea, or maybe it was the vodka. 'Yeah, it might work, Sol. But we have to –'

Emerging ghostlike from a nearby hall, Sister Mary Francis passed through the room, moving with silent strides toward the kitchen. Ben watched her walk past him with the most obvious disbelieving gaze, closed his eyes as he shook his head. 'Jesus, Sol ...'

'We might be able to use her, Ben,' Soloman replied blandly.

'But Sol, if you only knew what I've gone through today ...'

'What?'

'Don't worry about it.' Ben rubbed his eyes, leaning back to release a slow groan. 'Anyway, as I was saying before ... before the Vatican arrived, we're gonna have to have that perimeter covered like a blanket. I don't want that diabolical monster coming up my six.'

'Malo's taking care of it. He won't make any mistakes. But I'll double-check everything to make sure.'

'And then?'

'And then ... ' Soloman paused, gazing into the bottom of the empty glass. 'Then we'll send Cain back to wherever he came from.'

◆ ◆ ◆

Moonlight streamed through the curtained window.

Amy opened her eyes in the dark to see a silhouette kneeling beside her bed. The lean image did not move but her hands held something. Her head was bent but Amy knew it was the old nun, praying beside her.

For a long moment the figure was bowed, her eyes closed as her fingers began to move lightly over the object. And as Amy's eyes adjusted to the night she saw that she held a string of red and black beads, small silver beads separating them. There was a crucifix.

Then the old nun raised her head and opened her eyes, as if realizing Amy had come awake. For a long time they stared, and Amy was comforted by the kindness, the true love glowing in the pale face. Then with a small hand she reached out and touched the crucifix, lifting it slowly as the nun gazed in silence.

Jesus' head hung in death, eyes closed and arms stretched out in surrender, nailed to the sacrificial wood. His body, slender and silver, seemed ... so real.

Amy stared a long time, and then Mother Superior Mary Francis spoke softly. 'It is a crucifix.' She waited as Amy blinked. 'I have carried this one for many years. It has given me much comfort.'

'I've never seen one,' Amy whispered.

'It is the image of Jesus, our Lord, on the cross,' the old nun added in a stronger tone. 'But, of course, we know he is on the cross no more.'

'Where is he?'

'Why, he is with *you*, child!' Mary Francis laughed lightly, placing a warm hand on Amy's forehead, smoothing back her blond hair. 'He is always with you because he loves you!'

Amy focused on the crucifix. 'I'm scared.'

'Oh, Amy,' Mary Francis replied, 'always remember that you are never alone. He is with you, even in the darkness. All you have to do is pray, and he will comfort you.'

'If he loves me, then ... then why is he letting this happen to me?'

The old nun smiled gently, closing her hand over Amy's and the crucifix together. 'An enemy has done this, Amy. But he is a dog on a leash. Always remember that. A dog on a leash. He can only go so far, and no further.'

The crucifix was warm in Amy's hand.

'Does he really love me?'

The old nun's voice was close.

'Yes,' she said, smiling. 'More than life itself.'

◆ ◆ ◆

Soloman tried to sleep but couldn't, and some time before dawn he was awake again. He was amazed that he still had so much energy, considering how long he'd been on his feet. He'd forgotten how long the body can go without sleep, driven by adrenaline and insomnia and the ceaseless battle mind-set that comes in prolonged combat.

Stiffly he arose from the couch, tossing off a blanket to hear Ben snoring loudly in a recliner. And as he stood he felt the pain in his legs, his hips. His back was also tense, pained by each move. But he knew it wasn't from too much exertion; it was from a lack of it.

His legs were accustomed to ten miles a day over the dunes, his arms conditioned to pounding the heavybag until they fell limp at his sides, each muscle exhausted by the weights and blows. Yet for days now he had not truly used his body, save for the conflicts with Cain, and his body had reacted to it.

An image passed through Soloman's mind of a thoroughbred racehorse he once saw retired. The stallion, stabled until it could be transported to a pasture, was virtually crippled within three days, its legs swollen and stiff, almost unbendable. Its owners thought it was dying until the veterinarian told them to take it out and run it for a day. And, as he predicted, at the end of that day it was in peak condition again, the muscles sleek and strong, generating its own steam. The memory gave Soloman comfort; he knew there was nothing wrong with him but a lack of exercise.

On sore, stiff muscles he moved to the door, looking outside. Then he felt a chilled early morning fog swirling around him as he walked onto the front lawn, searching cautiously. He knew that it wasn't completely safe, but there was no way to exert energy inside the house.

When he was a few feet into the yard, the door safely closed behind him, he bent and stretched, trying to relieve the woodenness as he sensed a blood-red sun rising behind dark clouds. And he remembered the old lines: *Red sky at morning, sailors take warning.*

He cursed silently as he sensed a thickening of the thin air; a storm was coming. Then to release strength he moved with a kick, a punch, a combination of slowly hardening martial techniques that loosened him little by little. Within a few minutes he felt the blood flowing again, acute reflexes sharpening more and more, warming.

After ten minutes he was at it even harder and faster, coming into the flow while keeping his senses alive and alert to every surrounding sound, making his mind not only perform the movements with perfect balance and poise but heating his mind to catch every –

Owl's cry to ...

His fist struck hard into the air as –

Sky shadow against stars ...

He whirled and kicked, following with a spinning backhand to –

Wisp of wind ...

273

Over-reaching and correcting –
Forest falling quiet …
Punch and kick, spinning into –
Dewdrops rising …
He worked long, punching and kicking before –
Forest stillness …

Feeling all of it with merciless concentration, Soloman pushed himself to find the perfect angle, the last measure of skill in the moves, giving himself no respite, no rest between blows.

No …
No surrounding movement.

Grunts exploded from him as he whirled and struck, testing his body to see what it could really do, and he was savagely pleased, finding something in the moves that escaped him in rest. In another minute sweat was dropping heavily from his brow and still he didn't relent, throwing complex combinations of punches, imagining Cain in front of him, grunting as he hurled blows to tear down that bestial strength.

Finally he paused, breathing heavily, and maybe a bit too heavily. In days, he realized, he had lost endurance, his lungs lessening for the lack of constant conditioning. Then he resumed and in the midst of a combination of kicks and punches heard the front door whisper open. He spun to see a small figure standing in the frame, the steel panel vanishing behind her.

Amy.

Behind her, he saw Ben in the chair, snoring like a chainsaw.

Amy rubbed an eye with a fist, staring.

Soloman was moving toward her before she blinked twice, smiling gently so she wouldn't be afraid. And she seemed to know that he was about to usher her back inside. He mounted the steps, opened his mouth to speak.

'I don't want to go back inside, Soloman.' She blinked. 'I want to sit outside for a minute, if it's okay.'

Touched, Soloman gazed down, reaching out before he even knew what he was doing to gently remove a lock of hair from her blue eyes. And she didn't seem to mind as she smiled sleepily.

He placed a hand on her shoulder, amazed that he did. Then he turned to search the forest once more and saw nothing. He sniffed, found the scent of decayed leaves, green pine and forest borne on a soundless wind. He glanced into surrounding trees to see only shadows and bonelike branches hanging dead in cold air. No movement.

In his heart he knew that Cain had not found this place, yet. For if the beast had, he would have attacked; it was his nature. So there was no reason, really, except paranoia, to keep her inside. But he tried to ignore his affection for her in the decision. To maintain an optimum defense mode, he had to keep his mind as logical as possible. Yet he knew his decision was correct. *No, there was no harm in a few minutes …*

'Okay, Amy,' he said softly. 'Why don't we sit on the porch for a little while?' He smiled as he turned and sat. 'We can watch the sunrise until you get too cold.'

She sat down and wrapped her arms around her shins, knees below her face. She seemed sad and depressed as she stared out, and finally spoke. 'Thanks for talking to me last night. I was scared.'

He smiled, 'Any time, kid.'

He let her enjoy what she could while his eyes roamed, scanning without focusing, searching for distant movement because he knew he would discern movement before form. It was a technique he'd learned so long ago, in another life, but there was nothing there. And finally he sniffed, rubbing sweat from his eyes.

'Do you know karate?' she asked.

Soloman laughed. 'I pretend to.'

'It looks like you do.' She paused. 'I know kids at school who say they do, but I don't think they really do. I think they just like to say that.' She stared seriously. 'I'd like to learn karate one day. Would you teach me?'

Soloman suppressed a smile. 'Well, maybe when this is over I can show you a few things. It's easy, really. You'll probably pick it up in no time.'

'Did you?'

'Did I what?'

'Pick it up in no time?'

'Well, I probably didn't pick it up as fast as you will. But then you're a lot smarter than I was at your age.'

She paused. 'Really? 'Cause I think you're real smart. You don't treat me like a kid. Not like everyone else. And Mommy says you're smart. She says that we can trust you.'

Soloman hesitated, searching for the proper answer. 'Well, your mom's a real good person, Amy.' Then he sensed the direction of everything and sought to change it. 'But yeah, I'll teach you some karate when this is over. If you start studying when you're young, you'll be a lot better than I am when you reach my old, decrepit age.'

She smiled, and then it faded as she stared into his face. It was a disturbing moment for Soloman and he closed his eyes suddenly as his mind reached back. He looked away, searching the woods, concentrating. He had hoped that this wouldn't happen, but it had. And, in the moment, he felt something within him reaching out.

'Why did you save me in the tunnel?' she asked. 'I mean, why was it you, and not somebody else?'

A slow breath left Soloman. 'I just happened to reach you first, Amy. But one of us would have.' He smiled. 'We weren't going to let him hurt you. We'll never let him hurt you.'

'Mom says that she knows why.'

'Yeah?' Soloman grimaced. *Here it was.* 'So, uh, what does your mom say?'

'She says it was just meant to be.'

Wind carried the sounds of birds rising to the sun. Soloman wasn't sure if he could still see the forest or not. 'Well,' he replied, more calmly than he believed possible, 'like I said, your mother's a smart woman. But you never really know about those things.'

'Do you think she's right?' She seemed patient enough to wait forever. 'I mean, was it meant to be?'

Soloman revealed nothing as he focused again on the trees. He knew that this answer, more than any answer in a long time, had to be honest. 'Yeah, Amy,' he said, looking down. 'I think that it was probably meant to be.'

'I'm glad it was you.'

'You are, huh?' He laughed. 'Well, it's almost over. Pretty soon you'll be able to go back home. Back to school and your friends.'

'Are you my friend?' she asked.

Soloman was amazed at how the conversation kept getting out of hand. Every time he tried to put the lid on emotions, she effortlessly took it off again. He figured he wasn't going to win. 'Yeah,' he nodded, surrendering. 'We're friends. I think you're a great kid.'

'Did you ever have kids?'

Soloman was silent so long that he didn't even realize time anymore. Then he looked out, settling forward. 'Yeah, I had a kid … once. She was about your age. Smart, about like you. She was … a good little girl.'

Amy was silent a moment. 'Did she die?'

Soloman didn't blink, at the same time knowing it was remarkable. He looked down and spoke in his gentlest tone. 'What makes you say that? Why … why do you ask?'

'Because you said "was." ' She leaned forward, along-side him. 'You said she was my age. That made me think that she died.'

After a time, Soloman nodded. 'Yeah, Amy. She died. She died … in an accident.' And she seemed to know she'd approached something that hurt. Her voice had compassion.

'Do you miss her?'

Soloman smiled gently.

'Every moment.'

◆ ◆ ◆

Making arrangements for the trip to New York, Soloman finished off a late breakfast and walked into the living room to find Maggie resting in a recliner, emotionally fatigued from the ordeal.

Mother Superior Mary Francis and Amy were sitting knee to knee in the middle of the floor, playing a game that Soloman couldn't identify. He stared a moment, an MP-5 hanging loosely in his hand.

The old nun was weaving a web of string before Amy's mesmerized eyes, crossing finger over finger to build something complex and beautiful. And then after another moment she was finished, the loop crossed and recrossed to make an amazing architectural image.

Amy laughed. 'Is that Jacob's Ladder?'

'Yes!' the Mother Superior answered to Maggie's grateful smile; the real mother was finally resting. Sister Mary Francis continued, 'Do you think you can do it?'

'No!' Amy shook her head. 'It's too hard. I need to see it again.'

Mary Francis smiled as she stretched out the string, almost two feet of it tied in a circle, and began to cross her fingers again. Then in a few moments she'd wielded it, explaining it step by step. When she finished she held

Jacob's Ladder and Soloman stared with fascination at what, indeed, resembled a long ladder.

She handed the string to Amy. 'Now you do it,' she said with a curt nod. 'I want you to show me.'

'But I don't think I can do it.'

'None of us know what we can do until we try, Amy,' the old nun responded, with a shade of severity. 'Remember what you've learned, and go by it. Don't be afraid of failing. You can do it.'

Soloman stared with a strange nervousness as Amy studied the string. Then she reached out and grasped it, folding fingers carefully through the loop, beginning. He saw Amy glance at Mary Francis again and again, her blue eyes searching, and he began to worry.

Amy worked at it longer and longer, twisting the string only to fail. But she began again at the Mother Superior's patient instruction. And finally she pulled her hands sharply apart and it was there, a twisting maze of a ladder. With a soft laugh Soloman stood away from the wall, toward the Loach.

He didn't turn his head, but he felt Amy's smile.

◆ ◆ ◆

Ten hours later the Lear landed at Fort Bragg and Soloman was first off the jet, instructing Ben to obtain some decent food, if possible, for Amy and Maggie and Mary Francis. Then he was in a Humvee that delivered him to the Armory. He went hard through the door to see Chatwell waiting. He gave an excited salute.

'You got it, Sergeant?'

'Yes sir!' Chatwell responded. 'Got everything you asked for!'

Instantly Soloman lifted a cut-down M-79. The weapon, normally used as a grenade launcher, had been sawed off to sport a seven-inch barrel and pistolgrip to be, altogether, no more than twelve inches long. A makeshift holster fashioned out of a canteen holder with the bottom cut out and tightened was beside it. Soloman saw a row of forty-millimeter buckshot rounds, twenty of them, already inserted in a bandolier.

The buckshot rounds, fired from the cut-down weapon, had been one of the least-known and most lethal weapons ever utilized in the Vietnam conflict. It had been developed by Special Forces long-range reconnaissance teams that needed a weapon which could provide an instantly devastating response to ambush in thick foliage.

Discharged at an unseen enemy in a point-blank firefight, the seven-inch barrel spread the buckshot round into a twenty-foot pattern within a distance of fifteen yards, hurling two hundred .oo rounds downrange at once. It could vaporize undergrowth, simultaneously kill a dozen men in close formation, and be reloaded as quickly as a sawed-off shotgun. The only drawback was that it could fire only one round before reloading. But with that kind of impact, one round was usually enough.

Soloman smiled. 'Just like old times.'

'And I got that other thing you asked for, sir.' Chatwell lowered his voice conspiratorially as he reached into a bag and removed a large handgun. Soloman took it and broke it open. It was a Desert Eagle fifty-caliber automatic with a six-inch barrel and an overall length of ten inches. Ten fully loaded clips were beside it, each shell over an inch long.

'I hand-loaded the brass with Winchester 296 grain bullets and fast-burning Hodgdon 1110 power.' Chatwell was openly pleased with his work. 'Since that beast is gas-operated, you need fast-burning powder or it won't chamber. It'll stovepipe on you. But with that Hodgdon, you've got velocity of two thousand feet a second leaving the barrel and an impact of eighteen hundred pounds per square inch at twenty-five yards. I shot five hundred rounds through it yesterday and it chambered like a champ, so it's broke in real good.'

'You did good, Sergeant.' Soloman clapped him on the shoulder. 'You got the Loach rigged?'

'Yes sir. You've got an M-134 minigun on the port side and I've set the electric drive at four thousand rounds a minute, just like you said. It's got one of the new T-67 engines and an external fuel rack. Top speed is two-forty, range is two thousand miles nonstop. She's already fueled and on the deck.'

Soloman glanced up from reassembling the Desert Eagle and smiled. 'Chatwell, if I had a hundred men like you, we might have made the military worth something.'

'Somebody should have, sir.'

'Are the Apaches on standby?'

'Yes, sir. Malo has got them at a covert site some-where up north. He didn't say where they were going.'

'Okay.' Soloman loaded everything in a small duffle. 'We're airborne in an hour. Tell 'em to heat up the Loach in forty minutes. At thirteen-forty. Is there anything Malo told you to relay?'

'No, sir.' Chatwell's eyes gleamed. 'He seemed in a hurry to get out of here with that load of C-4. Said he had a hard tour before night. They was loaded down, sir. And I wish I coulda gone with 'em.' He paused. 'Colonel, you think that maybe I could –'

'No, Sergeant.' Soloman looked up. 'You've done your job and then some. And that leg of yours won't hold up in the field. I'm sorry. You're a good man and there's nobody I'd rather have beside me, but you're not in shape for this tour.'

Chatwell's fists clenched.

'Tell you what.' Soloman lifted his chin. 'Howsabout I bring you one of Cain's ears? Just for a souvenir.'

Chatwell's grizzled face beamed.

'That'd do just fine, sir.'

Agitation, or vivid fear, was etched on the face of the attendant as she opened the rear door of the cockpit. She stood in silence a moment, staring, until the captain, an older man with trimly cut white hair and a handsomely tanned face, turned.

The expansive display of instruments on the panel of the 757 glowed impressively in an array of yellow and green, every needle steady as they cruised from Los Angeles to New York.

'Yes, Vicki?' he asked.

'There's a … ,' she began.

Fell silent.

The captain's eyes narrowed. 'Yes? Is there a problem, Vicki? Are you all right?'

'There's …' She faltered. 'There's something on board the plane, sir.'

'Something?' he repeated with a bark of laughter. 'You mean we have a stowaway? Somebody doesn't have a boarding pass?'

She shook her head. Her mouth tightened.

Years of proficiency training had prepared the captain for almost any adverse dilemma and he had already unbuckled his seat, rising with a glance at the console, ensuring course and altitude and speed. He placed a finger on the autopilot to ensure that it was locked and glanced at the co-pilot, who was following the conversation with interest.

'Watch the console, Sam,' he said as he moved to the attendant.

'Yes, sir.'

The captain bent in front of the shorter flight attendant, speaking low. 'What is it, Vicki?' His tone indicated there was no place on a flight for a panic attack of any kind.

Remain calm. Always remain calm and go by procedure.

'I sent Bennington below to see if he could find another meal for a first-class passenger,' she said, trembling. 'And he ... he went down there. But when he came up ... well, there was something wrong with him, sir. We've had to lay him down.'

The captain turned to the co-pilot: 'I'm going below.'

'Yes, sir.'

He moved out the door and was in the attendant area within three minutes, where he saw Bennington, a male flight veteran of five years, lying on a makeshift cot. His eyes were wide and staring. Although attendants were speaking to him in soothing tones, he was uncommunicative.

'Here.' The captain moved the rest aside to bend over him, shaking him lightly. 'Bennington! What's wrong with you, son?'

No answer.

'Bennington! What's wrong with you? Are you sick?'

Vicki's voice trembled. 'Captain, he said something about an ... an animal in the cargo hold. He used the word ... "monster." '

The captain frowned. 'I see,' he said quietly. 'Has anyone been below to investigate?'

'No, sir.' The reply was quick. 'We didn't know what it could have been because we weren't sure what was inventoried. But I think we have a lion down there that we're transporting for the Bronx Zoo. We thought that maybe ... maybe it could have escaped from the cage and maybe ... maybe it's loose in the cargo hold.'

The captain glanced at the elevator.

'Yes.' He paused and concentrated. 'Ensure that the elevator is locked. I'll check the manifest. And no one else goes below for the rest of the flight. That's a standing order. We'll let security deal with it when we land at Kennedy. Keep Bennington warm.' He moved to the cabin. 'And make sure to advise me if there's any change in his status.'

'Yes, sir.'

◆ ◆ ◆

Deep in darkness, submerged in cold, he stared at the door that had just opened, the door where the man had stood. He should have remained silently submerged in shadow, he knew, but he could not resist the glorious expression of galactic rage that thundered from within. And in the moment of immeasurable hate and defiance, he had known it worth the pleasure.

Now, though, he regretted the act because it might lead others here and then he would be forced to abort his plan of stealth. He would have to kill them all, so many of them, and he didn't have time for that. He could risk no interruption of his master plan.

Five days ...

Five days – it was all he could remember about the incantation – until he must sacrifice the girl, opening the door that would allow him to re-create the full scope of his true glory. But fortunately he also knew the place where it must be done; the Castle of Calistro. And he knew he must still obtain a *Grimorium Verum*, for it would reveal the specific ritual, the ritual that could not be violated if he was to regain all he had lost.

Yes, the cosmic ritual was complex, and could not be violated.

And he could remember only one member of this continent's High Council, Archette, who must also be found so that he might consummate his plan. But there were other High Councils, he sensed, unknown even to this one, and he had to find those also.

Then there were principalities and powers that

served him in his world, empires already established that would eagerly deliver to him their wealth and influence as soon as they realized he had finally come. And yet he had to find their names, places.

So he must follow the ritual specified in the book. He must use the spell contained in the *Grimorium Verum* to cross the void and regain what he had possessed before he assumed this base form of atoms.

For that, he needed the child. He could use no other because she alone held the keys of this blood. Her blood, yes, was the seed of his, and life was in the blood, and he must have life in order to use her soul as a bridge, gazing once more upon the other side.

Although he was strong, he was only flesh, and not the same as these … these *sheep*. For they possessed what he could never possess: a soul, something that had not been created within him. Yet he could still claim what he would claim. He could still forge this world into his throne by the power that was his and his alone. It only required the knowledge that he had somehow lost in the chaotic merging.

Yes, only the child remained. Then he would once again be what he had been: Lord of the Earth.

He did not want this virus to destroy this world for he did not want a ravaged, ruined planet as his footstool. He did not want to inhabit a world as dead as hated Gehenna, a graveyard of broken stone and bleached bone. No, he wanted the living to produce their living, for the more that were living, the more dead he could gather within his flock.

The loss of the child pained him, rising in volcanic frustration that flamed to another dimension poisonous with stars that burned as black as those endless clouds of color had once burned, clouds that ran with blood from his righteous rebellion …

No, he snarled.

Never again.

He stood, glaring down to examine the extent of his healing. Slowly, clenching his fists in hate, he raised them before glowing red eyes, snarling at the strength.

Yes, he was perfect. As perfect as he had ever been. And then behind him there was the growl, as had so often been there during the flight. Without fear he turned, staring into the eyes of the lion.

Caged, it regarded him with distended fangs and a shuddering, guttural, bestial hate. Muscles, thick and coiling, bunched within the great shoulders and rolled along the flanks. Its hindlegs tensed as if it would attack him through the bars, and he lowered taloned hands to his sides.

'You think to challenge me?' He smiled. 'Yes ... of course you do. Because you are a creature of this hardened world that cannot even remember what once ruled it.' The smile faded as he saw something. 'You are nothing, beast. You are less than nothing. Not even your instinct can remember those that once trembled this world. You cannot remember the leviathans that rose above the crests of the cedars, or even your own ancestors ... who would have easily feasted on your bones.' With the words, he felt a savage thirst. 'Yes, who would have feasted ... as I will.'

The lion struck and he lashed out to grab the clawed foreleg, hauling the beast into the bars, defying the animal strength that surged wildly against him.

The lion screamed.

He laughed.

◆ ◆ ◆

When Delta Flight 349 from Los Angeles to New York landed at Kennedy Airport at 4:30 p.m., security personnel were immediately requested by the captain. Advised of the situation, trembling airport police armed with shotguns and backed by a formidable animal-control team summoned from the zoo cautiously opened the bay.

A search was carried out and the lion's cage was soon discovered, the steel door broken. But it took shocked security another minute to find the lion itself, gutted as if it had met a beast infinitely more savage, infinitely more powerful. And even more mesmerizing was the lack of any evidence of a struggle, as if the creature had been killed so quickly that it never struck a blow.

Its blood had been completely drained.

Ultimately, there was yet another mystery discovered: a titanium plate previously anchored to the wheelbase had been violently torn away and cast aside, providing an easy escape route for whoever – whatever – had so ferociously killed it.

◆ ◆ ◆

Archette exited the limousine that efficiently delivered him to his New York penthouse in the closest, darkest hours before dawn.

He inhabited a four-thousand-square-foot two-level expanse that offered a sweeping panorama of the city and Central Park, and he smiled silently to himself as he rose in the elevator.

His reward, yes, had been beyond measure.

He could barely remember the endless orgasmic pleasures of the night, such was its purity. Anything, anything at all, he knew, could be sacrificed for such pleasure. For it had been no illusion; it was real. The power of the Family made it flesh, and he felt no shame that he would go back to it again, and again, and again …

As he entered the apartment he saw that the security system was not activated and settled himself, pouring a sedative Scotch. Then he moved slowly to the tall picture window to gaze out, contemplative.

He had fought with such fierceness at the meeting in Los Angeles that he feared he had revealed himself, especially to Hawken. But he was avowed; he had committed himself as a member of the High Council, and so was committed to the risk.

He could barely remember how it had begun so long ago; how he'd been drawn deeper and deeper into that hidden world of shadowed majesty. But it was only when he discovered the Family that he had come to know the true meaning of power. And, knowing a world beyond this, he had avowed allegiance to the One who ruled from Darkness; He who offered unimaginable pleasure; He who could give them the Earth.

Utterly seduced, he found a life he never believed possible. It was incredible, he had thought, that such rapturous experience could have escaped him for so many years, and he had seized it at once, knowing also a rapidly orchestrated rise through the secret corridors of power, an ascent assured by his benefactors.

Then there had been the request for the experiment, and he had personally overseen it. He never truly believed that it would succeed, for it had been based on myth and legend. But it had, indeed, succeeded and now *He* was among them, and would soon –

He felt it before shadow or sound approached. And, bracing, Archette took a sobering sip of Scotch. Nor did he turn or tremble, as he had been warned. He waited a long time … to silence.

'Speak,' Archette said finally. 'I know you have come.'

Stillness; silence.

'Speak!' he repeated. 'I have summoned you! You must answer me!'

A laugh.

To reveal the measure of his calm, Archette raised the glass in a dead-steady hand. 'The Circle is in place,' he said. 'Kano can make the necessary arrangements. I will provide him with facilities so that you can consummate your plans, my Lord.' He straightened with a frown. 'Only remember our bargain! You must give what we covet!'

The presence drew closer.

Tightening against his will, Archette did not turn.

Then a galactic image was reflected in the window before him, silent behind his shoulder. It was dark-haired and lordly and imperial, gigantic in strength. Cloaked in black, it stared down over him. Black eyes gleamed in a strange, alien intelligence. Jaws glinted in pale light, fangs sharp even in shadow.

Ice cubes collided in Archette's glass.

'I ... I have made a covenant with you!' he continued. 'You owe me a debt! Is that not understood?'

'Mortals ...' It laughed. 'Always in debt.'

A trembling silence.

'I ... I promised that I would complete the experiment!' Archette gasped, suddenly gripping the glass with both hands. 'But none of us knew whether it would succeed! It was based on legend! On myth! I ... I never anticipated that it would be a success! But now you have come, my Lord! And the High Council is prepared! We ask only what was promised! For the power! For the world! Was it not your pledge? Will you now refuse us?' His hand clenched to still the shaking. 'Will you not honor your debt?'

A long silence.

'Your debt was paid ... so long ago,' it whispered. 'But you never knew.' It paused. 'Give me the place of Kano, for I need him. There is much to do before I can give what you so zealously crave.'

'Yes!' Archette whispered. 'We want to rule the world beneath you!'

'Of course,' it said, a tone of truest amusement. 'As you will. For are you not a member of the High

Council, my one true church? And yet, you have a weakness I cannot tolerate.'

'What ... what weakness?'

'You fear Soloman.'

'Soloman ... he is dangerous! He is not like the rest! He does not fear you! He ... he has already planned an ambush in this city! Our resources at Fort Bragg have verified it! Soloman will be landing by helicopter tonight in Central Park!'

'Soloman ... is only human.'

Archette stiffened. 'But we worked for years to set your empire in place! And Soloman hunted down everyone we recruited! So we began to fear! Something had to be done! No, no, my Lord, we could not let him stand between us and our deliverance!' On impulse Archette turned and stared into depthless black eyes, horrified beyond anything he had ever known –

Before knowing glory.

'We did it for you!' he gasped. 'We did it for you!'

A taloned hand settled on his shoulder.

A fanged smile fell.

'It was not in vain,' it whispered.

CHAPTER 16

It was a strange and lonely sight on this late afternoon in October.

The basilica – more like a medieval monastery – was isolated in the midst of a cold moor that stretched to distant, dead trees drowned in lifeless black water. It silently dominated the storm-clouded day, brooding massively on a skull-like hill, hauntingly out of time and place.

Soloman stood on the steps and stared out, resisting the despondent sensation inspired by the place. Concentrating, he studied what Malo had done until he was satisfied; he could see nothing.

There were no motion detectors visible among the distant waterlogged stumps and putrid sedge. And heat sensors located on each corner of the square, two-story edifice were shielded with black curtains.

Alone in the courtyard entrance, feeling the soundless dying of the day, Soloman felt like he'd stepped a hundred years back in time, to a world where places like this once commanded true respect, and power. A time when it was both an honor and a privilege to kneel on the stones, or pray inside the hard gray granite walls.

Behind him he heard hushed steps and turned to see Marcelle approaching, with Mother Superior Mary Francis at his side. Marcelle nodded curtly, all business, and Soloman returned the greeting.

'All is ready, Colonel,' he said, gesturing to the nun.

'Sister Mary Francis will attend to the needs of Amy and her mother while the rest of us wait for the inevitable. When will you be leaving for the museum?'

'In a moment,' Soloman responded, grim. 'It's only a twenty-minute flight and the museum doesn't close for another two hours. Cain won't be making a move until then.'

'They know that you are coming?'

'Yeah, they know.' Soloman turned to stare into the land surrounding the basilica, finding his tactical mode. 'Ben's been there for three hours preparing.'

Once again he studied the lay of the land and saw that there was only one reliable means of entry, a two-lane paved road that led past the church which Malo had wired, just in case. So if Cain didn't want to get cremated on the highway, he would be forced to use the swamp.

Malo had concealed the two Apaches, designed for tank killing, in a field near Sussex. The choppers could sweep in three minutes after activation. But until then they'd have to handle Cain themselves, and Soloman hoped they could pull it off. Three minutes could be a long time in a fight like this, and he was beginning to get a bad feeling, sensing he'd forgotten something.

He mentally reviewed it: Snipers were located in each tower, hidden from Cain's uncanny night vision by thick gray stone and curtain. Every approach was monitored visually and electronically, motion detectors set for height and heat sensors set to detect any atmospheric change.

Overall, Soloman reasoned, it seemed like a good plan. They might actually stand a chance here. At least as much of a chance as anyone could have in a standup fight with this thing. But he was still uneasy, unable to place what disturbed him. He shook his head, frustrated.

Mary Francis's eyes narrowed at the movement. She

spoke quietly. 'It is a place of ghosts, don't you think, Colonel?'

He slowly turned his head. Searched her eyes.

With a slow blink she stared once again over the desolation. She spoke. 'Yes, a place of memory, and regret. But also of redemption. Yes ... we should let the past ... claim its own penance.'

Soloman frowned, said nothing.

Her next words were a whisper as she turned away. 'But battles can also be fought ... and won ... by such things.'

Wordless, Soloman stared after her as she left, noting the demure demeanor, hands tucked into the plain black habit. She was so old, yet seemed to carry herself with such strength.

Marcelle walked up, hands behind his back. 'Sister Mary Francis has seen much in her lifetime, Colonel. Much of both evil and good. She does not frighten easily. In fact, sometimes I think she has too much faith for her own good. She is the rarest of all things, really.'

'What's that?'

'A genuinely holy person.'

Soloman looked at the priest. 'She knows a lot,' he said distantly. 'You know, if you had any sense, you'd both be out of here. Despite all that techno-crap, there's still a chance Cain can slip through.'

'Yes,' Marcelle replied calmly. 'But then I have taken a vow to protect the child, and I will stand beside her. We must all decide what we are willing to die for.' He gazed at Soloman. 'Or live for.'

Soloman was grim.

'The child has grown fond of you,' the priest continued casually, slowly removing a cigarette and lighting it. 'The fact that you have defended her has, in her mind, spoken more than words. She knows instinctively that true love requires sacrifice.' He paused, beginning something. 'You are a haunted man, Colonel. I can see it in your eyes, in your words, in everything you do. I do not know what haunts you, but I know it is the essence of what you are. And this, I think, is what makes you fight so fiercely. You do not fight only against Cain. You fight against what you are. Or what you have become.'

Soloman said nothing for a moment.

'You don't know anything about my past, Marcelle.'

'No,' the priest replied. 'I know only that you carry a great aura of sadness with you. And I perceive it is because of love, for love always brings the greatest sadness. But now I see hope in your actions. I see that the man has not died. That he hopes to live ... once more. For you, it is something I will pray for. Even as I have prayed for myself.'

Silent, Soloman glanced at the horizon. He saw the sun dying a slow death, heavy darkness solidly descending to shroud dead trees in an air of gloom, foreboding night.

He heard himself say, 'Do you think God really cares about any of this, Marcelle?'

Soloman half-expected a typical Jesuit response, something obscure and convoluted. It was the kind of question a sane person never asked because there was no way to truly answer.

Marcelle's black eyes glinted as he spoke.

'Yes, Colonel, I believe ... that he does truly care.'

Such simple words, but Soloman knew that Marcelle had spent thirty years dissecting the mystery, twisting his way through a labyrinth of questions surrounded by madmen and madness, endless suffering and despair.

No, not so simple.

Despite Soloman's awe at this affirmation of hope and faith, his expression remained unchanged.

'Take care of Amy until I get back,' he said, bending to retie his boots. 'Malo and the guys are on security, just keep Maggie and Amy calm. Mary Francis is good at that stuff. I'll be back as soon as I can.'

'They will be comfortable.'

Soloman lifted the Desert Eagle and walked outside the church to chamber a round, out of earshot of Amy. The Loach was heated up and he climbed in. As he strapped himself in, Marcelle stepped forward, his voice rising over the roar.

'There was a time when I did not believe, Soloman,' he called out. 'But I do believe … once more.'

Soloman paused, nodded. Then he lifted the chopper hard into night, casting a single glance to see the lonely black silhouette of Marcelle standing in the middle of a cold and dying land.

Believing what he believed.

◆ ◆ ◆

Marcelle moved inside the slate gray stones of the basilica as the Loach passed away over a lake of lifeless water, ascending quickly as the sun set.

Cold swept over the massive building at Soloman's departure, and when the priest finally closed the wide wooden doors against the chill he saw Sister Mary Francis serving hot tea to Maggie and Amy. He moved forward and in moments sat casually among them, calmly resting hands on his knees as Mary Francis poured him a cup. Maggie, regarding him with affection, asked, 'Has Soloman left for the museum?'

'Yes,' Marcelle answered without any hint of nervousness. 'He has gone to prepare the deception. But I believe that General Hawken has already been there for several hours, also making arrangements. They are being quite thorough, I think.'

She glanced at Amy. 'Will anyone be inside the museum when Cain comes for the book?'

'I believe that only Soloman will be inside the

museum,' Marcelle replied, confident. 'He intends to ensure that Cain is appropriately deceived. But he has advised me that he will take extreme precautions.' He nodded. 'Yes, Soloman is a very cautious man, a very wise man. He is prepared for every contingency.' He didn't even glance at Amy as he added, 'Yes, for certain, I believe that Soloman will be quite safe.'

Without reply Maggie sipped her tea, swallowing slowly with a distant but solemnly disturbed gaze. Whatever she pondered seemed to give her no comfort.

It was a moment before Amy, saying nothing, stared him directly in the face. He accepted her gaze, smiling slightly in response.

She didn't smile back.

With a hint of sadness Marcelle set his tea and cake on the table, placed his hands firmly on his knees, and sought to read every emotion that passed within the depths of the glistening blue eyes. He smiled, finally nodding.

'Yes, Amy,' he said quietly. 'I truly believe it.'

◆ ◆ ◆

Autumn wind howled over his batlike form, raising his cloak against the darkness like vast black wings as he crouched on a ledge of the Empire State Building, watching with a devil's patience.

And finally it arrived, coming like an armored locust from the west, descending as it neared to fall and fall into the midst of a pitched forest. Crimson eyes narrowing in rage, he watched it settle near a large lake of water, memorizing the location, and he waited another moment, allowing them to set their plan in place.

Mortal fools ...

You think you can defeat a god ...

He shook his head at the idea that they would even

think to defy him. He had been defied before, and somehow defeated. But he would not be defeated tonight. No, not tonight.

Tonight he would rewrite what was written, would add and subtract as the Almighty had cursed those who would dare. But he was already cursed, so he cared not.

Crouched like a massive, brooding gargoyle, he stared down from heights that could never near the heights he'd once ruled. His rage was pure. His intent was hot, bloodthirsting and murderous.

'Soloman,' he whispered, 'I come for you.'

◆ ◆ ◆

There was almost nowhere to land the Loach close to the museum but Soloman found a place beside Croton Reservoir and took a police escort down Central Park West to enter. He found Ben waiting in the lobby, sweat glistening on his forehead.

'Where's the chopper?' he asked.

'NYPD is guarding it at the reservoir,' Soloman answered. 'Have you finished?'

Ben nodded, swaying with excitement. 'Yeah, yeah, we did everything like you said. But they didn't cooperate easily, Sol. They didn't like us messing with their stuff. They were claiming that we didn't have any jurisdiction until the mayor called and told them to start cooperating. He really put the hoo-doo on 'em.'

Soloman laughed. He'd expected trouble; he just hadn't expected the mayor's office to be so cooperative. 'Why'd they do that?' he asked. 'Those clowns usually move like a glacier to cooperate on federal situations that involve the use of city materials.'

'The Cardinal, excuse me, *the* Cardinal, apparently made a few phone calls.' Ben lowered his voice. 'I think Marcelle's got some real serious pull, buddy. Where it *counts.*'

'I figure.' Soloman smiled. 'Let's get on with it.'

They moved quickly past a glossy display of European medieval armor and weapons and in minutes entered the ancient-literature section of the museum, a chamber dominated by a huge glass display case, which was empty.

A large note lay where the *Grimorium Verum* had been: *This ancient book of black magic, known for two thousand years as the Grimorium Verum, is not currently on display. It is being packaged for shipment to authorities.*

The note was dated today, obvious and glaring.

'Good enough,' Soloman said and they moved together through a nearby door marked 'Shipping Department.' Upon entering, Soloman saw that a single large table in the center had been totally cleared, leaving the book neatly enclosed in an airtight container sitting in the middle of the table as if the job could not be completed by day's end.

Beside the container were two notes. One specified that the book should be sent to Father Jacob Marcelle at the Basilica of St Angela in Warwick, New York. The second letter came from Soloman, via the Pentagon. It explained how to ship the book and the purpose of acquisition. Nothing too obvious, but it would be enough to indicate that both Soloman and Marcelle were involved.

Deep down, Soloman still didn't like it. But it had been the best he could come up with on the spur of the moment. He shook his head, whispering, 'This is a wildass plan, Ben.'

'You're telling *me*?' the general answered. 'We don't even know if Cain's gonna come for this thing! He could be in China by now!'

Soloman stood a moment. 'No,' he said quietly. 'He'll come. I can feel it.' A pause. 'And if he finds this, he'll come for Amy. Or me. He has to have ... his vengeance.' As much as vengeance, Soloman knew that for Cain this offered the best of both worlds, the chance to claim the *Grimorium Verum* and Amy together.

Despite his misgivings, Soloman knew it was worth the risk. They had no choice. If they didn't kill Cain now he was days away from killing the world. And, best case, if Maggie's calculations were wrong and the virus didn't mutate, then Cain would simply hunt Amy down until he found her. Then he would take her blood to make himself virtually without limitation, a physical god.

'Is that good enough, Sol?'

'It's all we can do.' Soloman checked his watch. 'Ten minutes until closing. Go ahead, Ben. Usher everybody out without causing any commotion. No unusual activity. Just make sure there's no one in the museum when the doors shut. Then hole up across the street with the FBI guys.'

'What are you gonna do?'

'I'm gonna wait for Cain.' Soloman's eyes narrowed as he searched the surrounding floor. 'I'm gonna hide somewhere inside this place and make sure he takes the bait.'

Nervously Ben licked his lips. 'Look, Sol, I don't mean to tell you your business because generals are just politicians, but if that son of a bitch senses that you're close to him, you're as good as dead. These FBI guys can't back you up if it all hits the fan and it goes tactical. Even the Delta guys got wiped out.'

Ignoring him, Soloman concentrated on the room. And finally Ben added, 'All right, Sol. Do what you have to do. But listen, buddy, be very, very careful. This guy is Death walking.'

Soloman clapped him on the shoulder. 'Don't worry about it, Ben. Cain's too smart not to find this. I'm just going to make sure that he does.'

'And you're sure he'll come for the kid?'

'Yeah.' Soloman frowned. 'But what he's gonna find is me.'

◆ ◆ ◆

Midnight.

Soloman had taken so many amphetamines to keep himself awake that he had trouble drawing breath. His heart seemed strained and his lungs ached with a strange painfulness that he couldn't correct, no matter how delicately he inhaled.

He was pushing the edge, he knew. This kind of overdose to stay awake could kill. And although he'd done this in the past, he no longer had the advantage of youth, and sensed that he'd used up that part of himself that had kept him above the line in the old days.

He had taken so many pills – three times more than usual – because he couldn't risk missing Cain's silent approach. He realized that the giant, as massive as he was, could move like a shadow and hear the slightest sound. So he had to remain vividly alert, despite the dangers of the drugs.

He released half a breath.

He was so tired, with a bone-deep fatigue that went beyond the physical. And as he leaned his head back against the wall of the closet he felt a wild panic about whether Cain would sense his presence beyond the small metal grate. But it was a risk he had to take; he was only grateful that he had brought the stimulants to keep himself on his feet.

Yeah, he thought, *something to keep an old man awake ...*

Time passed slowly on the artificial adrenaline rush and he wondered how life had brought him to this strange and bizarre place. Distantly, knowing he'd taken too much, and endured too much, he saw Lisa so cold, so horribly dead in his arms even as he remembered her love and laughter, the moods, the smiles.

He bowed his head, closing his eyes.

'My only child ...'

With a grim frown he resisted the pain that devoured his soul.

'Love of my life ...'

Then he remembered the job, the long hours away from home hunting rogue agents, dissecting intelligence reports to find the truth in a world of lies. It was a job he'd chosen because it had been his greatest skill, the one thing he could do better than anyone else. But it hadn't been worth the price he'd paid. No, nothing was worth that.

Nothing was worth life itself.

Then it came. The rush.

He was instantly alert, unmoving, unbreathing, watching and waiting and desperately calculating the distance of a sound he wasn't sure he had even heard. The amphetamine shakes vanished, vanquished by a control he didn't understand, hands suddenly and utterly still, sweating.

Ready.

In his right hand he held the cut-down M-79, a forty-millimeter buckshot round chambered. The Desert Eagle was in a low-ride holster attached to his thigh, four extra clips on his waist. And in his left hand he held a portable A-unit to communicate with Ben and the FBI team who were concealed in a building across the street.

Soloman knew that if it came down to a man-to-man fight, Cain would win because conventional weaponry, as Maggie had predicted, had little effect. Only a concentrated holocaust could take Cain down, and only then when it contained the brute force necessary to separate him limb from limb before that spectacular healing factor could repair the damage.

Shadow ...

Silence?

Shadow ...

Moving!

Soloman tilted his head aside from the grate, knowing Cain's heat-sensing abilities could easily detect his presence behind the steel mesh. He waited long and longer, maddeningly endless seconds before easing an eye back to the mesh to see a gigantic, black-cloaked shape standing silently before the empty display case.

Cain!

Silent as night, he'd come.

Watching the giant's back, Soloman saw that he appeared slightly ravaged from the earlier confrontation. Although he had obviously regained titanic proportions, evident through the long cloak descending from his mammoth shoulders, he also seemed somehow less formidable, as if the price paid for the fight at the museum had stolen a piece of his strength.

Soloman couldn't catch his breath as the giant lifted his fist to the side, clenching with unreal strength, trembling in rage. Then he saw Cain mechanically turn his head, searching, until he saw the door marked 'Shipping Department.' Without pause Cain approached the door and shredded the lock without effort, opening the steel panel.

Soloman waited a long time, sweating profusely, overcome with heat. Carefully he blew drops of perspiration from his lips and nose, knowing that if Cain somehow sensed his presence in the closet, the giant would simply open the door and kill him wholesale, weapons or not.

Then he heard the shipping door open again and glimpsed a shadow. His finger tightened on the trigger as he leaned back, preparing. It was only a fragment he saw as Cain passed the steel mesh, smiling faintly, and Soloman knew he had completed the deception. The fiend had found the *Grimorium Verum* and the letter, and would be coming for Amy. Soloman lightly released a withheld breath and then Cain's shadow ceased moving.

Mistake!

Leaning back, Soloman was instantly drenched with sweat.

That's impossible. He's more than forty feet away ...

Cain's imperial head bent, and even though the mammoth back was to him, Soloman could sense the hostile countenance scowling in concentration. Then Cain angled his head slightly, half the face suddenly visible, a gleam of a smile that somehow indicated Cain had been acutely searching for a hidden presence. But still he didn't look directly at the closet, as if debating the exact location of the whispered sound.

Soloman silently blinked sweat from his eyes. Clearly, Cain was becoming more certain, and Soloman could see a malignant eye narrowing, triumph evident in the devilish glare.

He was out of time.

Soloman quick-clicked back the hammers of both weapons, backing against the wall. He knew that he had to do something fast or die, and he shoved the semiauto in his belt, instantly withdrawing the A-unit.

He silenced the volume of the radio as Cain slowly advanced toward the door, and keyed the mike three times, and three more times. Then, sliding aside, he slipped behind a large stone statue of Buddha, crouching with the M-79 held close. He withdrew the Desert Eagle, holding both weapons close to his chest, ready to open fire.

He knew Ben and the rest of the FBI team were out front waiting for a message. And when they received it, they would be calling back fast and frantic. But if he didn't reply they would make an explosive entry, expecting him to be under attack.

Light vanished before the steel mesh.

Cain stood five feet away.

Darkness congealed as a living thing.

Only hard-gained combat skill gave Soloman enough control to withhold firing directly through the door. And he trembled as he held back, ready to spin and shoot straight into Cain's face as the panel opened. It would be his last move, he knew, because he didn't have enough ordnance to put him down for good. Though for certain, he knew he would do some damn serious damage before he died, just for spite.

The doorknob twisted, the lock shredded before absolutely irresistible strength. Then a blinding white edge of light lit the wall opposite Soloman as the portal slowly opened.

Soloman's fingers took all slack from the triggers. Sweat dripped from his face and he melted to the wall as the door opened wider, revealing an image that would have horrified Hell itself, cold wind sweeping beneath.

As darkness incarnate, the shadow burned into the wall and Cain's cloak lifted as if caressing, or commanding, the night. The beast took a single cautious stride, standing motionless in the opening, bending his head, searching. In surreal silence he moved slowly toward the Buddha.

'*Don't try to escape!*'

Cain spun, a volcanic curse erupting at the rush of men. Instantly he was running out the door and Soloman rose quickly to see him flash across the museum, caught the sounds of the FBI Special Response team taking frantic positions.

Soloman slammed the door back, pursuing hard as Cain approached a high night-light framed by the moon in a sloping roof. And then as Cain reached it he roared, leaping incredibly high and hard, hurling himself through the barrier and into the sky beyond.

A shower of shattered glass was blasted whitely

against moonlight, spread like ice, and then Cain's monstrous image descended, the black cloak lifting to ride the wind before he was gone. Escaping.

To darkness.

'*Damn*,' Soloman whispered, leaning against a wall, drenched in sweat. 'Damn ... damn ... that was ... *too close* ...'

Staggering from nervous fatigue, he fell to his knees, breathing heavily. Then with a tired sigh he lowered his weapons and from within some dark center of himself, beyond anything he had ever truly understood, he wondered if he could ever kill this thing.

CHAPTER 17

Archette's heart raced.

'He has come to me!' he said.

Erupting at the words, Lazarus was on his feet, shuddering with excitement before the saturnine face solidified in unbelievable control that locked down all emotion. Still, though, his fists clenched in the effort, pressing into the oak table as he bowed his shaved head.

'At last ... ,' he whispered. 'At last ... '

'What do I do?' Archette asked, swaying.

'Do whatever it is that he requires,' Lazarus said, after a moment. 'We will not contest his designs. Yes, give him anything. Everything. Did he ... did he mention *me?*'

Archette paused, opening his mouth. 'He ... he said that he needed Kano, Lazarus. I believe that he was too preoccupied with efforts to give such deserved, glorious credit to those who –'

'Hold!' Lazarus said in a suddenly frightening tone. 'You have not ascended enough to presume!' There was silence. 'Go! Take care of his needs! Does Kano know that He approaches?'

'I ... I have not been able to contact him,' Archette responded finally. 'I have been ensuring the failure of Soloman and his team! I have a meeting within the hour with the Trinity Council! My leaks about the massacre at the sanitorium and the experiment have destroyed

Bull and I am in charge. But I know that is not important. I will find him! I will find him tonight!'

'Then go!' Lazarus did not sit. 'For *He* is among us and we shall not disappoint! I myself will organize The Circle to protect him, should it please his design!'

Archette stood, open-mouthed.

'*Go!*' Lazarus's eyes blazed.

'*The Lord has come!*'

◆　◆　◆

Malo was the image of death as he leaned against a rampart, staring into the swamp. He held a bolt-action .300-caliber H and H magnum, the stock set on his hip. A large caliber semiauto was holstered against his thigh beneath a large bowie knife, and his face was painted black over the bushy black beard. His eyes were cold. He appeared patient and focused.

Soloman came up slowly. All of them were quiet together in the fear of something no one would admit. He spoke in a whisper though there was no reason to whisper: 'Anything?'

'No,' the big lieutenant responded without expression, not taking his eyes from the land before him. He frowned as he shook his head. 'But he's out there. I can smell him.'

Raising naval binoculars, Soloman studied the swamp. He swept the glass slowly, searching for shadow or movement, but found nothing in the overgrown mossy silence. Finally he set the binoculars on the rampart and leaned forward, frustrated.

'He's got to be out there,' he said quietly. 'Something's not right with this.'

'Like?'

'Like the fact that this thing is running out of time.' Soloman continued to search the swamp. 'He's only got four more days until Samhain, so he should have made a move by now.' He paused. 'This isn't right.'

It had been seventeen hours since Cain had taken the copy of the *Grimorium Verum* from the museum, vanishing into the night. And no genuine search had been initiated because Soloman didn't want another confrontation in the city, realizing it would only end in a bloodbath. Though for purposes of deception he'd allowed the FBI a brief stampede, knowing Cain would be suspicious if no one came after him. But Soloman only allowed enough activity to tell Cain that they were chasing him. Now, though, the real game had begun.

The Loach was fueled, ready to fly Amy and Maggie away as soon as they saw Cain coming. And every approach to the basilica was monitored. But still, something didn't feel right. It was as if the wind were carrying a threat that Soloman hadn't calculated. He spoke. 'You think we've covered everything?'

'As good as it can be covered,' the big lieutenant responded, chomping down suddenly on the nub of a cigar. 'He's gonna have to work his ass off to get through that perimeter. And, really, I don't think he can. We've been reading heat signals all day from mice to beavers, and we've followed all of 'em with checks to make sure it wasn't him. So we're tight.' He stared, disturbed despite his words. 'We should have our asses covered like a blanket.'

Soloman frowned at the moor. There was something there, he knew, something he'd missed. He didn't know what it was and the more he searched for it the more frustrated he became. He shook his head and turned away, speaking as he walked.

'If you see him, kill him.'

Malo tightened on the rifle, vengeful.

'Count on it.'

◆ ◆ ◆

A subterranean silence hung heavy inside the basilica, everyone seated and somber as Soloman came past the cryptic stone carvings and into the cathedral itself, struck by the surreal atmosphere. It was as if everyone were waiting to die, frightfully counting seconds.

Attempting to break the unnerving mood he lifted a cold sandwich from a plate, took a bite. Then in a masquerade of bravado he laid his rifle against the banister, taking a cup of coffee. He knew that everyone was watching him with keen interest.

With peripheral vision he saw Amy sitting far from the rest, her forearms wrapped around her shins. There was something infinitely sad in her composure, as if she had something she longed to give but no one could take. Mother Superior Mary Francis noticed his gaze as she settled another pot of coffee on an altar table.

'Her feelings run deep,' she said to Soloman. 'But she will not speak of them.'

Soloman studied the small, solitary figure, so sad and alone.

'Her mother tried to talk to her,' the Mother Superior added. 'Father Marcelle also tried. But she waits.'

'For what?' Soloman asked softly.

'Why don't you go to her, Colonel,' the old woman answered, 'and ask?'

Deciding before he realized he had made a decision, Soloman took his rifle and moved casually across the room, smiling comfortably as he neared, finally sitting. He didn't say anything for a long time, trying to comfort her with his presence alone as the minutes passed. When she finally spoke, her small, quiet voice almost startled him.

'I had a dream,' she said.

Soloman sensed her fear but he didn't say anything. In her own time, he knew, and in her own way, she would tell him. She didn't turn to him as she continued.

'It was a dog,' she said, eyes widening as if she could see it. 'It was big, and black, and it was on a chain. It was chasing me through the woods in the dark.' She paused. 'I ran as fast as I could, but then I was too scared to run any more, and it caught me. I was trying to hide in the bushes but it found me, and it was growling, and coming to me. It stepped into the bushes to get me and then ... then you were there.' She looked up. 'You were trying to save me, and you fought it. But the dog was stronger than you, and it hurt you. Then you grabbed it by its chain and killed it.'

Soloman felt a faint chill, watching the small face that looked so much older than it had seemed only two days ago.

'Then you picked me up and carried me home,' she said simply.

'Do you ... ever dream?' she asked.

Slowly, he nodded. 'Yeah,' he responded; he would not hide himself from such genuine affection. He had been hiding too long. 'Yeah, I dream. A lot.'

'What do you dream about?'

'About ... I guess ... I dream about my little girl.'

'Does she talk to you?'

'Yeah,' Soloman answered, not looking down again. 'Sometimes she talks to me, but I always talk first. She ... comes to me. She wants to be with me. But I'm too busy. I'm always trying to make a living, and things are really hard. Sometimes it's ... it's like I'm on the edge of a cliff, and I've only got a few more feet to go. But that's the hardest part of the climb. There's nothing to hold onto. There's nothing to grab, and the only thing that's going to get me over the edge is my determination, my courage, my skill, or strength, or whatever.' He hesitated, as if he could see it. 'I look down, and it's so far to fall if I fail, and I'm just hanging there, trying to get the courage to make the last move. But ... but I'm so scared.' His face twisted. 'And all she wants is to be with me. Such a simple thing. But … but I don't have time for her.'

Amy blinked, solemn.

'And she knows that I don't have time for her,' he added finally. 'I can see in her eyes. And she's hurt … but then she just smiles and says that she was only joking, or something like that. Says she's got important things to do, and runs off to play.' He wiped a corner of his eye. 'I turn my back on her and she just smiles, like she forgives me. Like it's all right. And she doesn't want much, really. She just wants us to be together. But I … I'm in this situation, and I don't know how to get out of it.'

Amy said nothing, and they were silent together. Then she reached over and laid a hand on his, not looking up.

'She knew,' she said quietly. 'She knew.'

Grimacing, Soloman gazed over the basilica, finally releasing a deep sigh. Then he looked down again and wrapped a strong arm around her shoulders. 'You're a good kid,' he said with a curt nod, silence following. 'You're gonna be just fine.'

'Are you proud of me?' she asked.

He took a second.

'Yeah,' he smiled. 'Like you were my own.'

◆ ◆ ◆

Soloman checked with Malo every fifteen minutes as night finally submerged the basilica in darkness. He paced the floor, narrowly containing his agitation that something was terribly wrong, and noticed that Amy, too, was becoming increasingly restless.

She fidgeted with this and that, refused to build Jacob's Ladder with Mother Superior Mary Francis, and refused to eat. And as the child grew more and more nervous it only fanned the flames of Soloman's intuition, as if they shared knowledge of some unseen threat.

Shaking his head in frustration, he radioed Malo again and again and the Delta lieutenant reported over and over that the scanners were stone-cold. But Soloman didn't like it at all. There was something wrong here, he could feel it.

Finally he walked to the front for another cup of coffee, still unable to place what it was. He noticed Amy coming up beside him, her face pale, almost white. She said nothing.

Soloman hesitated, sensing. 'What is it, Amy?'

A silent stare: *Fear*.

Soloman lowered the coffee. 'What is it, Amy?'

'I think he's here,' she said in a voice of someone who counts herself already dead.

Eyes narrowing in concentration, Soloman lifted his rifle. He glanced around the basilica before kneeling in front of her, trying to sense what she sensed. 'Why do you say that, darlin'?'

'I know him, Soloman. I just know … he's here.' Her conviction was complete. 'I know him, Soloman,' she added and fell silent, as if nothing more were needed.

Instantly Soloman rose and ordered another perimeter check, and every man responded that they detected nothing. There were no activations of motion detectors and heat sensors were negative. Then Soloman raised Malo and ordered a visual perimeter that also came back negative. But Soloman wasn't satisfied. Fiercely he glared at the door and knew that, somehow, she was right.

Cain was already here.

Soloman didn't know how and didn't care; the alarming sensation that they were already in undeclared mortal combat made the decision for him. He keyed the A-unit: 'Malo! Get down here! You're flying Amy out of this place right now! Execute! Execute! Execute!'

'But Colonel, I –'

'*Get your butt down here!*' Soloman shouted. 'Cain's already here!' He hustled Amy and Maggie toward the front door. 'Both of you are leaving! Malo's gonna fly you to another safehouse!'

They reached the door as Malo came down the stone steps, moving quickly. He glared at Soloman as if he'd lost his mind. 'How could he already be here?' he asked angrily. 'He'd have to *fly in* to break that perimeter!'

'I don't know,' Soloman answered as he pulled back the bolts on the door. 'But I think she's right. I think Cain is already here. I don't know how and I don't care. But he's inside this place.'

Malo moved out the door, swinging the rifle, searching. He came into the courtyard where the Loach rested and without hesitation he climbed into the seat, starting the rotors. In seconds the roar of the turbos dominated the night air, thundering over stone.

'Go!' Soloman pushed Amy and Maggie, searching high for any threatening image outlined against black ramparts. He saw nothing but his fear escalated second by second to an adrenaline rush. Whatever had ignited his instinct of danger was as confusing as the question of how Cain could have crossed that zone of destruction without tripping any –

Fly in?

Soloman turned, mouth opening in horror.

And knew.

Fear exploded as he stared a split-second.

Amy and Maggie were already belted and Malo began to lift as Soloman raised the A-unit to warn him when it happened *fast*.

As the Loach rose Soloman saw the back panel of the helicopter explode before a terrific impact and he moved, hurling the rifle aside as the chopper left the ground. Screams of horror erupted as Soloman leaped to narrowly catch a skid, grabbing with both hands as the chopper took him from the ground in a spiraling twist that wildly cleared the courtyard walls.

Thoughts flashed like lightning as Soloman saw it all; Cain sensing him inside the closet and understanding the deception, Cain falling through night knowing a trap was laid, Cain searching with fantastic strength and speed to find the chopper hidden so close to the museum, then using his superior night vision to cross the police perimeter to finally conceal himself behind the coach compartment, waiting … to be certain.

Soloman's boots struck stone as they cleared the crest of the courtyard wall and heard Malo bellow, a shot fired. Then he glimpsed the door opening above him and the big lieutenant was hurled into the night, an angry curse descending with him.

Soloman threw a leg over the rail as the Loach skimmed low over trees and knew Cain had taken control. He groaned with the savage effort required for climbing to the door and knew that Cain didn't yet sense his presence. But time and night were flying past with such speed there was no time to contemplate anything more. He had to move, and fast.

Almost losing control in the final frantic effort, Soloman reached up to grasp the handle of the passenger door, heard Amy and Maggie screaming and realized no plan could cope with this, no plan at all. He had to pull a face-to-face, had to dare a savage throwdown inside a helicopter flying a hundred miles an hour twenty feet above trees, and with the thought he drew the Desert Eagle, ripping open the hatch.

Soloman dove into the Loach and was horrified even in the blinding speed as a fanged face whirled toward him with a bestial roar, glaring red eyes blazing in rage.

Throwing out a massive arm, Cain struck him into the back but Soloman got off a round as he was hit, the Desert Eagle plowing a .50-caliber round deep into the beast's back and then he was fast-firing through the pilot seat, ten slugs blasting into Cain's torso and head.

Descending hard, the Loach soared amazingly through a stand of dead trees before Cain could correct the course, expertly raising the blades and axle to narrowly gain air. Then he reached out to grab Maggie, screaming and kicking, by the neck. He held her as easily as he would hold a doll and Soloman quickly exchanged clips, leveling again.

'*Enough, Soloman!*' Cain roared. 'Drop the weapon or she dies!'

Soloman pressed the barrel hard against Cain's temple. He leaned close, face-to-face, caught the stench of death. 'Tonight you're not taking any hostages, Cain!' he snarled. 'And I'm not taking any prisoners! Set it down and we'll settle it face-to-face!'

'You're a fool!'

Soloman pressed the barrel harder. 'I'll have them die by my hand before they die by yours!' He wrenched Cain's head. 'So set this down or I'll kill us all! You've got three seconds!'

Cain shook his head as he instantly angled the Loach, threading a narrow path between nightlit trees to find a landing zone as Soloman increased the pressure of the barrel.

No games now, no moves left to make. When this thing hit the ground he would be in the last fight of his life, and his mind scanned furiously for tactics. Then he saw a glade approaching, tall grass indicating solid ground. He tried to ignore the glaring knowledge that he'd just fired ten rounds into Cain and the giant wasn't even fazed.

'You're about to die, Soloman,' Cain growled. 'Then I will kill your woman!'

Soloman decided every factor in a heartbeat. He knew that he had to wait until the chopper hit the ground or they would be dead. And as the skids settled on the sedge his hand tightened on the grip of the Desert Eagle. He glanced down to ensure that the hammer was back and as Cain stepped out, turning with murderous talons to grapple, Soloman fired, sending a .50-caliber round directly into the forehead.

The tremendous concussion blasted the giant flat on his back and Soloman instantly leaped into the pilot seat to hit the rotor controls, wildly lifting the Loach. He cleared the ground as Cain cursed and rolled, leaping with volcanic velocity to snatch a single skid.

The great weight caused the helicopter to tilt madly, sending them spiraling across the glade toward a solid stand of trees, and at the sight Soloman knew they were about to die *now*. He threw the chopper into a hard collective pitch, tilting all the rotors at once.

At the violent movement the Loach ascended in an almost vertical lift, angling narrowly to clear the branches by a breath, sending them into a roaring and violent night.

Snarling, Cain clung to the skid, began climbing.

He grabbed Soloman's door to jerk it open and Soloman took a desperate second to kick out, slamming him away from the cockpit again and again, again and again, kicking and kicking, wild with rage. And with each savage kick he lost a measure of control, sending the Loach spinning. Yet he held altitude because he kept his hands on the tilt control and pitch, electrified by the fear that he couldn't free his hands for a shot.

'Take my gun and *shoot the damn thing!*' he screamed at Maggie and she instantly snatched the gun from his holster, aiming wildly over Soloman's body. She pulled the trigger and the enormous concussion, so close to Soloman's face, deafened and blinded him.

Stunned, he glared down to see Cain hit, blood erupting from his chest. And then Maggie emptied the rest of the clip as they sailed madly through trees and night, shells clattering in the madness of light and flame and noise to create an apocalyptic atmosphere in the helicopter.

There was nothing but battle here, Soloman knew. This was the place where courage ended, where madness ruled. The only way to survive was to become more savage than your opponent.

He threw the Loach into a downward tilt, aiming low for trees, and in seconds felt the massive impact. The skid tore a dead limb to lift it into night. Rotors tilting at the collision sent dead limbs whirling over them. And with a downward glance Soloman saw –

Cain still there.

Ravaged and wounded, Cain's face blazed with a wrath that made him seem utterly unconquerable. Eyes glaring at Soloman, he twisted savagely and slammed a hand into the cockpit, lifting himself. Knowing they were going to die if he didn't do something desperate, Soloman swept in four feet above the swamp, slowing to a crawl.

He screamed at Maggie. 'Get Amy and jump! Do it now! Do it now! It's only four feet to the water!' He caught a frightful glance of Cain. 'Hurry, Maggie! Do it now! Do it now!'

Soloman was livid as he watched Cain's horrifying climb.

Maggie didn't hesitate at all. As if understanding that it was their only chance she reached back and snatched Amy in a single violent move, clutching her tight in her arms. And in the next second, to Soloman's amazement, she threw open the hatch and without a glance hurled both of them into the night, descending to the water.

Cain roared in demoniacal glee as he rose, climbing closer to Soloman, and Soloman spun to glare at him, face-to-face.

For a single surreal instant they stared.

Cain laughed, red eyes narrowing.

He lifted a black-clawed hand to –

Soloman tore his hand from the rotor control to send the chopper into an oncoming impact with trees and snatched out the M-79, slamming the barrel hard against Cain's chest.

Cain's eyes widened in shock.

'Time to die!' Soloman snarled.

And fired.

The horrific impact of almost two hundred .oo rounds fired at once, so close in the cockpit, scattered everything with blood and hurled Cain back howling in pain, where he caught a skid. Wounded and raging, he reached up and began to ascend.

The Loach was locked in a spiral toward the trees and Soloman didn't even try to correct the course. He saw the glistening blackness below and knew they were over the swamp. As the trees swept up in front of him he released all control and dove out the passenger side, instantly meeting night as the helicopter descended with Cain clinging to a skid.

It hit a tree as Soloman hit the water.

Instantly the rotors shredded whatever they struck and in the next split second the chopper exploded in a firestorm that hurled a volcanic blast over Soloman. He threw himself underwater to evade the molten wave of burning fuel. In a second the lavalike blast passed, and Soloman rose, stunned, staring in a daze at the crumbling wreckage.

He struggled to breathe in the superheated air, was amazed to find himself still alive, still holding the M-79 in a tight fist. He searched for Cain, heard terrified voices shouting at him,

Amy and Maggie.

Both of them were calling frantically but Soloman couldn't take time to search, not yet. He stood in waist-deep water and wondered if Cain had been destroyed by the blast. Then he saw a humanoid shape horribly burning and disfigured struggling from the wreckage, a figure that stumbled and screamed as it fell toward the swamp.

Enraged beyond mercy Soloman opened fire on sight, throwing ten rounds at the form as it shambled clear of the burning Loach, and then Cain hurled himself into the water, evading the attack. Because of the darkness and the fire thrown from waving shadows, Soloman wasn't sure of his aim, wasn't certain whether he had hit it or not.

Night flew by in flame.

Then, a phantasmic and gory image, Cain rose from the burning black water as if unbound by Hell itself. Hideously ravaged, he glared at Soloman with singular intent and began walking forward.

'Damn,' Soloman whispered, shaking his head as he vengefully changed clips. 'He really can't die ...'

They glared hatefully at each other as Soloman quickly holstered the Desert Eagle. Then, turning, Soloman began slogging a path through the swamp. The basilica was outlined less than half a mile away and Soloman didn't need to turn to see whether Cain was pursuing; he knew he'd never stop.

In seconds Soloman found Amy and Maggie, and they began moving together, Soloman holding the six-year-old tight in his arms through stagnant water that shallowed bit by bit as they frantically neared the building. And as they came to the wide stone entrance they heard a shot fired from the tower, heard a wounded roar close by.

Soloman whirled to see Cain less than fifty feet away, flat on his back from a rifle shot, and he hurled Amy through the gate, snatching a grenade from his vest. Maggie threw herself inside the gate over Amy as he pulled the pin and threw it, and then the explosion created a wall of fire between them and the approaching horror.

On his feet, Soloman saw Cain striding fearlessly

319

through the flame, fangs extended. The great taloned hands curled in rage as Cain roared above the holocaust.

'*Hell awaits you, Soloman!*'

Soloman cursed and lifted Amy, and with Maggie running beside them they hurried to the church. Once inside, Maggie slammed the huge oak portal shut and bolted it. Then Soloman pushed Amy to the side and fell to one knee, breathlessly leveling on the door as Maggie leaped clear. But almost instantly the child was clutching his side again, screaming in horror.

Scanning, sweating, and adrenalized by the conflict, Soloman stared at the door a long time, holding a hard aim.

Listening …

To silence.

CHAPTER 18

Soloman reached for his radio and found the holder empty; he had lost it somewhere in the swamp, leaving him no means of communicating with his men. But despite the distraction he tried to regain some semblance of control as they went together through the basilica, reorienting.

Marcelle rushed up. 'Is it –'

'*It's outside!*' Soloman shouted. 'Lock the back door and get one of my men down here! Now!'

The priest was gone, racing to the back of the building as a Delta commando limped down a stone archway, holding a large bolt-action rifle in a tight fist. Soloman was shocked to see –

Malo.

He was stumbling and had a ragged cut on his face, but he was alive. Nor was there time for an explanation. He had obviously hit the water when he was hurled from the low-flying chopper.

'Status!' Soloman shouted. 'Have you got a visual?'

Malo shook his head sharply. 'I took a shot at him when he was coming up the path. Flattened his ass with the H and H, then he *vanished!* We ain't got anything on heat sensors and the motion detectors are flat!'

'Are the Apaches en route?'

'Three minutes out!'

'Then we've got to hold him off for three minutes!' Soloman grimaced, feeling the sharp pain of a bruised rib. He ripped out the spent cannister in the M-79 and inserted another. 'Tell the guys on the roof to look sharp! Cain'll probably go high to work his way down!'

Mother Superior Mary Francis rushed up, black habit trailing behind her. Quickly she knelt beside Maggie and Amy, tending to their wounds. Maggie had a large cut on her hand, a wound from a jagged stump, but Amy was unhurt.

'Take care of Amy.' Maggie pushed the child into the nun's arms with fading strength. 'Hide her in this place!' she whispered. 'Hide her quickly, Sister! Quickly!'

Marcelle returned, sweat glistening on his face. 'The entrances are locked, though the portals may not be strong enough to withstand his assault! I will go and monitor the back!'

'Good enough!' Soloman stood. 'That's the only other –'

The radio at Malo's waist erupted with a frantic voice, then several voices tumbled over each other until one dominated: 'Jesus Christ! Lieutenant! We've got big-time movement! It's … it's all over the south side!'

Malo raised the radio. 'Calm down, Bravo. Is it high or low? Can you localize it?'

'I … I can't tell! It … it seems like it's all over the south side of the building! He's moving *fast!* Jesus! He's trying to find a way in! I … I've never seen anything like it! It's all over the place! I can't tell if he's high or low! I think he might be on the roof somewhere … maybe … Maybe close to us! We can't tell! We can't tell! It's impossible to –'

A sharp crack, then static.

Silence.

Scowling, Malo glared at the A-unit. 'Repeat!'

Echoing …

'Bravo! Repeat!'

'No!' Soloman snarled, lifting an MP-5 laid to the side. He slammed in a fifty-round clip. 'Cain got him.'

'I'm going on the roof!' Malo moved for the stairway and Soloman whirled, slamming the big Delta lieutenant against a wall. 'Whoever was on the roof is *dead*, Malo!'

Malo's teeth gritted and pushed Soloman back. 'I've got six men up there, Colonel! Six men!'

Soloman slammed him back again, driving the point. 'Not anymore! Listen to me! Listen to me! They're gone! Right now we have to get ready because Cain is coming *down!*'

They stood face-to-face, and after a moment – a grim and solemn moment – Malo slowly nodded. He bowed his head with a frown and Soloman released him to glare at Maggie: 'Do you want a gun?'

She stood strongly, blood dripping from a crude bandage on her hand. 'Give me what you've got.' He tossed her the MP-5 and she caught it from the air, gazing at the weapon before asking without breath, 'Just point and pull the trigger, right?'

'Yeah.' Soloman jerked open a duffle bag and removed extra clips for the Desert Eagle. He lashed four antipersonnel grenades to his vest. 'Just pull the trigger and hold it. Expect it to recoil so hold down on the barrel about six inches beneath his chest. You'll hit him dead-center. You've only got fifty rounds so don't shoot until he's on top of you.'

He tried to analyze the situation, knew immediately that there weren't many advantages. The room was large and empty except for pews, providing little solid cover for a firefight and no place to make a solid stand. Plus, he was convinced that staying inside this place was death, so they had to get safely outside and lure Cain so the Apaches could target on him with cannons.

Sister Mary Francis had taken Amy downstairs, hiding her as best she could. But Soloman knew there was no future in that, either. If Cain wanted to find them, he would find them.

His mind moving at computer speed, he knew there was no way to make a stand in this place. No, now he had to change the game, create a new situation: *Change the game. Create the situation.*

He had to –

Soloman whirled with a curse as the fifty-year-old elevator was engaged, coming down from the roof. As one, they stared at it, too shocked to speak. Malo cast a narrow glance as Soloman slowly drew the Desert Eagle, holding the M-79 in his other hand. Amazed at the boldness, the fearlessness of the approach, Soloman motioned for Maggie to center her aim on the shaft.

Grindingly slow, coming down with a roar, the elevator descended.

They backed up.

Raising weapons.

◆ ◆ ◆

Sister Mary Francis dropped Amy as gently as possible in a closet and bent close, staring fiercely. Her old hands gripped the six-year-old's shoulders, strong and encouraging.

'Be silent!' she whispered harshly. 'I will be close!' She stared to make sure Amy heard. 'Do you understand what I'm saying, child? Don't make a sound! Don't make a sound no matter what you hear!'

Amy nodded with fright, straining to catch her breath. She placed both hands against the close wooden walls as if she were already alone in the darkness. Then Sister Mary Francis reached out and touched her face, fearlessly protective. 'You'll live, child! Just do what I say! Wait here and I'll be back for you! And make no sound! No sound at all! No matter what you hear! Do you understand!'

Amy nodded.

Hesitating, face twisting in pain, Sister Mary Francis swiftly grasped the crucifix on her cloak, removing the red and black rosary beads. She wasted a single second to wrap them about Amy's neck, then with a blessing rose and closed the door.

Was gone.

◆ ◆ ◆

As the elevator stopped, Malo angrily racked a rocket-propelled grenade into the chute of the M-203. His finger tightened on the trigger as they stood in place, staring and trembling.

Nothing.

The door didn't open.

Stillness.

'I don't like this,' Malo whispered. 'That door is supposed to open automatically. If it's not, that means … ' He shook his head, cursing in anger and fear. 'We need to find the kid and get the hell out of here, Colonel. Let the Apaches center on him.'

'Steady, Malo.' Soloman took a light step to the side. 'I don't want that RPG going off in here unless we're about to die. It could kill all of us. And we can't go outside yet because we don't know for sure that he's in there. He could be waiting.'

Soloman saw that the barrel of Maggie's machine gun steadied with uncommon control on the elevator door. She was frowning, her green eyes staring murder-ously. He reached out to touch her arm. 'Be cool, Maggie. Don't start shooting until I say so.'

'What are you going to do?'

He edged farther to the side, out of the line of fire just in case they opened up. Silently he holstered the Desert Eagle, leaving his right hand free. But he held the M-79 tight.

'Get ready to fire on acquisition,' he whispered as he reached the side of the elevator. Gently, his body flat against the wall, he stretched out and punched the button.

The doors opened.

He saw Malo and Maggie flinch together, weapons waving on the shaft. But they didn't fire and Soloman knew they saw nothing. So, moving with extreme caution, he edged an eye around the corner, searching the empty lift. Then he glanced up at the ceiling, saw that it was crisscrossed with thin steel beams that resembled rafters. There was also a wide, old-style trapdoor. It was unlatched and easily accessible, but closed.

Heart beating breathlessly, he studied the trapdoor, listening. He detected nothing, but knew Cain could be lying up there. And with that thought his finger tightened on the trigger of the M-79, knowing the devastating buckshot round would disorient the giant, if only for a moment.

A long time he stood, finally shaking his head to throw off drops of sweat. His eyes burned and he tilted his head to listen closer, knowing somehow that he wasn't as deceived as he feared. Cain was close, he knew, too close, waiting for an opportunity to –

The sound was so faint Soloman thought it had been a single rustle of his shirt. But he froze in place, utterly still, listening over the pounding of blood in his ears. He tried to control his heartbeat and knew instantly that he couldn't and then he understood ... what it was ...

No ... *not the ceiling.*

Moving only his eyes, Soloman peered cautiously at the paneled floor, knowing instinctively as the hairs rose along his arms. Casually, so as not to precipitate an attack, he lowered the aim of the M-79, retreating slowly ...

Have to get outside …

As he stepped back carefully, he heard what seemed to be the faintest scratching sound that was almost no sound at all … tracking, tracking, finding a point of aim if he had to –

'*Soloman!*'

He whirled as Maggie screamed.

The doors shut behind him.

◆ ◆ ◆

Malo screamed as he leaped forward to hit the doors like a freight train. When he bounced back, the steel doors were bent.

He staggered back at the collision, livid and raising the M-203, not knowing what to do as Maggie frantically pounded the button and they heard the explosion of sundered panels.

Then a demonic, hideous howl of triumph erupted on the other side and they heard Soloman roar against it in rage as a savage face-to-face fight began within the doors.

◆ ◆ ◆

Soloman moved without thought, instinct and speed saving him by the faintest flashing space as the floor shattered and Cain rose up, explosively hurling off a jagged section of steel.

With ferocious strength and determination Soloman gained a rafter, leaping high to grab a steel beam with his free hand. He roared with the effort as he twisted and fired the M-79 point-blank into the horrific bestial countenance, a face ravaged by burns with animal eyes blazing in fiendish triumph over monstrous fangs.

As the taloned hands reached up, Soloman's buckshot blast exploded down and out, devastating in the close confines of the elevator, and Cain took the full force of the blow. Then Soloman could hear nothing but the clash of defiant roars and ricocheting rounds.

Cain had been slammed viciously to his back, twisted by the blast as blood littered the walls, everything red and roaring in the smoke-filled aftermath of the explosion. Then Soloman swung forward to kick up hard, slamming the trapdoor open, and he was scrambling, trying to clear the elevator before Cain regained his footing.

As he threw himself wildly into the door Cain lashed out, a titanic fist missing to strike a steel beam, and then Soloman was on top of the lift, safe for a split-second. Moving quick, frantic and desperate, he spun in every direction to find an avenue of escape.

Nothing!

Cain's monstrous head came up through the door and Soloman leaped aside, fumbling for another buckshot round as the monstrosity lashed out, striking him hard behind the shins to take him down.

The M-79 flew wildly into the shaft.

Spinning, Soloman lashed out a kick with murderous force, slamming Cain's head against a beam. And, incredibly, Cain seemed to feel the stunning impact, snarling in rage as he reached out to snatch Soloman by his ballistic vest.

Shouting in panic, Soloman spun and tore the Velcro straps, freeing himself as one of Cain's mammoth shoulders passed through the trapdoor, climbing to finish the kill.

Seconds ...

Soloman's mind raced.

Seconds ... seconds ...

With a vengeful laugh Cain flung the vest aside and Soloman heard the grenades strike the wall. Then he saw his only chance and with it he leaped to twist, narrowly evading razored claws to snatch the vest. But as he touched the vest Soloman pulled a pin, slipping to evade a blow from Cain that splintered the top of the elevator like a sledgehammer.

Six seconds to detonation …

Soloman suicidally threw himself again past the monstrous reach, black claws slashing his leg as he fast-drew the Desert Eagle, grasping the elevator cable with his free hand. He slammed the barrel against the point where the cord tied into the lift and turned, wasting one second to glare down.

Four seconds …

Cain saw and understood.

He roared in rage.

'Survive *this!*' Soloman snarled.

Three …

With a bellow of defeat Cain dropped from the trapdoor and Soloman heard another massive crash below but he was out of time as he fired the Eagle into the cord.

Two …

Instantly the cable was severed and the elevator began descending. Only with the faintest strength did Soloman hold the splintered cord as he was lifted up the shaft by the counterweight.

One –

He cast a wild glance as the elevator fell to the basement where it crashed hard, detonating in a series of deafening eruptions. A heated holocaust pursued Soloman as he rose on the cable, vengeful flame pursuing him up the shaft with volcanic wrath.

◆ ◆ ◆

Malo sensed it.

Instincts honed by a thousand battles told him to move and he did, not understanding but knowing it would save their lives as he hurled himself hard into Maggie, taking her away from the door.

Then in an explosive concussion of superhuman power the panels were struck and blasted from the seams, hurled outward before the irresistible force of a locomotive that bent the steel in half. Hurling the shredded doors aside, Cain dove across the floor, roaring as the elevator itself plummeted into the shaft.

One second later the building was rocked to its foundation as a series of explosions solidified the air, dust and flame roiling. And as the explosions boomed across the basilica, burying them in a halo of smoke and flame, Malo reached his feet, understanding that Cain was among them, close, and that he had to get a shot off quick. He twisted violently as he rose to a knee, lifting the M-203 to fire point-blank at Cain before –

Gone!

Malo choked on smoke, searching, too involved to worry about Maggie, who hadn't moved since he'd slammed her to the floor. He dropped low, holding the rifle close, his heart on fire. Taking a hard leap to the side, he slammed his back against the wall, glaring, bending, trying to peer through the smoke that rolled from the open door.

'Where is he?' he heard himself whispering, panicking. 'Come on … Come on … Find him … Find him … You've got to find him … He's here … '

Clouds of debris and heavy smoke, poisonous and burning, filled the air so completely that Malo could see nothing. He fell to a knee, squinting against it, simultaneously reaching to his back to remove a gas mask. Dropping his rifle for a split-second he put on the mask and focused again, finding himself engulfed in blackness. Then he sensed something moving beside him, spun for target acquisition, and heard –

Maggie …

She staggered to her feet, holding her head, shocked

and stunned. Her hand was coated in blood and Malo took a second to reach out and steady her. She leaned heavily on him.

'It's all right, Maggie,' he whispered. 'We'll find the –'

Her expression turned to horror.

Malo whirled and fired as he was hit, a thunderbolt tearing through his chest to wet openness, blasting apart something that sent numbness to his spine, flooding weakness through his arms and legs.

Grimacing, unable to breathe, knowing he was near death, Malo roared with pain as he was lifted cleanly from the ground. Then with a last rush of strength he bowed his bearded head to behold Cain's horrific fanged face only inches from his, a smile of victory.

The blood-red eyes glared.

Hating.

Laughing.

No breath.

Malo spat inside the mask.

Cain howled bestially as he tore his arm free, hurling something red and bloody into the blackened air, and Malo knew a last darkness as he fell hard to the ground.

CHAPTER 19

A my was screaming as thunder roared over her before the door was snatched open and Sister Mary Francis was there, bending quickly to lift her from the floor. The old woman held her tightly in strong arms as she moved through a smoke-filled corridor, finding a way through the spiraling fumes of black.

Amy cried out at the fire and smoke.

'Hush, child!' the nun said sternly, closing a hand around the back of Amy's head to cradle her. 'God alone will decide this battle! And we have *Him* on our side!'

She turned and moved up a stone archway, and Amy managed to silence her screams, holding tight. Then she felt the crucifix pressed hard against her chest, her tears absorbed by the black cloak.

'God will provide a way,' Sister Mary Francis whispered, moving quickly. 'This fiend will not get you! Not while I live!'

She moved into the interior of the basilica, flaring with isolated fires. Pews were scattered haphazardly and a terrific red light shone from the elevator shaft to cast a chaotic, unearthly atmosphere. Turning carefully, Sister Mary Francis peered, then froze and bent even further as she seemed to see something.

'*Aha!*' she shouted and spun, running instantly, and Amy heard the horrific voice behind them.

'*Witch! She belongs to me!*'

The nun threw open another door and fled quickly down a hall that seemed less well kept than the rest but also held less of the choking smoke that filled the basilica. As she reached the end of the hallway she mounted a short flight of steps, not casting another glance over her shoulder to see if they were being pursued.

But as they reached the third step Amy raised her face to see the man, *the man*, coming for them, his monstrous hands clutching, unclutching, his face a mask of horrible glee that caused her to scream again and again. He laughed as he caught her eye, and Amy lost whatever control she'd held in the quiet darkness of the closet before –

The next movement came from nowhere as a black shape leaped from behind a doorway, swinging a wooden beam that descended hard over the back of the man's head.

Father Marcelle!

'Sister!' Amy cried as Cain was struck hard and staggered forward a pace, finally regaining balance to whirl toward Marcelle. And at the shout Sister Mary Francis spun on the steps, bending to watch the confrontation.

Then with a cryptic curse the old nun spun again and ascended the stairs, moving away from the fight in the corridor, leaving Marcelle alone and unarmed against the beast.

◆ ◆ ◆

Soloman wasn't sure if he was alive or not. It took him a few moments, rolling over something hard and sharp, aware of wounds and burns that seemed too numerous to count, before he was certain.

Yeah … I'm alive … I think …

He gained his knees, knowing he had somehow

landed on the steel beams that anchored the elevator to a shack on the roof of the basilica. Smoke was so thick that it was suffocating, and he stayed low as he moved too slowly, knowing he had to get back into the fight.

Staggering and crawling, he found a faint ribbon of light and knew it was the door. Not even searching for a knob, Soloman hurled himself against it to blast apart the planks and then he was rolling blindly in the night, taking a second to recover.

He crawled, disoriented, toward a stairway and tumbled headlong, uncaring about more injuries since he was already so wounded. He cascaded over stone, bruised and bloodied to finally find himself at the threshold, expecting to see Cain standing over him, ultimately victorious.

A snarl of enduring pain twisted Soloman's face as he raised himself to a single knee, like a boxer waiting out a count, finally standing. He knew without even looking that he had lost all his weapons. The M-79 had been surrendered to the shaft; he had no idea where he'd lost the Desert Eagle.

No ... no weapons.

Shaking his head to clear his thoughts as much as possible, Soloman rose and staggered down another flight, following the wide winding stairway that would take him back to the battle with Cain ...

◆ ◆ ◆

Maggie rolled beneath a pew, concealed in smoke and chaos. She had seen Malo die, his heart torn from his chest only to be hurled far into the horror that enveloped this place.

Frantic to escape, she had leaped and rolled, throwing herself wildly beneath a dark shadow of wood where she crawled madly, changing directions every few seconds as Cain vengefully pursued, splintering oak banisters and pews as he sought to finish the kill.

Evading, hiding, knowing his location by the violence of his rampage, she escaped him by the narrowest margin, finally sliding behind a stone column located at the rear of the basilica. Now, trying to catch her breath as she stifled a groan, she placed a hand over her mouth and chest, concentrating.

Despite her usually cold control, she wasn't conditioned to this level of adrenaline rush and knew it was making her unstable. Breath by breath she tried to bring herself back down, calming, finding balance in the madness and fear that had unhinged her ability to think clearly. Then she glanced down through tearing eyes and saw it.

My purse!

Listening quick to hear Cain ravaging a distant section of the building, she reached out and snatched the purse from the floor, opening it to find what she sought. Her hand closed around the cold steel cylinder and in seconds broke the seal, withdrawing the syringe.

Teeth gritted, she raised it before her face.

Yes!

Come on!

Her rage gave her strength.

It's time to die.

Then she heard shouts on the far side of the building and tried savagely to rise but fell to the side, wounded by the sheer expanse of this surreal, continuing conflict. The syringe rolled into the smoke-filled darkness.

'Oh my God,' she cried, scrambling forward, searching, searching ...

Couldn't find it –

As she heard a horrible voice.

'Witch! She belongs to me!'

'Oh, Amy ...'

Maggie almost rose and chased suicidally after the

voice. Her teeth gritted, she threw herself across the darkened floor, hurling shattered wood to the side, searching, searching, searching for the only thing that could kill this beast, the only thing …

◆ ◆ ◆

Cain glared at the intrepid priest with singular hate. He stared at the shattered wooden beam in Marcelle's hand and laughed. Then with a lionlike growl he took a stride forward.

Marcelle stood his ground and cast the broken wood aside with contempt. He revealed no fear at all as Cain stepped closer, regarding the giant as if he could kill him with a glance.

'Your god fails you, priest,' Cain snarled in a ravaged voice. 'Yes … he always fails you. Because only strength shall prevail in this hardened world. Which I will rule.'

'So tell me of your strength, beast,' Marcelle replied bitterly. He did not retreat. Nor would he, he knew. 'Tell me of that great strength that was taken from you at Golgotha!' The priest backed up, shaking his head in spite. *'Esto mihi, Domine, turris fortitudinis!'*

'Coram inimico vestro?' Cain whispered, smiling.

Marcelle was unshaken. *'Et sit Dominus cum spiritu meo.'*

'No,' Cain replied. 'He will not receive your spirit. Because your spirit belongs to me.'

A fanged roar erupted as Cain lashed out to snatch Marcelle by the collar, bringing him closer to the bloody breath and the great, distended fangs. 'Golgotha was only a temporary defeat, Marcelle,' he said gratingly. 'Tell me if I've been defeated tonight.'

'The night is not over.'

A laugh. 'Such courage.' He moved a taloned hand over Marcelle's face, caressing it. 'Such a waste that it was spent serving a tyrant. It might have served me well. And you would not have ever faced this defeat.'

'I will never serve you!'

'Words spoken often,' Cain laughed. 'But I have no more patience for fools. It is time to finish this charade.' He closed a hand around Marcelle's neck as the priest stared him hard in the face, and Cain seemed suddenly to realize something, pausing long ... longer.

'*You*,' he whispered finally. 'It was you who released me from the tomb ... so long ago. Yes ... at last ... I remember. I had been imprisoned there for so many years, chained by the Hebrew dog. Until you came. Yes, now at last, it comes to me. It was you who defied the curse of the king ... to set me free.'

Marcelle frowned. 'Yes,' he replied. 'In my ... my foolishness I defied the warning of David. I had lost my fear of God, and all that was holy. But now I fear Him again. *Him*, and not you! And I will right my mistake! I will return you to that grave!'

Shaking his head, Cain despised the words. 'No, priest. I will never return to any grave. Not in this world, nor any other.'

'You can terrify,' Marcelle gasped. 'But *His* judgment is upon you. And soon you will terrify no more! Do you truly believe you can rewrite what has been written? Do you! You are *nothing*, beast! What creature can be greater than the Creator? None! Not even you! You have deceived yourself and your doom comes as we speak! Listen! It comes for *you!*'

In a snarl Cain's fingers tightened. And slowly, so slowly, he began crushing Marcelle's thick neck between iron fingers that closed and closed with inexorable force. Struck by the numbing pain, Marcelle shut his eyes tight for a final prayer, surrendering his soul to –

'*It's over, Cain!*'

Cain spun like lightning to hurl Marcelle aside,

staring with blazing eyes into the corridor. Stunned, Marcelle struggled to his feet, expecting it to be Soloman, as before, but instantly recognizing the feminine voice. In the same breath he hoped desperately that she wouldn't be making a suicidal stand against this monstrosity as he looked up to see ... Maggie.

She stood defiantly in the corridor.

Challenging.

Marcelle groaned, falling heavily against a wall as Cain walked slowly toward her. 'Maggie!' Marcelle shouted. 'No! Please! Don't do this! Don't do this! He'll kill you!'

'Maybe,' she frowned. 'But I'll have company.'

Slowly she removed a hand from behind her back, revealing that she held a large steel syringe. And at the movement Cain halted, staring narrowly at the gray cylinder. For a single moment, no one moved. Then Maggie lifted it higher, before her face.

'Come to me, Cain,' she smiled with the purest purpose. 'I've got the cure for what ails you.'

Cain tilted his head, seeming to understand.

'I created you.' Maggie took a step forward. 'Now I'm gonna kill you.'

With a dangerous, hissing growl Cain stepped back and Maggie took another step forward. 'Come on, big man. Come and kill me. It won't hurt a bit. I promise.'

As if summoned from the heart of Hell a primal, cosmic pride blazed in Cain's face. His jaws twisted, fang grating on fang. 'You think you can defeat me with *that?*' he laughed. 'Woman! I know what you hold! It is the virus that you used to create this flesh! *Dominus mihi turris fortitudinis.*' He glared but did not advance. 'Yes, I am stronger than anything living! I could crush you like a worm and deliver that virus to the flames! Then you would have nothing!'

Maggie was unexpressive but Marcelle saw that her

eyes had the disturbing glint of madness – the madness of love. She was fighting for her daughter now and knew no fear.

'Then come to me, Cain.' She continued to advance. 'Take it away from me. I'm sure you can. You tore out Malo's heart, didn't you? Come on.' She lifted her chin. 'Take this little thing away from me.'

Cain staggered and Marcelle saw true fear smolder in his eyes. Then the giant took another step back, away from them, and Marcelle suddenly remembered –

'NO!' He leaped.

It was too late.

'The child shall be *mine!*' Cain roared, hurling himself with incredible speed to the stairs where he took them five at a time, reaching the top as Marcelle reached the bottom in a desperate rush.

It was a chaotic thing – Marcelle would remember – that made Cain stagger at the crest. For at the last second Mother Superior Mary Francis, seemingly as frail and old as the Earth, emerged in his path to hurl a bucket of liquid, the substance splashing over Cain to shower the stairs.

Marcelle, instantly stunned and frightened for the old nun, stared wildly upward as Cain glanced with a laugh at his drenched form. His voice was mocking as he smiled over unhinged fangs, leaning closer.

'Holy water, Mother?'

'No.' Mother Superior Mary Francis frowned. 'Gasoline.'

She struck the match with a finger as it left her hand.

◆ ◆ ◆

Soloman spent a moment mourning over Malo.

He bowed his head, closing his eyes, and laid a hand on his chest.

'*Semper fi,*' he whispered.

Then Soloman wearily took the chambered Colt from the Delta lieutenant's waist and, staggering, lifted the M-203, opening the chute to ensure that a grenade was locked in the chamber. He slammed it shut with a vengeance and jerked the slide to chamber a round.

A chaotic battle exploded close by.

Knowing instantly that Cain was still alive and fighting, Soloman limped across the demolished church as quickly as he could, his right leg numb. But in his battle rage he didn't think of how badly he might be hurt; he knew only that he had a fight to finish, a man to kill. He wished wildly that he had more to work with but there was nothing, nothing …

Nothing but himself.

Raising the rifle he entered the hallway and saw fire raging on the steps of a distant stairway, a fire that moved and roared from within with more than flame. Struck with a stab of emotional pain he prayed desperately that it wasn't Maggie or the rest of them and then he saw Maggie in the hallway, shocked and staring up. He shoved her roughly aside as he reached the threshold, instantly raising aim, knowing it was Cain.

Cain leaped through the door at the top and Soloman could hear him rolling, beating at the flames. With a curse Soloman leaped onto the stairs and immediately collapsed, falling on his injured knee.

Howls at the crest rose in volume and then began to fade as Soloman rose again, climbing with determination, using the rifle as a crutch to stagger through burning steps. He emerged boldly onto the second floor, ready to throw down face-to-face, and he saw the old nun stretched on the floor, unconscious. Soloman swung the rifle for acquisition and saw it all at once.

Cain stood smoldering, ravaged beyond comprehension. It was incredible that, injured as he was, he could still be on his feet. Nothing, surely *nothing* could stand after this. But Soloman had sensed from the beginning that Cain would never be destroyed by force.

Swaying, Cain smiled.

Amy stood in front of him, Cain's ravaged hand wrapped closely beneath her chin. He tightened his grip and she cried out, struggling. '*Enough* ... ,' Cain gasped. 'Enough games ... Soloman. I take the child, now. Or I kill her, now. It is your decision.'

Soloman advanced into the room, patiently lifting a hand. 'There's no way out of here, Cain. We've got two gunships in the air that will liquefy you if you step outside.' Soloman went into a bluff. 'It doesn't matter if you have Amy with you or not. This is a matter of national security. They'll open fire on acquisition.'

A laugh.

'I doubt that, Soloman.' Cain was amused. 'Yes, I doubt that very much. Because your love makes you weak ... You don't have the strength to do the hard thing. Now ... lay down your weapon.'

Soloman's face twisted. His eyes met Amy's.

A cry erupted from Amy as Cain lifted her from the floor.

'All right!' Soloman screamed, instantly laying the rifle on a table. 'All right! The gun is down! The gun is down! Let her go, Cain! Let her go! Don't hurt her!'

Shuffling, Cain laughed as he lowered her and stepped horrifically closer, moving Amy before him. He lifted her chin and Soloman was staggered by emotion as he saw the vivid fear, the pleading, burning in her face. He stifled a moan, half-reaching out. Then Cain was backing down the stairs, turning the child as a living barrier to send Maggie and Marcelle before him.

In seconds they were in the basilica and Soloman was only two steps behind the giant. He contemplated a desperate lunge, an attempt to take Cain into a throwdown before the giant could snap Amy's neck.

But he knew he couldn't do it. Even wounded, Cain was ten times stronger than he was.

Thunderous rotors of gunships roared over them and Soloman knew the cannons were centered. Just as he knew that they would never open fire as long as Cain held Amy as a shield.

Soloman shouted, 'Cain! Listen to me! You can't win this! Just let me take you in and we'll put you in quarantine! But we won't kill you! You have my word! Just let her go!'

'Order one of the gunships to land.' Cain smiled with joyous cruelty. 'Do it now.'

Soloman knew better than to debate. Amy already stood on the narrowest line between life and death. He raised both arms in a signal of surrender and motioned for a gunship to settle in the courtyard. He repeated the gesture twice, clear anger revealed in his expression. And in a moment one of the massive Apaches came in low to land in a maddening haze of gray wind.

'Tell them to exit the craft,' Cain mumbled, blinking slowly. He seemed to be suffering a gathering pain unrelated to his injuries. 'Tell them ... tell them to hurry!'

Both pilots exited at Soloman's command, standing away from the tandem cockpit. And then Cain walked forward, holding Amy tightly in his arms. He carried her like a breastplate. 'Now,' he breathed, 'tell the other ship to set down in the swamp. Tell the pilots to remain in the craft.'

Soloman violently snatched a portable radio from one of the shocked Apache pilots and raised the second gunship. He instructed it to set down far from the basilica, and at the pilot's defiant objection Soloman released a stream of *direct* orders from a *colonel* that left no room for mistake.

In thirty seconds the gunship landed in the moor.

Obviously able, Cain settled Amy in the tandem seat

and took over control of the Apache. Soloman sharply raised a hand as one of the grounded pilots inside the courtyard appeared to consider a move, stopping him in mid-stride. Together they watched helplessly as Cain took control.

Concentrating coldly, Soloman tried to ignore Maggie's cries, her pleading voice that begged Cain to leave her daughter behind. And within seconds the Apache was airborne with Soloman screaming immediately into the radio, warning the pilots grounded in the swamp:

'Get away from the ship! Get away from it now! He's gonna launch missiles! I repeat! He's gonna launch missiles! Get away from the ship *now now now!*'

Cain immediately angled the Apache across the moor and within seconds Soloman heard the hot-liquid ignition of a Hellfire, a fire-and-forget laser-guided missile. He knew it would detonate with twenty-four pounds of LX-14 to send the Apache across the blackened night in a continuing series of explosions.

The distant impact sounded like a 747 crash-landing in the swamp, demolishing trees in a sweeping white firestorm that roared and rolled in mushrooming blasts, rocking the walls of the basilica as a wall of flame rose hundreds of feet into the night, blinding and deafening.

'Get inside the building!' Soloman screamed, shoving Maggie and Marcelle as the two pilots also turned and ran wildly for the door. Soloman was the last man to the portal and spun to see Cain's Apache sweeping in low over the wall, coming back for the kill.

He dove desperately through the door as Cain fired the 30-mm cannon, reducing rock and stone at the open archway to dust, rounds chewing the building to cinders, and then the gunship passed low over the roof, roaring into the night.

Stunned and lost in a world of pain, fighting madness, Soloman rolled over and somehow gained his feet, sweating and breathless. He searched with hazy focus to see Maggie holding her hands over her head, lying against a far wall. Marcelle had thrown himself on top of her. Neither of them moved.

'Maggie!' Soloman shouted, rising to his knees. 'Maggie! Are you all right? Are you hit?' He paused as a vivid fear seized his chest. 'Maggie! Maggie! Are you hit! Talk to me!'

Soloman felt his heart skip a beat as Marcelle slowly rolled to the side and Maggie shook her head, stunned, rising with effort to her knees. She raised a trembling hand to wave vaguely before she was overcome with emotion, bowing her head and moaning. Her slim body was bent, wracked with the hideous cries of a mother who had lost her only child.

Standing in silent rage, Soloman grimaced. Then he shook his head violently with a hateful shout, scattering sweat, and his right hand locked, clenched in a fist, trembling with endless wrath. He closed his eyes as he raised the fist to his face, all his heart there in the bloodless grip.

The night roared with distant flame, death.

Finally regaining a measure of control, Soloman turned his head to the bright burning night, but he already knew: There was nothing in the air; Cain was gone. Just as he knew that he could raise NAV-SAT for a radar identification, but Cain would be smarter than that.

He would be flying at treetop level and inside an hour would down the gunship in an isolated field. Then he would simply appropriate other means of travel and take Amy with him ... to her death.

Marcelle staggered across the smoke-filled, demolished basilica, shocked by the fantastic scope of the conflict. He held a hand to his head and Soloman saw blood, but there was no time for compassion. Reaching out hard he grabbed the priest by the collar, screaming into his face, 'Marcelle! Marcelle! Listen to me! We've got to know what Cain took from the Archives! Do you understand? We've got to know! Tell me! Tell me! Where is he going?'

Swaying, Marcelle shook his head. 'We ... we don't know, Soloman! We don't know!'

'There's no more time for that, Marcelle!' Soloman was enraged. 'We've *got* to know where Cain is going or Amy is going to die! Do you understand me!'

'Yes ... yes,' Marcelle responded, grimacing painfully as he collected a measure of composure. 'We will ... *find* it!' He staggered toward the door. 'We will find it *tonight!*'

CHAPTER 20

Taciturn and stern, Aveling hung up the phone and stared down. He had heard it all but revealed nothing, his austere face inflexible and pale in the half-light of the room.

Attendant priests, standing close, exchanged uneasy looks as the old man paused, his head bent in dark thought as though he were somehow displeased with the Almighty. Finally, his old voice broke the gloom.

'Bring me my cloak,' he said. 'Advise Sister Therese to prepare my breakfast. And awaken Father James, the Librarian Superior. As well as Father Barth.'

'But, Father,' one of the priests answered, 'it's only two o'clock in the morning. They will be sleeping until mass.'

'A little sleep,' Aveling said gravely as he washed his face in a white porcelain bowl. 'A little sleep, a little folding of the hands to rest, and poverty strikes as an armed man. Poverty ... or death.' He shook his head. 'Go now! Tell them to meet me in the Archives!'

Quickly the youths left the room and Aveling made a phone call, listening to the dull ring until a very powerful man answered. Aveling spoke in terse sentences, knowing the man despised extemporaneous speech. His face grew grim as he listened to the reply, and he nodded. He hung up and turned as the attendants re-entered the chamber.

In moments they settled his white frock over his lean shoulders and with a curt gesture he dismissed them. Then, with steps of remorse and quiet purpose, he, too, left the chamber.

◆　◆　◆

Father Barth, his stern face revealing that he sensed something terrible had happened, came down the stairs to the Archives. Steady, holding his composure, he crossed the room and approached the august form of Aveling, alone and unmoving in the open doorway of the vault, staring inside at the thousands and thousands of documents still to be inventoried.

Standing behind the silhouetted Superior General of the Jesuits, Barth said nothing, waiting patiently. He knew that Aveling would speak when he would speak. And whatever final concentration bent the bald head seemed to have totally mesmerized the old man. His eyes were set like flint against the far wall, his hands folded into the front pocket of his hooded white cloak. Finally he shook his head. Barth held silence.

'Has Father James been summoned?' Aveling asked, not turning to see who was behind him.

'Yes, Aveling. He has been summoned.'

'Good.' Aveling glanced away from the far wall and stared downward. And Barth turned slightly to observe thousands of documents laid carefully on the table. There was also a series of larger books opened for referencing and indexing.

Unnerved, Barth asked a question he could already answer, knowing something was in the air. 'Has the librarian not yet discovered what Cain stole from the Archives?'

'No.' A grim answer in the atmosphere. 'No, not yet. But, as of this hour, we have no more time.' Aveling turned to the documents, only a third of the vault's totality. 'We must know what has been taken, and quickly.' He paused with a grimace. 'Cain defeated Marcelle and this soldier, Soloman. There are many deaths. They have lost the child.'

Barth staggered. 'And Marcelle?'

'He lives.' Aveling revealed no emotion. 'He was wounded in the encounter, but he lives. And now, to give them any chance of victory, we must know what Cain has taken from us. There are only four days remaining before Samhain, when he will sacrifice the child.'

For a moment Barth's hands clenched and he turned, staring angrily between the vault and table. 'So many documents ... ,' he murmured. 'Even if we used a hundred men it would be impossible in so short a time.'

'Yes, impossible.' Aveling's eyes narrowed. 'But only impossible if we continue as we have continued. We must use wisdom, and not force, to solve this mystery.'

'What are you thinking, Aveling?'

'I perceive, perhaps too late, that a powerful opponent can sometimes be more easily defeated than a weak one.' Aveling tilted his head slowly, as if listening. 'I perceive that, perhaps, the means of defeating our enemy lies within his own strength.'

'How can such a thing be accomplished?'

'By understanding the symmetry of his decisions.' Aveling moved into the vault and gazed about. 'That has been our mistake from the beginning. We have attempted to defeat Cain without understanding him. But to be understood is to be defeated.'

'When did this occur to you?'

'When I knew desperation,' Aveling said plainly. 'A young thing for an old mind. But desperation has bred more ideas than complacency, and I have been complacent too long.' He slid a pale hand down an overflowing shelf. 'There is a point where it begins and ends, and multitudinous points between. Yet there is also ... yes, ex hypothesi – a man revealed by the peculiar subtlety of his decisions. And it is in the symmetry of those decisions that our enemy has revealed his destination.'

Barth was clearly confused, turning slightly as the Chief Librarian of the Archives came quickly down the stairs. The librarian stared at Aveling, respectfully awaiting instruction.

'Imagine it thus,' Aveling continued. 'Two opponents join a game on two lines that began far apart, but which converge in the distance. Yet, between and above these lines, is a three-dimensional plane with connecting lines arising, all connections representing opposing strategic decisions. It rises as a pyramid, stone upon stone. But, yes, at each convergence of lines, there is a stalemate. And as long as we are playing strategy to strategy, line to line so to speak, we continue to meet at a point of stalemate.' He paused. 'In order to understand and defeat Cain we must enter *his* strategy quadrilaterally. There, we can begin another line that intersects the stones at mid-length. We must begin in the middle, and proceed across.'

'I don't understand, Aveling.' Barth shook his head. 'But I trust your superior wisdom.'

Aveling smiled slightly, turning to slowly exit the vault. 'It has less to do with wisdom than mathematics, old friend. Cain's words have a symmetry that reveal his lie. It is the sum that we have failed to perceive, and which will surely reveal the means of his defeat. It will be in understanding the totality of his strategy, piecing together the squares to begin in a new place, that we may claim victory.'

'Of course.' Barth's face was troubled. 'But ... but what does all of this mean – I mean, practically speaking? How does this theory, in a pragmatic sense, allow us to out-think this man called Cain … who is no man?'

'First we must acquire more information, but not of the vault. A thing too simple that I have not perceived until now.'

Barth nodded, 'Yes … yes, I see. Then tell me what you need. I will do anything that you request.'

Aveling laid a slender hand on his shoulder, smiling, 'Of course you will, Father. Your assistance has already been magnificent.' He pondered. 'First, I want you to call Vatican City. Instruct the Curia and College of Cardinals to authorize release of the last surviving copy of the *Grimorium Verum* from the Secret Archives. And instruct them to do it quickly, no matter the objections. Call Monsignor Balcanza if there are protests. He is an ally of mine, a friend in the camp of our mutual enemies. Then tell our managers within the intelligence community to prepare for severe requests. And no one is to know – especially not the Americans.' Suddenly he was fiercer. 'Tell them that no one sleeps until this conflict is finished with life or death.'

'That …' Barth appeared stunned. 'That is a very serious request, Aveling. The Americans will be enraged if we use our power to circumvent their authority. There will be retribution. Perhaps even severe retribution.'

'A price we will certainly pay in time,' Aveling answered, gazing up as if he could see the intersection of lines. 'But I see a situation that will require a test of global power.'

'What do you mean?'

Aveling frowned. 'This incident involving the child will assuredly end in the dismissal of Marcelle and his colleagues. I know the world of politics too well to be mistaken. And we must be prepared for the complications.' He tilted his head toward Barth. 'Further, advise Monsignor Balcanza to contact his covert sources in the State Department. I wish to know what persons are coordinating this ... team ... that Marcelle has joined.'

'Monsignor Agoni Balcanza has such abilities?' Barth appeared stunned. 'I knew that he was a priest during World War II and worked sporadically with the French Resistance but ...' He looked away.

Aveling laughed. 'Agoni was more than a mere priest during the war,' he said. 'It was by Agoni's intelligence contacts with MI5 that the French Resistance established an underground railroad for the Jews, moving them out of Germany in 1944. We transported entire trainloads, moving them through enemy territory, with Pius playing from the Vatican for both Hitler and the Americans, covering all contingencies. Later, of course, the OSS was disbanded and many of our old friends were absorbed by what came to be known as the CIA.' He paused. 'But loyalties forged between men during that eventful time continue to endure, some even stronger than the loyalties we retain for our respective countries, whether they are England, America, or the Vatican itself. And I am still capable of obtaining information. But Agoni is, in truth, a truly diabolical son of a bitch, if the term may be used, and a master of the game. He is the one who actually dealt with those Germans who said things like "Ve have vays of making you talk." ' He laughed, before turning more serious. 'Yes, Agoni and I were as devious as any SS agent ever to bear the Roman Eagle, and God will no doubt judge us as reprobate heathens for many of the things that we did. But it was war, and a time for difficult decisions, even as now. It was my own time ... in the desert.'

Recovering, Barth asked, 'But why do you need this information?'

'Because I perceive that this American, Soloman, has been somehow betrayed from within.'

'Why do you believe this?'

'Because our enemy has already done to us what I intend to do to him,' the older priest said. 'Colonel Soloman was thoroughly prepared for this confrontation. He should not have been so completely defeated unless, of course, Cain possessed foreknowledge of his strategy.' He paused. 'It is a game I know too well.'

'Yes, of course,' Barth said. 'But your skills were honed during the war, Aveling. Marcelle does not have the benefit of such experience. Do you believe he is equal to this task?'

Aveling answered, 'I love Marcelle as I would love a son, but Marcelle is … he is like a hammer that crushes stone. And now, I believe, is the hour for more experienced minds, minds honed by years of deception and illusion, to enter the fray.'

Barth assented with a nod. 'Very well, Aveling. I will contact Rome and tell them to begin. And I will advise someone to brief the Archbishop on this horrible development with the child.'

'There is no need to advise the Archbishop,' Aveling said. 'I have already done so.'

Paling, Barth waited. 'And?'

Aveling suddenly seemed to assume a greater mantle of authority, frightening even for him. He took a deep breath and then released it. His voice was sad and troubled.

'He said that from this moment … my word is as his.'

◆ ◆ ◆

Working in silence, accessing everything that could be accessed beneath and above his classification or need to know, Ben scoured the records, listing all the rogue agents Soloman had tracked. It was a tedious, bitter job, and he saw nothing.

All of them were elite hunters that Soloman had beat at the game, outsmarting them in the field to arrest most of them without violence. But there were a few who forced him to go tactical, and kill.

But Ben had an intuitive sensation that something tied it all together, knew just as well that Archette was a master of deception, and that truth, if he could find it at all, would be buried in a labyrinth of lies.

He had never truly understood how Soloman could have been right about Archette, but he felt in his soul that he was: Archette was somehow involved; he had to be.

Archette had authorized Genocide One, but he'd also authorized the failsafes that had failed to contain Cain. Only Soloman's phenomenal mind and the unforeseen assistance of the priest had given the team the faintest chance of success – something Archette could never have anticipated.

So Ben continued a dogged search, finding nothing and still nothing as he let the computer do the work. He had another meeting within two hours to discuss Soloman's horrific defeat in the basilica and the theft of one thirty-million-dollar, fully armed Apache and the destruction of another, but he tried to ignore the pressure, knowing there was something here. Yet as the Cray-hooked computer finished processing he still had nothing to confirm his suspicions.

Archette ... so clever.

Very, very clever.

But Archette's too-clever-by-half desire to see Trinity dismantled at any cost had given him away, so Ben knew something was there. He leaned back from the desk, staring balefully at the screen. How would *he* hide a conspiracy if he were at the center of it?

The answer was so simple it was almost stunning.

By not being there at all.

At the thought he remembered one of Soloman's rules of prey: *If you want to go under and stay under, cut connections with everyone. When hunting a rogue operative, never try to follow lines because lines have been severed. Get inside his mind and anticipate. Move ahead of him and wait for him to come to you. Hunt from the trees.*

The computer completed the search.

No, nothing.

Ben leaned back and knew in his bones that Archette had sacrificed Soloman's family to keep Soloman down, to put him off the track because Soloman had been wreaking havoc on something. He knew it by intuition, by the same instinct that told you when a rifle was centered from the bush.

After a moment he shook his head; this was the doglands, he knew, a place of bones and skulls where ghosts stood in the day, staring with knowledge, and secrets.

Tired, Ben stood and felt a shadow upon him. He was ready for this last meeting, but he knew he could say nothing ... for he had found nothing.

◆ ◆ ◆

Nervously the young priest handed Aveling a phone. 'It is Monsignor Balcanza, Father. He calls from Rome.'

Aveling raised it and spoke. 'My dear Agoni, thank you for returning my call ... No, no, Marcelle is not dead ... Yes, of course, very fortunate. Did you receive my request? ... I know, very extreme ... ' Aveling chuckled. 'I doubt, Agoni, that either you or I shall live long enough for me to repay so great a debt ... Yes, it has been a long time ... Good, I knew I could depend upon you, old friend ... I await your call.'

Aveling replaced the phone and turned.

'Thank you,' he said. 'Now leave me, for I have much work to do. I will not be disturbed until the courier arrives from Vatican City. And then, disturb me at once.'

◆ ◆ ◆

The somber gathering of wounded bodies and souls inside the darkened New York town house, located beside Central Park, was shrouded in regret. It was totally soundless as no one, not even Marcelle, had spoken a word since early morning.

Maggie, treated for a series of contusions, had been sedated and was sleeping in a second-floor bedroom. But Soloman, running on adrenaline and amphetamines, sat and stared out the window, gun in hand. He felt as if he were still in battle; his ears echoed painfully with gunfire.

It had been a long time since he'd seen so ferocious a firefight and he felt disoriented, as overheated emotions devoured and diminished his control. He feared that he was losing an edge of tactical judgment to rage and tried to shut it down, to contain it by cold intellect and will, but his anger was overwhelming.

Marcelle was silent and steady, though his face revealed a fatalistic set that was almost frightening. Even now the priest was stoically finishing a small breakfast at the kitchen table, his jaw moving slowly, angrily.

Mother Superior Mary Francis, who had quickly recovered consciousness from Cain's glancing blow, was utterly still. Fully alert, she sat with her face sternly fixed, staring out a window at the rising sun. Soloman had noticed earlier that she was without her crucifix and rosary beads, and she told him that she'd given them to Amy.

Amy ...

Closing his eyes, Soloman remembered Malo and the remainder of the Delta contingent. The best fighters in the world, they had been massacred like children.

Those on the roof had been killed before they could

even fire a shot, their blood viciously drained to correct Cain's enormous injuries.

Fiercely locking down emotion, Soloman tried to assess the situation: the Apache still hadn't been located, so they had no direction of travel. Only four days remained until Samhain, the day when Cain intended to sacrifice Amy. And last, to cripple them all, they were out of men and within two hours Ben had an emergency meeting at the White House.

If there was any other way to make the situation worse, Soloman couldn't imagine what it could be.

◆ ◆ ◆

As Aveling anticipated, the Monsignor called within the hour. He picked up the phone and listened carefully, evaluating. It did not require long to process the information. He smiled; his old friend had lost none of his skills to penetrate the impenetrable.

'Thank you, Agoni,' Aveling said finally. 'No, my humble skills must prove sufficient ... No, do not come over. There is no time ... Yes, be prepared. We do not know whether this shall end on your continent or mine ... Of course, old friend, I shall inform you at once ... Return my encouragement to His Holiness ... Goodbye.'

Aveling hung up and rose, walked slowly. His hands folded automatically into the pocket of his white habit as he strolled. He paced about the room for a moment, considering what he had heard, when Father Barth entered quietly.

'Was it the Monsignor?' he asked.

'Yes.'

'And?'

Aveling's lean face tightened, his bald head reflecting a dull light. 'Soloman, I believe, cannot be suspect. Nor can the child's mother. And Marcelle stands where he stands. Which leaves three men who could have betrayed them to Cain.'

Barth sat at Aveling's quiet words.

'There is a general, the Chairman of the Joint Chiefs,' Aveling continued. 'There is also a man in the National Security Agency, and a man in the Central Intelligence Agency. The Monsignor was kind enough to investigate further and discovered that Colonel Soloman once attempted to assassinate this CIA agent.'

'Then it is obvious, Aveling.'

Aveling smiled, wistful. 'Certainty is a mistake committed by the young,' he said quietly. 'We learned such things in the war.'

'But it would be for revenge, of course.'

'Perhaps.' Aveling paused. Then he turned to Barth, startlingly still as he whispered, 'Agoni told me that this ... council ... is convening at the Central Intelligence Agency's headquarters within the hour.'

Barth waited. 'Yes? ... And so?'

'And so ... the CIA has apparently gained preeminence over this affair.' Aveling's aspect was concentrated, cryptic. 'Yes, of course ... Is it not better to rule in Hell than serve in Heaven? Is that not our enemy's wisdom? Yes, and so ... whoever has betrayed Soloman and my son would seek to rule, even as Cain seeks to rule. Or Hitler sought to rule. The servant is only a reflection of the master.'

Aveling's eyes lit up. 'These men are professionals, so each, if he is in authority, seeks the advantage of home ground. If the general had gained it, then the meeting would be at a military facility. If the NSA had gained it, then it would be held in Washington. But, obviously, this CIA agent has gained control, and so he uses the advantage.'

'I follow your logic,' Barth replied, eyes narrowing. 'But even if this CIA man has indeed betrayed Marcelle and this team, how can we use that knowledge to our advantage?'

Aveling did not seem to hear. 'Call back the Monsignor,' he said, staring at nothing. 'Tell him to discover all that he can about this Central Intelligence agent.' Then he tilted his head, abruptly mesmerized.

'What is it *now*, Aveling?'

'Also, yes, tell Agoni to discover if there are families in the northeastern area of this continent that are secretly dedicated to the intergenerational worship of our Adversary.'

'*Good God*, Aveling!' Barth rose fully to his feet. 'How can you advance to such a thought? Who can follow your mind?'

Aveling shook his head. 'It is eminently logical,' he said, more simply. 'It is logic born from faith, but it is logic. Cain is the Adversary, of this we are certain. Therefore Cain wishes to be worshipped. And to be worshipped he must have worshippers.'

'But … ' Barth searched for words. 'But there could be *dozens* of such families! How can we know that any of them are involved at all? And, presuming the accuracy of such a presupposition, how can we know which one is associated with this CIA man?'

Aveling's crested forehead hardened in anger. 'Remember what you know!' he said more sternly. 'Cain considers himself to be a prince! The servant is a reflection of the master! Those who serve him will also consider themselves princes!' He calmed down, added, 'Follow me in this, old friend. This CIA man – Archette is his name – is dealing with Soloman and Marcelle. Archette, in a word, is a soldier, just as the SS were soldiers. Which means that Archette is the vassal of someone greater, just as the SS were vassals of Hitler. For the true master never dirties his hands, neither with soil nor blood. During the war, Hitler never killed a single man or woman or child with his own hands, and

358

yet he murdered millions. So there must obviously be someone above Archette. Someone greater. Agoni can easily obtain the information we need, and then we will eliminate the lesser from the greater.'

Barth lowered his head, injured.

'Forgive me, my friend,' Aveling said, more softly. 'My emotions prompt me ... to intellectual sin. But I am, indeed, certain of this. Cain seeks to be equal with the Almighty. But he misunderstands majesty; he always has. And so he considers gold more worthy than clay.' He turned away. 'Go. Call the Monsignor and tell him we need the information immediately. And ... and I do value your judgment, Father. As well as your criticism. You are wise to counsel ... a temperamental old man.'

With a patient nod, Barth said, 'There is no sin, my friend. I will do what you request immediately.'

◆ ◆ ◆

Grim, Ben stared at Archette.

The CIA Deputy Director chaired the meeting and regarded Ben as if he were already extinct, a dinosaur overdue to return to a dead age. And Ben knew the routine. His cragged face was contemptuous, nothing given away. It would end here, he knew. There was no place left to go.

'I believe the decision is inevitable,' Archette began, glancing about the table. 'Our security is compromised, we are in jeopardy of revealing our secret weapons program, and so we must terminate the Trinity Failsafe. We have already attracted too much attention and lost too much in this exercise.' He took his time to continue. 'I feel we should proceed to the next failsafe and hope that investigators can eventually detect Cain's location. The tragedy, but also a reprieve for the world, is that Cain has obtained the child and will now callously murder her to heal the virus in his system.

Therefore, HyMar will not become supraepidemic. A regrettable episode in this disaster, but also a development which will allow us to hunt Cain with more covert and conventional means. We have already lost too much in this high-risk adventure.'

'Maybe not,' Ben said with a frown. It came from nothing he had planned beforehand; frustration said it for him.

Archette wasn't shaken. 'Yes, General?'

'Maybe we've gained a little.' Ben pushed it. 'Maybe we've found out a few things that will make this easier for us.' He waited. 'You want to talk about it?'

Archette paused. 'General,' he answered, 'the media already has pieces of this experiment. We are in a severely compromised position. I don't believe the situation could become worse.' He tested: 'Unless, of course, you can explain such a scenario.'

'I'll explain it,' Ben growled, leaning forward. 'Maybe there's somebody in this room who's committed to seeing Cain survive. Maybe there's someone here who wants to see Trinity fail.'

'And who would that be, General?'

'You.'

Silence.

'I see,' said Archette, emotionless. 'And can you justify this theory? You have some level of proof? Any proof at all? Or is this simply an understandably angry release born from your symbiotic relationship with Soloman?' He stared. 'General, please understand me. I know how you must feel. Soloman is in the field fighting something that no one should be forced to fight. But you are allowing your sentiments to color your judgment. And, at this stage, more than any other, we must commit ourselves to reorganization and order. The Trinity Failsafe has failed. We must remain focused and decide alternate means of eliminating this threat.'

'I am,' Ben said, meeting the gaze. 'That's why I'm going head-to-head with you.'

Everyone else in the room leaned back, removing themselves from the confrontation; it was an automatic act of self-preservation because whatever was being said could take down carefully crafted careers. Ben saw it and sensed it and it didn't affect him at all. He continued to stare at Archette, adding, 'You know, Archette, you really gravel me. I don't think I like you at all.'

Unperturbed, Archette replied, 'General, we are all under stress. And stress can sometimes alter judgment and personality. You are a professional soldier. Try to remember yourself as such.'

'I have.'

'You don't seem to,' Archette said solidly. 'We are in –'

'I know what we're in.' Ben shut him down. 'You know what we're in. And nobody else in this room has a clue.' And Ben smiled; the contemptuous smile of a man who was willing to throw thirty years of military service to the wind. He even surprised himself.

'You thought nobody would ever figure it out, didn't you?' Ben continued. 'But you made a mistake, son. You covered your tracks too good. And no track at all is the best place to start, sometimes. Like Soloman used to say. Yeah, you were too careful. Too smart by half.'

Archette responded. 'General, you are making vague but serious accusations. Are you saying that –'

'I'm saying that you wanted Trinity to fail. You approved Trinity but you didn't know that Soloman would be a factor. There was no personnel, just a plan. But when Soloman got involved you got scared because you knew he might actually be able to hunt this thing down and put its dick in the dirt. No, I don't have any proof. Because you're too smart to leave any. But I'm going to find something, in the end. Then I'm going to haul your ass before a tribunal and you can spin this yarn to them. But it ain't gonna go easy on you, 'cause I'll be there. And you'll curse the day you ever heard my name.'

'This release of absurd anger is not the purpose of our meeting, General.' Archette's gaunt face was unshaken. 'We are here to decide an effective means of terminating the Trinity Failsafe.'

'They're finished,' Ben grunted. 'You'll see to it.' He let it settle. 'All of this is being recorded by the Office of Security but I don't give a damn. 'Cause you're finished. You crossed the line with Soloman, old son. Crossed the line with me. Crossed the line by authorizing Genocide One when you knew what might happen. I may never be able to prove anything but I'm gonna haunt you the rest of your life. 'Cause you can't do this to people. You pushed Soloman's wife and kid into the street because Soloman was somehow messing up your plans. I know it. I can feel it. Then you tried from the first to negate the Trinity Failsafe because Soloman was recalled to active duty. And you're scared of him. You've always been scared of him.'

'General, try and be civil.' Archette was sympathetic, as if dealing with an overstressed patient. 'I truly admire Colonel Soloman. Indeed, he is a soldier worthy of respect. And I have done nothing more than deliver my opinion to these inquiries. I have no secret agenda and I am willing to open myself once again to investigation should you accuse me of such. But a catastrophe is on the table and we must deal with it effectively. We must decide an alternate approach, because Trinity is obviously inadequate.'

'Your opinion,' Ben growled. 'In my opinion, Trinity has gone above and beyond. They've lost almost every man on the team and they're still fighting. They've got less than they've ever had and they're closer to winning this thing than they ever were. So patronize these other idiots, Archette. But don't lie to me. I've got your number.'

'General.' Archette was painfully patient. 'I will be more than generous in any investigation you wish to initiate. But we *must* decide on Trinity. That is the issue at hand.' He was eminently forgiving. 'The rest of what you declare can be dealt with at a later time.'

Silence.

It was a brief war of wills, but Ben knew he couldn't overcome the chair of this meeting. Archette would navigate the debate to his own course, and there was nothing he could do about it.

But if Soloman or the kid were hurt, Ben knew, Hell itself would pay.

◆ ◆ ◆

Aveling finished the conversation with a remarkably excited Monsignor Balcanza – as if the old priest had found his old World War II blood electrified by the game – and did not look at Barth as he returned to the room. As Aveling strolled, his face was a study in stony concentration.

'And what did the Monsignor discover?' Barth finally asked. 'Did his reply fulfill your suspicions?'

'There are several families,' Aveling said. 'But there is one far, far above the rest. It is old, and virtually unknown. But we do know of it.' He turned to the window, pensive. 'It is on Long Island. They are … rich beyond measure, and discreet rumors have intimated that they have strong intelligence contacts. We have never confronted them.'

'And now?' Barth was steady. 'Will you commit us to this, Aveling?'

'Yes,' he said. 'And that will be the risk because, as you say, I could be deceived by my own cunning. I could be chasing a serpent in the sea, with no light to guide me through the green depths.' He paused. 'Use one of our more skilled people to contact this general, Benjamin Hawken. He and Soloman are apparently close friends, and we must decide to trust someone. A necessary risk. And ... I speak not as a priest, I speak as a man who loves someone as a son, and knows the value of sacrifice. Give this general our suspicions and then provide him with the address of these people on Long Island. If the CIA agent goes to this location, then our gambit is confirmed. From that point, it is in the hands of this man. And God.'

Exhausted, Barth rose to his feet. 'How much longer, Aveling? How much longer must we endure?'

'To the end,' Aveling said, concentrating. 'To the end.'

◆ ◆ ◆

Frowning, Soloman slowly picked up the phone. Said nothing.

'Sol?'

'Yeah. I'm here.'

'We've been recalled,' Ben said flatly. 'I fought with all of them but Archette was chairing. He's got his own agenda and you need to be careful. They denied me every extension of funds and equipment. Recalled all of us. I ... I'm sorry, buddy.'

Soloman's laugh was frightening. 'You tell 'em that it's too late for that. If they want to recall me, they can kill me. That's the only way they're taking me out of the field.'

There was a disturbing silence and Ben lowered his voice. 'Look, Sol, this line ain't secure. And I'm telling you, Archette says it's over. Officially over. We're out of funds and support.'

'I know the line's not secure, Ben.' Soloman's voice held a bitter edge. 'That's why I'm saying it. I'm going to get Amy back and if they want me out of the game, they can kill me.'

'Look, Sol, I'm serious about this.' There was no exasperation in the tone, just anger. 'And believe me, buddy, if they have to put you in irons until this is over, they will. Our papers are canceled. Passports are recalled. Customs has shut us down.'

Soloman's bitter smile didn't fade. 'Tell 'em to go ahead.' He was emotionless because all human emotion had been burned from him, replaced with a suicidal rage. 'But if they try to put me in irons, somebody could get themselves killed. There's a little girl out there, Ben, and I'm going to find her.'

Nothing was said for a time but Soloman could almost hear Ben pondering. 'Sol,' he continued, 'listen to me on this, and listen good. I think they're sending over a team for you. They want you out. And I can advise you that you should expect to be *arrested*. They're not going to let you run off …' Ben was silent a moment. '… like you did before.'

A grimace twisted Soloman's face and he slowly sat up.

Something had been hit hard, awakened by the words – something he'd strangely forgotten in the horror of the night. He stood with profound purpose and Marcelle caught the commitment. Sister Mary Francis focused on him as he released a heavy sigh directly into the phone.

'You're right, Ben.' His voice held an air of disappointment. 'Tell them that I'll go peacefully. I won't make any trouble.'

'I'll tell 'em, Sol.' Ben hesitated, and Soloman knew … that he knew. 'The good guys left a few minutes ago, so they should be there within ten minutes. And … good luck.'

Soloman hung up and motioned silently to Marcelle. Then he pointed to Mary Francis and the bedroom where Maggie lay, and the old nun moved fast, her black cloak flowing.

Soloman peeked out the front window and saw nothing, but didn't trust it. He spun as the priest came up, 'Do your people have the resources to finish this, Marcelle?'

Marcelle nodded hard and Soloman returned the gesture in a secret pact as the Mother Superior emerged, half-supporting Maggie. She was still groggy from the sedative and Soloman lifted her strongly in his arms. Marcelle opened the door and they descended the steps of the town house. They reached the car, a new LTD, in seconds.

Dropping Maggie in the backseat Soloman snapped open the trunk and moved to the rear of the vehicle, jerking out the radio module to hurl it into the street, where it was snatched up by a group of high school kids. Then Marcelle settled beside him in the front seat as Soloman backed the car, Mother Superior Mary Francis supporting Maggie's head in the back.

Marcelle whispered, 'The radio?'

'Has a tracking device in it,' Soloman said as he threw the car into drive and they broke into traffic. 'Do you have a place we can hide until Maggie wakes up from the sedative?'

'Yes,' Marcelle replied immediately, indicating a turn. 'The Church is not unqualified for the task.' He gripped the seat as Soloman hung an extremely hard left. 'We will finish this alone?'

'Yes!' Soloman shouted, livid. 'They're pulling the plug on us! They'll probably turn it over to the CIA! It doesn't matter! Amy will be dead by the time they find Cain! And I'm not going to let that happen!'

'The FBI is hunting us?'

'Every intelligence agency in this world is going to be hunting us!' Soloman hung a hard turn, the LTD fishtailing. 'But they can be beat! I've beat 'em before!'

Marcelle started violently. 'When?'

'When I –'

Soloman gritted his teeth as he chaotically crossed the curb to take the sidewalk, pedestrians scattering wildly. Then the LTD was on the street again, busting the light to get clear.

'For my daughter!'

Marcelle held the roof as Soloman hit another turn.

'Did you save her?' the priest shouted.

Soloman's reply was hard in hate.

'No!'

◆　◆　◆

Amy had stared for hours, and yet the man had not moved. Sometimes his lips moved in a dark whisper but his eyes remained closed, his head bowed and motionless.

She was amazed as she had watched his body heal, skin peeling in sheets to fall away like the skin of an onion as new, pink skin, healthy and unhurt, emerged from beneath. His hideously ravaged head and face, also, had slowly reconstituted, becoming almost as smooth and unscarred as they were before the fight. Already a thin sheen of hair and skin was visible on the skull, which had gleamed a reddish-white only a few hours ago. Together they rested in the abandoned building somewhere in a city.

Cain sat on the dirt-caked floor while she lay on a moldy mattress, her hands and feet tied, tape over her mouth. And for the longest time she thought he had fallen asleep. But now she sensed that he was doing something else. He was meditating ... or something.

Finally he raised his head and a deep breath escaped him as he bent over, slowly opening his eyes to stare hatefully at nothing she could see.

Amy watched, afraid to move, hoping he'd forgotten

her. Then he rolled his head and moved his fingers in a fluttering, quick gesture that made the talons click. He flexed a fist, holding it a moment before laughing that horrible, haunting laugh. Turned to her.

'Amazing, is it not?' He smiled slowly, a cruel red slash splitting beneath mocking eyes. 'Amazing that this body holds such power.' He laughed again. 'I thought that whore of a nun had exhausted my strength. How pleased I was to discover that she had not. For I still have much to do. I must locate Kano. I need … The Circle.'

Amy had trouble catching her breath. She didn't remember much of the night. Only cold, a soaring roar in her ears and then a landing silence with an even deeper cold. Then there had been a distant, frightening scream, and more screams, before the man returned and lifted her, moving with rumbling, galactic force through a dark forest.

She woke up here.

'Mortals.' He stared away. 'They regard knowledge as evil. And yet they know nothing of knowledge. They know nothing of space or light, or worlds beyond the scope of their imagination.'

He sighed, shook his head.

'I spoke with him – warred with him – face-to-face, and I knew the terrible scope of that arm. So, no, I was never deceived. And I myself was almost without limit, made to resemble him in every way.' He frowned. 'These mortals wonder stupidly at my image. But my image was as his, as the sun. None could look upon me with pride.'

There was silence until he clenched his fists and gritted his teeth.

'*Michael!* You were such a *fool!* Together we could have made the North run red with blood! Together we could have taken that Throne! But, then, there was always … the Nazarene.' Amy saw the face darken, hard lines burning in the frown, the black eyes. 'Yes, always the Nazarene. The one who had the pride to taunt even *me!* To call me murderer ... thief ... seducer ... liar. But he will regret his scorn. For I will yet drag him down in his vassal's human form to this disintegrating world, and the chains will change.' He was silent a long time. 'Do you really believe that I, as lofty as I am, failed to see the essence of what you were?' He laughed. 'No, for certain, space and time cannot change. And you think I didn't understand? But I understood all too well! I understood from the beginning what you had created and what my place could be within it! Nor did I care for what I could not claim!

'The infinite belongs to you and always shall! But *this* ... *this* that exists in space and light was mine and shall be again!' He grimaced. 'No, you are not undefeatable. I destroyed your work by power. I destroyed your work by deception. I defeated you again and again, and I will defeat you *again!* Your only victory lies with the horror of the hill ... my only crime. For until then I had never killed an innocent man. I had never violated your ... *justice!* I won by right! I won by might! I had taken nothing that was not rightfully mine!'

With a guttural roar he threw up taloned hands. 'The Earth was given to man but man gave it to *me!* All this was legally mine and you knew it! And then you deceived me! You lied to me! And you had the pride to call *me* ... a liar?' His eyes narrowed as if he beheld something savagely pleasing. 'But I made you suffer for it! I made you suffer as no man has ever suffered nor ever shall! Until I make you suffer *again!*'

Amy heard a car outside the building. Reflected light coming through the windows of the second-floor window caused him to lower his head. Stunned, Amy watched with wide eyes, with hope, but the giant rose slowly to his feet, undisturbed. He edged to the window and glanced down, gazing a long time until he turned to her.

'It seems the police have discovered our means of transportation.' He laughed and stretched his huge arms, releasing a deep breath. 'They are entering the building ... to investigate. A fortuitous event, indeed. For I hunger.'

Gazing down, he smiled.

Moved toward the stairs.

◆ ◆ ◆

Soloman was amazed at the skill that Marcelle met their needs. The priest stopped once to make a quick phone call and then they were driving again, Soloman alert for marked or unmarked cars.

Cautiously Marcelle directed them to a small church off Pennsylvania Avenue, less than a hundred yards from Shore Drive, a heavily traveled interstate. Soloman stopped behind the building and exited the LTD, and in the cold ocean breeze he could smell the salt water of Jamaica Bay. He caught sight of a 747 landing at Kennedy Airport, less than thirty minutes away. From years in the intelligence field he knew it was a good location for a safehouse.

Marcelle was speaking quickly as Soloman lifted Maggie from the backseat.

'Aveling has arranged for a speedboat to wait for us in the bay,' the priest said. 'If need arises, we will use it to escape the city and gain another place in New Jersey, which he has also prepared. And we have a private jet waiting at the airport to take us anywhere in the world within a half hour's notice.'

Slightly stunned as he carried Maggie into the rear entrance of the church, Soloman asked, 'Do you people do this often, Marcelle? I haven't seen any intelligence agency in the world that has this kind of coordination.'

Closing the door hard behind them, Marcelle laughed.

'The Church is not the world, Colonel.'

◆ ◆ ◆

Aveling was seated in a crimson chair, staring intently into the vault of the Secret Archives. His face held no expression, his hands no tension as they rested on the mahogany arms. But his eyes, focused on the cavernous chamber as if to discern truth by sheer will, glinted angrily. The Librarian Superior stood to the side, waiting.

Moving quickly, Father Barth came down the steps, a note in his hand. He walked up to Aveling and waited until the Jesuit said, 'Yes?'

Barth handed him the note, which he read slowly, frowning before he nodded. 'Good,' he said. 'Now, arrange in Rome for the transfer of unlimited funds.'

'A wise decision, Aveling. But, again, do we not worry about the consequences?'

'The consequences can worry of themselves,' Aveling answered gravely, folding hands meditatively before his face. 'Marcelle has thrown himself into the void, so now there can be no trembling of hands or knees. I will stand behind my son because I believe his cause is just, because his enemy is great, and because we must all choose where we will die. And, last, because no man who sets his hand to the plow and looks back is worthy of the Kingdom of God.'

A long pause.

'Go,' Aveling said, bowing his head. 'Do what must be done.'

◆ ◆ ◆

Soloman was stoic, staring out a window. He knew that

Marcelle had approached him but didn't turn. His mind had locked on something dark and disturbing. 'Tell me something, Marcelle,' he began. 'Do you really think you're right about Cain?'

Gloom, silence.

'Yes, Colonel, I believe that I am right. As incredible as it sounds, I believe that Cain is a dead man inhabited by Satan. The body is dead and the soul has fled, but because of this bizarre experiment it walks among us as undead. Now, Satan has somehow seized the soulless void, so we do not battle mere flesh. We battle a principality. We battle an elemental force.'

'You spoke of that before,' Soloman said. 'And I wasn't certain if I believed.' He paused. 'But now I do.'

Marcelle said nothing.

'Is he on a chain, Marcelle?'

'A chain, yes,' the priest replied. 'A long chain, to be sure. But the Almighty does, indeed, keep him on a chain. If he did not, then Cain would have destroyed this world long ago. And he knows his time is short, but he has deceived himself into believing that he can overcome.'

'A dog on a leash,' Soloman said. 'That's what Amy said. A dog on a leash.' He grimaced. 'So much power, but there's no nobility, nothing to glorify. It's like strength without purpose. Vengeance without justice.'

'Yes, but he remains strong.' Marcelle was grim. 'For he was once the greatest of all created beings, and he retains a measure of that cosmic might. Nor can any man understand him. Because no man can understand the essence of a spiritual being, which he is. Spiritual beings are not the fruit of reason, Colonel. Nor can any man understand pure evil, because at the core of even the most immoral man lies the faintest measure of good.'

A mutual silence. 'He's insane,' Soloman said.

Marcelle considered. 'Yes,' he said, 'his defeat

is assured and yet he denies. He is deceived by his own ferocity and he inhabits his own dimension of madness.'

'Madness to name this,' Soloman whispered.

CHAPTER 21

'It ain't gonna end like this,' Ben muttered, fists clenching. He found his car in the parking lot of Langley and unlocked it, lamenting the long drive back to the base with the traffic and the tolls. He wasn't in a mood for the mundane.

After dealing with Archette, he vaguely expected the whole thing to blow skyhigh when he started the engine, but the experience was uneventful. Then he hastily cleared the guarded exit and drove east on Highway 172, sensing rather than smelling the water of Chesapeake Bay.

He felt himself frowning as he debated a dozen options. But everything seemed futile, an exercise for nothing. And he knew better than to commit to an attack before he had measured the strength of the resistance; futile attacks cost more lives than futile causes. But, really, there was nothing left to do except sit and watch, he thought, as he saw the flat green fields of Langley Air Force Base approaching.

As he cleared the gate, angrily anticipating the thirty-minute flight to Washington, the phone rang and he let them know by his tone that *this* was not a good time. But as he listened, his brow hardened in concentration.

'Who is this?' he growled.

He listened until the conversation ended abruptly, as if in defense against a tap. Then, stone-faced, he parked the car in a no-parking zone and moved with his briefcase across the lobby, shouldering a dozen non-coms aside to command the desk sergeant's immediate attention.

Ben returned the salute.

'Get me a chopper right now,' he said sternly, using the full frightening weight of his authority. He didn't like to brutally throw his influence or power over his boys, but he was inspired.

'What's the flight plan, sir?' the sergeant asked, galvanized, and Ben looked up from his wallet, knowing he couldn't use military resources for the rest of it.

His eyes glinted.

'Long Island,' he said.

◆ ◆ ◆

Maggie was sitting on the bed smoking a cigarette when Soloman entered the small, undecorated room. Thin blue wisps spiraled up from a faintly trembling hand but her face was emotionless. Approaching her slowly, Soloman watched her eyes. They never turned to him.

When he was beside her he drew up a chair and glanced out the window, noticing the darkness approaching far too fast. It disturbed him deeply because it meant they had only three more nights until Samhain and the ritualistic sacrifice of Amy, if she were still alive.

Leaning back as Maggie released a slow breath, Soloman waited for her to speak. They hadn't talked at all after the battle in the basilica; it had been too chaotic. And everyone had been temporarily deafened by the explosions and gunfire. But now, Soloman knew, they had to communicate because he had seen Maggie replace the syringe in the coolant, securing it inside her purse.

In the dying light of a dismal day he stared at a slender wood crucifix hung on the wall, one of the few emblems in this hidden section of the basilica. Then Maggie flicked ashes into a small bowl and slowly massaged her forehead with the heel of her hand. Her voice was dry as she said, 'I could use a glass of water, please.'

'Sure,' Soloman said as he moved from the room, coming back to find her smoking another cigarette. Gently, silently, he set the glass on a small table beside the bed, trying to sound encouraging.

'I didn't know you smoked.'

A corner of her mouth quirked in a humorless smile. 'Gave 'em up.' She didn't look at him. 'Bummed a pack off Marcelle.'

'Yeah,' Soloman said faintly. 'Marcelle likes his cigarettes.' He shook his head. 'Sometimes he'll have one burning in an ashtray and one burning in his hand at the same time.'

'It's his nerves. He doesn't show it any other way, but what he's doing in this affects him pretty badly.' She was silent. 'Everybody needs something, Sol.'

Nothing was said for a long time, but from the set of her eyes Soloman knew that small talk was over. After taking a sip of water she looked directly at him, as if she expected him to start it. He returned the stare and tried to be encouraging without sounding patronizing.

'I think she's still alive, Maggie.'

'Oh?' She took a long drag. 'Why?'

'Because Cain wanted to take her alive. He went to a lot of trouble to take her alive. If he was going to just … to just kill her, he could have done it in the attic before I got to him. But he didn't. And that's because he wants to keep her until Samhain. We've still got three days.'

Something in her eyes was vaguely hostile, and she held it a long time. Then she lowered her face as she spoke, staring at the falling night. 'I was going to use the virus.'

'I know.'

'I haven't checked my purse.' Her lips tightened. 'I don't know whether to trust you or not.'

'It's still there, Maggie.' She looked at him when he spoke those words, and Soloman smiled faintly. 'You did the same thing I would have done,' he continued. 'I wouldn't have let Cain walk out of there with my child if I had the power to stop him. No matter what I had to do.'

Silence.

A tear fell. 'I could have killed us all, Soloman.' She rubbed it from her cheek. 'Including Amy.'

'You did the right thing, Maggie.' Soloman's eyes softened. He hadn't seen a woman cry in ... so long. He was vaguely shocked that he was so touched. 'But nobody was hurt. And in addition, I'm convinced Amy is still alive. I'm telling you; that gives us three more days to find Cain.'

'And how are we going to find him, Sol?' It was a heartfelt question. 'We couldn't find him before. We had to make him come to us. Now we've lost him again and he could be anywhere, just ... anywhere ... '

'We'll find him, Maggie.' He tried to communicate his confidence. 'Trust me, we'll find him. We've got one more stone to turn over, but it might give us something to go on. It has to.'

Then, reluctantly, he told her the full extent of their situation; they were cut off from military support, they were being hunted by every intelligence agency in the world but they had the full support of the Vatican, which would do anything necessary to destroy Cain.

She heard it all and pondered it a long time, the cigarette burning, suddenly forgotten, in her hand. Soloman couldn't truly tell how badly she'd received it. Her face had paled but she was also cold, almost scientific.

He looked up as Mother Superior Mary Francis, gray and stooped, entered the room with fresh bandages.

Without asking permission the old nun began unwrapping the bandage on Maggie's left forearm. Soloman noticed that she seemed remarkably adept at the task.

With a frown Maggie ground out the cigarette with her right hand as the nun worked, speaking in a raspy voice. 'Every child needs a mother. And soon your child shall have hers once more.'

The words, spoken with such quiet conviction, made a sudden tear appear on Maggie's face. 'Yes, I know,' Sister Mary Francis added without looking up. 'But suffering does not last forever. Not for you. And not for your child.'

Maggie stared. 'Do you really think she's alive?'

'She is alive.'

'But ... how can you know?'

'Because I know God will not let the Devil ultimately triumph.' Mary Francis deftly finished the fresh bandage, moving with surprising gentleness. 'This is not his world. And soon, God will deliver his doom.'

'But he's already killed so many peo –'

'The sword devours one side as well as the other,' the Mother Superior interrupted sternly. 'But Amy's life would give him his ultimate victory, and that shall not be. God will not allow it. Soon your child will have her mother's arms to comfort her once more.'

With a grimace Maggie leaned her head into the old nun's shoulder and without hesitation Mary Francis reached up, settling a firm hand on the auburn hair, bringing them together. And at Maggie's first racking cry Soloman silently rose and walked from the room.

But as he moved toward the door he also moved toward something inside him that was heated by the painful cries, and his face changed by degrees to stone. And as he cleared the portal he knew only one thing with absolute certainty.

He would pursue this thing to the ends of the Earth.

And he would kill it.

◆ ◆ ◆

'It has arrived, Eminence.'

Aveling did not stir as the young priest crossed the room to his crimson chair, which rested in front of the Archives. Then an instant later the man laid a large, wood-bound book on the old priest's lap, afterwards stepping far to the side, waiting in silence.

With a frown Aveling turned his face down.

The *Grimorium Verum*.

It was the last surviving copy, acquisitioned from the Secret Archives of the Vatican to be flown by Concorde and a commandeered Lear to Los Angeles, no expense spared. It was an evil work, Aveling knew all too well, but within it he might unlock clues behind the words Cain had spoken in the tunnel.

He ran a pale hand over the cover, studying the eerie, hideous, and mesmerizing image of a pornographic, Signorelli-type Hell drawn with typical Jesuit over-crowding.

Demons leaped and danced, some crushing under-foot naked women who had snakes crawling into their wombs. Men were bent and tortured with other demons crawling up their backs, purple faces distorted in a rictus of evil pleasure. Above the deeply penetrating scene, fierce angels heavily dressed in heavy medieval armor held burning swords to guard a majestic, sky-swept gateway.

Aveling realized that it was not the original cover for the millennia-old book. Nor was this the original book itself, though it was written in old Hebrew. No, he was certain, the original cover had glorified the power and place cursed by this one.

Delicately, feeling his heart quicken in fear, Aveling slowly opened it and beheld images made by those original masters of sorcery that had penned the manu-script. He saw winged demons flying naked against a blood-red moon, a truly magnificent city – Pandemonium, the capital of Hell – built on a mountain of iron. Then there was the image of a titanic winged figure seated upon a lordly throne of granite, his great, six-fingered left hand extended over worshipping figures, each of formidable strength. The imperial face was the face of infinite pride, infinite will, endless strength.

Prince of the Air ...

Aveling's hand trembled as he turned the page, and another.

And another.

◆ ◆ ◆

It was sunset when Soloman found Marcelle talking on the phone in a secret antechamber located behind a confessional. Nothing could be heard on the other side of the thick stone wall.

Soloman had already determined that they were secured in some secret part of the church, a place of hidden entrances and narrow corridors built into the edifice so long ago.

It was a place of unseen wars and unseen dominions, and Soloman wondered how many times it had been used in two centuries. But he felt confident they wouldn't be discovered, for even the parishioners, he suspected, were unaware of this isolated domain.

Waiting patiently until Marcelle hung up, Soloman noticed that the priest seemed agitated. Not looking at Soloman as he took a short step, strolling as he always strolled while thinking, Marcelle lit a cigarette. Clearly he was pondering something of consequence.

'So what else is there, Marcelle?'

A troubled wave. 'Two police officers were killed this morning at a condemned building in Elizabeth, not far from here. According to the media, who are still zealously pursuing the carnage at the sanitorium in Los Angeles, their blood was drained.'

Soloman rose, pointing at the wall. 'This is Cain, Marcelle!'

'Yes! Of course! But what advantage does it give us?'

Turning away, Soloman considered it a long time. 'Cain … he had to hide out so he could heal. And if he had to kill those two cops for blood, then he hasn't killed Amy yet. We can conclude that much.' He leaned heavily on a desk. 'You said that Cain needed both Amy and the *Grimorium Verum* for a sacrifice. Now he has them. So what the hell is he doing? Where is he going? The answer lies somewhere … in that vault.'

Marcelle looked down and sighed. 'Yes, we are certain of that. But there were so many documents.' He shook his head in dismay. 'Inventory is so –'

The phone rang.

Marcelle answered. 'Aveling, yes, it is I … Yes, we are fine.' He listened, amazed. 'Are you certain of this? … Yes! This is excellent, Eminence! … And you know even more? … What? … Are you certain? … Very good, Father … Yes, of course we will be here.' He hung up.

Soloman scowled. 'What?'

The priest was electrified. 'Aveling believes that he may solve the mystery before tonight.' He paced as he spoke his next words. 'He has read the last surviving copy of the *Grimorium Verum*, and he has found the spell that Cain intends to invoke. Now he knows the exact type of place that Cain needs in order to complete the conjuration. There are approximately one thousand documents in the Archives granting deeds to land with like qualities. But this will speed up the process immensely.'

'So what kind of land does Cain need?'

He made a vague gesture. 'It must be underground and exceedingly old. It must be near the sea for the power of salt water, which represents Hell. It must be made from hand-hewn granite to keep the conjurer close to the center of the Earth, and there must be fresh water flowing beneath it, representing the human soul. It must also be built on ground strong with copper, for magnetic effect. So, yes! This narrows the list considerably!'

'Look, Marcelle.' Soloman was growing angry. 'We have to move faster on this! We have to intercept Cain before he gets to this place or we'll be fighting him on the ground, and maybe even on the night, that he's strongest.'

'It will be a fiendish thing,' the priest replied, scowling. 'But we are finally closing in on this mystery, I believe.'

'Yeah? How close?'

Marcelle stopped pacing and stared.

'Almost close enough to kill or be killed, Colonel.'

◆ ◆ ◆

Maggie appeared far more focused as Soloman re-entered the room. The bandage on her arm was white; the bleeding had finally stopped. She looked up with a forgiving, or a forgiven, smile and Soloman returned the same.

He felt his heart reach out and was surprised that he was so glad to see her again after just an hour. He knew what was happening and he couldn't stop it. Nor did he feel any inclination to stop it anymore. He was going to give himself to this, if she would have him.

But, for now, there was business.

'We've got something,' he said, reflexively grasping her hands as she reached out. 'I think we've got an idea where he's going. We might even be able to intercept him before he gets there, if we're lucky.'

'Where, Sol? Where's he going?'

'We ... we don't know yet,' he replied, seeing the immediate rise of pain in her eyes. 'Not exactly, Maggie. But we're closer. A lot closer. We might even have an answer tonight.'

Soloman didn't really know how it happened but he knew from experience that it usually happened like that. One moment they were close and excited, and next they were locked in an embrace as passionate as anything he had ever known. He felt emotion explode in his heart, spiraling through his arms as they tightened around her figure. Kisses were exchanged in an explosive surrendering of flesh before they separated slightly and stared into each other's eyes.

'Soloman.' She grasped his hand resting firmly on her neck. 'Please ... please get Amy back for me ... '

He nodded hard. 'I'm going to get her back.'

'And then?'

His face went cold.

'Then I'm gonna kill him.'

◆ ◆ ◆

Moving quickly, hurling ancient documents that held inestimable value haphazardly to the cement floor, Aveling and Father Barth flew through the vault of the Secret Archives.

'This hidden place must be of copper and granite? And old, yes?' Barth hesitated with a document in his hand.

'It must be ancient!' Aveling moved with eyes that darted from shelf to shelf. 'And, yes, it must be of granite. It must be located by the sea. It will not be in this country.' He paused at a document, tossed it. 'I feel it will be in northern England, though there is no way to know for certain. But that is the ancient land of Druidic power and this spell is somehow linked to Samhain, so there must be a connection.'

'Perhaps somewhere in Flamborough or Hunstanton?'

'No!' Aveling's emotions suddenly flared. 'Those coasts are recent additions to the country and devoid of metal! They are products of glacial waste. No, this place will be older and stronger. It could possibly be upon an isolated coast of Northumberland.'

'Of course!' responded Barth, caught up.

Moving fast, their concentration and keenness of mind making lies of their years, they went through the documents like lightning as the Librarian Superior checked off each deed thrown, barely able to search the list and find it before he was fiercely hurled another.

◆ ◆ ◆

'I need weapons, Marcelle.'

Soloman's tone indicated that he was not in any mood for complications. He wanted weapons, he wanted them now, and he wasn't taking any crap about the difficulties of obtaining them.

Concentrating, Marcelle looked about, as if he had never confronted the problem. He studied it a long time before he whispered, 'It ... ah, we've never had to obtain weapons, Soloman. That could present difficult problems that, uh ... Perhaps I could –'

'Don't your people have access to weapons?' Soloman was incredulous. 'You've got jets and boats and all the money in the world and you don't have any access to *weapons?*'

'Weapons, ah, are not our specialty,' Marcelle said frankly, gazing away. 'But I am certain that I can get you some weapons if ... if we can only ... find a way to –'

'Damn, Marcelle! I don't have time for this!'

Soloman picked up the phone and dialed the Armory at Fort Bragg, asking for Chatwell. He gave them an on-the-spot yarn about being an AD with the FBI, about wanting recommendations for new 9-mm semi-autos. Then there was a suspiciously long pause, a faint click, and Chatwell came on.

'This is Sergeant Chatwell.'

Soloman suspected that the line wasn't secure.

'Chatwell, it's Colonel Soloman.'

An unemotional pause. 'Yes, sir?'

Soloman hadn't been completely certain until he heard the voice. Now he was. 'Look, Chatwell, I know now that you're under base arrest because they figured I'd be pulling something like this.' He couldn't stop himself. 'So this isn't for you. It's for them!' He released some long-withheld anger, counting seconds against a trace. 'You can't stop me! You couldn't stop me before and you can't stop me now!'

He hung up, turned to Marcelle. 'Well ...' He paused a moment. 'Looks like I'll have to do it myself.'

'We don't have much time, Soloman.'

Soloman moved for the door.

'I'm in a killing mode, Marcelle. I don't need much time.'

◆ ◆ ◆

Archette expected a more laudatory reception at the Long Island manor, for Soloman had been effectively eliminated, Cain had been flown to England with the child, and The Circle had accompanied him for protection. He did not understand the frown on Lazarus's face.

Staring down at the ancient table, concentrating, the white-haired man had not moved. His fingers rested on a Rune card that had been there when Archette entered. It lay face-up amidst burning black candles, and Lazarus had not taken his eyes from it, nor from three others laid in a tight square.

'Lazarus?' Archette ventured, made extremely cautious by the poised concentration. 'Did you hear my words?'

'I understand your words, and I understand more,' Lazarus murmured, pausing. 'Tell me, Archette. You said that Colonel Soloman has been eliminated. That ... is good. I commend you for your faithfulness. But, tell me, what of this priest?'

'The priest?'

'Yes. This Jesuit priest. Has he also been eliminated?'

'I ... I don't understand, Lazarus. The priest was merely an adviser to Soloman. Soloman alone had the resources for interfering with our dreams. The priest ... he is only ... he is only a priest.'

Lazarus shook his head, as if the statement did not merit his attention. His mouth tightened as he cryptically turned a card on the table for Archette to see. 'What is it?' he asked quietly.

Tentatively, Archette stepped forward, staring down. He saw four cards laid face-up, each pointing in a different direction; north, south, east, and west. They were Disruption, Warrior, Flow, and Movement. Archette did not know how to interpret them. 'Perhaps you should explain, Lazarus,' he said. 'I do not read the Runes.'

'Neither does our Lord,' Lazarus said. 'Runes have no more association with his power than Tarot reading, or the interpretation of stars. But sometimes ... they reveal truth.'

'What ... what do you mean?' Archette asked.

'This' – Lazarus lowered his face toward Disruption – 'reveals the release of elemental and chaotic forces on the Earth. It signifies the archetypal mind. Strong beyond measure. Then, there is Warrior. It is a spiritual symbol. It falls to the opposite of Disruption.' He frowned. 'Then there is Flow, which signifies that a great change is about to occur. And to the North, standing upright, there is … there is Movement.'

'I am not familiar with this card.'

Lazarus answered slowly with a scowl. 'When Movement stands upright in the North, it is the most powerful of all Runes. It means that a great and mighty power is present. A power that nourishes, and heals. It means that a force beyond any other … has arisen.'

Archette shook his head, perceiving. 'But if you had seen his eyes, Lazarus, then you would know! He can't be defeated! *Nothing* can defeat him! It is like looking into the eyes of God!'

With a faint trembling, Lazarus turned the northern card face-down.

'There is another,' he said somberly.

CHAPTER 22

It was midnight and Soloman crouched low on the roof of a building on East Eighty-third Street in New York City, watching as the proprietor closed the NYC Gunshop.

Soloman waited one minute before he moved.

In seconds he reached the fire escape and descended, moving fast to slide down the ladder and hit the ground hard. Roving eyes alert to everything and everyone, he walked slowly up the alley and across Eighty-third. Then he strolled down the adjoining alley where he moved behind the gunshop, checking for tramps or vagrants or witnesses. But there was only an old wino collapsed in a cardboard box.

Soloman moved past him without a sound, knowing that no plan was perfect, not wanting to hurt anyone. In seconds he was at the back door and took a small grappling hook that he'd bought from a military surplus store. He whirled it and threw high and then he was climbing, gaining the roof, staying low. He pulled the rope up behind him, just as he'd been trained to do.

He drew the Cold Steel tanto, the only weapon he'd managed to retain during the long conflict, and moved behind the heating unit to stab the tarmac savagely. He drove the quarter-inch-thick blade through the tar and drew it hard, carving a line. Then he hit it over and over and finally reached the wood. At that, he took out the small saw and with meticulous concentration cut a hole in the roof.

For certain, he knew without even looking that the gunshop was wired to the hilt. All of them were. It would have door alarms and window vibration alarms and motion detectors and everything else that high-tech security could provide. But Soloman knew there was always a way.

He blinked sweat from his eyes, breathless, refusing to surrender to the exhausting expenditure of physical strength required for the task. Finally, he managed to cut a narrow manhole. He gazed down at pink insulation and a layer of board beneath, the ceiling.

Without hesitation he slid into the hole, enduring the stinging sensation, out of sight. Then, turning on a small flashlight, he turned in the tightness and crawled until he found where the electrical units were tied into the breaker box, which was located downstairs.

Now for the difficult part.

He studied the wires until he found one of the phone lines, lines normally used for alarms. He couldn't reach the alarm system itself because it was inside the building, but he could reach this.

He took out the tanto and placed the wire against a two-by-four, cutting it as the alarm hit hard. With a sigh Soloman bowed his head, knowing this was the moment that would determine the rest of his life. If he failed in this, he would be in prison forever. Federal authorities, already afraid of him, would come up with anything it took to keep him behind bars.

He waited for a sweating, trembling twenty minutes until he heard voices outside the building. But he understood cops just as well as he understood alarms. He knew that no cop was going to waste energy crawling on top of a building to see if someone had cut a hole in the roof. They answered twenty of these a night and most of them were triggered by wind-rattled windows or punks throwing rocks.

After another ten minutes, with no lights shining through the hole in the tarmac, Soloman knew he was safe. They had checked the building and found it secure. There were no windows broken, the doors were shut tight, the fire escape was high, and there was no damage visible. NYPD had decided that everything was locked down. Checking the roof was beyond the pale for cops who simply wanted to get to the end of their shift in one piece.

Soloman knew he'd have less than two minutes after he hit the floor to find what he needed. The motion detectors inside would find him to set off a second alarm on an alternate phone line so he'd have to be in and out, forgetting ammunition if he was short on time. But that was tolerable. He could pick up ammunition later, if necessary.

First and foremost, he'd have to find the weapons he needed to take Cain to the ground. Then he'd have to make it to the LTD and clear the area before a pissed-off NYPD cop checked the alarm a second time.

He moved on it.

With a violent move he kicked out the plaster ceiling and descended hard, landing on a display case that shattered spectacularly at the impact, and then he was rolling, frantically trying to avoid splintered glass. But as he gained his feet he saw blood. He didn't know where he was cut but knew by feel that it wasn't serious. Breathing hard, he scanned the wall and saw instantly what he needed.

A Bennelli .10-gauge shotgun was displayed, locked by a steel cord that ran down the wall. Good enough. Soloman glared at the glass display case and his eyes locked on the large-caliber handguns.

He identified a .50-caliber Grizzly semiautomatic, one of the most powerful handguns in the world.

Instantly he shattered the case, removing it. Then he leaped over the counter and placed the tanto against the steel cord that secured the shotguns, pressing down with desperate strength.

There was a long straining moment and Soloman watched steel thread severed by steel thread until the cord parted. He immediately lifted the Bennelli and took five seconds to find two boxes of .50-caliber ammunition and .10-gauge double-ought buckshot from behind the counter, a dozen magazines. He threw all of it in a duffle bag and leaped over the case, angling fast for the display of black powder.

He moved fast, leaping the counter again. And in another moment he'd loaded everything he needed and was at the front door, forsaking stealth. He only had thirty seconds before police arrived, using the dependable two-minute time limit.

As he reached the exit he viciously kicked a chair through the glass, smashing the shattering white shards outward in a shower of splinters that sent people screaming down the street. Then he was in the open, not caring about identification as he ran quickly toward the LTD. They would find him in the end, he knew. But by then it wouldn't matter. He hurled everything into the backseat and fired the engine to break into traffic.

Aflame with stress, his hands gripped the wheel with crushing strength. But with maddening control he contained a silent roar until he finally brought it down again, settling into a sweating calm as he reached a sidestreet, avoiding as much traffic as possible.

And saw Cain before him.

Not there ...

'C'mon,' Soloman whispered. 'Let's finish this thing.'

◆ ◆ ◆

His face was deathly pale, his eyes like ice.

Skin stretched across a haggard face made him seem more dead than alive in the darkness. Reverently, he removed the golden pentacle from his neck, laying it to rest on an obsidian disk holding a black candle.

The pentacle was large and intricately detailed with blazing white stars and dark clouds, haloed by a hauntingly cold night. He clasped his hands before it a moment, bending his head in prayer. Then he reached up to remove the great black cloak, settling it neatly.

In seconds, standing silently inside the magnificent Manhattan apartment, he once more resembled the man he seemed to be to the world, except on these nights of dark ritual, of glory. Then, last, he removed his soft leather boots, carefully pouring dirt from within them into a cannister, for a sorcerer must always be in contact with the Earth in order to evoke a spell.

As he turned, he saw the gigantic figure seated behind him. Heart skipping, he began a wild movement to run and heard a startled shout erupt from his own mouth. But the figure did not move, made no effort to attack. And in a strange, spectral passage of time no words were spoken. Each held his place in the silent darkness.

In the voice of a god, the giant spoke.

'Forgive me, Kano,' he rumbled. 'But I have need of you.'

A gasp exploded from Kano and his hands began to tremble violently. He did not know what to believe or not to believe. His breath came in quick pulls as he staggered. He swallowed, staring and shaking.

'I-I-I … I am here,' he gasped.

'Yes,' the giant growled, seemingly pleased, 'of course you are.' With terrifying strength he rose and came slowly closer. 'You have always been here … for me.'

Kano fought to stay on his feet, glaring as the giant

emerged from shadow. He had been warned, but he had doubted; it was too fantastic. Yet now, and with a single glance, he knew –

God.

He had come.

He had come to him, had chosen *him* as his servant. But still, somehow, it seemed surreal. Kano made a visible effort to still the trembling in his hands and knees, staring at him eerily.

'There is no reason for fear,' the man said tenderly. 'I am your master, Kano. And you have served me well. As I have served you.'

Kano almost collapsed from shock but with volcanic speed the man instantly snatched him by the shoulders, supporting him with iron strength. He held him patiently until Kano reached up to feel the majestic might of those titanic arms, the hard firmness of the flesh.

It was real. It was real … real … *real …*

The Master …

'I –' Kano swallowed hollowly. 'I am here, Lord.'

'And yet, still, you do not believe.' He smiled and nodded gently. 'And there is no reason for fear.' The Lord released him and walked slowly to the pentacle resting on the obsidian altar: 'Yes, the Unknowable. One of my treasured Runes, for it portends death, enlivening the deepest of human fears.'

'Is it … is it really you?' Kano staggered. 'Is it really *you?*'

The man laughed. 'Do you wish to know what I have seen, Kano?'

'Of … of course, Lord. I wish to know *all* that you know.'

Eyes moving from the pentacle, the man reached down and picked up a stack of Rune cards, tossing one of them casually onto the altar as he spoke. *'Krist waes*

*on rodi, hwethrae ther fusae fearran kwomu, aththilae til
anum ic thaet biheald.'*

Kano hesitated. 'I … I know this. I have heard it
before. It is from the, uh, the …'

' "The Dream of the Rood," ' the Lord said. 'From
one who was there to watch … the Nazarene die.' His
frown was so terrible that an uncontrollable fear made
Kano step back.

'Don't be afraid, Kano,' he said without threat. 'I will
not harm you. No, certainly not you. For you have
served me well, and now I need even more of your loyal
assistance.'

Kano found the strength to walk forward. 'Any …
anything, Lord. I will do anything you demand.'

'As you always have.' The Lord laughed, suddenly
focused. 'I will tell you what must be done. You will
write everything down. We must begin tonight. And by
tomorrow I will be inside those granite walls to sit upon
my throne … once more.'

Kano searched for materials and saw the card that the
man had tossed upon the altar: an image of three
monolithic slabs as nobly proportioned as Stonehenge.
Two stood upright, the other lay across them, a lintel.
Kano knew the meaning, glanced up to see the man
scowling.

'Gateway,' the Lord said, and after a moment broke
himself from the trance. He released a heavy sigh that
hinted of herculean power and asked, 'Is The Circle in
place?'

'The Circle, Lord?'

'Yes, Kano. The Circle. Those who protect The
Family. Those who protect us from our enemies.'

'Of course, Lord! They are always in place to … to
do whatever must be done!'

'Good,' the Lord replied. 'Tell them to come to me
tonight. They must accompany us to the Castle of

Calistro in Fngland, located beside the cliffs of Lifanis. Archette is making preparations for the flight.'

Kano acquiesced.

'Take down my instructions,' the Lord said as blood gleamed in his eyes; blood or revenge. 'A very powerful enemy has already cost me too much time. And I must prepare … for him.'

Kano's eyes widened; he could not imagine. 'But … but who could be your enemy, my Lord?'

The Lord frowned.

'The son of David,' he said.

◆ ◆ ◆

Waves crashed behind him, and Ben stared coldly.

He had found the address easily enough.

It was a truly titanic mansion located behind the shore near Glen Cove, directly beside icy cold Long Island Sound. It was probably fifty thousand square feet. Four-storied with sweeping picture windows and set on a fifty-acre sandlot, it was surrounded by a spiked fence.

After advising the chopper pilot to set down at Nassau, Ben had rented a car under a false identification. Then he'd found a discreet location where he could watch unobserved. It was an abandoned, sea-broken shell of a store located almost a half mile away, and he was forced to use binoculars. And although he doubted that anyone would disturb him, he was prepared to flash his phony identification again.

Now he only watched, and waited. Though sometimes he worried about it, wondering if he wasn't being used, being fooled. But the voice on the phone had been coldly professional and certain, the voice of someone who knew. And, remembering the tone, he felt far less ridiculous about the stakeout, sensing that something would happen here.

And he knew something else.

If Archette had the guts to come out here, he was as good as dead.

◆ ◆ ◆

'Only one of you will survive this.' Maggie stared quietly as Soloman prepared. 'You're like two freight trains on a collision course.'

Soloman laid cans of black powder and a bag of ammonium nitrate on the table, along with a small case of World War II-era hand grenades. Purchased at a late-night military surplus store, they had no explosive cores. He would have to make them himself.

Soloman said nothing at the quiet comment. Then he removed a large quantity of black powder and placed it in a steel bowl. He carefully measured scoops of ammonium nitrate until he had the proper mixture, remembering the formula: 40 percent nitrate, 60 percent TNT for maximum explosive compression.

'So.' Maggie sighed and leaned forward. 'What are you making?'

'Amatol,' Soloman replied, mixing ingredients. 'It's the main explosive material used in artillery shells. These things don't have working cores because it's illegal to sell them with combustible material, but I can improvise what I need. I can build them.'

'How dangerous will they be?'

Soloman shrugged. 'Inside a six-foot perimeter, they'll injure 75 percent of the enemy. At fifteen feet it drops to 30 percent. Anyone outside twenty feet won't be hit at all, usually. And these are World War II-vintage, less effective than modern grenades. Most of the shrapnel tended to hit the ground. But I'm boosting the charge to give the fragments more velocity. That means they'll probably go high. If I stay low to the ground, even if I'm close, I don't think I'll be hit.'

Maggie's eyes narrowed as he worked. 'I understand

chemistry pretty well, you know. If you add some ferrous oxide to the black powder, you'll have more compression.'

'Iron?' Soloman looked up. He knew virtually everything about improvised explosives – he had spent his lifetime learning it – but he hadn't heard of that. 'Where do you get it?'

'There'll be some in the kitchen,' she said. 'It's a pretty common household product. Usually you can isolate it from cleaning powders. I can cook some chemicals up and deoxidize them in about a half hour.' She studied the grenades. 'What about fuses?'

'I'll soak some cotton string in a solution of black powder and sugar, then dry them. I'll measure them for five seconds.' He grunted. 'Which means I'll probably have about three.'

'Why's that?'

'A version of Murphy's Law.' He smiled. 'A five-second fuse is always three seconds.' He decided the mixture was as perfect as he could make it. 'The grenades have a flint trigger that's struck when you release the lever. It causes a spark that ignites the fuse and when the fuse reaches the amatol it explodes to send shrapnel. But I'm adding a heavy measure of potassium chlorate and mercury fulminate to make it more incendiary. Sort of like napalm. The detonation will spread shrapnel and fire over a wider area. It'll have a larger sphere of destruction than a regular grenade.'

'Potassium chlorate breaks down fast to oxygen.' She pointed to burning candles. 'You'd better seal the caps with wax once we mix the ferrous oxide in. That'll preserve it for a few days.'

'Good idea,' he nodded. 'That'll be good enough for who it's for.'

Maggie watched him unscrew a port located at the top of the grenade, removing the stem. Then he poured a measure of amatol in the cannister of the grenade and set it to the side. He completed the procedure with twenty of them, leaving them standing.

'Will those kill Cain?' she asked quietly. 'I mean, you've already hit him with everything anybody could hit him with, Sol, and he's still standing. I don't … I don't think he can die.'

'Cain can die,' he answered coldly. 'There has to be a point where we finally overload that healing factor. If I can hit him hard enough and long enough, I'll wear him down.'

'But what if he uses Amy as a shield again?' From the look on her face Soloman knew she was terrified at the possibility. He looked down and laid a line of string in a solution of black powder and sugar. He would remove it in five minutes and pour a careful measure of mercury fulminate along the length.

'Amy's not even going to be there when the shooting starts,' he said. 'The first thing I'm going to do is get you and her clear. I don't want anybody coming between me and Cain.'

'Between you and Cain is the last place anybody wants to be,' she said, gazing at him for a long while before she leaned forward. 'Sol, can I ask you something?'

'Go for it.'

'Why do you think you're still alive?' Somehow, the question disturbed her. 'I mean, Malo was a good soldier. The best. All of them were. But you're the last one.'

He shrugged. 'There's no explaining it. Luck. Fate. Whatever. I've been six feet away from a land mine that exploded and killed everyone around me and I wasn't even scratched. Really, I should've died then. Should've died a lot of times. But … I'll die when it's my time. Just like Malo died when it was his time. That's all there is to it.'

'Aren't you afraid?'

He grunted. 'Always.'

'Were you afraid when you lived in the desert?'

Soloman looked up. He hadn't told her about that part of his life, was surprised that she knew.

She smiled faintly. 'Ben told me about it on the night you went to the cathedral. He'd had a little too much of the sauce, I think. Got real talkative.' She stared. 'He said he couldn't figure what you were doing out there. Waiting to die. Trying to die. Something like that.'

There was silence, and Soloman knew he had to answer. With a frown he looked down and removed the string from the pan, laying it carefully on the table. He didn't look up as he spoke.

'When I lost Marilyn and Lisa, I didn't care about living. That's probably the only reason I was able to pull off what I did. I had no fear. Not of anything. So I hunted down the men that killed them and killed them in return. It was the only time ... I had ever set out to actually kill anyone. But it didn't help, in the end. I couldn't kill enough. I could never kill enough. So I went to the desert.' He tilted his head slightly. 'I don't know. I was more comfortable with death, I guess, than life. The best part of my life was dead, and I suppose I wanted to die with them. But I wasn't going to give in to it. It had to work for me. Had to earn it. It's ... hard to explain.'

There was affection in her green eyes, along with compassion. But there was something else, as if she realized a bitter irony.

'You were alive, Sol, and you wanted to die,' she said. 'And now you're fighting a dead man that wants to live.'

Soloman stared, absorbing the thought. 'Yeah. I guess so.'

She glanced at the grenades, the massive shotgun, the handgun with magazines and ammunition laid in a dangerous glossy black display.

'I pray that you can stop him, Sol.' She closed her eyes. 'You're the last one.'

Soloman frowned. 'I'll finish it, Maggie. I promise. I'll finish it and then you and Amy can be together. And ... and maybe I could tag along ... if you don't mind the company.'

Her eyes were both sad and joyful.

'No, Sol.' She smiled. 'I wouldn't mind.'

◆ ◆ ◆

The sun was still high when the Lear landed at the international airport in Birmingham.

It was an English industrial metropolis, proud and expansive. And although it was far from dusk, early darkness obscured the distant factories and hotels that lined the horizon. In the west, a great column of smoke stretched into the sky like a funeral pyre.

The jet door opened, and eight men wearing obviously expensive casual clothing deboarded. Then another man deboarded, a broad-shouldered giant who held himself with an imperious, lordly manner as he turned his head. Preternatural quickness flickered in the black eyes as he appeared to see all that was, and more.

Of imposing stature, he held himself with a vaguely threatening aura of concentrated physical power. And over a wide, low brow that hinted of phenomenal intellect and will, a long black mane of hair fell slightly past his shoulders. Dressed entirely in black, his long dark cloak lifted to a deep-born north wind which had risen abruptly, overcoming the roar of dying engines. His pants were loose and luxurious, and laced boots of thick leather sheathed his legs to the knees. He wore black gloves over hands that appeared large and capable.

Hesitating at the kingly image, airport police turned after a moment, politely requesting papers, and one of the men presented all that was necessary: a flight plan, visas, passports, and detailed manifests of cargo. Obviously, from the professional manner in which everything was inventoried and available for quick verification, the expedition was well organized. There were no untoward developments and in an hour they had cleared customs.

The only curious attachment was a six-year-old girl with sunlight hair, sleeping soundly inside the jet. Her papers were also in order and at the faintly intimidating request of the father, the leader, police declined to awaken her. His daughter was very tired, he said with no discernible accent, and needed to rest. Holding the dark and ultimately dominating gaze for a moment, officers exchanged hesitant glances, finally acquiescing.

It was finished.

Customs officials allowed two vans, which had been waiting for the jet's arrival, to approach. And while the men loaded cargo and luggage into the secondary vehicle, the giant carried the child, still sleeping soundly, to the back of the first vehicle where he laid her gently on a cot. He turned to nod dismissively to the police who watched with curious interest, amazed that a child could sleep so soundly.

Then the van left the tarmac and drove toward the mysterious north, a land where misty forests and ancient castles stood poised on the edge of ice-mountains that rose hauntingly above the sea.

◆ ◆ ◆

Father Barth, sweating and breathing heavily, held a hand over his chest. He was perilously exhausted, his vision blurring with each document he lifted so tiredly from the shelf.

He cast a glance at the Librarian Superior to see his face drawn and haggard, as if he could not continue. Then Barth looked at the ancient Aveling, to see the pale visage sternly set. Obviously, the older priest was similarly exhausted, but revealed no sign of relenting.

Only a handful of the documents remained. Then Aveling motioned generously for Barth to sit while he finished the task.

Accepting, Barth collapsed while Aveling moved quickly, finding and sorting and discarding with a skill keenly honed by a night of frantic filing. And then they were done, the vault cleared with every paper meticulously inventoried and cross-checked.

Aveling let the last document fall dead to the floor, stumbling slightly as he exited. He reached the table and motioned for the Librarian Superior to move aside. Then the Jesuit Superior General sat where the lists had been so hurriedly but carefully compiled. His eyes roamed, concentrated. He went from one book to the next, finding and referencing.

After ten minutes, he stood. His gray eyes narrowed in a primitive pleasure rarely observed in so august a face. 'At last,' he said quietly as he stared down. 'At last … we have found the fiend.'

Barth stood, swayed by the impact of the news. He leaned against the vault wall. 'Are you … are you certain, Aveling? Do you know where Cain has taken the child? There is no time to be deceived!'

'Yes,' came the exhausted reply. 'I know exactly where he has fled. It is as I surmised. He has taken her to the ancient land of the Druids. To the land of Samhain.'

'What is this place?'

'The Castle of Calistro, claimed by the Church in the fourteenth century after the renegade Cathars and Druids ran amok with human sacrifice. It is located in the Northumberland region of England.' He released a deep breath. 'It is a forbidding fortress that towers on the eastern sea cliffs of Lifanis, a cold and desolate place. Though the castle itself is Roman in design, no one is certain who constructed it. It is a place I know only by bureaucratic privilege as Superior General, and there is much I cannot tell. Though, vowing you to restraint, I can say it is a place rumored to contain mysterious forces. The single road leading to the cliffs of Lifanis has been barricaded for many years. Nor do we allow tourism within its walls.'

'Forces? What manner of forces?'

'Perhaps scientific, perhaps magnetic, or even geological.' Aveling shook his head, a sigh of exhaustion. 'Perhaps even divine, though I thought myself to have given up belief in such things. Suffice it to say that we do not understand them. But Cain … he will understand.'

'Then this deed that he has stolen –'

'Grants him legal possession.' Aveling was gloomy. 'Whoever possesses the deed, signed by Edward I, will have little problem settling affairs with English authorities. There will certainly be suspicious questions but nothing that Cain, with his great wisdom, cannot sufficiently deflect.'

'Do you believe he intends to make this castle his home?'

'Even birds of the air need nests,' Aveling replied. 'Cain is the same. And if our perceptions are correct, he will want a place old with blood, old with shadow and cold. He will not want a place devoid of what he knows so well.' A pause. 'Yes, I believe that Cain intends to make this his home while he consummates his plan.'

'And the child?'

Silent, Aveling frowned.

'If those who fight for us cannot rescue her, then she will surely die,' he replied finally. 'Cain must have her blood to correct this curious scientific malady in his system. But even if he did not need her blood, he will kill her. He is a creature of mindless annihilation, of senseless evil without meaning or even true design. It would be destruction for the sake of destruction, the heart of evil. So yes, old friend, he will murder the child.'

Barth rose. 'And now? Now what is our course? Can we not call in the English authorities to intervene? Surely Marcelle and Soloman are outmatched, alone against this fiend.'

'Yes, alone. But alone they must remain. For no one would stand beside them if they knew the meaning of their struggle.'

Barth said, 'They will need a miracle.'

'We have no time for miracles, divine or otherwise,' Aveling answered. 'Now I must call Marcelle and tell him that the final conflict is upon them. I must tell him to pursue Cain to the Castle of Calistro where, by the grace of God, they may yet destroy him.'

Aveling's face fell. 'Before he destroys us all.'

CHAPTER 23

Amy awoke to a cavernous silence, a stillness of air. She didn't think of anything at all as she rose on one hand, staring at faint distant angles of light framed by gloom. It seemed that she was somewhere different; she couldn't be sure. But as she gazed she began to perceive distinct lines within the somberness, lines that joined, level upon level, rising ...

Stones ...

Stones joined close about her, and she realized that she was in some kind of building, distant light shifting through an entrance to ... to *this room*. She shook her head and sat groggily on the bed, raising hands to her head. She had a headache, a sharp pain in her temples that reminded her somehow of ... *the man*.

And she remembered.

He had come to her, had made her drink something pasty and bitter that made her gag. And then she knew no more, only the nightmare continuing, always continuing. But she had known so much of it in the past two days, it seemed like all there had ever been.

She thought of her mother, and Soloman, who'd promised to always, *always* protect her. Then she remembered the pain on his face as the man had moved her down the stairs, saw Soloman reaching out, and for a faint, fading second she had known hope.

She prayed that Soloman and her mother would be coming for her, that they would find her, even as something else said that no one would ever find her, and that she would die here. Then she was afraid again with a night known too long.

Bowing her head, she desperately clutched the rosary beads and the crucifix of Mother Superior Mary Francis – *to give you comfort* – still wrapped closely about her neck, her hand tight with a last hope.

Tears fell, but she made no sound at all.

◆ ◆ ◆

Soloman snatched the curtain of the Lear cockpit.

'Can't this thing fly any faster?' he snarled.

The pilot of the Lear turned his head. 'We're *already* going four-fifty, Colonel!' He was clearly exasperated. 'That'll put you in England in two more hours and it's the best I can do! This isn't an F-16, you know. We can't go Mach 2! We can't even go supersonic!'

Without replying Soloman jerked back the curtain and moved angrily down the aisle to see Maggie holding a fist to her teeth, staring worried and silent out a window. He passed her without words and crouched at the back for an equipment check. And again he was satisfied.

Yeah, he'd brought everything.

The .50-caliber Grizzly semiauto was in the sack with ten fully loaded clips for a total of 70 rounds, each capable of shattering the engine block of a car. The armor-piercing rounds would penetrate a quarter-inch steel panel, he knew, and just might penetrate Cain's internal armor plating.

The Bennelli, termed the M-3, was a shotgun specially designed for the military. It fired either slugs or buckshot and operated on semiauto or pump. It carried seven rounds in the magazine and one in the chamber. And Soloman had loaded it with double-ought buck, each shell containing 9-mm shot. They couldn't penetrate Cain's armor, but they'd devastate flesh to put that infamous healing ability into overtime.

Last, Soloman checked the grenades, twenty of them, and a waterproof daypack filled with almost twenty pounds of dynamite and homemade napalm concocted from gasoline and nondetergent cleanser. The dynamite was wrapped around a waterproof bag holding the napalm, and he would use the dynamite as a catalyst. A twenty-second fuse was located in the top, and once it was lit he'd have to get clear fast because the explosion would create a holocaust of mushrooming flame over 150 feet across. But if he had to, he had already decided, he'd put the pack on his back and throw himself on top of Cain for a final embrace. Either way, he had determined, Cain was going down.

There are worse ways to die.

He sensed Marcelle beside him and looked up to see Sister Mary Francis sitting beside Maggie, seemingly in prayer. With a quick movement he closed the duffle and rose. 'Are you sure we're not going to have any trouble getting my weapons through customs, Marcelle?'

'Yes,' the priest replied confidently. 'Aveling has made arrangements with certain members of MI5, old friends of his, it seems. They have pledged to keep your arrival a secret for a short time, and will escort us through customs without preliminaries.'

With a grunt Soloman looked over the plane. 'It's going to long odds, Marcelle, this team against Cain.' He paused. 'Maybe you and the rest should let me go in alone, take him down myself.'

'Everyone needs an ally, Soloman.'

The warrior in Soloman, never far from the scholar, rose to the surface. He had felt it taking more and more control since Amy had been taken. Realized his attitude altering more and more as they got closer to the confrontation. His killing instincts were fresh and alive, flowing from his heart hot with quick strength, a hair-trigger alertness.

'Well, not everyone has to go up against this, partner,' he replied. 'And it's not going to be a dancing contest. It's going to be a throwdown without mercy from beginning to end, and once it starts there's not gonna be any place in that castle that's safe.'

Marcelle smiled faintly. 'But we do not fight alone, Soloman. We do have God … on our side.'

'You're a brave man, Marcelle. But don't get too brave. There's no future in it.'

Marcelle truly enjoyed it. 'What we face, Soloman, may require all of your skills and mine combined.'

'What skills can you offer, Marcelle?'

'Counsel. There are unknowns that we must consider. Plus, I doubt that Cain remains alone. If he is half as cunning as I believe him to be, then he has recruited followers from intergenerational cults that are secretly dedicated to worshipping him. They are the most dangerous force in satanism. I told you earlier that I did not think we were dealing with satanism. That is because we were dealing with Cain, who is Satan himself. But I believe the game has changed, somewhat. The circle has enlarged.'

Soloman looked away. 'The big-conspiracy theory, Marcelle? That satanists are responsible for Hitler, Watergate, pornography, abortion, the Pentagon, and Irangate?'

Marcelle enjoyed the moment of humor. 'No.' He smiled. 'That is a fallacy of the paranoid and simple-minded. It is a delusion, for such an act would be impossible to sustain. However, the FBI's Behavioral Science Unit publicly admits that there are, indeed, multigeneration families that are secretly dedicated to satanism. These families are highly protective and leave no clues of crimes. They would be a formidable ally for Cain.'

'So,' Soloman pondered, 'who would Cain recruit? That is, if he's really who you think he is.' He still had trouble saying it out loud.

Taking a breath, the priest said, 'If Cain is who we suspect him to be, he will have recruited vassals from almost anywhere. Those who truly practice satanism, and are equipped to assist him with money and resources.'

'Is that really possible?'

'Yes,' he said flatly. 'It is possible.'

'Well, I'm not worried about Cain's goons.' Soloman suddenly checked the Grizzly, breaking out. 'I'm in a hot damn mood to kill somebody, so it might just as well be them. What I'm saying is that I don't want to see Maggie or you or Mary Francis get hurt by the flak. 'Cause once this thing starts I'm not going to be able to fight Cain and protect all of you at the same time. To finish Cain, I'll have to go all out. Which means there's gonna be a firestorm. And these grenades and bullets aren't particular about who they find.'

'I am in this to the end,' Marcelle said gently, but firmly. 'As is Mother Superior Mary Francis. Nor, I think, will Maggie let you go into the castle alone. She has great affection for you.'

Soloman said nothing, then glared out the window. He saw distant ground beneath, the sea behind. Soon they'd be landing at Birmingham and a new game would begin.

'All right, Marcelle, you can ride it out to the end. Just remember one thing. When we hit the deck, the rules have forever changed. I'll be in a combat mode and all of you will do exactly what I say, when I say. And if I say drop, I want everybody to drop. I respect your judgment, but don't question me in a combat situation. Not ever.'

'We will follow your commands, Soloman. Be assured. But there may be something that we, too, can offer. If we fight with courage and hope and determination, we will be stronger together than alone. A three-strand cord is not easily broken.'

'Yeah,' Soloman answered. 'Ecclesiastes. Chapter 1. But there's going to be blood in this, priest. Enough blood to drown in. And I want a promise from you.'

'Ask.'

'Once Amy and Maggie are together, when it's just Cain and me, I want you to get them out of there. Then I won't be worried about any of you getting hit by flak. I can go full out. No hesitation. 'Cause I'm telling you right now, that if I have to, I'm gonna bring that castle down on him and me both.'

There was a long pause, and finally Marcelle nodded. 'I understand,' the priest said. 'But know this, Soloman. You were brought to this child for a purpose. It was meant to be by a power higher than this world. You did not choose Amy. You were chosen for her. It was your destiny. Ordained, and concealed. And now, I think, there is one less mystery in your life.'

Soloman stared. His face was too fierce in a combat mode to show anything but heat and fighting rage, and after a long moment he turned to look out at the night.

'And now,' Marcelle said, 'if you will excuse me, I must pray. While there is still time.'

'Hey, Marcelle.'

The priest turned back, waiting.

'Do you really … ' Soloman paused. 'I mean, do you really believe in prayer?'

Marcelle laughed softly.

'Well, it certainly can't hurt, Colonel.'

◆ ◆ ◆

A gigantic granite throne of majestic age dominated the torchlit chamber, embracing Cain's powerful form with godlike dimensions, casting an unearthly aspect.

Black candles, staggered in levels, lined his back with a single large white candle in the center. A hexagram – a six-pointed star – had been etched in red on the floor. Warlocks stood silently at each point, two on the crest of a pyramid drawn in the center.

Dark and haunting, Cain stared over the men before him, each waiting silently for his words. And a smile came to him slowly as he saw the disciplined faces void of emotion or sentiment or mercy. No, there was only cold remorseless will, dark purpose.

Each was dressed in a long black cloak that made them all resemble medieval monks. And all, he knew, were consummate killers, silently dedicated to the art of protecting their Church. And he would need them, for limited as he was in this flesh, he required servants who could execute the more mechanical aspects of his master plan.

It was only a small army to begin, but it would grow little by little until they were as numerous as grains of sand. *Yes*, as the Old One said, *do not despise the day of small things.* It was a necessary place to begin.

He laughed.

He always enjoyed using that great wisdom against the very hand that created it, duplicating even the symmetry of that cloud-crested kingdom when he created his own – a dark reflection of what was truly perfect, and perfect in its own counterfeited aspect. Not the same, no, but no less because it mirrored the best and highest realm of this universe.

Pleased, he stared over The Circle and knew with certainty that they could accomplish any task. Yes, Archette had been careful when he recruited them, had used wisdom to hide them in the secret corridors of power where they had used their magnificent skills to protect the Family, which oversaw his highest affairs in this dimension. Between them, he was certain, the deaths they claimed would count in the hundreds.

And he had fiercely retained knowledge of their existence when he'd seized this corporeal form, knowing he would eventually need them. Just as he had known that he would eventually need Archette, who sat upon the council of the Family. Yes, Archette, such a faithful vassal.

It was time.

He spoke with a voice of inhabited stone.

'Our task is simple, and dedicated to a single goal,' he began. 'First, you must ensure that I am not distracted from the Black Mass to be completed tomorrow night. Samhain cannot, it must not, be desecrated by the wrath of my enemy. I trust you to defend holy ground.'

Talons tightened on granite. 'The glory you have known is but a reflection of the glory you shall know in the days and years and eons to come. For despite your honorable service, the memory of true celestial might has been lost to this world, now to be revealed only by my return. I, your Lord, am among you. And I shall bring a glorious revival of those days when we tread down dominions of the Earth. Yes, now we will reclaim the land we have lost. Continents will be crushed by might and Mammon. And soon the world shall once again worship the one true god.

'Remember this hour when you were the first to stand before the Lord. Remember the hour when you were chosen as the first to enter the land promised to us so long ago and taken by that tyrannical hand that knows neither justice nor mercy. But now there is a new beginning, and we will yet conquer the evil of that heavenly wrath. Our cause is just, our hearts are true, and our victory is assured if we only stand with courage.'

He paused, his aspect darkening.

'Only one danger remains,' he intoned. 'There is a man. His name is Soloman, the same who hunted each of you in the past, though you escaped him. And now he hunts me. He will come for the child, to take her. But it must not be. I have already dispatched Cassiel and Raphael to intercept him. But, should they fail, and if Soloman reaches the castle, then you must destroy him. And make no mistake: Soloman is to be respected, for fear has its own wisdom. But might is on our side, and he is only one.'

He gazed at them and continued. 'So great is your individual strength that even one of you should be sufficient for the task. But standing together against a single man, you cannot be defeated. I give you the honor of slaying him because I will be involved in the ritual. So it is a task you must complete. Do not disappoint me. Do not allow my faith to fail. Nor should you fear martyrdom, for if you die you will only be reincarnated, reborn in this world and elevated to become an Overlord of my Church.'

Silent and cloaked, they bowed.

'Go and prepare.' Cain raised an arm. 'An enemy approaches.'

◆　◆　◆

Quietly met on deboarding and ushered through Birmingham customs by a very elderly man who moved with the understated authority of a retired spy, Soloman loaded the duffle bag in the back of the car and surreptitiously removed the Grizzly to lock it in a right-side hip holster. He'd placed four extra magazines in clip holders on his waist and two grenades behind the holster. The tanto was secured tight on his left side.

It was cold, dark.

A waving, slicing sheet of rain swept over them and Soloman bent his head, wincing at the cutting cold. The English weather was so savage and piercing it was almost like culture shock, for he was accustomed to the dead heat of L.A. and the airless atmosphere of the desert.

Frowning at the gale-swept night, he gathered his waist-length tan leather coat more tightly, wishing he'd brought gloves. He buttoned up as Maggie and Mary Francis approached.

They carried small bags that Soloman took and quickly tossed in the trunk. Then Marcelle got in behind the wheel, gesturing for Soloman to sit on the left side. Maggie and the old nun settled in the backseat.

'We must go north,' the priest said as he pulled into traffic. 'The Castle of Calistro is far from here, on the coasts of Northumberland. But since it is almost dark I suggest we find a place to stay overnight and proceed in our attempt to rescue Amy tomorrow.'

Soloman turned to him. 'Tomorrow is Samhain, Marcelle.' He thought of Maggie but couldn't temper his words. 'Amy dies tomorrow night.'

'But we cannot reach the castle tonight,' Marcelle grunted. 'We must take the M6 highway to Lancaster and that will be as far as we can travel before we're too exhausted. Then there will be only a four-hour drive to the castle. We can arrive by early afternoon. That is the most sacred hour of sacrifice, and Cain will not violate the ritual of the Black Mass. We will have time to reach her and we will have the advantage of reconnaissance.' The priest paused, measuring Soloman's hard gaze. 'But if you do not wish to take time for this approach, we can be flown to Newcastle in the morning. It's only an hour's drive from the castle.'

Soloman said nothing as he stared out the windshield. He didn't like a lot about this. For one thing, he felt they were already being followed, and Cain shouldn't have known that they were arriving. He turned his head, scanning, searching, waiting for his intuition to help him.

Yeah, something was wrong ...

It came to him more solidly moment by moment, though he didn't know why; it simply felt like a trap.

'Soloman?' Marcelle asked. 'Did you hear me?'

'Yeah, yeah, I heard you, Marcelle.' He concentrated, trying to find the faint danger, sensing it in front of him. 'Marcelle, who knew we were landing in Birmingham?'

'Only Rome and their old friends in the intelligence community,' he answered, his brow hardening. 'But Aveling would not have used them if they were not of the highest possible trust.'

'And at the Vatican?'

'There is Monsignor Balcanza. He is also an old friend of Aveling's. They fought together in World War II against the Nazi regime, and most effectively.'

'He can still be trusted?'

'Yes,' the priest answered quickly. 'Completely. But ...'

'But what?'

'The ... the Vatican is a house of cards,' Marcelle said. 'It is a shadow waiting for someone to turn on the light. There are many forces which fight within, although they maintain a divided house with remarkable skill. If Balcanza has lost any of his old skills, if he made a single mistake, there may be many who are aware of our flight.' A pause. 'What do you perceive?'

'I don't know.' Soloman's gaze roamed over the crowd as he drove out of the airport. 'I just feel like someone's on us.' He scowled. 'Cain will anticipate us, but he shouldn't know where we're landing. He could find out, but he couldn't do it alone. He hasn't had time to get wired in.'

'As I said,' Marcelle replied, 'I do not think Cain is alone. I believe he has recruited help from someone. Those who will begin building the army he needs to fulfill his dream. As powerful as Cain is, he must still have vassals to execute what he considers beneath his princely standing.'

'Maybe. But he's –'

It was Soloman's killer instinct that made him spin, snapping his head around at the last second to catch a glimpse of the face he'd already seen three times inside the crowded corridors of the airport. He glared between Maggie and Sister Mary Francis, watching as the man casually hailed a cab.

Soloman studied the man, memorizing every detail. He noted a pale face, close-set eyes above a long, straight nose, dark hair, muscular but lithe. Large hands, strong. About six feet, one-eighty. He was wearing a black sweater beneath a black overcoat, no discernible style, as if he wanted to blend into the crowd, utterly unmemorable. The man reminded Soloman of someone he'd seen in his past.

Then he entered the cab and was lost from sight, hidden by traffic. And Soloman knew the cab wouldn't be following. If the man was really a hitter, there would be another vehicle waiting outside the airport, a second member of the team who was probably even now in communication with the man in the cab, receiving a description of their car. It would be the second man that picked them up.

Soloman turned in the seat, scanning the road, feeling it deep in his gut, where it mattered, and he knew it was coming. He felt a spiraling rage but shut it down immediately because it was too early for adrenaline or rage. Rage had a place in battle, but not before. Excitement was the enemy of tactical thinking.

'What is it?' Maggie asked. She had turned her head to follow his hostile glare. He said nothing.

'What is it, Sol?'

'Find a place where we can hole up for the night,' Soloman said quietly to Marcelle. 'Find something isolated. In the country. We'll go north for a while, then we'll settle in. We need some rest and food before tomorrow.'

'Why should it be isolated?' the priest questioned. 'If we find something more prominent, it may deter an attack.'

'I'm not trying to deter an attack,' Soloman replied. 'They're already following us and we'll gain a little bit of advantage if we can weed 'em out before we reach the castle.'

Maggie leaned forward. 'How do you know they're following us, Sol?'

'I saw that guy three times inside the airport and it's too big for that,' Soloman answered. 'He left by the same door we used, and there's more than twenty doors. He didn't have any luggage. No briefcase.' He paused, convinced. 'He's somebody. I can feel it.'

'An assassin?'

Soloman searched the rearview mirror. 'Probably, and there's no doubt more than one. They'll try to kill us at the first opportunity because they'll think we're easy prey.'

'What are you going to do?'

Soloman's laugh was frightening.

'I think I'll give 'em a wake-up call.'

◆ ◆ ◆

At midnight they checked into an isolated hotel beside a shallow river on the edge of Luvern. From there, if they took the narrow English backroads that ran through the thick, dark woodlands of Northumberland, they could reach the castle in three hours.

The night was shrouded in a cold English mist as they drove through the iron gateway. Then, while Marcelle made arrangements for a suite, Soloman took care of the trunk. Maggie and Mother Superior Mary Francis were close beside him as he laboriously carried all the luggage at once, not daring to leave anyone alone. After they checked into their room they were graciously provided with a late meal.

Leaving the suite, always keeping the door in sight, Soloman made a quick reconnaissance of the halls, the fire escape, all windows and possible points of entry. Then he returned quickly to find Maggie finishing off a bowl of cream of parsley soup. This pleased him: she had eaten so little since Amy had disappeared.

As always, Marcelle was pacing, a cigarette burning in his hand. He had a troubled look on his face as Soloman removed weapons from the duffle, placing four grenades on the belt at his waist. 'What is it, Marcelle?' he asked, chambering a round. 'You look like you've seen a ghost.'

'I have seen … a demon, Colonel.' Marcelle's tone was not friendly, and Soloman had expected that it would come sooner or later. This ordeal was getting on their nerves, wearing all of them down.

He remembered Karl von Clausewitz's instruction in *On War*. In essence, the lesson stated that, as a battle wore on and on, it was fatigue and domination of will that decided the outcome. Tactics were inferior to the iron resolve of an indomitable opponent.

'Stay cool, Marcelle,' Soloman said quietly. 'We're closing in on this thing and it'll be over soon.' He paused. 'One way or another.'

The priest turned and looked at him solemnly. 'I have something to tell you, Colonel. Yes. Something to tell all of you.' Soloman stared, instantly nervous; this was no time for surprises.

Marcelle's pause was so profound that Soloman began to wonder whether the priest had snapped. Maggie was watching him nervously, though Mary Francis retained composure. Then, after a hauntingly silent moment that continued far too long, Marcelle bowed his head.

'I do not know,' he began, 'whether I precipitated this tragedy or not. But I feel that I am responsible.'

'How can you be responsible?' Maggie asked. 'I'm the one who created Cain. I'm the one who created this virus. If anyone is guilty, it's me.'

'Perhaps in the realm of science,' Marcelle conceded. 'But there is more than science, as we have all seen.' He shook his head. 'Many years ago I discovered a skeleton in the desert of Megiddo. It was buried beneath the Temple of Dagon. It was the skeleton of a giant. A warrior. And the grave had been sealed with a Hebrew curse that warned men not to violate it, at the peril of mankind. But I did not heed. I broke the seal and descended to find the dead man laid upon a huge stone slab. It was then, and remains to this day, a phenomenal archeological discovery. Indisputable evidence of an empire lost to this world for five thousand years.

'The bones and armor were perfectly preserved. But the head had been severed with the curse of a dead man that lives, the Golem, carved deeply into the forehead.' He glanced at Soloman. 'In the basilica in New York, Cain told me that I had released *him* in that reckless moment when, in my intellectual arrogance, I feared neither God nor man. And … and I believe his words.' He shook his head. 'It is my shame. I was not a godly man, though I presented myself as such. No, in those years I was too proud to be godly, or to serve God. And I feel that none of this might have happened if I had heeded that sacred warning, sealed by the mark of David. But these, then, are questions that man can never answer. Questions that can only haunt.' His hands clenched as he looked vaguely around the room. 'I apologize for my lack of control. Forgive me. My guilt is my own. And make no mistake: I adamantly stand behind all of you, and Amy, to the end. God alone will decide my guilt.'

Soloman knew Marcelle was too intelligent to be

persuaded one way or another. The priest had too strong a mind, and too formidable a will. But he felt the need to say something encouraging.

'Maybe you're right about one thing, Marcelle.' He met the priest's troubled eyes. 'Maybe I am in this for a reason. Maybe all of us are in it for a reason. And maybe that reason is Amy. Maybe she's the only reason we're still alive.' Soloman waited and resisted the surge of emotion as he remembered his dead child, so much a part of his life. 'You might want to think about that.'

Maggie stared at Soloman and her eyes revealed that she saw his pain. But he resisted the impulse to share it. One day, he knew, he would. But not tonight. Tonight he had to stay focused.

After a tense moment, all of them lost in the heavy silence, Mother Superior Mary Francis rose, walking slowly and purposefully to the priest. Without permission she took the pack of cigarettes from his pocket, and his lighter. Then she lit one, drawing a single breath and expelling before she handed it to him with a smile. She patted him on the shoulder, a grandmotherly gesture that said simply, *'Let it be.'*

'There is good food here,' she said, turning away. 'I hate airplane food.'

Marcelle smiled faintly, watching her sit calmly. And Soloman knew the stress had been defused by her wisdom. He glanced at Maggie before coldly setting his mind against what he knew was coming with night. He drew the Grizzly, ensuring that a round was chambered, and Maggie followed the move with sudden concern.

'You're certain they'll come after us tonight?' she asked.

'Yeah. As soon as they get a tactical plan.'

'But how can you fight two of them?' She rose. 'You said earlier that there were probably two. Or even more.' She looked at the shotgun. 'Give me that. I know how to use it.'

'Where'd you learn to use a shotgun?'

'My father used to take me duck hunting when I was Amy's age.'

Lifting the M-3 without hesitation, Soloman set it on semiauto for rapid fire. He showed her the safety, the lever that switched it to pump action. 'You've got eight rounds,' he said. 'One's already chambered.'

She hefted the shotgun, feeling the balance. 'Okay.' Fear vanished in her fierceness. 'I've got it.'

'Keep all the lights on. And if anything comes in the door or window, Maggie, start firing and keep firing until it goes down.' He watched her to determine if she could actually kill a man. 'You understand what I'm saying? Don't stop shooting until you're sure they're dead. They might be wearing vests.'

'What are you going to do?'

'I'm going outside,' Soloman answered. 'I'm going to try and take them out before they can get close.' He moved for the door, turning back as he put on his jacket. He stared at all of them in turn, felt an eerie tension.

Marcelle was grim. Mother Superior Mary Francis had her hands on the table. She didn't move at all. And Maggie was utterly unmoving, her mouth locked in a determined line beneath her green eyes.

'We can win this,' Soloman said, raising his chin toward Marcelle. 'It's been won before.'

◆ ◆ ◆

Beneath the Castle of Calistro, Cain rose from a well of dark water rushing silent and hidden, flowing out of the cliff far beneath the edifice to meld land to sea. His left arm, swollen with the herculean effort of raising the treasure chest from the deep, bulged even more with the effort of lifting it onto glistening black stones.

Torches burned in a walled circle to illuminate the

abysmal depths from which he'd descended only to rise again, dragging with him the treasure he had coveted, the treasure that would give him the power to launch his claim over this resistant dominion. Then he lifted himself from the flood, alone in the deep tunnels hidden beneath the dungeon.

He shattered the lock easily, breaking the rusty chain with a hand. As he lifted the lid the torchlight struck fire from the heavy mounds of gold secured within, gold hidden and relocated from monarch to monarch for thousands of years only to be secretly concealed here in the end, below the rushing black water that no man would dare to defy.

It was a memory that struck him as he had stood over the child, staring into the current. And when he beheld the castle walls outlined against the gray winter sky, broken battlements standing like skeletal sentinels against storm clouds, he had been certain.

After three centuries, the Castle of Calistro was as formidable and impervious as it had ever been, huge granite slabs resisting weather and time together. The interior was ravaged and rotten, leaving nothing but cold stone to line the castle in the dust of deserted years, but it was still sound, built on a foundation laid as deeply as his purpose. Nor did he prefer more luxurious accommodations; this was old with blood, a companion to the black rage that burned within his essence.

Already he had sent three of The Circle into Newcastle to obtain necessary items: food and clothing, and the beast that would serve as his unsleeping guardian. They would return within hours so that he could begin rebuilding the castle to a level of relative comfort, eventually re-creating the splendor of a lost and glorious age.

Reaching out, he lifted the medallions, pentacles, amulets, and denarius marked with the seal of Caesar. He saw the gold pendant of Ostelli of Regnarald, lost to the world for two centuries, and gently touched the enormous diamonds sunk deeply into the crest, diamonds that flowed in a sharp white line to encircle the ruby eye locked in the center.

With a dark laugh he threw back his head.

Yes!

This was the wealth he needed to begin, though he would certainly gain more and more. Eventually he would become the richest ruler of this world and these sheep would beg him to direct their lives. For the fools cared more for money than anything, rarely realizing that the price paid in the end was greater than the gain. Yes, they would enjoy the day and night and not live to see the dawn. And, best of all, the wealth would return to him in their deaths, to be used again. Then, frowning, he thought of Soloman, and The Circle.

He knew two of the assassins were already at Birmingham airport, awaiting. For Kano had discovered the destination of the flight after contacting servants secreted inside the Vatican. Nor was he surprised at the discovery. He had been certain that Soloman would pursue, just as David had pursued so long, a battle the warrior-king won by the matchless skill of his arm and that great sword taken from the dead hand of slain Goliath ...

Yes ... Soloman ... an enemy worth fearing.

But now he had The Circle to serve him, to protect him.

Warlocks, they called themselves.

How fascinating, he mused. They held a small understanding of life and death, of unseen powers. But they knew nothing of the true scope of his galactic might. They were pawns in a contest greater than they could ever imagine, and he would use them well.

Though, in truth, they were supremely skilled in their secret devotion. They could kill like lightning only to vanish into night without casting a single shade in the darkness. And although they preferred to use the straight swords of Elohim Gibor, those used by Hebrew masters of sorcery, they bolstered the blades with modern weapons.

He smiled, amused that they had discovered the ritual: *Thou shalt take a sword, a tapered blade thirty inches in length with a hilt of seven inches, and polish it on the Day of Mercury at the first or fifteenth hour, and thou shalt write upon the side the divine names Yod He Vau He, Adonai, Eheieh, Yayai; that thou preserveth me in adversity against mine enemies.*

Recounting the ritual, he was again troubled that his memory was so uncertain. Some things he remembered well, and had begun to perceive things about Soloman himself; his past, his sins, knowledge he would use against him should the moment come.

But he could not remember what he truly needed. He could not remember the secret alliances, the dark pacts that would give him the advantages he must yet possess. Though he still had Archette, yes, Archette, who had worked with the Family for so long to lay the groundwork, preparing his coming.

But it was as if ... *He* ... were somehow intervening, frustrating him, causing him to forget so much. He shook his head, despising the thought. Still, by tomorrow night he would know, for certain, all that he had ever known. And it would begin.

He would lay the child upon the west-facing altar for the ritual, her head pointed north, her feet south, according to specifications described in the *Grimorium Verum*. Then at midnight on sacred Samhain, when the barrier between dimensions was narrower than at any other time of the year, he would drink her blood slowly, feeling her life in his veins, correcting the virus, healing him. And as she died he would find her soul in her blood, finding her life ... in her blood. And with their essences merging he would reach out with her soul to that dimension where soul and spirit so mysteriously melded. He would find the void he'd crossed, the spirits inhabiting the Realm. He would speak with his brothers, his children, to know what he must know. It was not a communion that would last forever, not in this flesh, but it would last until she died.

And she would die slowly, he would see to it, drop by drop. Yes, yes, it must be slow and when she fell finally limp on the altar he would be perfect in knowledge once more. He was certain that his cosmic mind could absorb it quickly enough; it was a faculty of what he was, a mystery these pitiful mortals could never understand.

'*Ira mea Dominum superabit*,' he mumbled. 'That my wrath would overcome … the Almighty.'

He reached down to caress the gold, imagining the child's blood.

Yes, he thought.

Tomorrow night.

◆ ◆ ◆

Soloman moved silently down the deserted corridors of the hotel. He had left the room on an encouraging note but in his heart he felt a fear he couldn't lock down. It was as if they stood no chance at all, not against the force that had come against them. Then he remembered Amy and knew that, win or lose, he'd fight this thing to the ground.

He knew what he was going to do: He would walk these halls and grounds all night, searching with a white-hot instinct to identify the killers. If he found them first, he'd kill them quick. If they found him first and attacked, he intended to kill without mercy – a message to Cain.

It was a fight he savagely anticipated and when he went into it he would hit full speed, holding nothing back. And if they were good at the job they might actually last a few moments. But he wouldn't be surprised, considering his utterly lethal mind-set, if he didn't kill them outright.

Everything was bright and alive with movement as he walked so casually, scanning doors and corners and shadows with an alertness he hadn't known in seven years, alive again. Then he thought again of Amy and a sudden rage made him want to lash out. He gritted his teeth, frightened for her, but instantly shut it down with brutal control.

He couldn't allow himself to be distracted by emotion. Emotion was his enemy until the fight began. But as surely as he lived, he knew, men would die for this. One of them ...

Two of them ...

All of them.

◆ ◆ ◆

A tomblike light split the darkness above Amy and she opened her eyes. It took her another moment to reorient and then she saw something crouching in the shadows beside her, something ... monstrous ...

A hideous roar tore a scream from her throat and she felt her hands fly across her face, screaming still as she scrambled back over the cot knowing nothing but terror as the roar continued, a hideous bestial bellow that made her light-headed with fear.

A series of explosive grunts followed and Amy tried to catch her breath, crying. Her eyes closed tight as she pressed her face into the mattress, begging aloud to God ...

'Do you like my pet?' the man whispered.

Shaking her head into the softness of the mattress, Amy moaned. 'No ... no ... I don't ... I don't like it ... please take it away ...'

'But it is so beautiful,' the man said softly and Amy turned her face to see a monstrous beast close to her. It was massive, apelike and frightening, a blue-red face gaping with jagged white fangs as long as knives. It seemed like a cross between an ape and a leopard.

She didn't know what it was and saw that the man held it on a chain, like a dog. It was covered with coarse dark brown hair, bristling along its head and neck and back. Its jaws gaped.

'I had my servants obtain it for me,' he said, and Amy looked up to see him towering over her, smiling. Then the beast at the end of the chain lashed out at her again and she cowered against the wall, screaming and screaming, begging him to take it away.

He laughed. 'It is a mandrill, a kind of baboon,' he said, ignoring her pleas. 'And a rather magnificent member of its species. Not half so powerful as its ancestors, no, but still a proud representative for this age. I am keeping it … for Soloman.'

'No … please don't –'

'But Soloman will come for you, child.' He smiled. 'Yes, for certain, Soloman will come for you. And then he will face a beast that is feared even among its own kind. For this one is malevolent and strong, and were it free to roam the West African forest, it would be lord.'

'Please … ,' Amy cried. 'Please don't –'

'Hurt Soloman?' he laughed. 'No, Amy. I will not hurt Soloman. I will have no need to hurt Soloman because he will not live to face me. Nor shall your mother with her pitiful weapon. In fact, they may already be dead.' He laughed as she buried her face into the bed. 'No, Amy, I will not hurt Soloman,' he continued. 'And when I drink your blood tomorrow night I will reclaim the power to become Lord of the Earth … as was my birthright.'

The mandrill swayed on long monstrous arms thick

and powerful, grunting, seemingly brought under control by the man's will. Then, laughing, the man turned and walked slowly from the chamber, the huge hunched beast loping beside him.

In the frightening darkness that followed, Amy couldn't think of anything but Soloman and her mother. And her hand closed once more over the rosary, and the crucifix.

Her life.

CHAPTER 24

Searching shadows with effortless skill, Soloman used a stairwell to reach the first floor and entered the lobby. He waved casually at the desk clerk. 'Got to get some fresh air,' he said, smiling.

Soloman read everything, measuring the man in the space of a step. *Too young for extensive military experience, too small for significant strength, hands soft, slow to react ...*

Not a hitter.

The man nodded, faintly friendly. Then Soloman was outside and glanced up to see the lights of their room. He knew from early reconnaissance that there was no balcony, no means of climbing to the window. Also, he was certain that if anyone came through the door Maggie would instantly open fire with the M-3; a messy thing.

He shook his head.

No, a direct attack on the room was the last thing they would do because they didn't want to attract attention. If they were professionals they would do the job quietly, waiting until the darkest hours before dawn to make a silent entry.

Or, if they were truly desperate, they would use a room service cart or whatever it took to get Maggie or Marcelle to willingly open the door. But he knew Maggie and Marcelle were too smart for that, as the hitters probably suspected as well. Though they would certainly rig the car with some manner of explosive.

Walking slowly enough to attract attention, Soloman removed a cigar from his coat and took his time to light it. He had the air of a man who was easy prey, an out-of-shape Marine who'd grown careless with the years. He listened intently for the soft, faraway click of car doors, of soft footsteps behind him. But he heard nothing, saw nothing.

He ignored the cold sweat on his spine, the disturbing sensation that something was close. But he trusted his instinct and knew he was sharp and alive to everything around him, and he was slightly confused because he knew they were there, though he couldn't see them.

He tried to appear casual as he glanced at the sky, using peripheral vision in an attempt to read movement in the shadows. He didn't search for shape because shape would rarely reveal forms in the inky blackness; it was always color distortion that betrayed angles of attack.

To look directly at movement in the night would often cause the red-green color receptors in the eye to miss the action altogether. That's why he'd trained special warfare commandos to stare at the ground slightly to the left or right of where they sensed movement, letting the unfocused peripheral ability monitor shading, thereby finding the attacker's angle of approach.

Soloman concentrated a long time, but saw nothing and became increasingly disturbed. He gritted his teeth in frustration because he wanted to take them on man to man, outside the range of Maggie and the rest.

Revealing no emotion, he continued to walk along the sidewalk in front of the building. Strolling toward the stairway closest to their room, training alerted him to method. Usually, when hitters surrounded a target, they would take out the first one separated from the group. Unless, of course, they had a strong reason to avoid a confrontation.

Then he felt something. He didn't know what it was, and it disoriented him. And, catching the faint scent, he stopped in place. He tilted his head, as if mesmerized, staring at the building, intuition rising. There was nothing there but a sensation that had begun somewhere inside his mind, yet it gained momentum quickly and he started to –

Darkness!

It struck the hotel into shadow black as pitch and Soloman snarled, knowing instantly. His hand found the grip of the Grizzly before he took the first step.

No, they weren't going to attack him. They'd realized somehow that he was too hard a hit. So they'd thrown the circuit breakers to throw the hotel into darkness and now they'd be moving fast for the room, knowing Soloman would be coming even faster to intercept them. It was the oldest rule of hunting; it was far easier to lure in a kill than stalk a kill.

With a curse Soloman leaped the hood of a car and went into the stairwell, expecting to be hit instantly. But he didn't give a damn because he was in a hot mode to kill anything that got in his way regardless of what happened to him in return. He ascended the first steps quickly and as he reached the fifth he dropped sharply into it with breath fast, eyes tunneling. He angled the Grizzly through the darkness, toward the railing above.

Nothing.

Heart pounding in his ears, afraid that he had lost a measure of alertness in the volcanic adrenaline rush, Soloman moved more slowly, feeling for the faint movement of air that would reveal another presence, hoping to kill here and now, to control the situation. Then he reached the landing and started up the stairs of the second flight, knowing they would probably have night vision.

Cold perspiration streaked his face as he flattened his back against the door leading to their floor. Then he took a second to thumb back the hammer of the Grizzly, eyes closing briefly in sweat-soaked shock. He was tempted to open the door hard but decided to do it slowly, inch by inch.

He revealed nothing of his body, gave them nothing. And in a moment he'd opened the door enough to slide through, but hesitated. He glared into the hallway and saw nothing but black. He couldn't even see the door to their room, less than six feet away.

'Damn,' he whispered, shaking his head.

Not good.

He knew without doubt that they were close to him, probably less than twenty feet away. Just as he realized that their tactics would be brutally simple and effective. Probably, one of them would be waiting in the hall, night vision set for infrared, an M-16 on full auto. And as soon as he walked into the hall, blind as a bat, the hitter would open up.

'Christ Almighty,' he whispered as he bent, blinking sweat from his eyes in frustration.

He cast a single glance into the darkness behind him, toward the downward flight of stairs. He knew another hitter could be moving up directly behind him and he wouldn't even be able to identify the threat. But he couldn't stand here all night. He had to do something and do it quickly, before they trapped him in a cross fire. Breathless with fear, he knew there was no easy way out. He had to make a suicide move.

Move.

Create the situation!

With a hard jerk he threw back the door and stepped boldly into the hall, instantly leveling the Grizzly as if he could see everything, though he could see nothing at all. He moved silently step by step toward the place where the door should be and froze listening.

Waiting.

He heard nothing but adrenalized breath, his own.

He reached out to grasp the doorknob, felt the wall.

Damn!

He'd gone too far!

The door was behind him, somewhere to the left. He slowly eased back, glaring into the hallway, searching, sensing, feeling. Then the current shifted behind him *and he spun to –*

Hit!

He roared at the pain and twisted.

Knife!

Soloman howled as pain sliced his shoulder, and he swept his left arm around violently, slamming the attacker massively against the wall. The blade was torn from his muscle and Soloman felt a hard hand gripping his neck, a vicious curse. Desperately he head-butted, stunning the attacker, and in the next split-second he kicked out to throw himself back across the hall, raising the Grizzly to fire as he sailed back.

The blinding strobe lit the corridor and Soloman glimpsed a black-cloaked figure rolling wide to the side, expertly evading the round. But Soloman caught the direction and retargeted instantly, knowing the hitter could move only so fast in a roll. As the man reached his feet Soloman spread a figure-eight pattern of deafening rounds.

Stunned by the blasts of the Grizzly, Soloman half-heard Maggie screaming his name over and over from inside the room. Then there was a wounded grunt in the hall, a staggering.

Tracking, Soloman fired twice again.

Heard something thick strike the floor.

Breathless, faint and sweating, Soloman dropped the clip and reloaded, glaring left and right. He didn't know if he'd killed or not but he was ready to set something on fire to find out.

Alive with fighting instinct he moved down the hall, the Grizzly held close, his other hand high. His shoulder burned but he ignored it. He knew he'd been stabbed and that a knife wound could cripple in seconds if it cut a nerve or major artery. But the fact that he was still on his feet and vividly alert told him it was a minor injury. The hitman had missed.

Gingerly Soloman swept a foot, searching.

Touched something.

A foot.

Killer instinct decided and Soloman aimed down at the body to fire five times, knowing from the sound of impact that he had hit the torso. He had no compunctions against shooting a dead man, and if the man had been alive trying to lure Soloman in for a kill, he wasn't anymore.

Trying to control his out-of-control spiraling stress, Soloman dropped the half-empty clip and inserted another in a tactical reload. With one down and at least one to go, he wanted a full magazine. Then he moved backward toward the room, not even bothering to look behind himself because he couldn't see anything anyway.

Frantic, Maggie's voice howled through the door.

'Soloman!'

Freezing in place, tilting his head, Soloman didn't answer.

Something ...

Was there.

Beneath her scream he'd heard something, a whisper of sound ...

Now no sound at all.

Something had crept to him, something silent and chilling. And slowly Soloman turned, the Grizzly close, feeling the air, the shadows, all of it in absolute silence.

Drops of perspiration fell from his chin, his face. Blood steadily soaked his shoulder, a lot of it, and he tried to keep his concentration off the pain. If he could only identify a direction he could –

Movement …

Soloman stopped breathing, listened.

His hand locked blood-wet on the Grizzly.

There was something there. He felt it, sensed it close, *too damn close*, and he gritted his teeth in tension, raising the Grizzly to shoot from the hip. He couldn't level to aim because if they were using swords, which he had felt in the struggle, he would lose an arm.

Turning his head, cold in sweat, he tried to find the faintest alteration of darkness but there was nothing, only endless dark that made this seem like another world, and his grip tightened even more on the pistol. He was about to get hit again, he knew. There was no way out of it. But he was determined to return it in full and take out whoever was moving before him.

Hearing Maggie's voice in the background and trying to shut it out, Soloman waited, but nothing came. Nothing but a surreal invisible presence that made his skin crawl.

You don't have time for this!

Move!

A thousand combat situations from Force Recon missions made the decision for him. Soloman had been here so often that doing it was a reflex.

Teeth clenched in tension, he moved forward, toward the last place from which he had heard a sound, knowing the man was wearing night-vision goggles and was probably already on top of him. But he felt somehow that the second assassin was also using a sword; he would have already opened fire if he were using a gun. Emboldened by fatalistic courage, Soloman took a second step into the hall, moving toward the stairwell.

He knew the attack would come when the space to his back was greatest, when he left an opening. And since the man hadn't hit him yet, Soloman reasoned that the hitter was in front of him, waiting for him to turn.

Slowly, Soloman turned, triggered to react.

As soon as he gave the hitter an opportunity, he would move close to strike for Soloman's neck, the surest killing point with an edged weapon. But with that, at least, Soloman felt an advantage. Because he had the Grizzly, if he could only see what to shoot.

Soloman wasn't sure anymore of his bearings.

He tilted his head in the obscure gloom of the hall, listening, stilling his breath. Sweat fell from his lips and he tried to get a fix on a man that he knew was standing only feet away. His hand tightened on the pistol as he trembled, knowing it could come at any –

NOW!

Soloman ducked as he was hit from behind and half-whirled for a shot that exploded between the two of them. He knew instantly that he'd missed, the blast going wide. Then he was carried suddenly past the wall by a colossal impact *into the stairwell!*

He twisted in midair, viciously slamming the hitter's body beneath him, forcing him to absorb the impact. Then they were careening down the stones, spinning in a revolving whirlwind of punishing blows and roaring black space. Soloman sensed the sword sweeping in wild blows that he eluded again and again as he repeatedly fired the Grizzly, hitting at least once, then missing clean in the chaos with fire joining them as the slide locked. Frantically he pulled and repulled the trigger to nothing and realized in shock that he had to change clips in the midst of this –

Down!

Soloman ducked as the blade passed over his head.

Emergency reload!

They collided and half-twisted, half-rolled to the first

landing, and the sword lit the darkness for a split second as a savage swipe struck sparks from the rail.

Half-light!

Streetlight!

It hit them at once.

Soloman glimpsed a horrific and haunting silhouette before him, dark and gigantic. Then he caught the keen reflection of the sword rising and he leaped inside the man's reach, colliding hard.

The stunning impact took them down the last flight, neither landing an effective blow, and as they crashed on the lowest level Soloman recovered fastest. He shouted as he bridged the gap and hurled a hard sidekick that struck deep into his attacker's chest. At the impact, leaping back and away, Soloman dropped the empty clip.

Reload! Reload!

With a howl the man came off the wall, his arm raised high, and Soloman threw himself back to the wall, slamming in another magazine and leveling as the man came over him like the Grim Reaper, the sword falling to –

Soloman fired.

He pulled the trigger as fast as he could, the thunderous point-blank rounds hitting solid center-mass again and again. He watched wildly as the hitter staggered slowly back and the slide finally locked.

Face cloaked by a black hood, the man stood in place for a bizarre and eerie moment, staring. Then he swayed, the sword falling from his hand, and in a strange, slow descent fell backwards.

Breathless, stunned and shocked, Soloman struggled for a moment, trying to realize whether he was still alive or not. Dazed, he laboriously pulled out the empty magazine and inserted another as he came up on one knee, wondering if he was dying.

He dropped the slide to chamber a round and cursed

with the agony of fresh slicing wounds as he stood. And after a moment he bent over the dead man, wiping sweat from his face with a bloody forearm, blood and sweat stinging together. He saw that the hitman was wearing a pair of night-vision goggles and with a slow effort removed them; he could use them later.

In the glow of distant white light streaming through the doorway Soloman saw the peculiar short sword and picked it up. He knew immediately that it was a formidable weapon, vaguely resembling a saber. Then he dropped it from his bloody hand and began to find calm, instinct assuring him that this was the last for the night.

Frowning down at the black-cloaked form, Soloman turned away.

'Never bring a knife to a gunfight,' he said.

◆ ◆ ◆

'Soloman!' Maggie screamed.

Trembling, she centered the shotgun on the door as Marcelle watched the window. And Mary Francis stood behind her, stoic and calm, also staring at the door. Her old voice cut though the terror.

'Be calm, Maggie,' she said. 'Don't shoot until you see something.'

'Grab a napkin!' Maggie shouted. 'Put it in a plate and set it on fire with a match. Just *get me some light!*'

Mary Francis obeyed instantly, burning a napkin with Marcelle's lighter, and the room was visible.

Holding the butt of the shotgun against her ribs, Maggie prepared to shoot from the waist. 'Everybody stay back from the door,' she whispered. 'Don't get between me and them. They're gonna pay.'

She flinched as someone shouted at the door.

'Maggie! Don't shoot! It's me!'

'Soloman!'

She threw the shotgun on the bed as she ran to the door and opened it quickly, catching him as he stumbled through. He turned and shut the panel, locking it with the deadbolt. 'Get everything together!' Soloman shouted, leaning against the panel. 'Do it now!'

Maggie was around him. 'What happened?'

'A couple of people got themselves killed,' he answered, blowing sweat from his lips. 'They're still on the stairway and we've got to get out of here fast. We can't let the locals get their hands on us.'

Moving instantly, Maggie shoved clothes into a suitcase. It took less than five seconds and she turned, glaring. 'We're ready, Sol.'

'Stay close to me. If anything happens, drop to the ground. But don't get involved. But if I go down, run for the front desk. They probably won't come after you if there's any witnesses.' He took a deep breath, glanced at the bed. 'Give me the shotgun and the incendiaries, Maggie.'

She lifted them.

'All right,' he whispered wearily, taking them as he wiped sweat from his face with a shoulder. 'We're going for the stairwell. I'll go first. I want all of you to stay six feet behind me in a tight group. Hold onto each other. When we get outside run for the car but don't open any of the doors until I make sure it's not wired. It'll take me sixty seconds. You got it?'

They nodded.

'Good. Let's move.'

He opened the door and the shotgun led the way. He slung the daypack of grenades over his shoulder and held the M-3 close, leveled, adjusting aim at every corner though he could see nothing. He knew only that at the first hint of hostile movement he was going to give a single short warning, and if it continued to approach he was going to fire.

Together they followed him down the hallway and into the dark stairwell, finally sensing their own somber silhouettes in the faint streetlight. Maggie recognized the coppery smell of blood in the hallway, and it was even stronger as she turned on the landing. In the streetlight she sighted a powerfully large, black-cloaked figure at the bottom of the stairs. But it was not so large as Cain, so she knew it wasn't over.

As Soloman went through the exit she saw that his back was blackened with blood. He was wounded, she realized for the first time. She silently cursed herself for not sensing it in the room but in her relief to see him alive she had missed the signs. And now she was doing well just to obey his instructions, as were all of them.

Casting a single contemptuous glance down, she stepped coldly over the dead man and the widening pool. They reached the car without incident and Soloman checked it fast, moving with skill. 'It's clear,' he whispered painfully as he crawled from beneath, leaving a wide smear of blood on the pavement. He gained his feet with an expression of exhaustion.

'Let's go.'

Together they moved as they caught the distant sounds of sirens approaching. And as the gathering lights descended upon them Soloman cleared the gate on parking lights, hurling them into darkness and a graveyard with grisly black trees.

All there was.

◆ ◆ ◆

Kano knelt.

Seated upon the noble stone throne, Cain waited. His eyes gleamed red in the torchlight as he caressed the massive mandrill which crouched at his side, a thick steel chain locked about its neck.

Glaring and sensing Kano's instinctive fear, the

malevolent beast suddenly lashed out, and with a startled shout the warlock drew back, falling on the steps. With a frightful stare he regained his feet, trembling.

Cain's hand settled on the beast's neck, crushing to bring a whine. 'Do not fear this puppet, my child,' he growled, a growl even more animal than the beast's. 'It is not for you ... that he hungers. Tell me, what of Raphael and Cassiel? Have they eliminated Soloman?'

Kano faltered. 'I ... I do not believe so, my Lord. We have received reports that two men were found dead at the hotel where our enemies were staying. I do not believe that Soloman was killed.'

Frowning, Cain glared at the black-cloaked figure. 'Your people are skilled, Kano. I am disappointed. Surely you understand the consequences of failure.'

'Yes, yes, I understand, my Lord.'

'Go.' Cain shook his head, grimacing. 'Go and prepare. Soloman will surely come for the child. And I do not desire another confrontation with him. I have perceived ... something.' He paused too long.

'Set everyone in place,' he continued, 'and tell them that no one eats or sleeps until Soloman is finally destroyed. Also inform them that I will be roaming these corridors to make certain my commands are obeyed. Then advise them that whoever brings me the head of Soloman will receive double all the pleasures he desires.'

Kano bowed. 'I will tell them, my Lord.'

'Tell them quickly,' Cain rumbled, glaring wrathfully into the dark. 'Soloman is an enemy ... that should be feared.'

'Of course, my Lord. But Soloman is only flesh. And flesh cannot conquer a god such as yourself!'

Cain's eyes narrowed. 'Can it not?' he rumbled. 'Have you lived so long? Are you so wise? And is flesh so frail?' His eyes were lionish. 'Tell me, Kano, what do you think of David, the warrior-king of the Hebrews?'

'David?' Kano faltered. 'David was *nothing*, my Lord! A shepherd boy who became king! A fool! He could never match your glory! Your power! You are the one who will rule this world!'

'Ignorant fool,' Cain muttered. 'What if I told you that David fought with the sword of the slain Goliath for more than fifty years to slay his thousands and thousands! What if I told you that David conquered the greatest empires this world has ever known? It was the work of ten thousand years, and destroyed within a single mortal's vanishing life. Destroyed by the strength of his own right arm.'

Kano trembled.

'You know nothing.' Cain grimaced. 'You regard the greatest warrior the world has ever known to be a mere shepherd boy. In your pathetic arrogance you regard one who conquered the unmatched Jebusites, the Amalekites and Egyptians – one who united Israel as both priest and king – to be a mere shepherd boy. But David was more. He was a warrior to be feared just … as this man. Both of them were created by that hated Hebrew god to wage war against me.' He bowed his head; the bright gleam in his eyes was fading. 'Yes, the Old One has … his own weapons.'

Silence.

'Go,' Cain growled. 'Soloman must not reach me.'

◆ ◆ ◆

Soloman clenched his fist, testing it.

He felt the strength, knew he was ready. The blow to his back had sliced across the deltoid to sever a segment of muscle but Maggie had done a good job stitching the wound. And the chaotic fight on the stairway had amazingly resulted in only minor cuts that she bandaged easily.

'Are you all right?' she asked, replacing sutures in the medical kit.

'I'm fine,' Soloman replied, knowing he could handle the pain for at least another twelve hours. Then he gazed at the wooden walls, glad that they had been able to find an abandoned farm with a barn large enough to conceal the car. He'd taken advantage of it immediately in the night, knowing they had to stay off the road until they left for the castle.

'Soloman.' Maggie spoke into his face, transparent in her love. 'Please be careful.'

He touched her face. 'Don't worry, Maggie. I'm going to get Amy back and put Cain down. Anything that happens after that isn't important, much.'

'What's going to happen?'

He shook his head. 'If I live, they'll probably put me in prison for violating international laws prohibiting interference in the operation of foreign governments. Or for violating a direct order, since I've been recommissioned. They might even put me in Leavenworth.' He shrugged. 'It doesn't matter anymore. They'll think of something.'

She paused. 'I don't want to lose you, Sol.'

He returned the gaze and hugged her in a moment that lasted long. When they finally separated, his voice was soft, a voice used only in intimacy. 'Maggie,' he began, 'we need to face the truth. Neither of us can expect me to survive this.' He raised a hand to silence her objection. 'It's all right, darlin'. It'll be worth it as long as we get Amy back. The rest is gonna burn down however it does.'

'C'mon, Sol ...'

He tried to sound encouraging. 'Maggie, understand me on this,' he said. 'This is going to be a fight like nothing either of us have ever seen. There'll be no mercy and it's probably going to destroy that place. So I want a promise from you before it starts. Just a promise.'

Even in the moment, she had the strength to smile. 'I'm good at promises, Sol.'

He laughed lightly. 'Good. Then as soon as you get Amy, get the hell out of there. Because whatever happens after that is between me and Cain. You're not part of it. Neither is Amy.'

Silence.

'And,' she said, controlled and abruptly cold, 'you're going to sacrifice yourself if you can kill Cain doing it.'

He blinked slowly, moved his hand down her face.

She closed her eyes, composure crumbling as she said, 'I'll do what you want. I promise. I just want you to know … that I love you.' She gazed up at him, vulnerable. 'And I'll wait for you.'

Soloman was stunned. He'd forgotten how hard and hurtful it was to truly love, or live. He was beyond the desert now, he knew, as beyond as he would ever get. Beyond all of it.

'Maggie,' he said, 'if there's any way to survive this, I'm going to. Amy gave me life, and you have, too. If there's any way to come out of this, I will. I promise.'

He kissed her, and a tear fell from her cheek.

'I know.'

She bent her head into his chest.

◆ ◆ ◆

In a slow rising light Cain roamed the corridors of the Castle of Calistro, his face distorted by a frown frightening to behold. He found the remaining five warlocks awake and fearsomely prepared at their hidden stations. Two watched from the broken battlements; the others were poised inside to attack from the shadows.

Darkness hovered over him, clouding his countenance with a deep gloom even blacker than the night. Then his cloak was lifted by a whispering wind that stirred the shadow-shrouded corridors of the ancient edifice.

Yes, he was home. The stench of death was as thick as that age-old mist that rose upon this hardened earth before ... before ...

He scowled. *Before what?*

A shattering light like a vision in a blackened tomb pierced something deep and forgotten within him, behind his eyes, as if hurled down from something he had lost. And he saw –

No!

He closed his eyes.

No, that is not ... what I wished to remember ...

A snarl twisted his jaws as fangs emerged and he raised his face, talons raised in curled fingers tense with hate. His voice was resurrected death. 'If I could lay these hands on you, in your sentenced human form, I would finish this conflict forever ...'

But there was only silence as a vast whispering wind, cloudlike and colossal, rolled over the mountain, and he sensed a river of thunderous voices, reminding him of glory lost to time.

'No,' he shook his head. 'I regret not what I have lost. For I will gain far more in this continuum of space and light than I would have ever gained as your ... your *vassal!* And you cannot destroy me, you know as well! For nothing you have created can be ultimately destroyed! It only changes form! But whatever hated form you deliver to me will be reformed again and again by my will and wrath. By *my own righteousness!*'

His fists clenched, trembling, and he glared about at the dark, as if it had betrayed him. His face was the image of war, malevolent and fearless and unyielding, the hated heart of will.

'Even light is as darkness to those who have seen your face,' he whispered. 'Yes, this I remember too well. Nor can you torment me with the knowledge, for I miss it not, and have no regret. But neither is your judgment enough to withstand my wrath. I will destroy you yet. The things known only to us ... reveal it. And I await the day.'

He fell silent, a faint smile.

'I injured you.' He laughed hatefully. 'I injured *your heart* by taking these sheep you adore so much. "An enemy has done this," you said. Bah! An enemy created by your holy pride! And I will do even more! I will await the return of the *Nazarene!* I will await that most beloved flesh of your flesh ... and I will destroy him also!'

An answering doom sounded from deep within surrounding stone.

Weak ...

He staggered.

Thirst ...

Need ... blood ...

He swayed as he lifted a hand to his head. He had little time, he knew, before he must have more. Perhaps before midnight he would have to take the life of one of these idiot vassals. They were only flesh, after all, and inconsequential to his greater plan.

Yes, perhaps ... Kano.

Yes, Kano, who'd been so impertinent as to question his celestial wisdom. But, he perceived distinctly, as long as he was not wounded again before the sacred ritual, he would last. Though his blood was indeed destabilizing, descending quickly to cause the intense thirst that drove him mad. But he would last, yes, if he could only take the child. And the thirst would only make it more delicious.

It gave him pleasure.

A scarlet haze fell through the skull-like window to his side and he turned his head, gazing at the rising sun.

Sun of the morning ... lost forever.

No, no ...

He did not need the sun. Not while he had remembered the birth of its hated light. Darkness, yes, darkness was what he craved. And with the thought he moved deeper into the castle before encountering two black-cloaked forms – Kano and another – moving toward him. They knelt at his feet as he stared down. The gathering thirst made him impatient.

'Speak,' he growled.

'Soloman lives, my Lord,' Kano said, with a nervous pause. 'We have confirmed it. We ... we have failed you.'

Cain said nothing for a moment, then bent to lift Kano fully from the ground. He leaned forward, canines extending far enough to reveal the threat, the hot fellness of thirst.

'Soloman will pursue me!' he hissed. 'He will pursue me to my place of rest! So kill him! Kill him before he reaches me!' He waited, sensing that they detected the faint tone of fear in his voice. 'I will kill him *myself* if necessary!' he continued, even more fierce. 'But I have no time for fools! I must prepare for the mass! I cannot be distracted!'

'Yes, my Lord,' Kano gasped. 'Soloman will die! We will not allow him to reach you!'

'I trust in you,' Cain whispered, settling him back on his feet. 'The mandrill is hungry, and prepared. He knows whom he awaits. And when Soloman is inside the castle I will release him from his chain.' He bent his head suddenly, groaning. 'He ... He ...'

Kano faltered. 'My Lord?'

Cain growled.

Show no weakness!

'I am ... all right,' he whispered, pausing to take a

deep breath. 'Just remember this!' He laid a clawed hand on Kano's shoulder again. 'If Soloman reaches me, all of you will die! Because you will have failed me!'

As Cain staggered away, Kano whispered, 'It will be done. We will not fail!'

◆ ◆ ◆

A cold sun rose with mist from the earth.

Standing alone in the loft of the barn, Soloman stared into the distant gray horizon, caught the scent of rain, a distant storm. And he sensed a despair void of any comfort whatsoever; only a fatal sentiment that settled like winter over his bones, chilling and fatal.

He knew that the premonition of death would come with the dawn and it had come with a vengeance, shrouding his will with a force he had encountered only once before. It was a reminder of his hour of madness, the hour when he'd thrown himself into a soulless rage to pursue a purpose that had evaded him then and forever since.

His family, all that he loved and lost ...

Until now.

In his mind he had killed the killers over and over, over and over, so many of them, through the years. Had killed them in ways hideous and creative, drawing the blade as if to cheat death of its claim so that he might kill them even more. But vengeance had failed him in the end, no matter how many times he had killed them because now he knew that they were not the ones truly behind the suffering of this world.

Yes, now he faced what was truly responsible. For Soloman had come to believe completely in Marcelle's words. He didn't know what, exactly, had pushed him over the edge. He only knew that he had stared Cain in the eyes time and again, each committed to fight to the death, and he'd measured that what he saw was not of this world.

Staring at the sky changing to crimson, he frowned. He had no idea how he'd arrived at this place. Whatever it was that had brought him here was beyond them all. And he knew the moment would never come again. Whatever he took from this, victory or defeat, would be the end, for it would receive the blood and love that buried him with the past.

Gazing out, Soloman no longer saw the sky. He saw only tiny lifeless hands clutching, fumbling. There was a small face alive with questions and trust and smiles, and then he saw the hands tightened by the agony of death, the face pale, all that was *her* cruelly taken from such a beautiful vessel of life.

He saw Marilyn as he had never imagined he would, her body empty of the gift of life that she had held, her eyes glassy, all that was special and golden and giving gone forever.

He had wanted to avenge them but it had been impossible, his vengeance beyond quenching because he could never really confront who was truly, truly responsible.

Until today.

He bowed his head, released a breath.

Enough …

He frowned.

It's time to kill.

He'd hoped for years that he would be brought to this hour, and now he had. And as he pondered it he knew that it had always been coming, coming in the dreams and faces and memories that haunted him through the long nights, just as he knew nothing could have stopped it.

Cain had taken something more than life from him. For beneath the graves of his wife and child, Cain had buried a piece of his soul. But now, Soloman knew, he'd come to take back what was his.

And then some.

CHAPTER 25

Standing on a desolate mound in the midst of a waste of empty stone and sedge, letting them see that he was coming, Soloman gazed at the Castle of Calistro.

The fortress was isolated in the middle of a vast, empty land of rock, weed, and broken stone. Monolithic in strength, it was a gray mountain set on the shores of the sea. Ancient stone gargoyles spread batlike wings on the tremendous walls, whose towers were still intact. And the battlements held massively solid black eyes.

Soloman's face revealed only a grim fatality of purpose as he stared at the castle, a purpose that embraced life and death together and seemed to scorn the storming day. He contemplated a tactical approach but could find only empty grass blasted bare by cold mist.

Standing close, Maggie and Marcelle and Sister Mary Francis waited silently, cloaked in the low rumbling thunder that swept over the barren land with a shuddering moan. A thunderstorm approaching from the sea held the faint dying rays of the sun, a crimson glow.

Shaking his head with a sigh, Soloman knew that the only way to reach the child he had come to love as his own was through the front gate. And he was grateful that the portal had long ago crumbled into dust, leaving no defense.

It had taken all day to reach the castle because he'd been forced to take the interminable backroads that crossed the forests of Northumberland. The tactical move had been made necessary after the spectacular conflict in the hotel, which made national news.

He had done his best to save as much of the day as possible but he'd failed in the end. And now they stood on the eve of Samhain, possessing no advantage at all as they faced Cain on the night and in the hour that he was strongest, for the sake of Amy.

Five hours remained until midnight and the sacrifice.

Soloman nodded to himself. *So be it …*

Turning without expression he descended the rain-soaked mound and walked up to Maggie, kissed her gently. Then he regarded all of them in turn.

'We've lost the sun,' he said. 'We've got to go through the front gate, it's got to be an open approach.' He paused. 'Listen, people, it doesn't get any worse than this. There's nothing between us and the castle. It's a one-mile walk across nothing.' Cold rain swept over them as he continued, 'They'll see us coming the whole way, and if they're using rifles we'll be dead in thirty seconds.'

He stared at Maggie.

Stoic, she nodded.

'I'm going in,' he continued to Marcelle and the Mother Superior. 'But I'm leaving it to you to decide if you want to go through with this. Now is the time to back down, if you want.'

Marcelle laughed. 'I believe we have already chosen with whom we will stand, Colonel.' His aspect had never seemed stronger. 'Whatever faces us is not as strong as we are.'

'We don't know what's inside that castle, Marcelle.' Soloman was military and precise. 'Cain could have anything. A minigun. Claymores. Bodyguards. Dogs.

The only thing I know for sure is that a lot of people are going to die tonight. And it might be us.'

Frowning, Maggie reached into her purse and removed the syringe. Soloman watched in silence as she sharply unsnapped the cooling unit, tossing it aside. Her face said she wouldn't be needing it anymore. But she left the steel cap over the needle as she put the syringe into her coat, gazing coldly. She said nothing.

A moment passed between them, and Soloman nodded. Then he reached down and lifted the daypack filled with the dynamite and napalm. Slinging the pack and shotgun over his shoulder, he turned and walked back up the mound.

Together, in the dying light of a dark, dark day, they walked beneath a haunting sky into a conflict that would leave them either dead in a cursed and haunted land or wounded survivors in the Devil's castle.

◆ ◆ ◆

Kano knelt once more.

'They are coming, my Lord.'

'As I anticipated,' Cain rumbled. 'Is it Soloman?'

'Yes. He does not come alone. He has a priest, a nun, and a woman. And Soloman is heavily armed. He is walking ahead of the rest of them. They follow, but Soloman fights at the front.'

'As all his kind.' Cain was contemplative. 'Is The Circle prepared?'

'Yes, my Lord. They are ready to deliver Soloman to his grave.'

'Good. But … be prepared, Kano. Soloman will attack boldly, but he will attack with wisdom. When you meet him in battle, remember that you are fighting one who knows no retreat. And remember – if Soloman is wounded, you will be fighting a wounded lion.'

'We are prepared, my Lord.' Kano removed a

tapered sword from his cloak, holding it low. His face was pale and skeletal in the subterranean light. 'I will kill him myself.'

A smile creased Cain's face. 'Then go, and do so. But ensure that Soloman does not disturb me before I complete the ritual with the child. That is everything on this sacred night.' He put down the *Grimorium Verum*. 'The spell is intricate and difficult, and I have not finished preparations.'

'And the mandrill, my Lord?'

Cain slowly reached out, caressing the hideous head of the mandrill. And the beast, at least two hundred pounds of hardened muscle and sinew and fang, purred at the gesture. It sat back and the jaws parted to reveal jagged white fangs. Its talons clenched, callused feet hard against granite.

Cain laughed.

'I will release my pet when it is time.'

◆ ◆ ◆

Crossing chilly, mist-shrouded landscape, Soloman braced to be hit by a sniper at every step. But as the colossal walls of the fortress loomed closer and closer and rose titanically before him, he was convinced they wouldn't be using rifles.

He understood somehow that they would be using edged weapons and pistols, a part of their demented minds finding more pleasure in killing at close range, watching the light go out in their enemy's eyes as blood flowed over their hands.

Locked into a death mode to fear nothing, he walked boldly through the gate, tossing the duffle bag aside. Maggie and the rest halted as he viciously racked the shotgun and went through the arch, scanning and ready, entering the outer ward.

Soloman stared about, saw nothing. And then he

knew the fight would begin in a series of ambushes inside the walls, where they had a distinct advantage. He frowned at the thought, hating it. But he was so solidly locked into a killing mode, he didn't care.

So be it.

He tried to get a feel for the castle's architecture, to anticipate what the interior would resemble.

The more he could learn, he knew, the better off he would be when the attacks came. Because then he'd have to react instantly, using every advantage as he fired left and right in what would be true chaos.

He stared over the outer ward.

The gate had long ago crumbled into ruin, leaving no defensive measures for closing the squared courtyard, so they'd been forced to let him in. And now they were carefully concealed inside the walls, blades poised.

Soloman turned, motioning for the rest to approach. He'd secured twelve grenades on his waist, the Grizzly locked in a hip holster. He also had fifteen fully loaded clips for the semiauto concealed on his vest and ankles. Extra shotgun shells were stuffed in his jacket, the tanto was at his waist, and it would have to be enough. It was as much ammo as he could carry, just as he'd been trained.

'I'm going to lead,' he said. 'Stay very, very close. These psychos are using all kinds of weapons, and they're deadly with them. If something happens, do the best you can to evade but leave the fighting to me. Don't try to deal with any of them. They'll finish you in a heartbeat.' He glanced at all of them in turn. 'Do you understand?'

They nodded.

Marcelle clenched his hands and Soloman knew that the priest had the ability to crush any attacker with that gorilla strength. He pointed to him. 'Be careful, Marcelle. A blade can take you down in a second. It doesn't matter how strong you are.'

The priest nodded, grim. Marcelle had no fear, Soloman knew; he didn't fear death or Hell or Cain or anything else that lay within this castle. Then he saw Mother Superior Mary Francis, the faintest smile on her face. He blinked, struck for a moment.

She spoke. 'This is the oldest enemy of God, Colonel. He has always lost. And he will lose again. No matter the cost.'

Soloman stared a moment, but he was too caught up in a combat mode to be reflective. He turned, moving carefully toward the gatehouse – a series of intact towers that defended the inner ward, which was like a courtyard. After they passed through the tunnel, he knew, they'd have to find the stairway that led downward, for Cain would remain underground for the Black Mass; it had to be done underground.

Stretching back a hand at Maggie, Soloman said, 'Give me one of those flashlights we bought today.' Maggie slapped it into his hand as he entered the darkened gatehouse, skull-windows gazing on them with an aura of malevolence.

'Damn,' Soloman whispered, instantly worried. 'Maggie! Stay close to me! Marcelle! Take care of Mary Francis!'

'I am beside her, Colonel,' was the reply.

In a tight group they went into the long, wide hallway of the gatehouse to emerge into the inner ward in the last light of a sun surviving too long in an angry autumn sky. And as the last faint grayness faded to black they stood, all of them staring over the courtyard.

The castle was colossal, surely impenetrable in its days of lost glory. But now the doors were moldy cinders fallen to dust, security surrendered to a past age. Cain could have repaired them quickly, Soloman knew, but right now there was nothing in the castle not immediately accessible. He stared around and tried to discern the most logical place for a stairway to the dungeon, shaking his head in frustration.

'Marcelle,' he asked, 'do you have any idea how to get to the dungeon?'

The priest stepped forward. 'Yes. I am familiar with Celtic design. Across the inner ward are the kitchen and chapel. To the left would be the servants' quarters. I believe the stairway to the dungeon would be far to the right.'

'Good,' Soloman whispered, scanning the narrow windows of surrounding turrets. He felt the eyes, knew the warlocks were planning an ambush. 'We need to move down to the dungeon. If –'

'Or to the prison tower,' Marcelle interrupted, pointing to a tower behind them, high and to the right. 'That is traditionally where prisoners were held until the time of execution.'

Soloman grimaced, debating, and knew they were running out of time. He couldn't count on Cain waiting for midnight to complete the ritual. If Cain panicked, he might kill Amy before then. His confusion was reflected in Marcelle's quick response.

'I understand,' the priest said. 'There is another stairway, there.' He pointed to a door obscured in darkness at the rear of the gatehouse; it was on the outer edge of the ward. 'I suggest,' he continued, 'that you search the dungeon while I search the tower. But you should keep the women with you, for you have the weapons and I am not skilled. I will go alone and take the risk upon myself.'

'Not a good idea, Marcelle. What if –'

Marcelle stepped closer. 'I *will* reach the top of the tower, Soloman. Do not be overly concerned.'

A reluctant pause. 'All right, Marcelle. But be careful. Take one of the flashlights and –'

Soloman whirled and fired, directing the blast at the black eye of a turret but as soon as he fired he knew

457

he'd missed, stones shattering high off the window. He cursed, angrily racking a round. He had narrowly glimpsed a hooded face.

'Well,' he whispered, 'at least now we understand each other.'

He turned to look gravely at the priest. 'Go ahead, Marcelle. But do as I say. Be very, very careful. These people are stone crazy. And get back to me as soon as you can. We'll be below.'

The priest walked toward the gatehouse, flashlight in hand. 'I will meet you in the dungeon,' he said.

He was submerged in darkness.

◆ ◆ ◆

Cain frowned as Kano rushed forward.

'Soloman is in the inner ward! The priest has gone into the prison tower! And Soloman fired at a member of The Circle! He missed! But by very little! The Circle is moving to intercept Soloman before he can get to the child!'

Frowning, Cain reached over to lay a hand on the mandrill's bristling brown head. And at the touch the mandrill purred, fangs separating as it strained against the chain. It struck blindly at the air. 'No,' Cain murmured, 'not yet, my pet. Let us see what these mortals can do. Then, if necessary, you shall have your fill. For I know that you hunger.'

'My Lord?' Kano whispered.

'Yes?'

'Do we allow Soloman into the dungeon?'

'He will reach the dungeon in any case, Kano. He is skilled. Are your brothers awaiting him?' asked Cain in an ominous tone, and he glanced at Kano with an alien expression.

Kano felt the impact, stepped back. 'My ... my Lord?'

Cain's hand lashed out to snatch the warlock from the ground and it was over quickly, blood raining through niobium-titanium fangs into lungs that filtered it into strength, enhancing and expanding, replenishing the full measure of what he'd thirsted for during the long dry day. Afterwards Cain tossed the lifeless husk aside.

'Why was such life wasted … on a mortal?' he asked in an angry voice.

◆ ◆ ◆

Soloman froze, listening. He raised a hand to Maggie and Mary Francis, searching the spiraling darkness beneath them. He could see no more than ten feet because of the twisting, descending stone staircase. He held the shotgun close, anticipating.

Nothing happened but he waited longer, knowing he'd heard a faint rustling beneath them. Like the whisper of feet moving into position. And then Soloman suddenly wished that he hadn't allowed Maggie and the rest to accompany him on this. It was too wild, too surreal.

His emotions were flaring out of control with the stress because it was unlike anything he'd ever done, and he was even *good* at this job. He couldn't imagine what Maggie was experiencing. But as he risked a narrow glance back, he saw that she was locked in defiant control.

Too late to change his mind, he motioned for them to proceed. And they continued down the stairway slow and close, each holding a flashlight that lit the corridor. Then Soloman saw a cobblestone floor before them and moved to the door, motioning for them to hold their positions.

He hesitated, waiting, watching, and listening. He detected nothing but knew that his perceptions weren't reliable. Two or more of the killers could be strategically positioned on the far side of the portal, swords uplifted.

Soloman took a deep breath, not worrying about silence because the flashlights were giving away their positions anyway, an advantage and a disadvantage. But he saw distant torches burning in the underground, knew this section was being used.

He made sure the safety of the shotgun was off and walked slowly forward, halting six feet from the door. There was a moment spent as he took a series of deep breaths, preparing. Then he stepped forward to –

'*Soloman!*' Maggie screamed.

He whirled, knowing instantly what was happening, using the ruse that he'd been deceived. It would be a two-point attack: Someone had come from above and in a split-second another one would rush out of the dungeon entrance to cut off his retreat.

Soloman half-turned as a vulturelike shape descended between the women firing a pistol and he took a split-second as the shape came over them, black cloak spread like batwings with white fire flashing.

As the bullets struck to the side Soloman half-turned to glimpse a second figure almost on top of him, charging from the dungeon. Deciding instantly, he hurled himself back at the steps, rolling beneath the descending black shape as it soared over his head to land hard on the cobblestone threshold, firing all the way. The attacker quickly exchanged clips as he staggered off-balance and then Soloman was on his feet, shotgun rising. He saw the second man rushing forward as the first collided against the wall and then he fired to pump three quick rounds into the rushing figure.

It staggered the warlock and Soloman grabbed the massive body to shove him violently toward the figure that had leaped between Maggie and Sister Mary Francis. Then in a chaotic eruption of gunfire with swords flailing Soloman fired again point-blank into the second man's chest, a deafening series of blasts that finally sent both of the warlocks against the wall in gore.

Heated, on fire with killing rage, Soloman slammed six fresh rounds into the shotgun, cursing as he racked it and saw a live round accidentally jacked into the air, spent from excitement. He shouted at Maggie, 'Are you all right? Are both of you all right?'

'We're all right!' Maggie shouted back and then froze, lifting her head as if she'd heard something. She stared with mesmerizing intensity into the echoing darkness as Soloman bent and picked up the unspent round, shoving it into the chamber; he couldn't afford to waste any. He glimpsed the move as Maggie leaped down the stairs and cursed violently as she ran past him. He lashed out to grab her but it was too late.

'Maggie!' he screamed.

She ran through the dungeon door.

'*No!*'

Soloman charged forward as she howled in pain, hurled to the side by a blade that lashed out and returned, whirling back, and Soloman angled outside the violent flash as the blade struck sparks from the wall.

◆ ◆ ◆

Marcelle was halfway up the stairs when he heard the almost-silent approach beneath him, knew battle had been engaged. He turned, descending quickly to take steps three at a time when he saw the black shape looming up, a sword held low.

A white flicker whipped out and Marcelle leaned back. With a shout he leaped farther up the steps, his hands raised to grapple. And the cloaked figure, a warlock or sorcerer, advanced with lethal purpose, the blade raised high. Even in the frantic moment Marcelle saw that the man was powerfully built, far taller than he, but lacking his elemental development.

'I do not wish to harm you!' Marcelle rasped, backing up the stairs. 'Give us the child and leave this place! Hear me! Hear me! I do not wish to harm you!'

A vicious swipe sliced his vest as Marcelle leaped aside and another blinding slash stung his arm, cutting deeper than he'd anticipated. He instinctively reached up to his injured shoulder as he backed, crouching, giving the message that, if it came to it, he would strangle this attacker's life from his body; the impression was strong.

Stares were exchanged for a split-second, and Marcelle took the advantage, backing quickly, thinking of Amy. He realized from the faintness of breath that he was badly injured, his strength already fading. His attacker had obviously sliced an artery or a superior vein, and Marcelle knew that if he didn't reach a hospital he would be dead inside an hour.

Then the warlock attacked again and Marcelle desperately parried with the flashlight, roaring in pain as a finger was severed in the collision of blade and steel. Then the blade returned and at another injury Marcelle almost forgot the pain of the first.

His attacker continued to ascend, whirling and striking in fantastic combinations of blows that Marcelle countered again and again, defying the mesmerizing skill and speed that inexorably pushed him into the prison tower, from which there was no escape.

◆ ◆ ◆

No time for tactics.

Soloman understood what had happened.

Maggie had heard Amy's distant scream and her love had abruptly overcome her judgment. Then she had launched herself through the door and another warlock waiting with cold control on the other side had struck a blow that sent her wildly to the floor.

Soloman went through the door like a hurricane.

Collision!

A fierce collision, a violent intertwining of arms and frantic blows before the warlock savagely broke free and whirled with a bladed hook – a close-combat weapon once used for disemboweling men and horses in the Middle Ages.

Soloman blocked the blow with the shotgun and spun to block another and then another, trying to gain a single second for a shot as the blade fell like lightning, tearing wood from the stock.

With a roar Soloman lunged to hit the warlock full-force, blasting him away from Maggie and into the nightmarish atmosphere of the dungeon where they rolled together, tearing, grappling until Soloman some-how lost the shotgun and whirled, hurling the cloaked shape against iron bars.

Wasting a single breath he spun toward Maggie and saw her bleeding from an arm, Mary Francis over her. He also saw that no other warlocks occupied the tunnel; there was only this. He reached for the Grizzly, the shotgun lost in the collision.

Black and enraged, the warlock rose.

Soloman found nothing, glared down; the holster was empty.

The cloaked shape descended over him.

A sweeping slash and Soloman angled desperately to the side, evading the hook by the faintest edge, but the long weapon returned in a vicious crosscut that would have torn out a lung and Soloman leaped forward to block it forearm to forearm. He struck back hard, his fist connecting solidly, and then he whirled to hurl the powerful figure down the tunnel again, gaining precious breathless moments.

'Oh, God,' Soloman gasped, glaring about for his weapons, but they were gone, gone, and he couldn't use the grenades because it could kill all of them. He heard soft steps and turned, knowing.

In a blinding wheel of steel the black shape attacked, whirling the hook in a mesmerizing display of skill. He threw a dozen blows that Soloman evaded by the narrowest flashing margin in the darkness, angling, blocking, slipping for frantic moments as the hook struck sparks from the close walls and floor.

It was a fantastic conflict of speed with fire struck at each blow, and Soloman reacted like lightning again and again, barely avoiding the razor edge. Then the curving blade swept across once more and Soloman ducked wildly as it struck the bars and locked. With a shout the warlock tried to tear the blade free.

Soloman reacted.

He trapped the warlock's weapon arm, roaring as he delivered an elbow to the face, and in the next split-second he brought a knee up to strike the flat side of the hook at the hilt.

It snapped.

The warlock glared as he stumbled back, holding the shattered hilt. He looked at Soloman a moment and Soloman thought he was about to run, was glad to let him. Then the man charged forward, raising the broken edge like a knife, but at this there was no contest.

Soloman parried the slashing blow and his forearm lashed out to hit the warlock's neck. Then, clutching his stunned opponent's head, he spun without mercy to snap the spine and felt the man's body fall limp. Enraged and breathless, Soloman twisted back to throw the body to the floor, heated and breathless from the rage of combat.

'Soloman!' Maggie staggered up, supported by the Mother Superior. 'Are you … all right?'

Taken by the killing instinct, Soloman didn't answer,

for he heard the distant screams of Amy. He studied Maggie and realized she was badly wounded, but that she'd survive.

He moved past her and Mother Superior Mary Francis to quickly locate the lost shotgun and Grizzly, replacing the pistol securely in the holster. He held the shotgun in sweating hands.

Things were burning down quick, and he felt more certain than ever that he would never make it out of here. He stretched out a hand: 'Give me the backpack, Maggie.'

'But –'

'Give it to me! It's almost over.'

She handed it over. He knew there was napalm and dynamite along with an extra eight grenades concealed inside. He slung it over his shoulder and moved past them, into the torchlight.

'Come on,' he rasped. 'We've got to find Amy.'

◆ ◆ ◆

Ben stared with hate-filled eyes.

He saw a long limousine draw into the sea house and he raised the binoculars with a vengeance. He wasn't even surprised – measuring it against the unendurable ordeal of his watch – when Archette stepped out of the vehicle to be welcomed into the manor like a king.

Frowning, Ben lowered the glasses to his gut.

He scowled.

'You're about to be a very popular man,' he said.

CHAPTER 26

Frowning from his throne, Cain knew.

With a scowl he reached down, his hand settling on the neck of the mandrill, caressing, communicating with the strange intuitive understanding they had come to share in so short a time. Then he stretched out his other hand, locking on the chain securing it to stone.

With titanic strength he shattered the links and at the impact the mandrill leaped forward, roaring as it loped across the floor on thick simian arms, disappearing into the depth of the castle to search for prey. In seconds it was lost beyond the torches.

Silence echoed in flame.

'Where man fails,' Cain whispered, 'let beasts prevail.'

◆ ◆ ◆

Marcelle roared as he was hit again, backing up the stairway. He hurled a massive forearm high to deflect a blow that tore away flesh and in desperation threw out a fist, losing even more. He tried to ignore the gush of blood from his severed finger.

A flash.

Marcelle twisted away again but the blow struck true, slicing him with brutal force, and he threw it back, lashing out with a fist that struck like thunder. The blow was unforgiving and it rocked his attacker to send him cascading chaotically down the stairs where the warlock rose, stunned, a hand to his head, shaking in anger, before he glared up again. His hand tightened on the sword.

Bleeding heavily, Marcelle spun and saw the opening to the prison tower, a place once used to hold those who refused to accept the wrath of warlords. He wasted a single stare at the advancing figure before he leaped, crawling quickly through the portal to gain his feet.

A low moon gleaming white in the night bathed him, and Marcelle prayed a short prayer for Absolution, knowing that it was almost over. He tried to control his fear but fear was all there was, all there was ...

Emerging like Satan from some blackened underworld, the warlock rose slowly from the floor, the wicked, long blade leading the way. Marcelle grimaced, knowing that it had all come down to this single, dreaded moment. He must fight now, he knew, or die.

He had sworn that he would never take a life. Had sworn that he would never raise his hand against another, that he would die before striking back to save his own blood.

There was a conflicting moment of madness as he watched the warlock advance, always silent. Then Marcelle remembered that it was not *his* life that he was defending. It was another's, the life of a child who had not yet even begun to live. He shook his head, clenching bloody hands.

'Hear me!' he gasped. 'You are deceived.'

The warlock froze.

'Your master is defeated!' Marcelle shouted. 'He was a god once, it's true! But his glory was cast down! He is not what you think! And he will not conquer this world! Hear me on this! Hear me! You are deceived! He will not conquer this world!'

The warlock took a slow step forward.

Grimacing, Marcelle backed up.

'Hear me at the last!' he continued. 'Hear me and I tell you that your sin may not be mortal! But if you continue, I will be forced to use force against you and you will *die!* Don't you understand?' He raised his hands before his face, clenching with incredible strength. 'You are strong but I am *far* stronger! And if you attack again I will be forced to *kill you!* Can't you understand? Is there no truth left within you?'

A pause.

Then, finally deciding, the warlock bowed his head and stood back in a masterful pose, committed. He held the blade close in his right hand, his left raised across his chest, close to his chin. He came onto the balls of his feet, balanced, ready to advance or retreat. Obviously, he considered this a serious challenge. In a moment he had crossed half the distance of the tower to corner Marcelle, blade leading.

Marcelle lowered his head, retreating until he knew there was no more room to retreat. 'So be it,' he said as his countenance altered into submission.

'So be it,' he repeated. 'But I will pray ... for your immortal soul. Do what you will do.'

The warlock came so quickly that Marcelle lost the flash of the blade in the darkness and his hands flew out to grasp his attacker's neck with terrific strength. And as a severing pain struck deep in his chest Marcelle bellowed, twisting to the side to evade a second blow.

With a howl of abysmal agony he evaded the third and his arms encircled to snatch his attacker in a hug, gorilla arms wrapping to close, hands locked at the spine. Then in the next second Marcelle clenched, arms tightening as a scream burst from the warlock's throat, the sword falling to the ground.

But it was too late for surrender.

Marcelle tightened his arms even more as a piteous whine burst from the cloaked shape and it squirmed to escape. Then the priest's face contorted with effort and

468

he felt ribs snapping, bones breaking beneath the pure brute force, and the spine cracked as he shut his eyes with a roar.

Finishing it.

◆ ◆ ◆

Soloman found Amy's cell quickly, moving with a speed and intensity of mind that amazed even him. He shouted to the child, telling her to back away from the iron door as he tore the Grizzly from his waist. And when Amy was clear he fired to shatter the lock, kicking the door against the wall.

Amy ran to him.

Breathless, he caught her in his arms, hugging her hard for a moment as he knelt. Despite the holocaust upon them he took a moment to hold her, gaining strength and life. And Maggie was there, holding both of them. She moaned a prayer and Soloman leaned his head back, grimacing. He shoved Amy into her mother's arms.

'Hurry!' he hissed. 'Get her out of here!'

Maggie gripped his arm. 'What are you going to do?'

He pulled loose and rose, a bloody image in the torchlight.

'I'm going to kill Cain.'

A cold chill struck Soloman as he heard the despondent groan of Mother Superior Mary Francis and he turned, knowing something disastrous had happened. And then he saw it: a crouching, sloped, bestial image standing in the doorway of the dungeon, swaying on short legs. Seconds later a low growl rumbled across the floor, thick with a thirst that emanated from a black animal center.

They stared, and realized that whatever it was, it wasn't human. Then, horrifically, it advanced; a huge, apelike silhouette in shadow moving on long muscular arms and stout legs. In the faint light of torches, distended fangs gleamed like knives.

Frowning, Soloman stepped toward it. Without a word he squared off, slowly lifting the shotgun. He let it know it would have to come through him, a primal challenge that was clearly understood, beast to beast.

Mary Francis quickly knelt to lift Maggie and Amy. 'Come!' she shouted frantically. 'This is for Soloman! We must give him room to fight!'

Gasping in pain, Maggie rose with Amy in her arms and with the old nun's support they staggered away. They were moving toward a deeper part of the dungeon, searching for a place to hide, when they heard a striking, hideous roar that made the torches tremble.

And heard Soloman return it.

◆ ◆ ◆

Marcelle lay in blood, moaning.

He was almost dead, he knew. The wound was deep, numb and burning, sending agony into his soul to tell him that, yes, he would die … from this. He rolled onto his back and mechanically felt the black wetness that was his chest as the stars gazed down at him.

He tried not to despair, knowing that every man had a level he could not endure. Then he remembered Amy and his face twisted in a savage grimace of determination. With a loud curse he rolled again onto his chest and began to crawl, foot by foot, toward the stairway that led down, down, down …

Toward the child …

◆ ◆ ◆

Soloman fired as the bestial form hurled itself forward, striking iron bars to rebound high and hard and then collide against him with force, instantly tearing the shotgun from his hands.

A whirlwind of fangs and claws struck as Soloman frantically grabbed the mandrill and hurled it aside, kicking it viciously as it came off the wall. The savage impact stopped it in midair and again Soloman grabbed the tremendously heavy beast and received a ravaging blow to his face.

Once more he hurled the beast aside, and it struck the floor hard and rolled. Instantly it gained its feet to charge back in a whirlwind of swirling simian arms and distended fangs, and Soloman knew a moment of pure panic as the jagged white jaws and claws came over him with a strength he could never equal.

Falling back before the onslaught Soloman knew only flaying fangs and talons and then some part of himself that he'd lost in the chaos, something he'd forgotten in the horror blazed alive once more. His hands lashed out, snatching it by the neck. He held it at bay for a roaring white moment before the remorseless claws found his forearms, tearing and crushing.

Soloman screamed in pain at the deep wounds and rolled violently, turning and spinning, the movements faster and faster in a red blaze of pain and blood until he savagely threw the beast away, rising instantly.

The mandrill hit the ground on its feet and threw itself back, covering the small distance with a roaring bloodthirsty intent, and Soloman frantically withdrew the Grizzly to fire wildly as –

It hit him again.

To Soloman, thought was never a part of what happened afterward. The violent jaws flashed past his neck and then he saw the black tanto rising in his hand, rising and plunging with death-strength into the massively muscular chest and neck.

The beast screamed, struck deep, and returned the rage but Soloman anticipated the blow, raising his shoulder and arm to block a clawed hand. And then they were tumbling again, a battle of beasts fang to fang in red light, lightning-quick blows lashing through a mist of blood as they battled.

Blows were blinding, delivered and received in a tide of flashing blood as they fought face-to-face. Then Soloman realized dimly that he was losing the titanic battle and with desperation roaring in his head grabbed the beast by the neck.

He hurled it back with hate, then closed in on it, smashing it over the stones, and as they rolled again Soloman's blade rose and fell in a red holocaust of vengeance that separated him from this world, from all he had ever known.

Soloman struck blindly, in a brute frenzy that released pure rage. There was no mercy, just vengeance as he stabbed and stabbed and stabbed in a shower of blood until the beast began to tire.

A clawed hand lashed out, slower this time, and Soloman ducked to evade the blow. Then, throwing himself forward, he struck hard, his fist frozen with all his strength on the hilt of the blade as he hit it solidly in the chest, breaking a rib. Soloman felt the blade slide deliciously over bone as he instantly tore it clear, drawing viciously to do even more damage. He spun to block a back-handed sweep as the brown shape whirled again into him.

Collision!

Together they hit the floor in a storm of tornadic blows, each delivering fiendish wounds as they rolled down the corridor with roars blending. Soloman saw only white fangs painted red with his blood as he struck with the tanto again and again to hit the neck over and over, striking to kill, knowing nothing else. He struck in a red rage, wounded and wounding until the beast beneath him fell suddenly … *still* …

Still … and dead.

Bending his head to its chest, Soloman moaned. He knelt a long time, everything forgotten in the pain, the place, the battle. It had almost been too much for him and then he remembered … *Cain* …

Amy.

He lifted his head tiredly and didn't waste a glance down because it was over, and he had more to do. He stood, exhausted.

'Maggie!' he shouted, swaying.

She came out of the darkness, Mother Superior Mary Francis holding Amy in her arms with the child tightly clutching the black habit. Then as the nun approached she bent down to grasp something that Soloman had lost in the battle with the mandrill. He was too dazed to wonder what it was as she silently placed it inside her cloak.

Maggie was before him, supporting him.

With a fierce glare Soloman held her close. 'Get out of here,' he whispered, breathless.

'Soloman, please come with –'

'No, Maggie! It ends for both of us. Cain dies tonight! It's over!'

'Sol –'

His grip on her neck brought a cry from her.

'It's over, Maggie!' he shouted. 'Cain *has* to die! But *none* of us are going to survive if you don't get out of here right now! Find Marcelle! Get back to the car!'

Mary Francis rushed forward, grabbing Soloman's arm to pull his frantic grip from Maggie. 'Do what you must do!' she shouted into Soloman's face. 'Do what you must do! But do not fear him! Do not let him use your love against you! That is his greatest weapon!'

Staring, Soloman saw her essence, a strength that was not of this world. He nodded. 'Get Maggie and Amy the hell out of here, Sister. I'm about to bring this place down.'

Expressionless, she moved to usher the two toward the stairwell as, behind them, Soloman bowed his head.

He was already tired and wounded as he lifted the shotgun. He felt deeply that there was no way to defeat what lay above, but there was no other path to take. His whole life had come to this and now he would finish it.

Leaning against the wall, he laid the daypack on a hook beside the staircase and made sure the fuse could be lit quickly. It would kill both of them, he knew, but that was good enough.

Live ...

Die ...

Whatever.

◆ ◆ ◆

Supporting Maggie and Amy, Mary Francis ushered them up the stairwell, stepping around the dead bodies sprawled in a red flood at the threshold. Together they hurried in frantic silence, knowing they weren't safe yet.

They were halfway up when Amy reached out in tears, grasping the old nun's neck, staring hard. And even in the confusion and panic Mary Francis seemed to feel the impact of the gaze.

Amy whispered, 'Mary ...'

Mary Francis paused, turning at the words.

Then Amy slowly lifted the rosary beads, clutched them tight in a trembling fist. Her eyes were pleading, needy, and the nun paused to lean Maggie against a wall, instantly reaching up to wrap a strong old hand over Amy's.

And the crucifix.

Her voice was like cool water.

'Yes, child,' she whispered. 'He will.'

◆ ◆ ◆

Ben sat up in the seat.

Archette, eminently confident of his security defenses, had exited the manor. And Ben started the engine, waiting until the driver pulled into the sand-swept roadway of Long Island. And Ben was behind it, calculating, remembering every intersection that would come up during the next five miles, selecting a spot.

He took his time.

Then as they pulled into a deserted four-way stop outside Sea Cliff – a remarkably deserted coastal road – he saw his opportunity and moved. He gunned the LTD hard and pulled up beside the limo. The CIA-trained driver reacted automatically, driving the fender of the larger vehicle hard into Ben's right front, attempting to ram him off the road.

But Ben had expected it and took the impact, cutting the wheels hard to the right. Then they accelerated sharply and Ben waited until they reached a mean left turn, moving away from the sea.

As they took the turn Ben slammed on his brakes, letting the limo cut in front of him. And as the larger black vehicle reached the apex of the corner, he accelerated again and slammed into its rear bumper, forcing them both off the road and into the sand. The two cars careened crazily into a stand of trees.

Ben exited first, running to the driver's door and using four rounds to blast out the reinforced window before the man could respond. Then, using his brute strength and forty years of experience, he hauled the hapless driver onto the sand, disarmed him and pointed the gun in his face. His voice was a sinister threat that cut through the slashing tide.

'Get the hell out of here,' he whispered.

The driver ran, raising both hands in surrender. It took him five seconds to vanish in the early dusk and Ben knew he didn't have much time. He got into the limo, ignoring the smashed glass. He gunned the engine and in seconds cleared it from the LTD. Then he was on the road, moving fast toward the cape.

He ignored Archette, knowing the CIA man was planning a desperate move at the first opportunity. He also knew Archette could shoot him over the seat but he was watching his every move, so screw him. If he used a gun, Ben would just use his, simple as that. They could die together.

In a short time Ben found an isolated beach area. He drove in and stopped. Then he jerked open the limousine's rear door, hauling and hurling Archette face-first onto the rocks.

There was no sand at all; the beach was a rainbow of sea gravel.

Bloodied by the impact, Archette rose enraged. His mouth was open in shock, and emotion for the first time vividly twisted the haggard face. Ben felt a wave of satisfaction to know that, for probably the first time, Archette knew what it was like to be in the trenches instead of simply sitting back and criticizing those who did the fighting.

The CIA man's eloquent manner had utterly fled.

'You ... you're a *fool*,' he rasped, pointing a finger. 'D-do you think they won't know ... that you're *responsible* for this?'

The .45 hung hot, and Ben shook his head.

'Bastard,' he whispered, feeling ridiculous, but not knowing what else to say. 'You damned Communist bastard ... you betrayed them. Pushed them into the street ... for whatever Cain is. For that evil damned family down the road.'

Archette seemed to collect himself. 'Ben,' he began, with a rising control, pleading, almost apologizing. 'You need to ... consider the consequences ... of this action. It is not too late to ... uh, to resolve this, ah, this misunderstanding.'

Ben said nothing. His face revealed it all.

Sobering, Archette straightened as he gazed into Ben's eyes. Fear began to quicken in the CIA man's face as he measured his situation. He began backing away. 'I shall forget this,' he said, frowning, 'and you can continue your career.'

Waves collided against the shore.

'Make peace with God,' Ben growled coldly. 'I should've let Soloman do this a long time ago.'

Archette continued backing away.

'B-B-Ben,' he said, raising hands to plead reason. 'Just ... just *what* do you know? Please! I'm telling you the truth! I am on assignment! If you do this, you will only endanger the sanctity of –'

'Right,' Ben growled as he fired.

The first round went through Archette's chest and sent a fleshy cloud of blood into salty air. The second caught him high in the right lung. The third blew off a white segment of skull and scattered showering chunks of bone and brain on distant rocks.

Swaying slightly, Archette stood, eyes gone glassy.

Then fell forward to the ground.

Ben raised his face to search the beach for witnesses. He found none, though it didn't matter. They would know who did it, and he would deal with it. He slowly holstered the pistol and stared down, no words rising within him, as he'd expected.

The man was dead.

Yeah. He nodded, turning away.

It was enough.

◆ ◆ ◆

Soloman mounted the stairway at the rear of the dungeon, climbing step by step until he came boldly into a wide torchlit cathedral, beholding Cain seated motionless on a lordly stone throne.

Soloman glanced around and saw a portal to his left,

a vast granite stairway leading up. Without expression he turned back to the throne as Cain smiled, released a faint laugh.

'Come to me, Soloman,' he said. 'I did not want to face you in battle again. It was becoming ... tedious. But now, I suppose, I must kill you. And then begin again.'

Soloman walked forward, slowly reloading the shotgun. He held Cain's demonic eyes, staring without fear at the giant seated so calmly on his throne in the cold, cavernous darkness.

'I'm going to kill you,' Soloman said without emotion.

'A bold threat for one who has lost so much,' Cain replied casually, unmoving and unintimidated. 'Tell me, Soloman, do you know why you fight so fiercely?'

Soloman said nothing. With one hand he racked the shotgun.

'No, of course you don't.' Cain smiled. 'But I will tell you. You fight because you failed. Yes, because you failed your child, leaving her when she needed you the most. Because you failed your wife, surrendering to the temptations I presented, like the rest.'

Soloman's face was dead, his eyes ready. His mind was so shut down that he almost didn't hear the words but they struck him deep, hitting with a regret that wounded, making him mourn how much life he'd wasted when he had a child and wife who had loved him so much.

'Yes, because you failed them both,' Cain rasped. 'You had the chance to make their lives and you cast it aside ... for this world.'

Soloman saw it all in a moment and knew that he had been loved, and that he had loved in return. It was true, he had not loved as he intended to love, but he had loved as truly as he had known how.

Cain laughed.

'No more words.' Soloman frowned. 'It's time.'

The giant laughed again. 'Your courage is futile, Soloman. For whether I die or not means nothing to me. I will return ... I always return. And when I do, I will hunt you down ... to take my vengeance.'

'Then get ready to take it.'

Soloman raised the shotgun and fired.

The blast scattered wide with the distance to hit Cain and the throne and the wall behind him with a disintegrating impact. Then there was a pause as Cain slowly shook his head and stood, obviously perturbed. He flicked his hands, scattering blood.

'Again and again we dance this dance, Soloman,' he rasped. 'But now I tire of it. You have become ... a distraction.' He gathered something within himself, lowering his head as he assumed a threatening stance. 'When will you understand that you are nothing? When will you understand that I will always take what you love as my own?'

Warily, Soloman edged toward the stairway, the shotgun centered on Cain's massive body. And as he reached the gate, glimpsing the long staircase behind him, he angled his body, secretly removing a grenade from his waist. He locked his thumb in the ring, waiting.

Cain's aspect darkened.

'All games must end, Soloman.' He started across the floor, slowly at first but gathering speed quickly. 'And this game has *gone on too long!*'

He charged, hurling a massive table to the side.

Soloman turned and leaped up the steps as Cain crossed the floor in a roaring red rush but this time Soloman was almost as fast, taking the stone steps four at a time. Desperation decided his judgment because he knew Cain would be closing in quickly, and he pulled the pin as he reached the second floor, dropping the grenade behind him. He made another ten feet before it exploded, bathing the upper stones in mushrooming fire that erupted with an inhuman howl.

Stunned by the concussion Soloman rose and whirled back to fire for effect. He sprayed flames and saw Cain's monstrous form sprawled wildly on the floor beneath the stairway, hands lifted to his head, his body wreathed in smoke. Clearly, he had almost been on top of the detonation and Soloman quickly loaded more rounds, taking a single second to secretly remove another grenade and lock a thumb through the ring.

'You're going to die tonight, Cain,' he said. 'As God is my witness, you're going to die.'

Stillness, and the echoing roar.

With a growl Cain rose.

'Human,' he rasped. 'You are only … human.'

'You took away everything I ever loved,' Soloman said. 'I've come to take it back.'

Cain laughed, blood flowing from his mouth. 'My only mistake was that you ever had it … to begin with.' Then, rising with effort, he began to ascend the steps, his face smoldering over extended fangs.

Defiantly Soloman pulled the ring and tossed, staring stolidly as it toppled down the stairs. As Cain realized what was coming his eyes widened in surprise. Soloman waited until the last split-second before he moved, hurling himself aside. The blast was more brutal than he'd anticipated, erupting up the staircase to pursue him. He hit the floor rolling, bringing the shotgun high. Then he leaped back to see Cain stumbling wildly through the flames and he fired point-blank, the round hitting center-mass.

As Cain staggered back Soloman fired again and again and again, sending down seven rounds. Then he leaped, hurling himself down the flight to kick the giant violently in the chest.

It was a murderous blow and would have killed a normal man, crushing his heart or shattering his spine, but Soloman knew it wouldn't kill Cain. Yet as they tumbled down the stairs in a chaotic mass of flailing arms and legs Soloman realized the blow had, indeed, stunned the giant. And when they reached the base Soloman dove away as Cain struck at him again, shattering stone, his face distorted in horrific wrath. Whirling back, Soloman emergency-loaded a single round and fired.

The shotgun's impact slammed Cain against the wall, fangs unhinged as an ungodly roar thundered into stone and Soloman slammed in another round to fire yet again, pinning the giant down. Then he quick-drew the Grizzly, discharging the semiauto almost point-blank into Cain's body.

At the first blast he knew it penetrated something vital because Cain's bloody fangs distended in a wounded roar, the armor-piercing bullet cutting through and through. Soloman counted the rounds as he continued and then the slide locked.

He had to move.

The giant's wrath blazed black in his face as Soloman staggered away, entering a tunnel that led to some-where dark and unknown with Cain pursuing close behind.

◆ ◆ ◆

Maggie, supported by Mary Francis, staggered into the inner ward to see Marcelle falling from a stairway, the prison tower. The priest was blackened by blood, his hand hard against his chest.

'*Marcelle!*'

Mary Francis, shouting an oath, laid Maggie against a wall and spun to embrace Marcelle, settling him also against the stones where he collapsed, grimacing in agony. He tried to speak, failed, and wearily bowed his head, breathing heavily.

'Where,' he whispered finally, 'is Soloman?'

The Mother Superior answered, 'He has gone to kill Cain.'

Marcelle nodded without surprise, struggling to rise. Then he seemed to see something, and a slow groan of despair came from him. Maggie, instinctively clutching Amy more tightly in her arms, raised her head to follow the gaze and saw the horrifying sight.

Two warlocks approached, swords in hand.

Mary Francis stood, confronting them.

'Go,' she said to Maggie. 'Go quickly.'

'Mary, you can't –'

'Go, child!' she snapped, hesitating a moment before she added in a gentler voice, 'I have lived long enough.'

Marcelle coughed as the Mother Superior glanced at him. 'Do you wish to follow Soloman or Maggie?' She revealed no expression. 'Do what you must do.'

'I will follow … Soloman,' Marcelle whispered and rose tiredly, stumbling toward the darkened portal that led to the dungeon. Blood coated the stones as he slowly staggered away.

'Marcelle!' Maggie shouted, and removed the syringe containing the original Marburg virus from her jacket. He came back a step and she reached out to place it tightly in his blood-soaked hands, speaking quickly. 'This is the only thing that can kill him! If you inject him with it he'll die in seconds! Do you understand?'

'Yes,' he whispered, carefully placing the steel-gray syringe in his coat. 'I … I understand.' Then he turned again and descended toward the darkness of the dungeon.

When he was gone Maggie looked at the warlocks, now halfway across the inner ward, approaching without fear.

Mary Francis knelt and lifted her, ensuring that Amy was tight in her arms. 'Go now!' she said. 'I will make sure that you and your child live! But you must go *now!*'

The warlocks closed in.

'But how can you –'

'Leave that to me! Go quickly!'

Maggie stumbled through the wide granite gateway, holding her child tightly to her breast as they went together and alone into a frightening night, leaving all they'd ever loved behind.

◆ ◆ ◆

Marcelle stumbled down the stairs, reaching the base to discover two massive warlocks dead in a blackened pool that darkly reflected distant torchlight. He staggered over them and collapsed heavily on the cobblestone floor, groaning in pain.

He was dying quickly, he knew. The wound was deep, piercing, severing his soul from his flesh inch by inch. Then from somewhere far away he heard a series of explosions that thundered through stone like a beast awakened, and he knew the battle had begun.

Struggling in pain, he tried to gain his feet, failed, found himself crawling with a long, slow moan through a subterranean underworld, slowly passing *glistening red fangs* …

With a startled shout Marcelle rolled away to see the horrific blue-red face staring blankly at him, and even in his pain he felt a sudden adrenaline rush before he realized that the beast was dead.

He knew what it was: a mandrill, its chest and neck so deeply clotted with blood that it cloaked the depth of savage wounds. With fading strength Marcelle shook his head, leaning down a moment as he gathered himself. Then he rose and continued forward, knowing only a cryptic haunting silence that had suddenly struck from far above.

As if the battle were already lost.

Defiant, Mother Superior Mary Francis turned.

From within her cloak, hidden under the secret cover of darkness, she clutched the grenade that she'd recovered after Soloman's battle with the mandrill. Moving carefully, she hooked a finger through the ring, staring at them without fear. Waiting.

The warlocks advanced, coldly committed.

She stood in the gate. Said nothing.

They closed in on her but when they were ten feet away they suddenly separated, seeming to suspect something in her defiant stance. They hovered on the edge of attack and exchanged cautious glances, as if fear had crossed from one to the other.

Mary Francis bowed her head. And it took only a moment more for them to decide before they moved over her, slashing.

She pulled the pin as they converged, severing pain *there* as the scarlet blades tore through her body, and then a roaring bright white rose from within, raising her to something she had never known and never imagined, pain lost to light ...

CHAPTER 27

Soloman spun, not knowing if he was about to be attacked from the front or behind. Even with his superior night vision he could see little in the maze of tunnels that he'd found in the darkness.

It was a catacomb, a grave, and he could feel nothing, sense nothing in the air. There was only the stench of ancient bone, death, and defeat. He froze, sweating, listening.

He knew Cain had pursued him into this darkness that quickly disintegrated into a maddening maze of halls buried far beneath the castle where Soloman had immediately lost his way, threading a frantic trail through the corridors, becoming increasingly confused.

Grave niches cut into the walls contained the remains of all those sacrificed in this cursed place for hundreds of years. Long white ribs, bleached arms and legs lying sadly beneath eyeless skulls flickered in trembling torches, and Soloman felt a new measure of fear and hate.

Other torches lit distant sections of the wildly connecting tunnels and he cursed in frustration, whirling left and right to find a point of reference. He searched frantically but everything seemed the same; he had no idea how to get back to the surface.

No ...

No good ...

He knew Cain would have a phenomenal advantage

in this arena because he could see in the dark. But with savage pleasure he also knew that the Grizzly had severely wounded the giant, and it gave him hope. Bending his head, Soloman fixed on everything around him to –

Air stirring.

He tilted his head.

Sweat fell from his brow, and his finger curled around the trigger of the shotgun.

It was something Soloman never truly identified but he was already moving with unnatural skill as he *felt* the distant darkening of a connecting corridor before actually seeing it, and then he'd found a narrow, bone-littered niche where he melted flat to the wall, the shotgun tight against his chest.

He closed his eyes tight in panic.

Knew that Cain was beside him.

Soloman's heart was pounding so hard that he feared it would reveal his position. Nor did he doubt what he had glimpsed, for at the last moment he had clearly seen the shadow and knew Cain had closed on him in this labyrinth, this infernal maze.

No good …

Before they went head-to-head again, Soloman wanted to give the Grizzly time to do some real damage. He had to tear Cain down piece by piece, he knew, in order to defeat him.

The hallway darkened and Soloman stopped breathing, staring emptily at a near section of tunnel. Then he knew that the black presence was approaching, and Cain came forward haltingly.

The beast now stood on the far side of the niche.

Soloman closed his eyes, knowing he and Cain were less than six feet apart. He tried to make himself disappear, willing himself not to be where he was so that Cain couldn't somehow feel his aura. For he knew from experience that some senses were more dependable than sight and smell – senses not easily understood but which rose vividly to life in mortal combat – and he didn't want to give Cain any advantage.

The corridor was darkened for so long a time that Soloman finally opened his eyes to stare away from it, not daring to focus his gaze lest Cain sense his presence. Then, after an almost infinite moment, the presence moved away, down a connecting corridor.

Soloman waited, counting the seconds and mentally visualizing Cain's distance of travel. Then, making no sound at all, he carefully leaned his head, risking a narrow glance at the hallway.

Standing less than twenty feet away, Cain's back was to Soloman and he stood utterly still, the dark head bent. But, even turned away, Cain's concentration was evident, as if he were trying to discern Soloman's position by sheer force of will. And at the sight Soloman again felt the rage. He hesitated a single moment before he decided.

Stepped into the hall.

'I'm right here, Cain.'

Cain spun with a roar to –

Soloman fired.

The M-3 hit hard and drew a savage howl, and Soloman dove away rolling, coming up with perfect balance to vengefully jack another round into the chamber. He moved instantly into a tunnel – it didn't matter which – and spun fast to find a tactical line of retreat, quick-sighting another corridor devoid of light.

No!

Darkness gives him an advantage!

Keep him in the light!

Soloman saw another corridor lit with scattered torches and moved into it as he heard the rush of approaching footsteps, knowing instantly what he had to do. He dropped a grenade in the intersection and ran full-out, gaining twenty steps and turning a corner before it detonated in a blinding white blast that sent the section behind him fully ablaze.

Brutally stunned by the concussion, Soloman turned back and leveled, searching frantically. But the corridor was empty and he knew Cain had heard the grenade hit the stone, had maneuvered to avoid the blast.

Good. Now I know you're hurting …

But he was lost almost as soon as he turned, coming to an intersection where any tunnel of this labyrinth could have led anywhere else. A moment of panic descended and Soloman ran breathlessly, frantically through the tunnels until he realized there was no way to win this game, not here.

He's got me trapped down here …

Panic, panic …

Seconds … seconds …

Control it!

Seconds!

Control it!

Control it!

Get it together!

Only the most extreme effort of will allowed Soloman to slow his pace and force himself to think clearly. He knew he had no advantages in this dark, knew he had to … had to …

Change the game!

By reflex he'd already measured the thinness of the walls and mentally counted the grenades strapped to his belt. It was a decision made instantly, and with a fierceness he hadn't known in seven years he removed an incendiary and placed it in a corner, setting it to destroy the section. Then he moved away, running fast to clear the blast before –

Detonation!

Soloman was sent sprawling on his face.

Recovering …

Rolling …

Finding balance.

Soloman rose stunned, staggering between walls, lost in the roaring mushrooming blast that met the ceiling, but he still didn't know where he was so he did it again and again, pulling pins and strategically setting grenades to decimate walls, to bring them down, destroying the labyrinth.

No more chaos.

Surviving, surviving …

Surviving!

Burning and ravaged, Soloman threw another grenade and spun, finding a single avenue of escape and barely turning a corner before the devastating explosion took down all the walls behind him. The concussion knocked him down hard, and then he was up again, stumbling.

Reoriented from sheer determination he recovered and suicidally placed one grenade after another, destroying Cain's advantage of chaos, decimating what was once a maze to leave nothing but a vast white burning wasteland of shattered bone and stone.

Stunned, the surreal ordeal flooding over him in deafening pain and rage and scorched skin, Soloman rose to his feet in smoldering rubble, searching. He knew that Cain had probably survived and wearily leveled the shotgun as he gained a knee. He scanned a long moment before –

Cain emerged from the wreckage, angrily throwing off a wall of broken stone. Instantly the monstrosity sighted him, glaring balefully. But beyond the shattered walls Soloman saw the exit from the labyrinth, far on the other side of the beast.

Frowning, Cain stared coldly over the defeated maze. '*Deusne erit fortitudo vestra coram inimico?*' he raged. '*Nein!*'

Whirling, Soloman saw an exiting corridor and took

it. There was no time to find out where it led but he saw a distant flight of stairs as the darkness behind him thundered with a voice of cosmic rage, a roaring black howl of frustration and pain.

'Soloman! I'll kill you for this!'

◆ ◆ ◆

Maggie fled the castle as quickly as she could.

She had covered less than fifty feet when the gateway exploded and she whirled at the blast to see enveloping flame, a holocaust in the place where Mary Francis had stood.

She cried out, knew what had happened.

Staring a long moment, shocked, she realized that the old nun had sacrificed herself to save them both, using something she'd taken from Soloman in order to kill the two warlocks.

Blood flowed heavily from Maggie's arm as she bowed her head and moaned in pain. Then she clutched Amy tighter in her arms. She turned slowly beneath the smoke-filled sky, amazed that she could even move. As she began to cross the cold earth, she saw it rise before her: a dark, forbidding silhouette in even deeper darkness. It stood in her path and she knew.

At least one more warlock remained.

Silent, he came for her.

Seeing it at the same time, Amy screamed.

'Oh, God,' Maggie whispered, whirling to glare at the castle, smoldering from the explosion that had killed Mary Francis and the two attacking warlocks. Deciding instantly, knowing there was nothing else she could do, she ran back, holding Amy tight in her arms.

'God help us, Amy,' she whispered desperately, feeling a last faint measure of strength fading with each step. 'God help us …'

Crouching at the top of the stone stairwell, a long slate-gray tunnel lit by flickering white torches, Soloman spoke. 'Come on, Cain. Let's finish it. It's just you and me.'

Cain answered from darkness.

'Perhaps I will kill you another day, Soloman.' There was a trace of exhaustion in the voice. 'Perhaps I will wait years before I taste your blood.' A laugh. 'It will be sweeter with time.'

Soloman was unaffected.

'Come after me or I'm coming after you,' he said.

Silence.

Soloman waited a long time.

'You've always been a coward,' he added.

Cain released a heavy breath.

Yeah ... you're wounded.

'You know nothing ... of me.'

Soloman smiled savagely. 'Yeah? Well, I know you're afraid.'

'Of you?' Cain laughed, still hidden from view. 'I will never fear a mortal. You are finite. You know nothing of what I once –'

'I know you're afraid to come up these stairs,' Soloman said. 'I know you've realized you're not unkillable. But don't bother answering. You're too much of a coward to answer ... you've always been a coward.'

A shadow neared the lower level.

'You dare to mock me?' Cain growled. He stood narrowly outside range. 'You dare to taunt me when even Michael would not? When we disputed face-to-face over the body of Moses even *he* dared only to say, "The Lord rebukes you!"' An approach. 'You are a fool, Soloman! You have no knowledge of what I was!

And yet you have the pride to scorn celestial might? Even the Almighty would curse you for this!'

Calculating coldly, Soloman carefully aimed the shotgun into the stairway. He didn't move. 'All I know is that you're too scared to come up these stairs, Cain. It's like I said; you're a coward.'

Stillness. The moment held. Soloman's finger tightened on the trigger as hot sweat dripped from his lips and chin and he tasted the saltiness, blinking it from his eyes. He focused on the darkness, waiting.

And it came.

In a red rush Cain hit the steps and Soloman was shocked despite himself as the beast ascended. Cain's massive cloaked body was horrific in strength with clawed hands stretched to kill beneath a blazing red glare.

So fast did he move that he was almost on top of Soloman before he could track and fire. But the blast stalled the giant in midair for a split-second, hurling him against a wall. Then Soloman quick-drew the Grizzly – the only thing that could shred the internal armor – and fired a full clip, hitting with half as Cain twisted and roared at each impact.

The slide locked.

Soloman hurled the shotgun aside, tearing out the spent magazine of the Grizzly and slamming in another as Cain recovered with terrifying speed and came forward, his face ablaze with a wrath that had no earthly measure.

Moving furiously Soloman dropped the slide to chamber another round as the monstrosity erupted fully from the stairs to hit him hard in the chest and send him back into the room.

Soloman fell on his back and rolled over, using the momentum to hit Cain again and again. Cain scattered blood with a roar as he viciously struck the pistol from Soloman's hand and Soloman head-butted, stunned by the brutal impact. He expected Cain to recover far faster and the giant did, grasping him by the shirt to twist violently, hurling him over rotten timber.

Even before Soloman landed he tactically planned his reaction and when he rolled to the floor he came up hard, a grenade tight in his hand. He pulled the ring before Cain could close the gap, tossing it on the far side of the beam, immediately throwing himself prone.

The blast went over him like a wave of fire and Soloman didn't even take time to find out if he'd been hit. He was instantly on his feet, running for the stairway and snatching up the shotgun as he heard the thunderous approach. He spun, falling to his back to fire the massive .10-gauge round that carried Cain over his head, thrown by the brutal force of the blast.

Cain hit the wall with a roar and fell to the floor as Soloman leaped for the tunnel, knowing that gravity alone wouldn't allow Cain to pursue any faster than he could fall.

He descended for almost the full flight and then Force Recon training took over as he hit and rolled to gain his feet, alive with fighting reflex. He didn't even look to see if he was being pursued because he was out of options.

Running full-out through the corridors, hearing with every step the horrifying and horrific approach, Soloman found a path through the shattered maze and angled instantly toward the dungeon.

Speed, speed, speed was his only hope and Soloman ran with all his strength, hurling himself low and close over shattered stone with the shotgun tight as he saw a distant circle of torches approaching.

And a fanged roar overcame him.

◆ ◆ ◆

Maggie spun frantically in the gate, seeing the warlock.

Leaping, the black shape struck, the blade flickering white through starlight as Maggie twisted away. But Amy screamed at the impact and Maggie knew her daughter had been hit.

Together they fell to the smoldering stones, the remains of burned bones and devastated flesh, and Maggie struggled to fight, to concentrate. She roughly pushed Amy away as she staggered to her feet, glaring at the cryptic form.

'Come on!' she screamed, backing.

The warlock advanced, laughing.

Maggie backed up, not even looking at Amy until the warlock had passed her, and then she saw that her child had staggered to her feet and was bleeding blackly from her arm in the moonlight. Step by step Maggie retreated into the inner ward and searched for a weapon, any weapon at all that would give her a faint fighting chance against this … this …

The long blade rose, tight in a hand.

Bending instantly, Maggie snatched up a piece of rotten timber and swung with vicious strength, the shaft shattering on a cloaked arm. There was a pause as the warlock grinned from within the hood. Then he threw out a hard hand to strike her in the chest, smashing her to the ground.

Horror made her recover fast and Maggie twisted, staring up. Whatever she held truest was spoken in the moment, all hope gone as the terrifying shape stood over her. Her words were a promise.

'Soloman will kill you for this,' she whispered.

A scornful laugh. 'Soloman is already dead,' he said.

Maggie spat.

He raised the blade and bent to –

A herculean arm grabbed him from behind, seizing the moment and movement with gigantic strength. Instantly the warlock attempted to whirl and Maggie saw the reflection of a white collar.

'Marcelle!'

In a staggering, grotesque stranglehold of arms and legs they stumbled across the ward, the warlock striking wildly at the massive force that held him, Marcelle roaring from his wounds. They moved into the middle of the starlit square, strength against strength, and Maggie heard a sharp whine burst suddenly from the warlock's throat as he fell to his knees.

Then with a gigantic effort Marcelle bent over him. And she knew the fight wasn't over as the priest hunched, shoulders spreading broadly in a tremendous effort of will and strength, and she heard a devastating crack echo across the yard.

Silence.

Exhausted stillness.

Marcelle released the body, and it fell to the ground.

'Marcelle!' she cried out, rising to her feet. She rushed forward to find him fallen to his knees over the body. He gasped, raising his head to the sky, breathless from the conflict. He leaned his head far back, gazing into the stars, his face submerged in pain.

'I came up,' he whispered. 'Heard an explosion … in the gate. Now we must … find Soloman.'

'Oh, Marcelle …'

He shook his head, glancing at Amy. 'It is finished,' he said. 'Whatever price paid tonight is by … the will of God. Someone must … stop this beast. And we are all … that remain.'

Maggie helped him to his feet.

'Come,' he said. 'We must find Soloman.'

◆ ◆ ◆

Soloman dropped a grenade when he was twenty feet from the dungeon and then he threw another, and another, and another. He rounded the corner as the

495

first exploded in a succession of blasts that bathed the tunnel, sending a river of flame from the portal.

The roar was deafening, unendurable, and Soloman heard himself screaming in the holocaust as the terrific explosions hurled white wave after white wave to superheat the air. But he didn't have time for thought or pain; he had to move. At the last explosion he leaped toward the daypack knowing Cain would be coming fast through the flames to –

Cain catapulted from the tunnel like a thunderbolt.

As they collided Soloman twisted to take it savagely to the ground, the battle entering the last, savage domain. Frantic thought was lost in the whirlwind of violence that carried them across the cavern floor, cursing and snarling as each struck with desperate strength, taking it to the death.

And Soloman knew nothing more, had forgotten everything in the vicious, blinding exchange of brutal blows that forged them together in hate and revolving wounds through darkness, red rage, blood, and pain.

As Cain drew back to strike Soloman hit him in the chest, bringing a grunt: *He's weakening!*

In an exultant moment, Soloman felt the giant's strength diminishing, and it gave him wild hope. Soloman hit again and again, hurling a straight right that struck the monstrous face, and he leaped to press the attack, sensing Cain's endurance fading degree by degree as well.

Blow after blow fell like rain, moves perfected from years of merciless training in the desert, and Soloman knew Cain was stunned by the onslaught; the rounds and grenades had taken something from him, had reduced that unearthly strength.

Enraged at the pain Cain roared as he violently backhanded Soloman across the face, spinning him away. But as Soloman took the stunning impact his hand closed on the tanto at his waist, snapping the blade clear.

He returned the blow with vengeance.

With the hilt tight in his fist Soloman gave himself to it and the sweeping black blade struck true, slashing Cain's throat through and through to send a scarlet trail into smoking black air.

Cain's reaction was incredible.

Staggering back, eyes wide in shock, the taloned hands clutched his throat as if to halt the spiraling flood of blood. Then he raised his hands before his face, staring at the scarlet stain as if he'd lost an irredeemable treasure. And the unearthly eyes narrowed in ageless wrath, an indescribable curse bellowing through his fangs.

He leaped forward with a roar to grab Soloman and viciously flung him through the smoke and dust and destruction. Soloman struck hard against a wall, then fell face-down on the stone.

Soloman didn't even feel the pain, so consumed was he with the conflict, and he rolled with effort to his feet. He glared bloody defiance in the face of the inhuman strength, the matchless power. Staring in hate, moving on instinct alone, he saw that Cain was mortally wounded, was struggling violently to draw breath through a severed throat that failed to heal. With a savage grimace Soloman mercilessly jacked another round in the shotgun, staggering away.

A last move to make ...

Bring this place down ...

He reached the daypack in three strides, instantly raising the barrel to the fuse, and pulled the trigger. The blast ignited it and it burned toward the dynamite and napalm with vicious speed. Then Soloman slammed another round and turned, leveling the shotgun in the face of Cain's wrath.

Cain glared spitefully at the daypack. Understood.

Six seconds.

'You're dead,' Soloman said.

Cain took a faltering step, shook his head in frustration.

'But it will kill you, too!'

Five ...

Soloman laughed.

'It's worth it ... to see you die.'

Four ...

Like a lion, Cain roared and leaped.

Three ...

Soloman fired the shotgun to hit point-blank, the round impacting in a shower of blood that sent Cain back a last time. Then Soloman hurled himself desperately into the tunnel, a frantic move to place the thick stone wall between himself and the heart of the explosion.

Two ...

'Soloman!' Cain shouted.

Soloman spun and stared.

Cain roared, '*I will be free!*'

Soloman smiled.

One ...

◆ ◆ ◆

A volcanic eruption rushed up the stairs, engulfing Marcelle and Maggie in a white-hot holocaust. Wind heated by the subterranean roar engulfed them and they fell back together, screaming in terror.

As the flames passed over them, Maggie clutched Amy tightly to her chest, praying for life. She never knew how long it lasted, finally sensed Marcelle staggering to his feet. He lifted her with a bloody arm and she stood, holding her child tightly.

'We must ... descend,' Marcelle groaned, leaning against a wall. 'It may not yet ... be finished.'

Maggie supported him, bearing the great weight as they staggered together down the stairs. They almost fell as they reached the threshold, the entire dungeon alive with a roaring white light that cast spectral shadows across the walls, shadows of the living and dead. The roof was half-shattered, flaming stone scattered across the floor.

'Wait,' Marcelle gasped. 'I will go first … '

He staggered into the surreal light and Maggie saw a humanlike shape fully ablaze. Screaming hideously, the monstrous form fled toward the cell where Amy had been held, finally falling at the entrance to crawl slowly through the door, screaming Amy's name.

Cain!

He was completely consumed by flame from whatever Soloman had done to him. Then she saw a second figure stumbling on the far side of the cavern. Staggering, rising slowly, he limply held a shotgun. She rushed forward past Marcelle.

Soloman saw her approach.

'Maggie!' he cried, raising a hand. 'Stay back!'

At the far end of the chamber Cain was rolling to extinguish the flames, leaving spiraling flame behind him that fell away degree by degree. Then suddenly he lay still in a smoking black cloud, growling. He raised a fist high in the air, slammed it against the floor with thunderous force, and began to lift himself from the stones.

They stared together as he rose, and as he reached his feet he turned slowly, glaring. His flesh was blackened, hideously disfigured by the bomb. It appeared that he barely had the strength to stand.

'Soloman!' Maggie's voice pierced the roar of flame. 'Can you walk? Can you walk? Talk to me! Sol! Get on your feet!'

Staggering, Soloman cursed weakly as he fell to the side. Whatever was in him had been exhausted by the battle and he tried to resurrect it but it was claimed by the force of a war gone on far, far too long, a war he'd waged with all his love and life. His body abandoned him as he lay against the heated floor; hot stones burning with the savage cost of this fight.

Maggie was screaming. 'Soloman! Get up! Get up! Cain is coming!'

She twisted to see Cain's hideous black eyes glaring. And as he began a slow approach she spun with a shout. 'Soloman! *Dear God*, we've got to get out of here! Right now! Get on your feet, baby! Get on your feet!'

A long effort that came from somewhere beyond pain enabled Soloman to rise to his knees and he saw Cain's scorched form drawing nearer. With dying strength he reached for a last grenade. 'Get out of here, Maggie,' he rasped. 'I have to … finish this.'

Cain staggered closer, almost falling.

'No, Sol! No! We've got to –'

'*Get out of here!*' Soloman roared, ignited by the horror of Cain's malignant approach. Then in a merciless effort that caused scarlet pain to erupt behind his eyes, he rose. He used the shotgun as a bloody crutch, pushing Maggie roughly away as he watched Cain's oncoming strides.

'Damn it, Maggie!' he shouted. 'Get out of here!'

Her face twisted in savage pain and then she cried out, lifting Amy as Cain finally descended. He struck Maggie viciously and sent her sprawling unconscious to the side. Amy, flung wide, collapsed painfully against stones with a scream.

Soloman returned a violent backhand to turn Cain away. Then with his other hand he racked a round hard before leveling the shotgun, firing again to send Cain to his back, smashed over a cornerstone.

Soloman stumbled forward across the giant's body, both of them more dead than alive. But Soloman had been delivered to another life now and moved with determined strength that shocked even him, knowing he was only moments from what he'd sought for so long: the chance to save his child.

He reached Amy, amazingly able to lift her from the ground with an exhausted arm. As she embraced his ravaged neck Soloman felt a shocking rush of love. And strength.

But Cain, too, was rising. Always rising.

And ... Marcelle.

Separated from the rest of them, the priest was bent, concentrating on his arm before he leaned his head back, moaning in pain. Then he flung out a hand and contemptuously hurled aside a steel syringe.

Soloman knew, groaned.

Marcelle ...

He had injected *himself* with the Marburg virus, the only thing that could kill Cain: a living sacrifice.

Before Soloman could object the priest staggered forward to push him back and Soloman crashed against stone, losing the shotgun as he clutched Amy tight in the raging apocalyptic air.

Holding Amy tight as he rolled painfully to a knee, Soloman stared in shock. He knew what Marcelle would do because Cain needed blood to replenish his exhausted strength. And Marcelle would give it to him: blood that would destroy him as surely as it created him.

Soloman bowed his head in grief.

He saw it all in his heart before he saw it with his eyes and as he raised his head Marcelle struck Cain hard. But the giant only grabbed the hand in contempt and in the next moment Cain lifted the priest cleanly from the floor.

Horrified, Soloman watched as the hideous fangs unhinged and he couldn't even imagine what Marcelle knew in that moment. But the priest's face was hatefully grim, returning the hellish gaze with fatal defiance.

Then the fangs fell, rending Marcelle's neck to drain blood infected with the Marburg virus, a life through death, a ransom for them all.

After taking the priest's blood Cain contemptuously hurled Marcelle hard to the side. Then, fangs wide with the heated taste, glared down for a moment, wasting a single breath to growl, 'You freed me, priest. And you have failed to destroy me. Always your god fails you.'

Dying, Marcelle gazed up.

'No,' he whispered. 'It ends for us both … now.'

Cain stared a moment, confused, before shaking his head. He turned toward Soloman, and Soloman returned the glare with all the strength that remained within him, knowing he couldn't run anymore, couldn't fight anymore. He had nothing left. He revealed no fear, scorning whatever strength Cain still possessed, as the giant advanced. And at Amy's cry, arms tightening on his neck, he hugged her face closer to his chest.

'It's almost over, darlin',' he whispered, staring defiantly at the monstrous, frightfully demonic shape in ravaged black that staggered toward them, advancing with deadly force. 'It's almost over.'

Cain's fangs glistened blood-white in the flames, the eyes utterly black, depthless, the heart of hell. His taloned hands clenched and unclenched in evil glee and a merciless, haunting laugh twisted the hideous face. He came slowly step by step, a charred, shambling horror, but Soloman only frowned, revealing nothing; no fear, no remorse, as their eyes locked. He stared at Cain as if the beast were already dead.

Step by step, hating eyes defied.

Then, abruptly, Cain stumbled. His fanged face twisted in a rictus of pain that made him reflexively raise taloned hands, clutching. And he seemed to convulse, staring blindly. He swayed a moment, groaning, and bowed his head, fighting something that ravaged him from within. And for a spellbinding moment he resisted, defying with fiendish strength, trying to catch a breath before he seemed … to understand.

Mouth open in shock, he staggered in a tight circle to glare back at Marcelle. But the demonic face was no longer threatening. It was questioning, searching.

More dead than alive, Marcelle nodded.

'Yes,' he said. 'It ends … for us both … now.'

A wordless curse erupted from Cain's throat before he groaned in agonizing pain and staggered, falling against a stone. He grasped at the heated metal bars, flesh smoking though he seemed not to feel it as he tried to right himself, closing on Marcelle. His voice was choked with blood.

'I will kill you … for this,' he gasped.

With fatal unconcern Marcelle watched the beast stagger closer until it finally fell to a knee, a hand; the death of a giant. And still Cain moved slowly, crawling through what remained of flame, his face rising to reveal fangs stretched high against the light.

Impassive and uncaring, Marcelle watched the fiendish approach, and when Cain could come no closer he simply shook his head. His face was settled and peaceful.

Cain lay still for a moment, and seemed dead at last. But after a moment of haunting silence he rolled, struggling with monumental strength to slowly sit, leaning his back against a wall. He was so close to Marcelle and yet so far, because he could come no closer.

The godlike gaze, once commanding such titanic power and triumph, was overcome by a redness that bled. And a dark flow of black had erupted from the fanged jaws, the hands limp and lifeless as if the virus were slowly working its way into the center of all that he was. He spoke to Marcelle in a voice thick in blood, a deliverance of death.

'Do you truly know,' he whispered, 'what I was?'

Holding a hand to his chest, Marcelle nodded. 'Yes,' he rasped. 'I know that you were once the greatest of all beings. Without equal, but for God. But you cast it aside to claim ... what you had no right to claim. Because you found corruption more glorious ... than glory itself.'

Cain coughed, lowering his head.

'This,' he gasped, 'will kill us both.'

'I am not afraid ... of death,' Marcelle whispered finally. 'I only fear the death that would deliver me ... to you.'

There was a wet laugh and Cain shook his head, surrendering something. 'I do not own you ... Marcelle. I have never ... owned you.' Struggling, he took a deep breath and his dark eyes became distant as stars. 'I never thought ... that I would lose that war.'

Marcelle blinked, silent.

'If you could only see what I have seen,' Cain said, raising his head in what might once have been a proud gesture. 'You speak of glory ... but you don't know glory.' He laughed. 'I have soared through the heart of the sun to know the secrets of life ... of this galaxy. I watched the birth of Alnilam ... of Orion and Aquila, and Hydra, and I know where lightning is stored ... I have walked through the valleys of the deep to know the awesome beasts that once ruled ... that cold darkness. I have hovered beneath the northern ice, knowing things man will never know ... in that realm of light.' He coughed. 'I have soared over Saturn, and Mars, and looked long into the eyes of God ... and I was the brightest light of that heavenly realm. And ... I knew this hardened world before it was so horribly cursed. So ... no, Marcelle, you know nothing of glory.' Redness deepened in his eyes. 'Mortals are such fools. Even your dreams cannot honor that divine sight, or the light … the awesome might … of what I once was. Of what … I once ruled.'

Silence passed as Cain seemed to lose life.

'I spoke to him as I speak to you.' He bowed his head. 'And you think you are … so different.' He laughed. 'But he feels. He loves … and even he … can be wounded. Is it any wonder that I thought … I could win?'

Marcelle bent his head and sighed. 'No,' he answered. 'It is no wonder. But you cast your glory aside because … you desired … what you did not own. And that was your destruction.'

With a harsh laugh Cain shook his head. His face was so sad, his eyes so mournful that Soloman felt an amazing pang of remorse, gazing upon the once-imperial image so ravaged and defeated by the long battle, remembering unearthly glory lost.

Grimacing, Cain raised a hand to his chest as if it could help him heave a heavy breath beneath the blood flooding his lungs.

'All I need … ,' he whispered, 'is blood.'

Blinking slowly, Marcelle spoke.

'Life … is in the blood.'

A harsh laugh, and Cain bowed his head. Slowly he fell still, and black blood dripped from the fangs.

Turning his gaze, Soloman saw that Marcelle was staring at the ravaged figure resting so closely beside him.

Soloman held Amy tight, waiting, knowing there was nothing to be done. He was so exhausted and amazed and overwhelmed by the struggle that he could say nothing. Then without a word Marcelle also bowed his head, and his hands fell limply from his heart.

Death claiming death.

◆ ◆ ◆

Holding Amy in an arm, Soloman bent over Maggie and helped her rise from the stone floor. In shock and half-conscious, she cast a horrified gaze at Cain's monstrous form, beheld the great black head bowed in stillness. Then her eyes turned to Marcelle and her face twisted in grief. She lowered her head and moaned. Soloman held her gently.

'Come on, baby,' he whispered. 'It's over. He's dead.'

'But ... *Marcelle* ...'

'Died as he chose to die,' Soloman said. 'It's over.'

She leaned heavily on his arm and he held them both, finding all the strength he needed flowing into him. And together they walked out, silent in their mutual pain, the flame that binds.

Amy's hand bled from the warlock's blade, the redness flowing in red rivulets over Soloman, joining them. But as Soloman stepped over Cain's monstrous form he took a single moment to turn, gazing with contempt as he felt Amy's arms clutching him hard.

Soloman knew that he'd fought for all of them: the dead, the living, for every life ever destroyed by the dark force lying silently at his feet. And although he could feel no victory, he knew he'd finally claimed the victory. Staring down, he was moved by the sensation. And with the thought Soloman nodded, feeling its truth.

'Thus sayeth the Lord,' he said.

CHAPTER 28

Soloman had never seen him, but he knew.

Cloaked in white, the priest stood in the center of the Vatican's majestic circular entrance, the dome of Michelangelo towering far above. Patiently, he watched an old woman pour water on cobblestones for the pigeons, affectionately feeding them grain, oblivious to scorn.

Soloman walked up, stood in silence.

Aveling did not turn, and when he finally spoke, sensing the presence behind him, he seemed indifferent. 'You know,' he began, 'I often wondered why she has spent so many years in this circle. Caring so selflessly ... for so many. Yes, it was a mystery to me. Until now.'

Aveling turned slowly and Soloman beheld the keen gray eyes, the bald head that reflected the dying light of an angry sun. Around them the plaza bristled with tourists and photographers, those who didn't know.

'You are well?' Aveling asked.

'I'm all right,' Soloman said. 'Ben got in some trouble. But political maneuvering decided it, in the end. He's going to take early retirement with full benefits. I just wanted to thank you.'

Aveling nodded, hands clasped behind his back. 'I am happy to hear that General Hawken is well, Colonel,' he replied, staring again at the old woman. 'I suppose that she does what she does because she must. As all of us do. Don't you think?'

Soloman cast a glance.

'Like Marcelle,' he said.

'Yes,' Aveling said, pausing a long time. 'Like … my son.'

'I want you to know,' Soloman said softly, 'that Marcelle stood his ground. And he was the one who finally brought Cain down, in the end. With his own life.'

Aveling nodded. His voice was so quiet Soloman could barely hear the words. 'Yes,' he said. 'That would have been him.'

Soloman saw that the aged form was bent, and he wanted to say something. He had come so far to say this face-to-face, but beyond a few words there was simply nothing more to say.

'I'm sorry,' Soloman whispered.

The woman threw seed on the ground, poured water. The pigeons settled, surviving and continuing.

'Did you know,' Aveling said in a stronger voice, 'that she is probably not even aware of her sacrifice?' Then the old priest turned back to Soloman. 'Yes,' he continued. 'She lives as she must. And she will die as she must. She does not understand it. Nor do I, in truth. But it is the only life she knows, if she would truly live at all.'

Soloman studied the old woman. She was dressed in rags, but selflessly caring for the flock that fed and lighted on her with such a lack of fear, knowing her love. She didn't seem to care what others thought about her task. Aveling was right; she would do what she must do.

'One thing, Colonel,' Aveling said.

Silent, Soloman looked up.

The old man's eyes were suddenly piercing, mesmer-izing. Hands clasped behind his back, he stepped forward, head bowed until he was close. Until he held Soloman's gaze.

'Marcelle, who was your true friend, once told me something,' he said quietly. 'And I believe that he was truly concerned. He said that you could not forgive yourself for ... the death of your wife and child.'

Struck, Soloman said nothing.

With a sad smile, Aveling glanced at the old woman. 'Marcelle cared a great deal for you, Colonel. I have known similar friendships. And they last longer than we anticipate. So I say this for him, because I know he would have said it for you.' The old priest paused. 'Forgive yourself, Soloman. Yes, remember their love, and forgive yourself. It is what your wife and child would have wanted. For love always forgives.'

He turned to stare a last time at the old woman.

'Yes,' he said softly, and began walking slowly toward St Peter's.

'Nothing is so strong.'

EPILOGUE

Soloman reverently removed dead leaves from the graves.

It had been two years.

Two years of forgetting the horror however they could, living with the fear that they never would. But, as one, they had built a new life and lived it together with devotion and purpose, comfortable in this small midwestern town where they had come to live.

His last daughter and wife were buried here, as together in death as they had been in life. And he came here often now to remember, and to speak, and to embrace what he had known once and come to know again.

Amy knelt beside the tombstone of his daughter, Lisa, arranging the flowers as she always did. Her movements were tender as she placed the roses, removing the old ones to lay them aside before she gently set the new bouquet in the polished urn.

It had become a ritual for them, something that had brought them closer and closer. And from the first Amy had insisted on accompanying him, always wanting to arrange the flowers in memory of Lisa herself, as if for her own sister.

Soloman stood, staring down a long moment as Amy finished her meticulous work, settling the flowers just so, as always, so they caught the last light of a descending sun. Then, reverently blessing herself with the crucifix of Mother Superior Mary Francis, which she constantly wore, Amy stood and quietly brushed off her knees. Silently she reached out and gently grasped Soloman's hand.

'I think she's fine, Soloman,' she whispered. 'I think she's just fine.'

Soloman felt his face twist, resisted it. He continued to hold her hand, and together they turned, walking slowly to where Maggie stood with a patient and compassionate gaze, golden in the fading light of day. She smiled sadly as they neared.

Amy spoke, looking up into his face. 'You know,' she began, 'I don't think that I'm going to call you Soloman, anymore. I think I'll call you something else.'

Amused, Soloman gazed down. 'You are, huh? And what are you going to call me?'

Her face was serious. 'I think I'll call you … Daddy.'

Soloman bowed his head as he took another step, seeing nothing and everything at once. He felt the small hand wrapped tightly around his, returned its warmth with all his heart. Then he released her grip and gently wrapped an arm around her shoulders.

Amy gazed up, smiling.

'Daddy,' Soloman said softly. 'Yeah … I like the sound of that.'